You Came Back

You Came Back

A Novel

CHRISTOPHER
COAKE

VIKING
an imprint of
PENGUIN BOOKS

VIKING

Published by the Penguin Group

Penguin Books Ltd, 80 Strand, London WC2R ORL, England

Penguin Group (USA) Inc., 375 Hudson Street, New York, New York 10014, USA

Penguin Group (Canada), 90 Eglinton Avenue East, Suite 700, Toronto, Ontario, Canada M4P 2Y3
(a division of Pearson Penguin Canada Inc.)

Penguin Ireland, 25 St Stephen's Green, Dublin 2, Ireland (a division of Penguin Books Ltd)

Penguin Group (Australia), 250 Camberwell Road, Camberwell, Victoria 3124, Australia
(a division of Pearson Australia Group Pty Ltd)

Penguin Books India Pvt Ltd, 11 Community Centre, Panchsheel Park, New Delhi – 110 017, India

Penguin Group (NZ), 67 Apollo Drive, Rosedale, Auckland 0632, New Zealand
(a division of Pearson New Zealand Ltd)

Penguin Books (South Africa) (Pty) Ltd, Block D, Rosebank Office Park, 181 Jan Smuts Avenue,
Parktown North, Gauteng 2193, South Africa

Penguin Books Ltd, Registered Offices: 80 Strand, London WC2R ORL, England

www.penguin.com

First published in the United States of America by Grand Central Publishing,
a division of Hachette Book Group, Inc. 2012
First published in Great Britain by Viking 2012

001

Copyright © Christopher Coake, 2012

The moral right of the author has been asserted

This book is a work of fiction. Names, characters, places and incidents are the
product of the author's imagination or are used fictitiously. Any resemblance to
actual events, locales or persons, living or dead, is coincidental

Printed in Great Britain by Clays Ltd, St Ives plc

A CIP catalogue record for this book is available from the British Library

ISBN: 978-0-670-92125-6

www.greenpenguin.co.uk

MIX
Paper from
responsible sources
FSC
www.fsc.org   FSC® C018179

Penguin Books is committed to a sustainable
future for our business, our readers and our planet.
This book is made from Forest Stewardship
Council™ certified paper.

ALWAYS LEARNING   **PEARSON**

For Stephanie Lauer, my love: I promise you're nowhere in these pages.

Acknowledgments

If you would like to imagine the author of this book as a solitary fellow, working alone and friendless, please close the book now. I am neither, however, which is why I need to thank many people whose love, advice, and/or interest helped bring this book into the world.

Thanks to:

Family: My mother, Jan Coake; my sister, Whitney Coake; and all my Lauer in-laws.

Early Readers: James Mardock (thanks and thanks again), Michael Kardos, and Lori Rader Day.

(A surely incomplete list of) Friends and Supporters: Emilie Meyer; Catherine Pierce; Taylor Snodgrass and Michael Snodgrass; Heidi Hesse; Greg Harris; Wes and Tory Herron; Doug Bowers and Stephanie Suen; Claire Vaye Watkins; Curtis Vickers; Gabe Urza; Ben Rogers; Jason Ludden; Cameron Filipour; David Higginbotham; Grant Peterson; Michelle Herman; Paul Martin, Deb Spieker-Martin, and the crew at Bibo Coffee Co.; Justin Gifford; Erin and Ben James; Lynda and Patrick Walsh; Jane Detwiler and Beverly Lassiter; Eric Rasmussen; Don and Heather Hardy; Stacy Burton; Aaron Santesso and Esra Mirze; Rob and Elizabeth Trupp; Tim Johnson and Maura Grady; Kelly Bahmer-Brouse and Andy Brouse; Kami Bevington; Cari Cunningham and Trannon Mosher; Aaron Linfante; Joshua Jay; Okla Elliott; Andrew Scott; Scott W. Berg; Tony Lacey; Francis Geffard; Peter Wild; Kacey

Acknowledgments

Kowars; Matt Weiland; John Freeman; Dan Chaon; Otto Penzler; Ray and Barbara March; Dr. Miles Congress; Shaun Griffin; Christine Kelly, Dan Earl, Michael Croft, and the staff of Sundance Bookstore; and Steve Davis and Christina Barr at Nevada Humanities.

Good dogs: Dashiell Hammett, Kona, and Nada (RIP).

Special Thanks:

To Ian Jack: I acknowledge you.

To my colleagues at the University of Nevada, Reno, and to all the students, past and present, who've made mine a dream job.

To the students and faculty at Ohio State University and Miami University of Ohio, past and present, who keep inspiring me.

To all the journals that have published my work: *The Journal,* the late and lamented *Three Plum Review/Central Ohio Writing,* and *The Frostproof Review; Five Points; The Gettysburg Review; The Southern Review; Epoch; The Jabberwock Review;* and *Granta.*

To the PEN American Center—especially Thomas Beller, Victoria Redel, Heidi Julavits, and the family of Robert Bingham, all of whom gave my career a huge boost.

To Ann Patty, who told me how to make this book shorter, and kept telling me until I listened.

To my agent, Marian Young, the gunslinger.

To—of course!—Grand Central Publishing, especially my fabulous editor, Deb Futter.

And finally: thanks, more thanks, and all the love in the world to my wife, Stephanie Lauer, for putting up with me while I hid in dark rooms, making this thing.

Author's Note

I lived in Columbus, Ohio, from 1996 through 2004, and have incorporated into this book a number of locations and neighborhoods with which I am very familiar. However, I have taken license with the city as the story demanded; locations and street directions are not always accurate, for instance (if not entirely invented); and the inside of the Franklin Park Conservatory is ever-so-slightly warped from true. Nevertheless, no harm to the city or its resident Buckeyes was intended.

You Came Back

I

His New Life

One

Mark Fife was being watched.

He realized this in a coffee shop three blocks from the town-house where he and his girlfriend, Allison, lived, sitting in a stuffed chair with his back to the front window. It was early on a weekday morning; all of central Ohio had woken to four inches of new snow, and Mark and Allie had decided to take a morning walk, ending here. Just before rush hour, the Cup O'Joe was full, noisy, the air warm and humid from snow melting off scores of boots. Allison had left Mark alone to use the restroom, and he was pretending to read the *Dispatch* while he waited. And then came the prickle at his neck, the sudden shock—as though a sly lover had drawn the tip of a fingernail across the short hairs of his nape.

He lifted his eyes from the paper and scanned the shop, but no one was looking his way. Then he turned around in his seat and was startled again: A woman—a stranger—was peering through the window at him.

The woman was older than he was, forty-five maybe. Her face was round, unnaturally tan for December, and wrapped in a silver scarf; what hair escaped was curly and very dark. Her eyes were wide: she seemed surprised to see him, in a way he recognized, and that soured his stomach.

Mark might have ignored her, but the woman was too odd—too nervous and frenetic—to ignore. Her mouth hung open; her gloved hands were twisting together in front of her. She wasn't simply surprised to see him. She was afraid.

He raised his hand, automatically, and she flinched—as though, instead of waving, he'd held up a gun.

Was she really afraid of *him*? He turned back to the shop, but the only other person in the woman's line of sight was a young blonde, wrapped in a shawl on a nearby couch, frowning at her textbook.

When Mark turned back to the window, the woman had vanished.

He stood, peered out onto the sidewalk. At that moment maybe a dozen people milled outside, all dressed in dark coats, converging and scattering, getting in and out of cars, puffing steam. The silver scarf, that hair—he searched for them, but saw nothing. The woman was gone.

~

He dropped back into his seat, trying to place her, failing. He told himself that she must have made a mistake. She'd thought he was someone else. Or she could simply be a crazy; Columbus had its share. Still, her appearance and departure left Mark oddly shaken, maybe because the strange woman was of a piece with a morning that had already done its best to unnerve him.

Not forty minutes before, Allison had woken him from an endless nightmare—the pressure of her fingers in his hair as gentle, as unreal, as the sensation that had alerted him to the strange woman's gaze.

It snowed, Allie had said, when he'd opened his eyes. Come see.

Mark had been dreaming of his son, Brendan, who had died on a cold January day several years before, just weeks after his seventh birthday. The dream was an enemy whose tactics were familiar, intimate. In it, Mark and Brendan's mother—Mark's ex-wife, Chloe—were still living in their old two-story brick house in Victorian Village, on the far side of downtown. In the dream their old, rambling home had become a labyrinth: Floors had traded places; new hallways branched into shadows; doors had been smoothed over into plaster walls. Brendan was still alive, running from them, laughing, calling them, always out of sight, but in this strange new house they could never catch him; they could never tell him to be careful, to wait for them, to take his time on the stairs.

And then Mark was awake, and seven years had passed, and instead of Chloe's tear-streaked, panicked face beside him, he saw only Allison's peering down at him, her dark eyes alight, excited by the snowfall.

Allie had spent the first eight years of her life in Southern California; even after more than two decades in Cleveland and Columbus, snow was still exotic to her, special. *Whatever Ohio doesn't have,* she liked to say, *it's got snow and fireflies.*

Get dressed, she urged him. Come play with me.

He didn't want to. Allie knew about Brendan, about Chloe, as much as he could bear to tell her—but how could he make her understand that a second ago Brendan had been lost, that Chloe had been crying? That even though Mark was awake, he could still *hear* them?

He couldn't make her—anyone—understand a thing like that. So he dressed, pulled on his boots, and did as Allie asked.

They lived in German Village, an old, historic neighborhood just south of downtown Columbus; they'd moved into their brown-stone townhouse the previous summer, six months after they'd begun dating. The streets here were cobbled, and the brick houses were all a hundred years old, squared and serious and rising porch-less from the streets; the sidewalks were overhung by enormous, steadfast trees. This morning's snow, flat and heavy, gave the air a weird closeness, as though Mark and Allie walked across a sound-stage. Strings of white Christmas lights glowed in their neighbors' windows—but not yet in their own; they'd been too busy with work to decorate—and on the light poles at the corners. If not for the single set of tire tracks dividing the road, Mark wouldn't have been surprised to see a horse-drawn carriage clattering by.

Allie kicked at the snow, shrieked away from clumps shed by tree branches, with a kid's joy. Mark followed her, freeing himself from the dream, remembering himself.

He was thirty-eight. Chloe had left him six years ago, not long after Brendan died. He loved Allison Daniel now.

Mark couldn't help his dreams, but his years of lonely grieving had taught him how to pull his mind back from its gray chasms and thickets, into the world where his body moved, where his heart beat and his lungs breathed in cold air; where a woman he loved frolicked ahead of him in the snow. This was his life, now. His new life.

He wasn't so naive as to think anyone could simply *choose* to be happy—that was bullshit of the highest order, and he'd thought so even before his son had, in an instant, fallen down the stairs and out of the world—but one could choose paths that *allowed* for happiness. One could choose to accept any happiness one found. How many times had he and Allison, herself divorced, talked about this? Neither of them had planned for the other. Planning was impossible. Their lives, now, were wild improvisation.

Allison lifted a hand and smacked a low branch; snow sifted down. Watching her, he felt aching gratitude that, on a morning like this one, he was not alone.

Allison Daniel, he said.

She turned. Her cheeks and lips were a violent red; her black hair was speckled with snowflakes. Mark Fife? she said.

He reeled her in for a kiss. Her lips cold. The barest warm touch of her tongue.

What's that for? she asked.

For weeks he'd been thinking of proposing to her. He could have asked, then; the words were close to the surface. *Marry me. Please.*

But he didn't. That's for Allison Daniel, he said.

You speak in riddles, she said. She thumped his chest with her palms. Come on. Let's get coffee.

Just like that, his happiness clouded. Why hadn't he asked? He had been sure, for some time, that Allie wanted him to. He followed her to the Cup O'Joe feeling as he had in his dream—silenced, as though a magician's spell had sealed his lips.

Just before the strange woman stared at him through the window, Mark had been steeling himself, again, to ask. As they'd drunk their coffees he'd found his humor again; he had just been trying to convince Allison to call in sick to work, to stay home with him—Mark designed websites for local businesses, working out of his office at the townhouse, and his schedule was his own. Finally Allie had smiled and asked, What's it worth to me?

She knew, he thought. *Ask.*

His hesitation registered; Allie's smile faltered. And when, minutes later, she left for the restroom, he was sure—for a long, free-falling moment—that she had finally given up on him. That none of his thoughts were hidden from her. That she was really calling her sister from the alley, was right now telling Darlene, *He'll never ask. I'm wasting my time.* Mark had to fight back an overpowering urge to weep.

But then the stranger had appeared. A cold finger had touched his neck. The unknown woman had stared at him—into him. Whatever she'd found there had caused her to run.

⁓

Allison returned now from the restroom, the soles of her snow boots squeaking; she picked up her coat from her chair, then saw his distress. "What's wrong?"

His first instinct was to lie, to say, *Nothing.* But he made himself tell her about the woman. "She scared the hell out of me," he said. "The look on her face—"

"Someone you knew?" Allie said. "Someone—"

"No," he said.

Allie pulled a white knit cap over her black hair, tugged on her mittens. She was trying, still, to read the look on his face.

"It's all right," he said.

They walked the three blocks home, holding hands.

Someone he knew before? That was what Allie had meant. Only a few days earlier, she had been with him at the grocery when, by accident, they had run into the mother of one of Brendan's old baby-sitters in the checkout line. The woman had been too slow to real-ize Allison was *with* Mark, that they were buying supplies for two. To remind herself that he and Chloe had split. When she finally had, she'd given both of them a quick, sour look of appraisal. A look that seemed to ask, How could a man like him—a man who had lost so much—dare to be happy again?

Allie had seen it, too. In the car she told him, It's the judgment that gets me. Like anyone has that right.

She wasn't judging, Mark told her, though he knew better. When the woman in the checkout line had last seen Mark, he had been sobbing at his son's funeral. And now here he was: trim from two years of working out, wearing an expensive sport jacket and shiny shoes and horn-rimmed glasses, standing at the side of a woman not only obviously younger than poor Chloe, but untouched by grief.

Mark tried to bury thoughts like the one he'd had, then: that Allie didn't know what judgment *was*.

⌒

The snow on the streets was bright; the rising sun's light caught hold of every flake. Mark took Allie's mittened hand; he steadied her, his fingertips touching the small of her back, as she climbed the steps to their townhouse door. He concentrated on these things: touching her, smiling. Again, he brought himself back.

What had happened this morning did not matter. He would ask Allison to marry him. She would say yes. Allie had trusted him enough to love him, and he owed her all of himself. He promised himself, then, that he would ask the right way—he would buy a ring, drop to one knee, say something to her profound and true. He would find the ring this afternoon while Allie was at work. She deserved the full ritual, the best gesture, not some half-assed declaration over morning coffee.

It wasn't until Mark was pulling the door shut behind him that he noticed the extra footprints leading from the sidewalk to the door. His and Allie's had come and gone from the left. But another pair of prints—the size of Allie's, or even smaller—approached their steps from the right, in and back out.

He glanced across the street, right to left. Then he closed the door. Before turning to Allison, he locked it.

Two

Mark didn't buy a ring that day, after all. By nine o'clock in the morning his work voicemail had amassed several messages—emergency calls, clients panicked by the impending holiday—and he ended up spending too many hours trying to figure out why a website selling imported balsamic vinegars wouldn't display any images of the bottles.

In the afternoon Allie called from work to tell him two of her college girlfriends were traveling through town, on their way east to New York. Did he want to go out with them tonight? He didn't; he disliked most of Allie's college friends, though he tried to keep that from her. He was relieved, in a way, to say no—if he stayed home to work he'd have no reason to feel guilty about ring shopping, either. He told Allie to have a good time.

But the prospect of the empty townhouse, with nothing but work and cold drafty air and his cowardice and footprints in the snow to think about, proved to be too much for him. He had been a hermit for far too long after Brendan's death; even when he wanted to be alone, now, he often failed at it. So when he knocked off at five he called his old friend and college roommate Lewis, then drove out to the recording studio in the neighborhood of Grandview, fifteen minutes away, where Lew worked as an engineer.

He found Lew smoking a cigarette beside the studio's side door, halfway down a slick and shadowed alley; the ice by Lew's feet was littered with cigarette butts, each sunken into a tiny crater, like dud shells on a battlefield. Lew had shaved his massive head cue-ball-bald, and it glowed whitely beneath the security light. Mark exclaimed over it as he knew Lew wanted him to, as they walked inside, down a narrow hallway and into the booth. "I'm an old man," Lew said. "This hair-growing business is for kids." Lew eyed Mark's own hair, made a face. "I'm glad you called, stranger. I'm bored to fucking tears in here."

Mark had roomed with Lew at Ohio State for three years, first in the dorms and then in an apartment off-campus; Lew had, in fact, dragged Mark to the party where he had met Chloe, had doubled with them on their first date. Since moving in with Allison, though, Mark had barely seen him. He had been troubled by this without making much of an effort to rectify it. But in Lew's presence now he felt an old, welcome comfort. Going through college with Lew had been, much of the time, just like this: happy, profane talk; access into secret places, cool places, where shy, quiet Mark could never have found entry on his own.

Lewis was, really, the only friend from his old life Mark had kept. The only friend from that life who'd ever truly been *his*. Lew came with his issues—he was an unrepentant drunkard, for one, and Mark wasn't—he didn't drink at all, anymore—but Lew had been Brendan's godfather, and had loved Chloe nearly as much as Mark had. Lew, more than anyone except maybe Mark's father, knew the depth of his grief. Lew had spent countless nights with Mark after Brendan's death, after the divorce, bringing Mark food, making him play video games or watch movies instead of brooding alone. Lew knew the depth of the pit out of which Mark had climbed. He knew what Mark's happiness had cost him.

Mark understood, now, why he'd called. He hadn't simply wanted company; he'd come to tell Lew he was going to propose.

They sat side by side in the control booth. Lew laced his fingers behind his gleaming head, his big wedge of a torso barely contained by a torn Stooges T-shirt. He told Mark about the band whose record he was mixing (terrible, just terrible), about other music he did like; as usual, he made Mark surrender his iPod, and while he talked he loaded music onto it from his laptop. Then he told Mark about his new girlfriend, a mechanic. "Her hands are calloused like a man's," Lew said. "I'm really questioning myself, here."

"We'll have to double," Mark said. "Allie would like that."

Lew's palm rasped over his skull. "How is Allie? I haven't seen her in ages."

Mark hesitated. When Lew had first met Allie, last year, she and Mark had been on the tail end of a fight. Lew, maybe sensing this, hadn't liked her at all, and Allie had been sharp with him when he told a dirty joke. The next day Lew had emailed him: There's plenty of people you can fuck, if fucking's all you're after. So why pick a mean one?

The two had warmed to each other since. Even so, he and Allie almost never invited Lew over for dinner, and Lew, for all his promises, almost never invited them out. Mark hadn't sat with Lew like this in, what—two months? There'd once been a time when Lewis crashed two nights a week on Mark and Chloe's couch; when Brendan had run eagerly down the stairs every morning to see if his uncle Lewis was there and needed waking up.

The acoustics in the booth made Mark's every word immediate and echoless. "Funny you should ask. I think I'm going to pop the question."

Lew sat up straight. "For real?"

"I'm buying a ring tomorrow."

Lew didn't hesitate. He rose from his chair and wrapped Mark in his arms, slapped Mark's shoulders. Up close he smelled of sweated-out beer. When they separated, Lew's eyes were moist.

Mark began to tell Lewis about all the thinking he'd been doing. How much sense his plans made.

Lew laughed, shook his head. "You're whispering!"

"I—I guess I'm nervous."

"Why? Allie's not going to say no."

"Probably not."

"Cold feet?"

Mark shook his head.

Lewis smiled, sly. "You were nervous about Chloe, too."

"Bullshit."

"What bullshit? The week before you asked her, you were like some dude on his last three days in Vietnam."

Mark wished Lew hadn't brought up Chloe, not now. He remembered telling Lew, all those years ago, that he and Chloe were engaged; he remembered saying, I need a best man; he remembered how crazy these sentences had seemed—and yet, at the same time, how they had felt ancient and right, as though the words *I am engaged to Chloe Ross* had the power to transform his puppet-self into a real boy.

"Just ask," Lew said. He regarded Mark seriously for a long second. "You have my blessing, if it matters."

Mark felt himself grinning. Apparently it mattered a great deal.

Lew insisted they celebrate; he locked the studio and they walked two blocks down the street to his favorite bar. There Lew ordered a beer for himself, and a Coke for Mark, and when he had his drink in his hand he shouted to the room that his oldest buddy was getting married, and a dozen drunken strangers whooped and toasted. Mark turned and bowed, wishing, as he always did in bars, that he still drank, that he hadn't promised his father—and Lew— that he wouldn't, ever again.

An hour and several drinks later Lewis embraced him again, heavily. "I'm so fucking happy for you."

Mark rubbed the prickly top of his head. "I'm happy you're happy I'm happy."

Lew looked at him for too long. "So you gonna tell Chloe?"

Mark only hesitated a moment before saying, "I'll have to, Lew."

Lew's smile contained as much maudlin tragedy as joy. "What'll she say?"

Chloe and Allison had only met twice. Chloe had a boyfriend, a serious one, but even so she'd done everything possible to avoid referring to Allie in Mark's presence.

"She doesn't get to say anything," Mark said, suddenly angry, as though Chloe had already begun to make the protest he knew she wouldn't. Lew offered another sad smile—he knew Chloe well enough to know exactly what Mark was imagining—then drank deeply from his beer, and for a moment Mark was close to ordering one for himself. Why shouldn't he? He was a different man than he used to be, a different man entirely.

But he did not. If he was different—if he was happy—it was because of decisions just like this one: hundreds of them, one after the other. And because of his father, who'd made him promise not to drink again, and because of Lew, who never pressured him, no matter how many times the two of them had gotten happily drunk together before.

He grew silent at the bar. The appearance in his mind of his father's face, stern and kind, had shamed him; Mark realized he had to tell him this news, too. He was shocked, really, that he hadn't talked to his father *first*. Maybe he could sneak away over the weekend to Indiana, where his father still lived alone in the same rambling farmhouse where Mark had been raised. He tried to imagine the look on Sam Fife's face when he told him the news, and was seized again by unreasonable fear.

Mark looked away from the television behind the bar—he'd been idly watching a Buckeyes basketball game—and found Lew gone. The noise in the room rose up, like flooding water, and his throat closed; he looked right and left, and finally—there—saw

Lewis outside on the sidewalk, talking with a woman in a long leather coat, smoke streaming from his nostrils.

Mark sat back down on the stool, his heart beating too fast. For the second time that day, he wondered how on earth he'd managed to become the person he was: a man who felt like weeping whenever someone he loved left the room.

Three

Mark spent the next morning, a Friday, at home in his upstairs office, debugging a website for a store that imported wooden toys from Holland—cups and balls, floppy wooden dolls with joints made of string, little horses with manes of yarn and painted-on smiles. He didn't care for the store, or the job. He had visited the place in September, and made a show of admiring the dolls before taking digital photos of them. The owner, an old Dutchman, had smiled to see one of them in Mark's hands.

You have children? he'd asked. Please take. With compliments.

No—no children, Mark had stammered, too loudly. Sorry.

The man's eyes had softened with sadness, with pity, and Mark had only communicated with him over email since.

But his work today was pleasant. Mark's visit with Lew had reinvigorated him; he had promised himself that if he slammed through the morning's calls, he would take the afternoon off to price rings. Lew had even offered to come along. And Allison had kissed him deeply on her way out the door—a promise, Mark was pretty sure, of lovemaking to come that night.

But at midmorning he remembered with a lurch that he owed Chloe a call. In less than two weeks it would be December 18— Brendan's birthday. For the last few years—since they'd decided to be civil with each other, to be *a part of each other's lives*—they'd had dinner together on that night. If his plans came to fruition,

16

he might very well have to go to that dinner and tell Chloe he was engaged.

The thought dropped into a black hole in his mind. He didn't place the call.

A plan came to him. Instead of ring shopping this afternoon, he would do what he ought to have done days ago: He'd drive the three hours to Indianapolis and surprise his father at work—Sam taught history at Butler University, but had no classes on Fridays; he'd be holed up in his office until the evening, working on his latest book, about the politics of the Colorado gold rush—to tell him about Allison.

Immediately Mark felt better. He had spilled his plans to Lewis; they were real now, and his heart sped up as he imagined telling his father, too. He'd been neglecting Sam too much, and now he could make amends. He could be the good son his father was always telling him he had.

He called Allison from the road to tell her what he was up to. "Are you okay?" she asked, after a pause.

"I'm fine," he said brightly. "I just haven't seen Dad enough lately. This will be a nice Christmas present for him."

Allison and his father had met a few times; Sam, in fact, had driven to Columbus to help them move into the townhouse. She's a peach, his father had said that night, as he and Mark stood sweaty beside the moving truck. Sam had thought awhile longer, then added, A real peach.

"Promise me you're all right?" Allie asked.

He wished, for the thousandth time, that he wasn't as transparent as everyone in his life found him to be. That he wasn't the sort of man who would always have to reassure people he was fine.

"I'm just fine," he told her. "I promise. And maybe me and Dad'll shop for you."

This cheered her. "Give Sam my love," she said. "And get me something good."

⌒

The drive from Columbus to Indianapolis followed a stretch of I-70 so straight, Mark could have safely slept behind the wheel. Cold rain and sleet pattered on the windshield. He drove past mile-wide fields, black frozen soil speckled with bent and broken cornstalks. Small towns that seemed embarrassed by their own off-ramps. A wide, straight brown river, like an interstate flowing south, its banks harboring occasional pockets of ice. An exit with a truck stop and a Stuckey's. Mark plugged his iPod into the stereo and played loud rock and roll—Led Zeppelin—and sang along to keep himself awake.

An eternity later the Indianapolis suburbs appeared in the west like Columbus's in reverse—the same strip malls, the same truck stop and Stuckey's floating out of the rain. The same endless suburbs. Finally he crested a rise and saw the buildings of downtown Indianapolis, clustered and glittering.

Mark loved Columbus, his home for so long, but the sight of Indy's skyline still warmed him. When he'd been a teenage boy— skinny, long-haired, fancying himself an artist—he used to flee the cornfields and tool around the downtown streets in his rattletrap Dodge Challenger. He'd imagined himself an adult, living in a warehouse loft, someplace with high ceilings and billowy curtains and a procession of beautiful young women in his big bed, admiring him while he painted.

He could never pass the city without remembering this. Every time he did, he felt guilty, but not because of the foolishness of the fantasy. He felt, rather, as though he'd run into an old girlfriend in line at the bank, someone he'd cruelly left, who'd cried when he'd done so. Who wasn't ready, now—who wouldn't ever be ready—to hear him say, *I'm getting married again.*

The interstate curved north, away from downtown. To the right of the highway loomed Methodist Hospital, which Mark could never see without thinking of his mother; she had been treated for lymphoma there, had succumbed in a room on one of the upper floors, when Mark was a senior in college. Mark and Sam and Chloe had all been with her. Sam had held one of her hands; Mark had held the other, his eyes closed, listening to her shallow breaths. Finally the next breath had failed to come, and the moment had stretched out longer and longer, and his father had said, Oh, no—

Mark knew, now, why he'd been hesitating to propose.

His mother had been dead more than a decade and a half, yet his father had chosen to remain single. Mark had decided upon a course of action that Samuel Fife, PhD, had never seen fit to take.

Chloe had told Mark, once upon a time, that he was just like his father. He'd protested; then, as now, comparisons to his father alarmed him. This was during the summer after his mother had died, when Mark and Chloe had lived with Sam at the farmhouse for the summer months, taking care of him. When Chloe had told him, they'd been alone in the house, curled together in the narrow guest room bed while Sam was away on errands. He'd been staring at the ceiling, Chloe's head tucked against his chest, worrying aloud about his father's state of mind.

I see where you get it, Chloe said suddenly.

It?

Your ability to love, she told him. The people you love, you love completely.

He hadn't known what to say.

I'm sad for your dad, Chloe told him. But I'm glad we're in love like he was. Is. I mean, this is pretty rare. Don't you think?

He had thought so, had told her so then and there. At the end of the summer he vowed it, slipping a ring on Chloe's finger in a Columbus rose garden.

But Chloe had left him. They hadn't even made it a year beyond Brendan's death when she'd cast him loose. We're not the people we were, she'd told him. If we ever were.

Mark was not a husband. He was not a father. Not anymore.

He was free. The thought came sneakily, as it always did, but when it had arrived he could only clench his teeth and accept it: His wife and son had left him alone. He was a new man. His own man.

He could do whatever he wished.

⌣

Ten minutes later Mark had parked the Volvo on Butler's campus and was inside the long, low limestone edifice of Jordan Hall, climbing wide stone steps—slightly concave, slippery with wear—to his father's office on the third floor.

Sam Fife had worked in this building since before Mark was born. If the downtown skyline had regressed him to sixteen, the inside of Jordan took him back even further, to the age of ten. The building, he'd told his father then, smelled like thinking. It did still—a happy smell, of books and people and their heated thoughts. History, the parts of it they'd never scrub or remodel away: decades' worth of pipes and cigarettes, once smoked openly; musky perfumes and colognes; industrial cleaners; heavy paper, glue, and leather; spilled ink; tweed in need of a wash.

From twenty feet down the hall he saw that his father's door was open. Laughter burst out of it. Mark stood in the doorway, summoning his younger self's doubtful courage. His father sat at ease behind his desk, fingers laced behind his head, loafered feet propped up one of his open drawers. He wore a terrible multicolored sweater, and—he did this every winter, and every winter it never failed to surprise Mark—he had grown a small white fringe of beard, at odds with his ever-balder head. His desk, as usual, was neatly organized and dusted. Shelves of books lined the walls, so densely they might have been painted on, all the way into the corners.

Another professor, Mitch Doyle—round and asthmatic, wearing a black sweatsuit and a Colts cap—sat in the stuffed chair in front of the desk, his cane across his knees. Both men smiled, at Mark's appearance—was he a student, needing something?—and then his father dropped his feet. "Mark! Oh my goodness!"

"Hey, Pop," Mark said—his father hated the nickname, but Mark could already see worry seeping into his face, and he wanted to calm him. "I was in the neighborhood—"

"Mitchell! It's my boy!"

"So it is," Mitch said, struggling to rise. "Good to see you, Mark."

"Oh my," his father said, and came to Mark's side—as always, comfortingly tall.

"I'll see you, Fife," Mitch said, wheezing out the door. "We've got graduate committee on Monday, anyway."

"If I'm interrupting," Mark said.

"Oh no," Mitch and his father said all at once. "Sit, sit," his father said, and Mark settled into the vacated chair, while his father shut the door. He rolled his eyes. "Thank you," he said. "Did I tell you Mitch is our new department head?"

He had, but Mark made a face anyway. "What's that like?"

"A roiling, acid hell. Good Christ, the meetings take forever now."

"*You* should be head," Mark said.

His father didn't want to be in charge of anything, but he liked to be told he ought to be. "Six more years to retirement," he said, smiling grimly. "Mitch is a small price to pay for routine. But who cares! You've driven out to see me."

"I have."

"Something's wrong." Sam's face tightened. "Has something happened with Allison?"

"No! We're fine, Dad. I just wanted to talk some things over. Get out of my head a little."

This was old code. Sam had been the first to use it, in the year after Mark's mother died. Later, after Brendan, Mark adopted the phrase himself.

Sam squeezed Mark's forearm. "Of course. Would you like to walk with me? Final papers are due—if we stay here we'll be beset."

His father shouldered on first his sport coat—green tweed, shot through with brown—then an overcoat. Mark followed him down the hallway. A dozen students, milling at the top of the stairs, brightened, and his father greeted them all.

They walked outside into a speckling of cold rain. His father touched Mark's elbow, guided him down a branching sidewalk to a side street, toward a coffee shop he liked. "It *is* Allison. When I said her name I saw it on your face. Tell me."

Sam was bracing himself for bad news. He had seen Mark's mother through a year of cancer; he had answered the phone seven years ago to Mark's choked voice telling him Brendan had died; he had seen Mark through a divorce from a woman both of them had loved. Now Sam only wanted to know that things, always and forever, would be all right.

"I'm buying a ring," Mark said—though his throat tried to close around the words. "So yeah, I guess we're all right."

"You *guess*?" his father said. He used the Voice—the timbre, dripping with friendly sarcasm, that brought students to full attention—*Mr. Shields, you're paying attention. Please define* noblesse oblige. *You guess? Or you're certain? Take your time. This is history; it's not going anywhere.* "You guess," his father said again, laughing. "Stop."

Sam embraced him. His father's coat smelled like the farmhouse, like mothballs in the closet, like safety, like *Sam*; Mark closed his eyes, grateful, lost. "I'm so glad," his father said. "You deserve this."

Sam drew back, his eyes blinking rapidly behind his glasses. *Deserve*, Mark thought, and fended the thought away with a sudden, snappish fury. It left in its wake the bleary sadness with which Mark was too familiar. They walked along in silence, Sam's hand on Mark's shoulder.

The café was a small, square shop inside a bland, featureless storefront at the eastern edge of campus. Inside, though, it was close and warm; the smoky, greasy smell of roasting beans hung close to wooden rafters deeply carved with generations of initials.

As they waited in line, Sam asked, "Will you be staying tonight? I could cook—"

Mark's plan had been to drive to Indy and back in a day, but now that he was with his father, he was tempted; he missed the farmhouse, its high ceilings and plastered walls and rooms full of books, his father's turntable playing crackly jazz.

He had spent years, now, saddened by the thought of Sam alone there. His father wasn't a hermit by any means—he went to dinners with colleagues; he went to concerts. But most nights he stayed at home, sitting in a deep leather recliner, grading papers or listening to his records through old headphones he'd bought in the seventies—they dwarfed his head—and drinking a single martini made with scientific precision. His nearest neighbor was half a mile down the road. Which was still dirt.

"I can't stay," Mark said, with genuine regret. "Allie's going to want me home tonight."

His father nodded, but his disappointment was evident. They each filled a mug, then took a seat by the window. "Now," Sam said, "will you please tell me everything?"

Mark laid out his case: He and Allison had lived together for six months. She was thoughtful, calm—older, it seemed sometimes, than he was. Her divorce, he thought, gave her some common ground with him. But she was playful, too, and sharp as a tack. With her he felt something like peace.

"I love her," Mark said. Again, louder: "I love her a lot."

His father's eyes flicked up to Mark's, then back down to his drink. "What will Chloe say?" he asked.

Mark was stung, just as he'd been when Lew asked the same question.

Sam said, quickly, "I shouldn't have—"

"No, it's okay. I don't know. Chloe's got Steve now—"

"The restaurateur." His father pursed his lips carefully around each syllable.

"Still," Mark said.

Sam still called Chloe on her birthday and on holidays, to check in, to tell the mother of his grandson that she was still a part of his life. Mark would never have known about these calls if Chloe hadn't mentioned them. Chloe still loved her father-in-law, too. That summer after Mark's mother died, when they were all holed up together in the farmhouse, Chloe had taught Sam how to cook; she'd gone through Mark's mother's clothing for him, boxing it up for Goodwill. Sam loved to read aloud, and every night after sunset, the three of them sat on the big stone porch and drank wine and listened to his father read *Great Expectations*, Sam always sitting on the left side of the porch swing, as though his wife would, at any moment, emerge from the house and fill the empty space to his right.

There'd never be a good time to broach this. "Dad. Can I ask you something?"

"Of course."

"You never remarried."

Sam's brow knit; he frowned into his coffee.

His father had had dates. He'd mentioned them in passing,

with an odd formality: *So-and-so mentioned that to me at dinner, one night last July.* He was a good-looking man, well known and well liked. Once Mark had become an adult, he'd realized his father had a dirty mind, that he was capable of the same appalling jokes with his friends that Mark traded back and forth with Lewis. He and Mark had seen each other through losses they'd each barely borne. But after all this time, Sam still never mentioned his private life to Mark, as though he worried that the tending of his emotions was business too private for his son. Mark had never found a way to tell him otherwise.

"Ever been tempted?" Mark asked.

His father looked briefly from side to side—a simple reminder of where they were, how much he could say. Figured—Mark had finally gotten the guts to ask, and he'd done so in a place where Sam had an automatic out.

But then Sam said, "Well. I've been meaning to tell you. I'm seeing someone. At the moment. Now."

Mark rocked back from the table. "You are?"

"Yes. And"—his father had blushed a deep crimson—"I don't know how to describe this. We don't want to marry. But we've discussed, ourselves, what we're doing, in those terms. We've spoken of . . . of permanence."

"*Who?*"

"Helen Etley." After a pause, he added, "Political science."

"How long—"

"A little over a year." His father crumpled his napkin into a ball, rolled it between his palms. "I'm a coward."

Now Mark was peeved. "What's so goddamned scary about—"

"*Everything's* scary. Good Lord, Mark. Think about it."

His father's most cutting phrase. In other words: *Don't be stupid.*

His father kept spilling details. Helen was twelve years younger—

"Cradle robber!"

"Keep your voice down!"

—and she'd been hired three years ago, from Penn State. She'd looked for a job in Indianapolis because her elderly mother, newly widowed, lived in town. Helen was smart, classy—his father used that exact word. They went to plays and jazz concerts together. She had no interest in living outside town, but they had begun to consider living together, in some fashion. Those negotiations were ongoing.

"In some fashion," Mark said.

"Do you disapprove?"

"Dad! No, I don't disapprove. Maybe, you know, if I had a chance to meet her, that question might actually mean something—"

"I want you to meet her."

"I'd like to."

His father let out a tremulous laugh. "I'm happy," he said quietly, as though he might be arrested for it.

"Dad. It's okay." And it was. It absolutely was.

"Mark," Sam said, still blushing. "You're happy, too? Tell me you are."

Mark swallowed a lump. "Yeah."

"I like Allison," his father said then, catching his eyes. "I see in her what you do."

Relief weakened him. "Thanks, Dad."

"Bring her out soon. Please? And—we'll have dinner with Helen."

Mark raised his mug; his father raised his; they clinked the rims together.

They fell silent then. Mark looked around him, at the chattering, impossibly young students. He watched a couple some tables over; they were stripping off their wet coats, smiling at each other with rapt intensity, unable to contain the joy in each other's company. The girl—the woman—was a tall, willowy blonde, smiling wide, her glasses still dotted with rain. The boy beside her was spindly, hunched, blinking too fast, his hand never leaving his love's elbow. As though, if he stopped touching her, she'd vanish.

Mark couldn't watch them. He turned back to his father—but Sam was staring out the window, holding his mug halfway between the table and his lips, smiling a private smile.

Sam canceled his office hours, then drove Mark to nearby Broad Ripple, to a store that sold good antique and secondhand jewelry, owned by a friend of Helen's. Sam stood by the door, his hands in the pockets of his overcoat, while the owner—a short, plump woman with long salt-and-pepper pigtails and a merry smile— showed Mark tray after tray of rings. His father had guided Mark well—Allie would love this place, and the woman who ran it. "Do you know the size of Allison's finger?" she asked. Mark shook his head no. "Don't worry," she told him. "It can be resized. The right ring is the right ring."

Finally he saw it: a small sapphire on a platinum band. Both colors fit Allie; her look was wintry in all the ways her heart wasn't.

The ring was elegant, understated, not too expensive, but certainly not cheap. He handed the woman his credit card; she smiled warmly, winked, and he remembered planning his wedding with Chloe—the way everyone they'd dealt with had offered them signs and codes, as though they were joining a cult. *You'll know all our secrets soon enough.*

When they were in the car, Mark forced out his last question: "Would Mom like Allie?"

His father clicked his seat belt into place, his eyebrows drawing together. "Of course she would. Allie would make your mother laugh. They'd play euchre." Sam grasped Mark's knee and shook it from side to side. "Mark. It's okay. We trust you."

We.

⌒

Mark beat Allison home by forty minutes, but well after dark. In that time he took a shower and put the ring into the pocket of his jeans. While he waited for her, he opened his phone. He'd gotten one message while showering, from a number he didn't know.

His nerves got the better of him; his mouth was sour; he quickly ran upstairs and brushed his teeth again, then swished mouthwash between his cheeks. He patted his thigh; the ring was still there. Then, pulling aside the downstairs curtains to check the street, he dialed his voicemail.

The message began to play: He heard a woman's voice, high-pitched, hesitant. "Um. Mr. Fife. I really need to speak with you. My name is Connie Pelham. I have—I have an issue to discuss with you. It's very important. My number is—"

She recited it, carefully, but her voice shook, as though she was near tears. In the background Mark thought he heard the voice of a child. Then a long silence. Perhaps a deep intake of breath. "Please call," the woman said.

To erase this message, press seven. To save it, press nine.

He pressed nine, confounded. The woman didn't sound like she had business for him—and no one who did ever called him this late in the evening, not on a Friday. She'd sounded nervous...

He remembered again the woman who'd stared at him through the window of the coffee shop. The one who had run away from him in fear. This couldn't be her, calling, could it? The thought was ridiculous, and yet he found himself uneasily mulling it over, all the same.

A key turned in the front-door lock, startling him. Allison stepped through the door, bundled in her coat and bearing armloads of shopping bags, shivering theatrically. She saw Mark standing at the top of the stairs, and smiled.

Mark put the phone in his pocket. His fingers touched the thin, cool surface of the ring.

And this was why he had done the right thing, why the strange woman didn't matter, why his doubts didn't matter: because here was Allison calling out, "You're home!" Here was Allie, climbing the stairs, meeting him. His Allie, holding out her arms, smiling, kissing him, taking him in.

Four

They did not sleep for many hours.

"You're sure?" Mark repeated, at one in the morning, Allie naked and straddling him. "Say it again."

"Yes," Allie said. She stared into his eyes, bent forward, bit at his lips, dug her nails into his shoulders. If he concentrated he could feel, against his bicep, the slight ridge of the ring on her finger. She ground down against him. "Oh, yes."

At two thirty in the morning Allie got up and rustled around in the kitchen downstairs; sex made her ravenous. Mark lay sleepily on his belly. He was engaged—but even now, inside his head, the words sounded unreal, the wild hope of a child. He thought back to the tawdry way he and Allie had met—they'd trysted in a hotel room in New Jersey, after knowing each other all of six hours. Now look at them.

Ten years ago he'd been married; he'd had a toddler for a son. If a time-traveler had told that long-ago Mark Fife where he'd be in a decade, what lay between him and his future, he might have cut his wrists in the bath.

Allie returned to the bedroom with a glass of water for him, and a glass of wine for her. She brought with her the sharp tang of sex, of sweat; it mixed agreeably with the wine's bouquet. She sat beside him; he kissed her dry knee.

She said, after a sip, "You know it's okay with me if you have some wine."

He remembered how close he'd been to ordering a beer last night with Lew. Whatever danger he'd felt then was gone now, banished. He had come all the way into his new self; a little wine couldn't hurt him. "I only ever get wine," he said. "That's got to be the deal, okay?"

He'd never told her much about his drinking—only that he didn't like himself drunk, which was true enough. That for a long time he'd been drunk too much.

Allie studied his face. "Okay."

He sipped from her glass. It was a good red—Allison made a study of wine—and he nearly shuddered in pleasure. "Tell me what I'm tasting," he said.

"Wine," she said, shrugging. "Merlot. I'm not one of those people."

He laughed. "Yes, you are."

"I'm not supposed to *tell* you. You're supposed to decide for yourself."

He took another sip.

"Boysenberry," he said.

"You're also not supposed to make shit up."

"It's oaky?"

She took the glass back from him. "We'll go to a tasting."

"Sure."

She reclined against his chest. "So I said yes."

"I remember. Thank you."

"I've been wanting you to ask," she said. "And I wanted to say yes before I asked you some things. I wanted you to know I want this, more than anything."

She'd turned serious just as he'd made himself relax. "Ask me what?"

"Well…are we having a wedding?"

He was abashed not to have much of an opinion. He'd envisioned himself asking, envisioned them living together—but a ceremony?

"Your call."

She turned toward him. "I'd like to have one."

Now Mark did have an opinion, which was that his last ceremony had driven him nearly crazy and cost almost twenty thousand dollars. "You okay with small and cheap?"

She laughed. "I'm very okay with that."

"Excellent. So where should we do it?"

He was thinking about some small, bland public office; a bland public officiant.

"Tahoe," Allie said, without hesitation.

So much for cheap. But he said "Sure" anyway.

Allison loved Lake Tahoe, and had hung pictures of it all over her old apartment. She'd gone there for a vacation, by herself, after her divorce, and had fallen in love with the mountains, the waters. She told him she'd thought seriously about making a clean break, moving to Sacramento or even Reno.

Mark had never even been to California. The thought of the wedding, though, excited him. It was going to be a good time. Almost no one he knew besides his father and Lewis and maybe an uncle in Portland would make that trip.

"Blue skies and water," she said. "We could rent a cabin and honeymoon there, too."

"Hell," he said, "We could move out there."

She made a quick, surprised noise. He was as shocked as she was, but he didn't retreat.

"Why not?" he said. "Everything's wide open for us. You know?"

"Wide open."

"Yeah. I mean, why are we staying in Columbus? I can do the business anywhere. You hate your job—"

"Wait," she said. "Colorado."

"You'd like that better?"

"I like Denver," she said. "A big city. Better for business. And the mountains are right there."

"Vancouver," he said. "Let's apply for Canadian citizenship. Get the fuck out of Jesusland."

"New Zealand," she said. "Citizenship's harder, but they might need tech professionals."

"There you go," he said. "It's settled. New Zealand."

She nestled closer, took the glass back from him, and drained it.

"Okay," Allie said. "Here's the tough one. I don't even know—"

He smiled. "Ask anything."

"I just want you to know, I don't know which way I'm leaning. There's not, like, a right answer."

"Okay," he said, mystified.

But then, in the pause, he guessed it.

"Kids," Allison said.

He'd thought this over before. Of course he had—a thousand times since Brendan had died, yes, but in particular during the last few months with Allie.

They'd even discussed it once. Allie had been off the pill when they met, but went back on when they agreed they were serious. Mark had told her, then, that he wasn't sure he could ever think about children again. It's not a priority for me, Allie had told him. I mean, who knows?

Which wasn't the same as saying she didn't want children at all, was it? He wished there was more wine in Allison's glass.

"What do *you* think?" he asked. Because he was a coward.

"I might," she said finally. "Right now, no. I always figured if I did, it would be later." She lifted his hand and kissed the tip of his thumb. "But hey, I'm thirty-four—"

"Almost an old woman."

She curled tightly beside him. "I mean, could you—do you want to have another one?"

She misunderstood his hesitation, and winced. "Mark, God— *another one*. That sounds so—"

Plenty of times before, he'd been driven to rage by the exact same question. But never with Allison—and not now. "It's okay," he said. "In the spirit of honesty, I have no idea how to answer."

"Bill wanted kids," she said. "I kept putting him off."

She'd told Mark this before; Allie liked, or needed, to tell him what an utter disaster her marriage to Bill had become. He'd always wondered if he was supposed to reply by cutting down Chloe. Sometimes he did—Chloe had left him; he had a lot to complain about—but most of the time he didn't. Couldn't.

She said, "Now I don't know. Over the past few months—" She sat up straighter. "All of a sudden I can see it. I mean, me with a kid." She waited a long time before saying the next part: "*Us*, with a kid. I mean, I *know* you're a good dad. I think we'd be good parents. Together."

His mouth was dry. "You think so?"

"Yeah. I do." She met his eyes. "I wouldn't want to get married if I didn't think we could pull it off. Parenthood. If."

He chose his words carefully. "I wasn't as good a father as you think. And I wasn't as good a husband."

Allie started to disagree, but stopped herself. She had barely met Chloe, but he'd told her plenty about the end of their marriage. Certainly Allie saw the trouble on his face every time he came back from one of his and Chloe's infrequent dinners. Allie's marriage may have been awful, and the one time Mark had met Bill he hadn't taken to him, but he'd never been tempted to hate the man. A bad match, that was all, and if Bill ever asked him, he'd say so. Mark, however, suspected Allison had an entire manifesto prepared for Chloe: *Let me tell you about the ways you fucked over Mark, you crazy bitch.*

"You're too hard on yourself," she said, her voice husky.

He kissed the top of her head. The few sips of wine he'd drunk had left a faint, warm cloud of serenity behind his eyes. Had going dry all these years left him so much of a lightweight?

"We'd be good at it, right?" Allie said. "If?"

He had to give her an answer. It wouldn't be fair, if he didn't. And at the moment the answer was easy to give.

"We'd be great," he said. "But not yet, okay? I want some time just for us."

Her eyes were damp. "I want that, too," she said, and turned to kiss him.

⌒

Mark had expected the wine to put him to sleep, but instead he lay wide awake, Allison snoring beside him, thinking about the strange woman who'd called him. He thought about his father and his father's new girlfriend. He thought, for as long as he could bear to do it, about having a child with Allison.

Mostly he thought about Brendan.

In fact, he did what he was often prone to: He lost himself in a guilty fantasy, one that both pleased and sickened him. In this fantasy Mark and Chloe had divorced, and Brendan—who had never died—lived with her. And because it was a fantasy, Brendan had not aged, either; instead of a quiet, withdrawn teenager (because, had he lived to see his parents' divorce, he surely would have become one), the Brendan whom Mark imagined was still seven, still the spindly boy he'd been the day he fell down the steps. His hair was still unkempt, needing a cut; he was still wearing the gray

Buckeyes sweatshirt and jeans he'd had on when Mark found him at the base of the steps, crooked and boneless and still.

But he was alive, this Brendan, and Mark was visiting him and Chloe at the old house, where they still lived, and he and Brendan were sitting side by side on the old porch swing, and it was springtime and the trees were budding, and Brendan had his hands folded in his lap, and wouldn't lift his face, as Mark explained that he was going to marry someone new; as Mark told him, You're really going to like her; as Mark said, You don't ever have to call her your mother; as Mark said, I've been lonely without you and your mom, you know that. Inside the house, Mark knew, Chloe was crying.

He said to Brendan, Maybe someday you'll understand, but by then Brendan was gone from the swing, and inside the house, at its center, where the stairwell was, Chloe's cries built to a terrible, grinding scream—

Mark started awake. Allison shifted beside him but didn't open her eyes. He'd drifted off without turning out the bedside lamp. Allison's ring glinted, where her left hand lay flat across his chest. Chloe, wherever she was, was not screaming. Mark was here, in his new life, happy. And his boy—the truth of it descended upon his chest like an iron bar—was still dead, still gone.

II

❧

*The Little Boy Who Used
to Live Here*

Five

Mark and Allie spent the next week cementing plans for the wedding. They called friends and family—mostly Allie's—spreading the good news. They nailed down preliminary details: They'd be married at the end of the coming summer, on September 5. The ceremony would be held on the western shore of Lake Tahoe, in a private lodge overlooking the water; they'd been lucky to book the place, even this far in advance. The guest list would be small. Lewis would be Mark's best man; Allie's sister, Darlene, would be the maid of honor.

By Saturday night they'd hastily developed a plan to introduce Mark's father to Allison's family. Sam drove to Columbus the following afternoon, and that evening both families toasted Mark and Allison's good fortune over dinner at the townhouse. As always Mark admired his father's civility; Sam charmed Allie's mother and sister, and managed not to argue with Allie's father about politics— he chose, instead, to tell folksy stories about the Colorado gold barons that Mark could tell were really about the Bush administration. Mark spent much of the night talking with Darlene's dreadlocked boyfriend, Tim, who asked him for business advice—Tim and Darly were thinking about acquiring chickens, selling organic eggs. After dinner Sam helped Allison with the dishes. Mark heard them laughing in the kitchen: Allie chastising Sam for not bringing Helen, his father's embarrassed protests.

It wasn't until Monday that Mark listened again to the message the strange woman, Connie Pelham, had left on his phone; he did so while walking across the OSU campus, killing an hour while his father had lunch with an old colleague. He listened again to her sad, tentative voice, the sound of her child in the background.

By now he had convinced himself that Connie Pelham was someone who thought he owed her money. He'd been over and over his records, had found nothing—but he'd made mistakes before. Two years after Brendan had died, Mark had worked for a friend's web-design start-up; it had failed after only a couple of months, bankrupting the friend. Mark's name had turned up on forms it shouldn't have, and he'd had to hire a lawyer to disentangle himself. Maybe Connie had something to do with that mess.

It didn't matter. He had done nothing wrong; he wasn't going to go out of his way to seek her out. He deleted the message, and her number.

And anyway, he had a much more unpleasant call to make.

Mark sat on a bench by Mirror Lake and dialed Chloe. She wouldn't answer; she was teaching her second graders. Even so he struggled, leaving his message. He told her he was sorry he hadn't checked in on her in a while—and, right away, wished he hadn't; she would hate that kind of language from him: *checking in*. He told her he hoped she was well. That he hoped they could have dinner soon, to catch up. A week from tomorrow was December 18, Brendan's birthday (and here Mark stumbled, as he always did, even though they'd almost always met on that day); he really hoped she'd have the time to meet, around then. If she wanted.

When he'd finished he sat watching the water of the lake, the semi-circle of ice that obscured it. As students he and Chloe used to walk here, holding hands, kissing when they were alone. They'd probably sat on this very bench and made each other promise after promise.

I'll always want you. I'll love you forever. Of course I want kids.

Had he picked this spot in order to make himself sadder? He was capable of it.

It took her two days, but Chloe finally left him a message in return. Sure, she said, let's have dinner. I'm free—I'm free that day. Tuesday. She sounded frustrated, her voice pinched, a little hoarse. I've got to run.

She paused a long time, and his heart beat faster and faster. Was something wrong? Did she know about Allison already? What was she about to say?

Okay, she said at last, like the closing of a door. Bye now.

⌒

The following Sunday night, while Mark browsed alone at the Barnes and Noble at the Easton Town Center, killing time while Allie shopped for her mother at a crafts store nearby, Connie Pelham appeared in front of him.

Despite a nice dinner out, and the lingering excitement of the engagement, Mark was enjoying his solitude. The past week and its phone calls and its endless planning—not to mention a dozen emergency jobs his clients had called in between Wednesday and Friday—had exhausted him. An evening shopping for books and maybe a new CD was exactly what he needed.

His enjoyment ran deep. In the chilly, numb year after Chloe left him, Mark had gotten into the habit of visiting any number of bookstores around town, especially in the evenings, when he was most often at loose ends. He liked to wander the shelves, nursing a coffee, picking up books—fiction, usually, or history—without even looking at them. He'd close his eyes and lightly run his fingertips across the spines, until a book felt right, pushed subtly back. He'd stay until the bookstore closed, before returning, reluctantly, to his tiny apartment, or to an all-night diner (anyplace where he had to seem normal, composed—anyone but the man he was), where he read whatever he'd purchased ravenously, without allowing his own thoughts any time or space to intrude.

He was glad to be back in this place, now, as himself: happier, more relaxed, needing no trickery to distract him from his life. Even so, he had to admit he missed those old days, just a little. Especially that odd period of months when he had begun, slowly, to accept what had happened to him. When the pain had begun to subside; to recede, tide-like.

Once, during the spring when Brendan was five, Mark had taken him to Goodale Park, to learn to throw a Frisbee. Brendan, while running headlong across the grass, had turned an ankle; fifty feet away he'd collapsed as though shot, and had begun to wail. Mark had run to him, put his arm around Brendan's shoulders, let him sniffle into his chest—and then Brendan had surprised him.

It feels so good, he said.

Twisting your ankle feels good?

No, Brendan said. That hurts worse than anything. But when it goes away? That feels *better* than anything.

He'd laughed, turning his ankle from side to side, the laces on his sneaker flopping and dirty. Mark had laughed, too.

A woman's voice said his name, then: "Mr. Fife?"

Mark turned, startled, and saw her, five feet away: the woman who'd stared at him through the coffee shop window. Here in front of him, she was younger than he'd thought—younger than he was, maybe—but this was the same round, tan face; the same narrow brown eyes; the same dark halo of curls. She wore the same black coat. Only the color of her scarf had changed, from silver to cerulean.

She still, however, looked frightened of him. Her eyes darted across his face; her hands worked and twisted. He wondered if she wasn't just a random crazy, after all, about to harangue him about the evils of the Democrats, or to ask him over and over what time it was. The crazies liked bookstores—he'd noticed that, when he was crazy and spending a lot of time in bookstores himself.

"I'm Mark Fife," he said.

The woman drew back—fearfully, Mark thought. "I'm Connie Pelham. I called you?" Her voice—it was indeed the same voice that had left him the odd phone message—was high-pitched, quavery. It sounded, he thought, like her hair—curly, too large, out of control.

She offered her hand, awkwardly, and he nearly fumbled his coffee trying to shake it.

He didn't know what else to say, so he asked, "Connie, have we...met?"

Connie Pelham glanced out the bookstore window, toward the parking lot, at the cold rain that had fallen steadily all evening, refracting each headlight in such a way that the window seemed broken into jagged shards.

"No," she said. "I'm—no. We haven't. Not really. I'm—I'm doing some amateur detective work, I guess, but I'm not very good at it." She took a deep breath, as though summoning will. "Can I buy you a cup of coffee, Mark?"

Detective work? "What's this about? Do I owe someone money?"

"No! It's not like that. I don't work for anyone." She smiled. "I'm just me."

And who was that, exactly? A woman frightened of him before, frightened of him now. Any curiosity he felt was undone by deep misgiving.

Connie glanced at the window again. "I'm sorry," she said, when she saw him staring. "My—my ex-husband is due soon. He's dropping off my son."

He remembered the child's voice, speaking behind hers on her phone message. This strange woman had a child, and he did not.

43

"Ms. Pelham, what's this about?"

She nodded, as though listening to a voice inside her. "I'll just say it. Mr. Fife, I live at One Fifty-six Locust. In Victorian Village."

He started. Connie had just given him the address of *his* house—his and Chloe's old house, from the old life. The place where they'd lived with Brendan, where Brendan had died.

She said, "My—my ex and I bought it nine months ago from Margie Kinnick. I—your name was on the papers. I found your picture online, on your website? I've been thinking about whether or not to call you. Then I thought, no, I ought to tell you in person. I saw you at the coffee shop when I went to find your address, but I saw you in the window—you remember?—and I got nervous, and I thought, I can't do this, I should leave this poor man alone—"

Her voice hitched, as though she might cry. His misgivings curdled into alarm, and he scanned the store, hoping to see Allison, returning for him.

"—But then tonight, I saw you walk in through the door, and I thought, that's *him*, and then I thought, maybe it's meant to be, you know? Maybe I'm *supposed* to talk to you?"

Connie smiled, then—suddenly, weirdly hopeful. "Do you think things are supposed to happen?" she asked. "Like in fate?"

Mark heard this question more frequently than he could bear, from friends and strangers alike, as though it might comfort him. They asked the man whose mother had withered to a moaning skeleton before dying whether he believed God had a plan. They asked the man whose son had broken his neck falling down the stairs whether or not he believed things happened for a reason. They asked a man whose wife had abandoned him for her grief what he thought about fate.

"No," he said tightly. "I don't."

Connie frowned. "Well, I do. And seeing you here is—I guess it's no stranger than anything else that's happened."

He heard his father's voice: *You guess?*

Mark could guess, too. Connie could only want to talk about one thing, couldn't she? Weeks after Brendan's accident, he and Chloe had put their house on the market—they couldn't bear being in it anymore, surrounded first by their son's toys, his strewn clothes, and then by the absence of them. They couldn't bear the walk, every day, up and down the narrow stairs. Their own echoing voices.

But no one would make them an offer. Turned out there was a law—for three years, you had to report to buyers if someone had died in the house. Mark and Chloe had resigned themselves to a year—but three? Three seemed impossibly cruel.

Then after six months of silence, their realtor, Margie Kinnick— dear Margie, who'd been so friendly with them when they bought the place, who for years had stopped by to visit whenever she was on their street—had offered to buy the house from them. She was in the market for a place in the Village, she said; she'd always loved their particular house. Her heart broke for them, she said. Why not make a deal that would help everyone? They'd sold the place to her for less than its value, with relief.

Mark hadn't spoken with Margie in ages; he'd simply assumed she still lived at the old place. Just last year he'd gotten a Christmas card from her, with 156 Locust as the return address.

So Margie had sold the house to Connie Pelham. And—Mark guessed—she hadn't said a word to Connie about its past. Some- one in the neighborhood must have tipped Connie off, told her the history of her expensive new house, the tragedy that had occurred there. And now this woman who believed in fate was playing ama- teur detective. Seeking him out.

"Mr. Fife," she said, "can we sit down?"

He wanted to run from her.

"Sure," he said, his voice soft, conciliatory. His angry-client voice. "Sure, Connie."

She led him to the café at the front of the store, and asked again if he wanted a drink, then looked so sad and dismayed when he held up his coffee cup that he almost ordered another just to keep her from crying. She left him to stand in line, casting nervous glances both at him and out the front windows.

When she was in line he took out his phone and texted Allison: Come get me. Urgent. A middle-aged man with a ponytail was setting up an acoustic guitar amplifier in the corner of the café. The music would provide a good excuse to break away, even if Allison didn't come.

Connie returned with a mug of tea and smiled. "I wish I could have coffee, but it's too acid."

"Ms. Pelham," he said, "look, I—"

"I know. I'm a crazy woman and I should just go away. I know. But I have to ask you something. Something really important."

She placed her hands around her mug and looked down into the steam. As though it contained a sign. God's plan, just visible in the depths.

"Mr. Fife. Did you have a son? A little boy?"

So he had been right.

"I did." His voice measured. "My ex-wife and I lost our son in 2001. His name was Brendan."

Connie lifted a hand to her mouth. "Oh God."

"Ms. Pelham," Mark said, "you have to understand. I really don't like to talk about this."

She closed her eyes. "And it happened—there? In my house?"

Her house. The same old voice that had spoken to him during his long years of grief offered up its familiar whisper: *Unfair, unfair.*

"Yes," he said. "It happened at the house."

She was crying, now, tears rolling out from the corners of her eyes. "Where?"

"The stairs," he said. "He fell down the top flight, onto the landing."

46

She was shaking her head.

"Look," he said, "I had no idea Margie would—would choose not to disclose something like that." He added, quickly, "It's not the house's fault."

Connie dabbed at her eyes with a napkin. "It's a good house. And I sank—my husband and I put a lot of money into it. It's a good school system. I mean, we wanted that for our son."

"Yeah," Mark said. "So did we."

Didn't she know about libraries? Couldn't she have looked up the article in the *Dispatch*?

"Ms. Pelham," he said, "I'm sorry, but I really don't like talking about this, okay? You have to understand—"

Connie plunged forward as though he hadn't spoken. "My son, Jacob. He's almost nine. Two weeks ago I got a call from Parkhurst Elementary. From Mrs. Dane?"

Mark didn't know her. Brendan hadn't lived to be nine, to have Mrs. Dane as a teacher. But he nodded helplessly.

"Jacob kept falling asleep in class, and he told her he was too scared to sleep. So I asked him about this, and Jacob—he tried to lie, and tell me he was sleeping fine. But I kept pushing him, and pushing him, and finally he told me the same thing—that he was too afraid to go to sleep. So I asked him, Why was he afraid?"

Don't say it, Mark thought.

"And Jacob said, 'Because of the ghost—'"

He stood, too quickly; his chair clattered backward. "That's enough."

"—The ghost of the little boy who used to live here."

Connie's frightened moist eyes. His own breath. The slow bubbling murmur of the voices around them. A guitar string plucked, plucked, tightening into tune.

"Never speak to me again," he said, then turned and left.

An older couple at the next table was staring at him; the

woman's hand covered her mouth. He walked quickly past the registers to the front door, a sick taste tightening his throat. Connie Pelham might have said something to his back as he pushed through the doors. Outside the cold wind had strengthened; sleet cut at his cheeks. He looked back; Connie was walking toward the doorway after him, her eyes sparkling with tears.

He reached into his pocket, to call Allison, but then a horn honked to his left: Allie pulling up to the curb in her Honda, peering at him through the streaked windshield. He jogged to the passenger door—slipping briefly on a patch of slick black ice—and ducked into the warm car.

"We have to go," he said.

"What's wrong?"

"Just go, okay?"

"Okay," Allie said. She put the car into gear and pulled away from the bookstore. Connie Pelham emerged, her face twisted, Mark thought—he watched her in the passenger mirror, the reflection threaded over with quicksilver rain, cold and sluggish—twisted up in rage, or grief, or both.

⌒

On the drive home he told Allie what had happened. She listened carefully, frowning, and when Mark told her the worst part—when the word "ghost" left his lips—she erupted:

"Oh my God! She didn't say that."

"She did."

"What did you tell her?"

"Not much." He shook his head. "I ran for it."

"She just came up to you?" Allie glanced over at him. "How'd she *find* you?"

This was a good question. Connie Pelham knew where they lived; those had to have been her footprints he'd seen, just after she'd spotted him at the coffee shop. Mark had never told Allison about them, and now he began to feel a little sick. *Had* Connie been following him? Things happened for a reason, she'd said. He bet they did.

When Allie parked in front of the townhouse, Mark half expected to see Connie Pelham already standing at the doorway, wringing her hands. But when they walked to their door, no shadowy figures emerged from the alley. He locked the door behind him, and shut all the downstairs blinds.

In the bathroom he pressed a scalding washcloth to his face. Replayed what Connie had said to him: *The ghost of the little boy who used to live here.* Brendan, a ghost.

Preposterous. Worse. And yet the implications of the idea— ocean-size, icy-cold—touched at the shore of his mind, and he felt an appalling fear, old and familiar. The horrible crash on the stairs. The silence. The world he knew suddenly crushed to flinders in the palm of a giant's hand.

He breathed in and out through the washcloth until it cooled.

When he entered the kitchen, a few minutes later, Allison asked, "What did she expect you to *do*?"

"I didn't talk to her long enough to find out."

Connie had told him she was waiting for her son. A young boy—the one he'd heard on her phone message.

"I bet the kid heard something at school," he said.

"What?"

"She has a son. He goes to Brendan's old school. I bet he heard something. Or one of the neighbors told him. 'You live in the house where that kid died.' Something like that. And then he ran with it."

The more Mark thought about this, the more he was sure of it. The adults in the neighborhood would only speak about what happened among themselves, quietly, respectfully. The neighborhood children, though—the news that a little boy had died would have been passed down among them, in the back of the school bus, at slumber parties. Brendan's old friends were just starting high school, now—but that didn't mean they, or their younger siblings, would never cross paths with Connie's boy. And if Jacob Pelham was young enough—how old had Connie Pelham said he was? Nine?—he could easily have lost himself in a story like this. Lying awake, staring into the shadows of his high-ceilinged room, thinking about the little dead boy.

Mark said, "It makes sense. The kid's folks are split. He's alone with his mother in a big old house. He made it up."

"Sure." Allie was still mad, her brow knitted. "But for that woman to—to just say that, to your face. I want to call the cops on her."

Mark thought of all the times Chloe had gotten a hair up her ass, taking offense at some slight against Brendan, real or imagined. The ferocity she'd unleash. "Maybe Connie's just—I don't know. You get protective of your kid. If she truly believes this—"

Allie gave him a look. "That doesn't excuse her."

"I'm not saying it does. But parenthood's a weird place."

Her voice tightened. "I'm not saying it isn't."

Since the night of their engagement, they hadn't talked any further about the subject of children—not even when Allison's mother had looked into Mark's office and cried, Oh! This would make a wonderful nursery! But he hadn't avoided the topic on purpose, and just now he hadn't meant to shut Allie out. He'd only been thinking of Brendan, of all the times *he* used to wake in the night, afraid of imaginary monsters. Of all the times Mark himself had woken, panicked by Brendan's cries.

Allie began to wipe down the countertops. "Do you think she'll try to contact you again?"

"Allie, she's come to the house before."

"What?" Allison turned to him. "When?"

Mark told her then about finding the second set of footprints, the morning Connie had spied on him through the coffee shop window.

"Call the police," Allie said.

"I don't know if that's necessary."

"She can't come here again, Mark."

"No, she can't. But—look, what would I even tell the cops?"

He remembered, then, the young policeman who'd come by the house when Brendan had fallen; he'd shown up moments after the ambulance had. The cop had been young, Mark's age, with thin rust-red hair. He'd said he would drive Mark to the hospital, behind the ambulance. He'd gripped Mark's arm when he tried to go up the narrow stairs to the landing. Mr. Fife, he'd said, Wait for the paramedics to finish. Let them do their job. Mark heard the paramedics on the landing, the fizzy crackle of their radios. He could see Brendan's foot, canted toward the top step of the bottom flight, his dirty sneaker pushed off his heel. The laces untied.

I have a son, too, the cop had said, his grip painful.

Again, Allison asked, "What did she think you'd do?"

He held up his hands. "I really need to stop thinking about this. Okay?"

Allie searched his face, then gave in. "Sure. Sure. Want me to make some tea?"

He didn't, but he nodded.

Allie put on a pot of water to boil. She readied a mug for each of them, and went upstairs to change into her pajamas. Mark remained at the table.

The little boy who used to live here.

The very word. *Ghost.*

The teakettle whistled; Allie filled her mug. Steam rose up from between her hands.

Allison must have seen the anger in his face. She placed her hand, hot from the mug, across his wrist. "You don't even believe in ghosts. Do you?"

Of course he didn't. His father was an atheist, and Mark's mother had been something like a Buddhist; as in most matters, Mark had decided a long time ago that Sam Fife's view of the world served him just fine. For as long as he'd been a functional adult, he hadn't believed in heaven or hell, or souls—and if you didn't believe in souls, you couldn't believe in ghosts, could you? You couldn't believe in an afterlife at all.

How many times since Brendan had died had he explained this to people? So many well-meaning relatives and friends had told him, at the funeral, Brendan's in heaven now. Or: He's in a better place. If his father and Chloe hadn't been standing beside him he'd have argued with every one of them: *No! He's gone. He's utterly and completely gone. Don't you get it?*

He was something, and now he's nothing at all.

Mark worked the rest of his tea down his tightened throat. "I'll be all right."

Allie said, "I have to ask. Chloe, does she..."

Does Chloe need to know? Mark hadn't thought that far, yet. But Chloe would have to be told, wouldn't she? She had signed the papers on the house, just as he had; she could be found, too, by someone playing amateur detective.

But she had signed those papers as Chloe Fife. Since the divorce she'd gone back to her maiden name—she was Chloe Ross, now, C. Ross in the phone book. She barely ever turned on her computer, let alone left any sort of trail on the web. She'd be a lot harder for Connie Pelham to find than Mark had been.

"We're having dinner Tuesday," he told Allie. The day after tomorrow: Brendan's birthday. His throat closed. "I guess I'll tell her then."

How, he couldn't begin to imagine.

⌐

They went upstairs to bed, but Mark couldn't sleep. He was heart-sick, in a way he hadn't been in years—not since the year after the accident, when everything he saw, every noise he heard, every scent and texture in all the wide world, reminded him of Brendan's absence. That Brendan was dead. The very word a slow bubble in tar, expanding and popping and swelling again. *Dead. Dead. My boy is dead.*

Connie Pelham had returned that word to him. Allison, tonight, had held him, kissed his cheeks, stroked his face. He could have made love to her; she would have welcomed it. But he would have hovered over Allie's warm body thinking *Dead, Dead.* Tomorrow, when he tried to work, he would think *Dead,* he would think *Gone,* he would think *Ghost.* If he called his father. If he lay perfectly still. *Dead, Gone, Ghost.*

On Tuesday, Connie Pelham would make him say *Ghost* to Chloe, and then the disease would spread to her.

He couldn't. He couldn't tell Chloe this.

Two weeks after Brendan died, he'd found Chloe in Brendan's old bed, knees pulled to her chest, clutching fistfuls of his sheets to her mouth. Mark had wanted to lie down beside her, to press his belly to her back, but even then she would not have allowed it; already Chloe had begun to jerk away from his touch.

I thought I heard him, she said.

Soon after, they began to argue about selling the house. Brendan was everywhere, there; they'd given away his things, but still stumbled upon objects they'd missed: an action figure beneath the armchair, a Cheerio on the windowsill, a mateless sock tucked into the folds of a towel.

Both of them were having nightmares. Both of them dreamed of Brendan, laughing in distant rooms, crying in the middle of the night. They traded off episodes of insomnia, wandering the hallways in shifts, as they had when Brendan was an infant, squalling for comfort every two hours on the dot. Chloe cried; when Mark woke in the night, he walked downstairs to the kitchen and poured himself a drink.

When he finally asked her if they would be better off leaving, Chloe had erupted, begun to beat her hands against him. We can't! We can't!

You can't make me leave him. You can't.

But he had. Slowly he'd made her agree that the house was a danger to them, that its memories were too potent—that if they were going to have any chance, the two of them, they had to move on. But his gambit hadn't worked. Not long after they moved out, Chloe had left him for good. And then Mark returned to the house, by himself. He'd spent a week alone there. He'd drunk whiskey by the bottle. He'd had terrible, vivid dreams.

Mark slipped his arm from beneath Allison's. "What?" she murmured, into her pillow.

"Nothing."

"I thought—"

"Shh," he said. "Nothing's wrong."

He pulled the covers over her bare shoulder, then stood and crept downstairs. In the living room he turned on the television, the sound lowered, and watched a movie about a giant, tentacled thing pulling swimmers down below the surface of a lake.

He remembered the end of that solitary week at the old house: Waking. Not knowing himself. Finding his father cleaning the kitchen, a box of empty bottles beside the door.

But sometime before Sam had come looking for him, Mark had woken up alone, in the dark. He'd been sleepwalking—how else to explain that he was in the upstairs hallway, kneeling on the floorboards, out of breath? He'd been talking, he thought; the sound of his own voice had woken him. He felt he'd woken up in the middle of a secret, at the edge of a revelation. He was just outside Brendan's room, and he'd been talking, and then he had been awake in the dark.

Because he'd been drunk, far too drunk.

And ghosts weren't real. He did not believe in ghosts. Ghosts made no *sense*.

When he was Brendan's age, though—when he was the age of Connie Pelham's son—he *had* believed. Mark had been an early, avid reader, and, until he was twelve or so, he'd believed nearly every story he found in a book—especially if these stories involved the supernatural, the unseen, the monsters that—he was sure—inhabited the shadows of his room, the recesses of his closets, the half-empty spare bedrooms in the upstairs of the farmhouse, ticking with silence.

One book had especially terrified him: a collection of essays about haunted houses across the world. One such house was Borley Rectory, in England—he could still remember a photographic plate at the book's center, showing a pale smudge on the Rectory's staircase that was supposed to be the specter of someone lost. Who? He couldn't remember, now. Someone dead and gone, descending the stairs, over and over, playing out an old misfortune. That photo made him consider what it might be like to be a ghost. To do nothing but walk his house, alone at night. To reach for the people who lived there. To understand they could not hear you.

Brendan had believed in ghosts, too. In the old house, he had often woken, crying out for help—especially during his fifth year, when Chloe's grandfather had died, and Brendan had first learned about death. Thereafter, their old house was alive with threats from the beyond: Branches tapped his window, pipes rattled in the walls, old timbers flexed in a stiff wind. One "ghost" Brendan claimed to have heard groaning down the hall had been—Mark was pretty sure—Mark himself, straining atop Chloe.

Finally—at two in the morning, after Brendan had woken screaming for the second time in as many nights—Mark had a long talk with him. He told Brendan about how there were no such things as ghosts; about how their big old house was scary in the dark, but when you turned the lights on, it was okay. Mark sat on the edge of Brendan's bed, beside Brendan's small form, wrapped tight in his covers. He flicked the switch just above the headboard: the Ghost-Killer.

See? Now it's dark. But here are the lights—and look!

Their house, their friendly happy house, all its rooms painted in cheerful yellows and turquoises and pumpkin-golds, returned.

The ghosts are in your imagination, Mark had said. I promise.

Brendan, unblinking, the covers pulled to his pointed chin, said, I believe you.

Two nights later, however, Mark woke again to Brendan's panicked cries.

After that he tried another strategy. If you see a ghost, he told Brendan, just say, *You're not real, and I'm not afraid of you.* Over and over, until you don't see it anymore.

And that works? Brendan had asked doubtfully, his eyes still wild and red-rimmed.

Sure it works, Mark told him, his voice rich in fatherly confidence. Even inside of dreams.

And, miracle of miracles, this *did* work. Brendan was a serious boy, full of doubt and fear, but he learned to vanquish his ghosts. That week Mark often heard him, murmuring the words like prayers: *You're not real, and I'm not afraid.* The words gave him enough courage to sit up and flip the Ghost-Killer, and flood the room with light.

Mark stood, turned off the television, plunging the townhouse into darkness.

He remembered waking, kneeling in the hallway, his head ringing with the echoes of his own voice, and, just maybe, Brendan's—

No. This was ridiculous. So, all together now:

You're not real. I'm not afraid.

He walked upstairs and climbed back into bed. Allison didn't wake.

Maybe, Mark thought, the mantra had been his mistake. Maybe he hadn't gone far enough. Maybe what he should have done was tell Brendan there were ghosts everywhere: in the closets; in the walls; in the attic; in the basement; on the narrow, creaking stairs. Especially on the stairs.

He should have said, The ghosts live anywhere I'm not. You're only safe with me. Stick close to Dad, okay?

Stick close, and I'll keep watch.

Six

That next day, Monday, Mark could barely concentrate on his work. His anger at Connie Pelham had intensified overnight—curdling, it seemed, even during the spare two hours of sleep he'd finally managed. Once he was up and dressed, her own ghost seemed to hover just outside the house, threatening him with its story. He skipped his usual midday coffee break at the Cup O'Joe—Connie, after all, might be waiting for him there. He clenched his jaw every time his phone rang. All afternoon, as he typed at the computer, he felt the open curtains at his back.

I'm not afraid of you, Connie Pelham. You're not real.

Yet he kept probing her words, like a sore inside his mouth he couldn't stop touching with his tongue.

The little boy who used to live here.

He couldn't help himself: he imagined a shadow-boy, a shape cut out of the air, standing silently in Brendan's old bedroom, gazing down at Connie's boy.

You're not real.

The very thought of Connie Pelham and her son, living in the old house, alarmed him. He had never gone to visit Margie Kinnick, when she'd lived there; when he thought of the old house at all, his only comfort was to imagine it as a place he and Chloe still inhabited. A place where the three of them still lived, happy, safe. Their usual clutter on the floors and counters.

How could Margie have sold the place without telling them? This, above all, felt like a betrayal.

When Mark and Chloe had been vulnerable, they'd trusted her—with the house, with the memories of Brendan there. I'll take care of it, Mark remembered her saying, as they'd signed the papers. Don't you two worry. But what had she done, instead? She'd sold the house without telling them, to the worst possible family. Because of this, Mark would have to tell Chloe, at Brendan's birthday dinner tomorrow night, about Connie, about her son.

Chloe, I'm marrying Allison. Also a crazy woman thinks Brendan's haunting our old house. How's Steve?

A vision began to preoccupy him. In an hour he would be meeting a client only a few blocks from the building where Margie Kinnick worked. He imagined himself, afterward, marching into Margie's office, confronting her, making her hear the same words he'd heard. Making sure she understood the consequences of what she'd done.

And then, as he was putting on his coat to leave, he knew: He would really do it. He'd trusted Margie, and she'd betrayed him, and Chloe, and even Allison. Connie Pelham had caused so much suffering—why shouldn't Margie Kinnick suffer, too?

﹀

An hour later, heart beating too fast, Mark climbed the steps of the two-story brick office building in Grandview—no more than a mile, in a straight line, from the old house, and closer than he liked to go—that housed Margie's agency. Not a thing had changed since he and Chloe had walked inside almost sixteen years before, clutching a flyer for their house at 156 Locust, hearts in their throats. The same reception desk squatted past the vestibule; the same spotless green carpet swallowed up his footsteps. The same troubling smell of money filled the air. In 1992 he and Chloe had come into money—much to their surprise—but it had terrified them, as though instead of an envelope full of bank statements, they carried a bagful of snakes.

No, he didn't have an appointment, he told the receptionist now. But he needed to talk to Margie urgently. And he'd be happy to wait right here. The receptionist, a young man wearing suspenders over a pale blue shirt, frowned and told him to have a seat.

While he waited Mark looked through a binder of available houses, organized by neighborhood. The past year, it seemed, had been just as brutal for real estate in Victorian Village as anywhere else; the houses weren't going for much more than they had six years ago, when Mark and Chloe had gotten out.

He waited a long while. A man with silvery hair, wearing an expensive overcoat, walked past him, greeted the receptionist jauntily. He was followed by a black couple in their early thirties, trim and handsome. They were buying for the first time, Mark thought—the man spoke too loudly; the woman kept her hands in the pockets of her long coat and looked straight ahead. Both of them wore dazed, frightened smiles. They had seen their dream house. They were in love.

Mark watched them with a deep, tricky pain. The woman reached out and stroked the man's shoulders, through his coat. They were dressed in expensive clothing; the man carried a leather briefcase. They'd earned their good fortune. They were lucky—but nowhere near as lucky as Mark and Chloe had been, when they'd first walked through these doors.

A month before they bought the house, neither of them had dreamed such a thing could be possible. They were each twenty-three, newlyweds, living in a tiny apartment in Clintonville, together pulling in a little over fifty thousand dollars a year. They'd planned to rent and save for five years at least, maybe more; then they figured they would look for a little ranch house in the northern suburbs and put in five years there. And so on. A big house in

Victorian Village, they would have said, was for bankers, executives. People born into money.

Then one night Mark's father had called and told him, in the same chatty tone with which he might tell Mark about the rain, to be on the lookout for a check arriving from his attorney.

When Mark asked what it was, Sam said, Well. Your mother left you some money.

Mark's mother hadn't been dead a year, then; his father still held the words *your mother* in his mouth too long, like he'd learned them in another language. Mark didn't know what to say. It seemed wrong to admit Sam had said anything at all, let alone that what had happened to his mother had been of any benefit to anyone.

But he and Chloe, then, were eating most of their food out of cans, and spending too much time listening to their neighbors scream at each other through their apartment's too-thin walls. Sniping at each other over the length of time the other spent on the toilet.

How much is it? he asked.

A little over two hundred and twelve thousand dollars, Sam told him.

In answer to Mark's stunned silence, Sam explained: Some of the money had come from life insurance; Mark had been his mother's sole beneficiary. The rest had come from investments. Molly, Sam told him, had gotten an inheritance from Mark's grandparents, the last of it some ten years before, and had played it on the stock market. She owned a little bit of Microsoft, Sam said, a smile in his voice—I didn't know, myself, until just before she died.

Mark's mother had been small, still, quiet; she'd been the head librarian at the old Carnegie library in the little town of Westover, three miles from the farmhouse, and Mark had never imagined someone more dispositionally suited for the job. When she'd met Sam, Molly had been a San Francisco hippie; in the library she wore glasses and long shapeless dresses and her hair in a braid. At home her favorite place was a papasan chair on the back porch, where she'd sit through dusk in the warm months, books spilling from her lap. Mark couldn't remember his mother even holding money in her hand. The idea itself—his mother, wealthy!—seemed crass.

He had just been freed—from his debt, from his youth, from his tiny apartment, from a hundred different limitations on his and Chloe's future. But he could think of nothing better to say than: I can't.

Your mother wanted this, Sam said. What else would she do with it? Give it to me? When I kick the bucket you'd get it anyway.

Incredibly, his father laughed. Mark realized: Sam was happy. He'd loved calling up his only son, saying, *Two hundred and twelve thousand dollars.*

You want my opinion? Sam said. Buy a house. Your mother would have liked knowing you did.

When Mark hung up, he didn't tell Chloe about the check. In fact he couldn't bring himself to say a word about it until it arrived—that preposterous number confirmed, grooved into the check beneath his shaking fingers—until he'd deposited it, after an ever-friendlier chat with one of the bank managers, in their joint account. And Chloe, then, was so worried about money that he had to argue even to take her out to a fancy dinner, in order to give her the news.

At the restaurant he slid the deposit slip across the table to her, saying, Surprise.

Chloe stared at it for a long time in disbelief. Is this a joke?

No. He was still shaking as he explained. And then Chloe was shaking, too.

Oh Molly, Chloe said. Oh sweet God, thank you.

Before dessert arrived they'd agreed with Sam: They would

use part of the money on a down payment toward a house. Then for weeks afterward, they took long walks at night through neighborhoods they liked: German Village, Dublin, Bexley, Old Town East. Victorian Village, just south of campus, especially—as poor students they'd both rented here, had dreamed of its big rambling homes. On a recommendation from Chloe's principal they called Margie Kinnick, an agent who had worked the neighborhood for years.

You're lucky, Margie had told them, smiling, not long after they first walked through these same doors and told her their story. If you choose wisely, you can buy the home you'll have all your life.

By the time the receptionist called Mark's name he was near tears. *Don't do this*, he told himself.

But he climbed the stairs anyway. He found Margie in the same office, seated behind the same big oak desk, in front of a window that overlooked the bare whipping branches of a tree—when he and Chloe had been here, those branches had been thicketed with lush green leaves; the office had glowed emerald. Margie had gained weight, and had quit dyeing her hair; she was gray now, square, her face almost craggy. A deeply shadowed line formed between her eyebrows at the sight of him. Bangles and charms hung in a tangle from her wrists; her arm tinkled when she offered her hand.

"Connie Pelham called me yesterday," she said, right away. "She told me she'd talked to you. I was going to call you this afternoon."

Margie was lying about that last part, he was sure. "She... confronted me last night," he said. "She's been to my house."

Margie briefly closed her eyes. "I wish she hadn't done that, Mark."

"Did she tell you what she told me?"

Margie kept her voice neutral. "She said the two of you... discussed Brendan?"

Margie spoke like his former therapist, Gayle, used to, with a little curl upward at the end of her words, tossing the statement back
to him as a question. Making *him* say the crazy stuff aloud.

"She says the house is haunted."

Margie sighed. "She told me that, too."

Mark sat down in one of Margie's plush visitor chairs. He made
a gesture: Go on.

Margie only pursed her lips. She was giving him nothing—like
someone guilty. Fine, then. "I was a little surprised to hear you'd
sold the house," he said.

"It was time," Margie said evenly. "The market's been brutal.
There was a lot of turnover in the neighborhood after you left. Sally
Watson sold the apartments next door, the new guy rents to students. The Upchurches' place was foreclosed on. I look up, I'm surrounded by strangers. If I wanted to get out with a profit, I had to
do it right then." She frowned, maybe seeing the disturbance in his
face. "I'm sorry if you're upset, but I made the right choice."

"You could have told us." He shook his head. "You could have
told *her.*"

Margie's eyes narrowed. "No, I couldn't have. You know that
better than anyone."

He opened his mouth, but shut it before anything came out.

She said, "You said it yourself, back when you were trying to sell
the place. *It's not the house's fault.* And it isn't."

"Even so—"

"Come on, Mark." She lowered her voice. "What was I supposed to do? Let you and Chloe screen the buyers? It wasn't your
house anymore." Anger filled her voice—a tone he'd never heard
from her before. "Do you really think this was the first house I've
sold where—something unfortunate happened? People die in
houses."

"I know that—"

Margie waved him off. "In Victorian Village? Those houses are eighty, a hundred years old. Everyone wants to buy there because the houses have *character*. But you know what character is? It means a hundred years ago people got laid out on a table in the parlor for three days before they were buried. I'd bet you Brendan wasn't the first—"

"Margie," he said.

Her eyes were wide. She tapped her nails on the desktop, but swallowed the rest.

She said, "I see why you're upset. I can only imagine what you're thinking, now. But I bought your house because I saw it as a good investment. Okay? And yeah, because I felt for you and Chloe. But I'm not Mother Teresa, Mark. I'm not sentimental. I never told you I'd live there forever. I just took it off your hands. That's all."

It's in good hands, she'd said to him and Chloe, as Chloe had begun to weep.

Mark, his face burning, said nothing. Margie wasn't wrong, but he'd be damned if he said so aloud.

She pushed her chair back from the desk, but didn't get up. "Look. I'm sorry Connie felt the need to find you. A reasonable person wouldn't have. I told her so on the phone. If it's any consolation, I didn't tell her nicely." Margie shook her head. "She threatened to sue me."

"Can she?"

Margie screwed up her face, then shook her head again and stood. The meeting was over.

If he'd gotten to her at all, the effect had been momentary; she was as business-like now as when he'd arrived. He tried to remember the happy, joking woman who'd come to dinner with them after they'd first moved into the house. Who'd rubbed her nose against baby Brendan's when they'd brought him by her office. Who'd left them a poinsettia on their porch steps, in the first week of every

December. Several other houses in the Village got them on their porches, too.

But he knew: Margie was no different now than she'd ever been. She'd never *had* to be different.

"Mark, I'm sorry, but I have an appointment coming up."

"I'll go," he said.

"Connie Pelham's a crazy woman. Put her out of your head."

He could only nod.

Her face softened, a little. "Mark, I'm sorry. I hope you're well?"

"I am," he said. Then: "I'm getting remarried. In September."

"Good," she said, and smiled. There was warmth in it. "Oh, that's very good."

A few minutes ago he'd been shaking with anger, and now he was lingering.

Margie dropped her voice to a whisper. "So I probably don't have to say this, but I will. In all my time in the house, I never—"

"I know," he said, quickly.

She walked around the desk and took his arm. She accompanied him out her door, down the hallway, all the way to the front doors.

"You deserve better than what you got," she said. "I hope you know."

She smiled at him, then leaned forward and kissed the air next to his cheek.

⌒

Mark was too ashamed of himself to mention his meeting with Margie to Allison that night, but she certainly sensed his mood. After watching him stare silently at the television for a while, she suggested they go out for Chinese food for dinner.

When they'd taken their seats at the restaurant, she watched him gravely for a while before asking, "So what can I do? Tomorrow?"

He was surprised, and then doubly shamed. Of course Allie

had been aware of Brendan's birthday—she knew why he was having dinner with Chloe, and he'd told her often enough that the day could make him a little crazy. Somehow he thought he'd been keeping that a secret from her, too.

"I'll be all right," he said, meeting her eyes. Tell her about Margie, he urged himself, and didn't.

"I was thinking I'd go out tomorrow night," Allie said. "See some friends while you're out with Chloe. But only—only if you—"

"That's fine," he said. "I'm going to be okay. I've been through a few of these."

Allie smiled and squeezed his hand, and—for the first time that day—he allowed himself to smile back.

After Allie went to bed, Mark went to his office and shut the door behind him. He woke up the computer. It was now eleven thirty at night, December 17, 2007. Mark didn't much care for ritual, but he'd developed one for Brendan's birthday. He could follow it in the morning, he supposed, but he also knew sleep was a long way away, tonight. He could stare at the television, still stinging with the afternoon's embarrassment, or he could do this.

He waited until the clock on his computer screen turned over to midnight. Then he retrieved supplies from his big metal file cabinet on the far wall: a large sheet of paper from a sketch pad and a box of charcoal. He taped the paper onto the drawing table beneath the window, then turned to his computer and spent a few minutes deciding on music. Once he'd tried to listen to songs Brendan had liked, but he didn't have many of them on his hard drive anymore. His boy had had good taste, though; he had liked folky stuff, men and women with acoustic guitars: Nick Drake, Neil Young, Tracy Chapman. Had been crazy about "Pink Moon," for kid reasons— he'd liked the idea of a moon that was pink. Mark's serious, introspective boy had thought poor, suicidal Nick Drake was funny.

None of that now. Mark settled on something droning, contemplative—Lew had gotten him hooked a couple of years back on music that let him sink out of his own mind, into his work. He liked—according to Lewis—post-rock, and ambient electronica. Obscure stuff. That idea pleased him too, just as it had in college, when he and Lew used to skulk around Used Kids Records, buying punk and grunge. Now he listened to bands with names like Tortoise. Godspeed You Black Emperor. Mogwai. Explosions in the Sky.

If he were alive, and fourteen years old, Brendan would be hip to post-rock. It pleased Mark to think so—that Brendan would share his music, just as Mark shared music with his father.

Mark upped the volume as much as he dared, then turned to the drawing table, picked up a piece of charcoal, and closed his eyes. Spindly guitar prickled out of the speakers. He took a breath, two, and tried to pull Brendan's face from memory. Brendan at seven.

His son, alive.

He had a favorite memory, for this exercise. One night not long before Brendan died, Mark and Chloe had rented *Searching for Bobby Fischer*, and Brendan had stayed awake and attentive throughout, fascinated by the chess-playing kid, by his ever-more-harrowing matches. When the movie was over Brendan had turned to Mark and asked, Do we have a chess set?

They did, upstairs in the guest room. Mark and Brendan had gone upstairs to get it, Brendan—as he usually did—scrambling bug-like ahead of Mark up the steps.

The narrow staircase at the house's exact center, hairpinning at a landing barely big enough to hold Brendan, let alone Mark.

His son, sprawled at the foot of the steps. Mark hovering beside him, his cries—*No No No*—vibrating between the narrow walls as he waited for the paramedics, aching to cradle Brendan's head but fearful of his kinked neck. Touching only his warm upturned palm—

No. Not Brendan that way.

This way: Brendan sitting across from him at the dining room table. The chessboard set up between them, made of thick good wood, the pieces glossy like rich chocolates. Mark taught Brendan the moves, they played one practice game, and after that Brendan made his moves without help.

Brendan approached chess the way he approached any problem—his face a knot of fear and supreme concentration. And while he focused on the board, eyes darting among the pieces, Mark had watched him.

His hair had been a dusty straw color, the exact muddy middle ground between Mark's own dark brown and Chloe's yellow-blond. His face a long oval, with a surprisingly pointed chin. Lips parted and full. Cheeks pale enough to show the blue vessels just beneath. That quality, peculiar to children (but surprising, to him anyway, in boys), of not just fragility but impermanence—as though, if he brushed a finger across Brendan's cheek, he could wipe the skin away, like dust from a moth's wing.

Brendan's eyes a deep oceanic blue (Chloe's, exactly), narrow, elongated—a touch longer and they'd have an almost Asian cast. A long narrow nose, a smallish mouth. An aristocratic face, Mark often thought—Sam's face, maybe even more than his own, and Mark had always thought that when Brendan was in his forties he'd lose his hair, have that same high forehead full of ponder. Sam had seen this, too—he and Brendan had, that last year, started calling each other "Professor Fife," nodding, solemnly, over and over, as though endlessly acknowledging each other in the hallway outside their offices, until, always, Brendan cracked up and collapsed.

Brendan's eyes sweeping across the chessboard. Eyebrows drawn slightly together. Lower lip pouched out. Tiny, even teeth.

Looking up at last, perplexed. Saying, Dad, I don't think I'm a chess prodigy. Mark hadn't known whether to laugh or cry.

That face.

Mark opened his eyes and began to sketch. He tried not to pause, not to consult memory. That wasn't the point, was it? No. The point was to remember well in the first place. To keep Brendan from becoming a black hole in his mind. A shadow in a darkened room.

Forty minutes later he thought he was done. He allowed himself to pull his eyes away from the particulars, to see the entire drawing. And there was Brendan, looking up from his game, ready to speak.

Mark swiveled back to the metal cabinet. A thick pile in the bottom drawer comprised the accumulated drawings he'd made of Brendan before he died. But a smaller stack, in a manila folder on top, held all the sketches he'd made since.

He hadn't begun this ritual until two years after the accident. By the time of Brendan's first birthday, after, Chloe had just left him; Mark was living with his father, barely alive. On the second birthday he had been dating a graduate student at OSU with the unfortunate name of Harriet Martin. They had spent the night of December 18 at an antiwar rally on campus—Mark had insisted; this was in 2002, he'd been in therapy for months, and the ever-escalating stupidity of the Bush administration had helped to rouse him from his long, numb stillness.

That night he was trying his best to be alive, to do something, *anything*—but in the middle of the rally his mind had kept sliding to thoughts of Brendan; he'd thought, clearly, that maybe it was better his little boy hadn't lived to see this future. When he and Harriet returned to her apartment, the guilt that had flooded him in that thought's wake had broken him down; he'd fled without much apology, had left a message for Chloe—they weren't speaking, then—that had shamed him, and had stayed up for a long time, awaiting a call that never came. In the middle of that long night he'd panicked, wondering—with a wrenching, shivering fear—whether he could even remember his son's face.

Mark now laid out the sketch he'd produced that night—and the four he'd produced, once a birthday, thereafter—side by side on the drawing table. At the bottom of the pile was a photo he'd taken of Brendan on his seventh birthday, glancing up from a book at the camera, surprised. His face was fuzzy around the edges, but it was still a shot that got the kid, that caught him unawares, unguarded. Six Brendans, now: one real, the others echoes.

Not much had changed in this new drawing. A narrowness in the bridge of Brendan's nose, but that might just be a slip of his hand, a too-thick shading. The eyes were too long. But apart from these minor flaws, Mark could look down and recognize his son.

He flipped through the drawings, then again, quickly. He'd made enough, now, for an animation; as the pages whickered by, Brendan's expression changed, his eyes opening wider, as though he'd been startled.

Mark stacked the new drawing with the others and shut them all away in the drawer.

Seven

The following evening, Mark drove to Dublin—Chloe's neighbor-hood, on the north side of the city, outside the 670 loop—to meet her for dinner at a Mediterranean place they both liked. It was a forty-minute drive for Mark during rush hour, but at least Chloe hadn't suggested her boyfriend Steve's restaurant downtown.

Before leaving, Mark had lingered for a while in front of his closet—what did one wear, when one had news such as his to deliver? He chose khaki slacks, a black buttondown shirt, a sport coat: the sort of clothing he had never worn when they were married.

He and Chloe did this sort of thing, now—they dressed nicely for each other.

On the drive he thought about Chloe sitting beside Brendan's grave. She usually spent Brendan's birthday with her parents, who lived an hour northwest of the city; eventually, along with her mother, she'd go to the hilltop cemetery in Marysville, where three generations of her family had been buried, to leave flowers at Bren-dan's headstone. Mark used to go with her, even after the divorce, but he'd given that up. The grave meant far less to him than his drawings, than his dinners with Chloe. He'd said that to her, once: I just don't *feel* him there.

Mark had said this, too: I'll grieve in my own goddamned way.

But he still imagined Chloe, shivering against the cold, kneeling in the snow and murmuring—he knew she did this—to their son. He saw the picture clearly, and felt a terrible ache.

And then, even though he tried not to, he imagined Brendan, in the old house, looking down at Connie Pelham's sleeping son.

All afternoon Mark had tried to come up with a plausible reason for canceling tonight, but he couldn't. Even with a week's head start, he didn't know how to tell Chloe any of what he had to say— about the engagement, about Connie Pelham. After ten years of marriage and six of divorce, he could not predict Chloe's response to either piece of news.

Still, Mark looked forward to seeing her, to sitting across the table from her. Despite her cruelty, during the divorce and after, despite Allison, he wanted very badly to see her. He had long ago given up denying that for the rest of his life he would need to be aware of her: her life, her storms, her infrequent happiness. Chloe, he believed, needed him, too. They had tried not speaking, for over a year—and in the end they'd buckled. They had shared a decade, Brendan, his loss. No one else alive had known him like they had; no one could return that faint submarine ping.

Chloe was late. In the restaurant lobby Mark paced, too nervous to sit at one of the benches. His phone buzzed in his pocket. Allie, texting him: Thinking of u. xoxo.

He turned off the phone without replying. Despite Allie's thoughtfulness earlier, she'd tensed up tonight, while they readied themselves to go out. What are you going to tell her? Allie kept asking, until finally he'd admitted—more angrily than he'd wished— that he still didn't know. Her text—which really meant Don't forget your fiancée—deserved to be ignored.

He'd just deleted it when Chloe walked through the front doors in a long gray coat; she smiled gratefully at an older man who held the door for her, and he turned his head to follow her passage.

Chloe's eyes touched his—and there, right away, Mark knew:

Something was wrong. She might be smiling, but her eyes were shifting, full of chaos. Had Connie found her?

But then she smiled—the lopsided, slightly pained smile he'd gotten used to, since. She walked to him, brushing back her long, straight hair—back to its original blond, now, from the muddy red-brown she'd been dyeing it. He was surprised to see her narrow, black-framed glasses; she'd never needed them. Not surprisingly, they looked fantastic on her.

It was always like this: He saw Chloe, and his heart lifted—as it always did, because she was so beautiful, still, because he had loved her for so long—and then, immediately, his heart sank, because she was so beautiful, because he had loved her for so long, and didn't any longer. Couldn't, any longer.

She opened her arms to him. "Hey," she said.

Chloe almost never spoke his name.

They embraced. He closed his eyes, breathed her in. She still smelled of the same perfume—a French name he could never remember—and beneath it he could make out the scent of the detergent she used to clean her clothes, of the conditioner she used on her hair, the particular smell of the blush she used—it had never been necessary; he could never convince her. He rubbed his hand across the rough wool of her coat, between her shoulder blades, and which of them paused an extra second, held the other close, he could not discern, except to know that it had happened.

"Chloe," he said. That old magical spiral. Her name a spell, cast.

She handed her coat to the hostess. Beneath it she wore dark blue jeans and black high-heeled boots; over a gray blouse she wore an odd, cropped yellow-and-black checkerboard jacket that looked as though it belonged on some poodle-skirted fifties teenager. In the past Chloe could have made clothing like this work through sheer force of personality, but tonight? If he didn't know her, he might have thought: Here's a woman pretending.

But then, he now wore a goatee to mask his slight double chin, his drooping jowls.

"You look good," he said.

"Thanks," she said, averting her eyes.

She never said, *You too.*

The hostess led them down a narrow set of stairs, past a series of wooden booths. Mark looked into the faces of the men and women seated there: an old game, dating all the way back to his and Chloe's first night out. These strangers watched Chloe pass, then turned to him, the man who got to walk with her. The lucky guy. Even though he knew he shouldn't, he felt again the old giddiness, the old sense of magic good fortune. He should have answered Allie's text.

The hostess sat them at a small table against the back brick wall. She lit the candle, and then left. Chloe's face was softer in the candlelight—ghostlier, and fuck him for thinking it.

Her eyes were puffy. She had been at the graveside, crying.

"So," Chloe said, brightly. "How've you been?"

He wasn't ready. Not yet. "You first," he said. "Long day."

Chloe gave him an old, old look. The you're-being-weird look. "How've I been?" she said, wincing. "Wow."

She was about to say more, but then the waiter came for their drink orders. Chloe turned to him with relief. She ordered wine; like Allison, she was into wine now, thanks to Steve and his expensive restaurant, with the *best goddamn cellar in the state of Ohio*—and then, when the waiter had gone, she looked over her menu, frowning.

"Something's wrong," he said.

Her pale lashes fluttered. Three years ago she might have snapped at him: *Apart from our son being dead?* Now she only shook her head. "I guess I should just say it, huh? Steve left. He's gone. We're—we're done."

"Chloe," he said. "God. I'm so sorry."

He wasn't. Of course he wasn't. Mark had hated Steve from the first. Steve was from New York City, and seemed to have devoted his entire life to acting out the cliché of a New Yorker trapped in Cowtown; he'd curse the provincials, and then, in the same breath, pretend that all of Columbus had gone apeshit over his *très chic* little bistro, named—subtly—Gotham. Mark and Allison had had dinner with Chloe and Steve there—this was the last time he had seen her, and he had never figured out what possessed them to try it. Steve—big and thick-necked and glowering, with too-white teeth— had been unable to sit still, had gotten up endlessly to inspect dishes coming out of the kitchen, to shake the hands of regulars, to insist he had a better bottle of wine stashed than anything on the list. He ordered for Mark and Allie, explaining, I want you to eat the best we got tonight, on me. He'd slung his heavy arm over Chloe's shoulders, the implication clear: *Except you don't really get the best. Not anymore.*

How could Chloe, Mark had thought, have loved both of them? Was he flattering himself, or torturing himself, to think she'd deliberately chosen his opposite? Had he done the same with Allison?

It didn't matter. Steve was gone, Steve was gone.

"Do you want to talk about it?" he asked. "Or I can pretend you never said anything."

Chloe shook her head, which he thought was probably as much a denial of threatening tears as it was an answer. He could see her sitting on the edge of a long drop—knowing she had to talk, wanting to collapse, unwilling to do either in front of him.

"It's all right," she said.

He couldn't stop himself. "How'd it go down?"

She said, softly, "This has been coming for a while."

"Did he—?"

Chloe's mouth twisted. "The short version is, I'm never going to be Jewish, and I'm a bad person for grieving Brendan." The cords in her neck pulsed. "He said he was worried what sort of mother I'd be."

Chloe had met Steve at her school; she'd taught Steve's young daughter in her class. Chloe had loved that girl; Mark's theory had always been that she loved the child a lot more than the man. But calling Chloe a bad mother? He wished he believed in a hell, so he could condemn Steve to the flames.

"I'm sorry," he said.

Chloe's eyes were moist; she was obviously not seeing a word on the menu. And now he was supposed to tell her about Allie? About Connie Pelham?

"You didn't have to come tonight," he said.

"I'm thirty-nine," she said. "I'd like to think I'm beyond collapsing over a guy."

He scanned this for criticism, found everything and nothing.

"Come on," he said. "Like we're not allowed to ever be sad about anything else?"

A line of Gayle's, probably. He always hated himself when these sorts of sentences popped out—especially in front of Chloe, no stranger to therapists, either.

The waiter came back. Mark ordered something full of lamb and oil, and a salad and an iced tea—he ached for a glass of wine, but he'd tried hard, these last years, to show Chloe he didn't drink anymore. Chloe, ever the rabbit, ordered salad, as little falafel as they'd serve her, and a martini. He thought the words before she said them: two olives, dirty. She gave a sweet smile to the waiter. Even in her dismal state of mind, the smile transformed her; the waiter grinned back.

I love you, Mark wanted to say. *I've always loved you, and I love you still.*

This happened every time he and Chloe went out. He weathered it, let out a breath, made himself step back into the world.

"So," Chloe said, her voice brighter. "Let's change the subject. What's new? How's Sam?"

His father was always a safe topic. Mark told her about Sam's book, about the new girlfriend—who, Sam had promised them, would be coming out to Ohio with him for Christmas. Chloe didn't seem bothered at all by the thought of Helen Etley; she laughed to hear of Sam's embarrassment.

Then she asked: "And Allison?"

He took a sip of his tea. "I'm not sure this is the right time to talk about her. Considering."

Chloe frowned. "I'm a big girl, Mark."

An old slight. He condescended to her, apparently. Well, then: "We just decided this week. We're getting married in September."

Chloe took a deep breath, drew back from the table. Almost as though he'd slapped her.

"September," Chloe said.

He might have been imagining it in the low light, but he thought she had blanched.

"I finally got up the guts to ask."

She shook her head. He was, oddly, excited. The news hurt her; news about him *could* still hurt her.

Ask me to come back, he thought. Come on. Beg.

And what would he do, if she did? If Chloe stood up and said, *I love you, I've always loved you, don't do this?*

He didn't know. All he did know was that he wanted to say her name—to cast the spell of her again. To reach for her. To comfort her, like a husband did. He'd spent half his adult life holding her, rubbing her back, her hands, her feet. Telling her that her mistakes were forgivable, apologizing for his own, receiving forgiveness. Why couldn't he do it now?

Because he'd put a ring on Allison's finger, that's why.

He couldn't go back, now. But for all these years, throughout all these awkward dinners, he'd always assumed that someday he might.

Unbidden, he remembered the first night he and Chloe had made love, back in college. They'd only known each other two weeks, yet still they were twisting together on her bed, fumbling at buttons, gasping. But Chloe had hesitated, just for a moment, as he lowered his weight. A sudden strangeness was in her eyes. Like panic.

I'll never hurt you, he'd told her.

She'd let out a long breath. Smiled. I believe you, she said, and pulled him down, in.

And here they were: Chloe in front of him, hurt and hurt and hurt again. Their story a complicated stitchwork of hurt.

"Would you like me to go?" he asked.

"Yes." The speed of her answer surprised him. She dropped her forehead into her hand. "I'm sorry. I can't do this. Not tonight."

Numbly, he stood. Chloe was still covering her eyes. He wanted to bend over, to hug her goodbye. And say what, then? *I'm sorry? I hope you can be happy for me?*

So. "Goodbye, Chloe."

He turned and walked upstairs, stopping only to tell the waiter to cancel his order.

He was halfway home, his thoughts a whirl, before he remembered he hadn't told Chloe about Connie Pelham.

⌒

When Mark unlocked the door he found the townhouse empty; a note on the counter, in Allie's scrawl, read: *Went to salon with Yancey, back eight???*

He winced. That Allie had picked Yancey for company meant the salon would be just a starting point, and that *eight???* would be more like midnight or after, and she'd be coming home in a cab.

He found some leftover soup to reheat and ate it while watching basketball on television. He thought for a while about calling his father, but he didn't want to tell Sam what had just happened. For that matter, he hadn't told Sam about Connie Pelham, either—a task as impossible, in its way, as telling Chloe would be. He closed his eyes, wishing fervently he could erase the last week from his memory.

An hour later the buzz of his cell startled him awake. He was so expecting Allie to be on the other end he didn't check the number. "Hey, you," he murmured.

"Mark," Chloe said. "I'm so sorry. I had no excuse to talk to you like that."

Her voice was thick with misery. He sat up. "It's okay. Don't worry about it." He was nearly whispering, as though Allie was upstairs, and might hear him.

"No, it's *not* okay. It's been six years. I walked out on you. I don't get to—to throw a fit when you're happy."

"I shouldn't have told you today," he said.

She ignored this. "Mark—if we're going to be in each other's lives, we need—I need—to be happy for you."

What else could he say? "Thank you."

Some sort of magnetic strangeness caused a long whine to rise and fall in his ear. Then Chloe said, "Steve left me for someone else."

Mark lifted his eyes to the ceiling. "I'm sorry, honey."

Honey. He'd called her honey.

Chloe didn't seem to have noticed. "Some girl he met at the fucking gym," she said. He heard then what he should have when he answered: Chloe had come home from the restaurant and gotten very drunk.

"Christ," she said. She was crying. "And then it's Brendan's birthday, and you tell me this, and I—"

She never finished, and Mark wondered—he couldn't help but

wonder—if what she wanted to say, truly, was, *Don't marry her. Come back to me.*

"God," she said, "I miss him so much, and then to hear you—"

If Mark ever wrote the history of the two of them he'd include a chapter on pauses like this one: on himself waiting, a phone clutched to his ear, for Chloe to break his heart, or mend it.

She let out a long, wavering breath. "Be happy, Mark. That's all I want for you."

"I want it for you, too."

I want you, too, he could have said.

He waited for her, now, to say the last thing. The important secret he heard impending in her voice.

But she only said, "Good night, Mark," and hung up.

Eight

Mark didn't go to bed until Allie came home, at nearly one in the morning, spilling rubber-limbed through the door into his arms.

"It kind of turned into a bachelorette party," she told him, and laughed wetly, and then began naming women she'd seen at a bar with Yancey: old friends and sorority sisters who, it turned out, had all conspired to surprise her. He led her to the kitchen for a glass of water, and she swayed in his arms. "I sang your praises all night," she said, "O man of mine."

He'd spent the last two hours picking over his memories of Chloe's phone call like some kind of carrion bird. "Mm," he said. "Thank you."

"How was dinner?" Allie asked, still swaying. "I forgot to ask you that."

"It's safe to say Chloe was unhappy."

"Well, fuck her," Allie said. She drew back and looked blearily into Mark's eyes. "I mean, not her. Fuck me." She put a hand over her mouth. "Is that okay to say? I mean, today?"

He told her it was, and he would. But Allie was waylaid in the bathroom. The last thing he'd wanted to do, this late on this day, was hold her hair out of her face while she puked into the toilet, but he ended up doing exactly that. "I'm sorry, I'm so sorry," Allie kept saying.

"It's okay," he said, rubbing a circle between her shoulders.

This was his penance, he figured, wringing out a washcloth, digging under the counter for bleach to pour into the toilet—cosmic penance, for longing after his ex-wife.

He was jealous of Allie. If ever there'd been a week since Brendan died when he had deserved a good mind-erasing bender, wasn't this the one? He'd happily trade any of the last few days for a good heave into the toilet, a spinning head, someone to put him to bed and stroke his hair and whisper—as he did now—"Just sleep. Sleep and it'll be okay."

The next day, after Allison—greenish, wincing at the light—had staggered off to work, Mark kept drifting away from his own. He couldn't stop thinking of Chloe's call—which he recalled hazily, as though her voice had been a kind of liquor—and about Connie Pelham.

He had to tell Chloe. He should call her, say: *There was something else I needed to tell you yesterday. Brace yourself, it's nuts.*

All along, as he'd imagined telling Chloe, he had figured her response would be the same as his own: indignation, outrage. But today he wondered whether she might take the news a different way.

He remembered her lying on Brendan's bed. *I thought I heard him.*

Mark got up and splashed his face with cold water, then went downstairs and made himself another cup of coffee.

At one in the afternoon he gave up. He went to the living room and lay down on the couch in front of the television. And finally, for the first time since Connie Pelham had appeared in the bookstore, his mind let him loose; he thought he'd closed his eyes only for a heartbeat, but then Allison was shaking him, and outside it was dark.

"Sleepyhead," she said. "Look at you."

She was still in her coat, carrying shopping bags. He struggled to sit up. "What time is it?"

"Seven."

He'd sneaked a full night's sleep into the afternoon. Steel cables creaked in his neck and shoulder blades.

Allison said, "So there's a house for sale a few blocks over—one of the big ones? That looks out on the park? They're having an open house."

"Now?" he said. "God."

"It's going until eight." Allie sat down next to him on the couch and bounced with excitement, a tic she only sometimes employed with irony. "It's like two blocks from here! It's just gorgeous."

"You seem to have rallied."

"I'm still young," she said, nudging him. "I talked to the agent. I told her I'd come back with my husband, the doctor."

This was a game they'd played before, but he sure wasn't in the mood for it now.

Allie said, "And I told her I was a lawyer. Come on—this place is unbelievable."

He stood, barely in control of his legs. "What happened to Colorado?"

They had decided that their honeymoon wouldn't only be devoted to sex and relaxation, but also to reconnaissance; they'd joked before about leaving Columbus, moving west, but more and more (and especially after the winter had dug in its claws) the idea had gained traction. Why not leave town? If they could up and get married, why couldn't they pick a whole new place to live? Since Connie Pelham had appeared, the question had taken on, Mark thought, a new urgency.

"Colorado's still there," Allie said. "Trust me—this place is so far out of our league." She grinned and bounced again. "But maybe not for Doctor Marcus Fife and Allison Daniel, Esquire."

"Honey—"

"Okaaay," she said, in full pout. Another tic he wasn't especially fond of.

"I'm just—I'm still asleep."

"Can't we just go see it? I owe you some fun, after last night."

She owed him, he thought, more than that. She owed him a hell of a lot more than dragging him out of the house to play a silly game she liked better than he did—

But he was being an ass. He hadn't worked so hard, all these years—hadn't tried so hard to be alive—just to lose himself at the snap of Connie Pelham's fingers. At the sound of Chloe's voice over the telephone. He agreed to go.

He put on nice clothes: a jacket and tie, shiny shoes. Brushed his teeth and shaved and combed his hair. When he came downstairs Allie looked him over, smiling, and ran her hands down the lapels of his coat. She was still in her suit and heels from work—she didn't have to do much to look the part of a young, ambitious lawyer.

They took the car: They were two professionals who'd worked late, who were just going to pop by before a late dinner. The air was insidiously cold and filled with mist, exactly the sort of unsettled winter damp he was willing to move west to escape; every street-light had a cotton-ball halo. The curbs were crusted with black-speckled snow.

She was drumming her fingers on the wheel, singing something indistinct. Allie loved playing make-believe. He ought to love it, too—or else why would he and Lewis have wasted so many nights in college playing Dungeons and Dragons? And being Dr. Fife, now, carried with it an entirely different benefit—his and Allie's make-believe hadn't started with realtors; it had begun in bed, and, if he wanted, it could end there tonight. He glanced sideways at Allie, the lovely lines of her dark hair, the happy curve of her lips.

Allie pulled up to the curb, right in front of an OPEN HOUSE sign.

No balloons for German Village: The agent had instead set out a couple of tasteful paper lanterns on each side of the sign, lighting it in pale gold. Allie was right—this was a beautiful house: two narrow stories, flat-roofed and brick. Four symmetrical windows glowed warmly; a wreath hung upon the front door. Across the street was the wide, knolled expanse of Schiller Park.

The agent met them at the door. She was in her fifties, tall, with lacquered blond hair. She wore a navy suit and pearl earrings and absurdly pointed high-heeled shoes. "Allison!" she cried. "Come in, come in." To Mark she said, "Dr. Fife, is that right? I'm Lorraine."

Mark smiled thinly at Lorraine, began arching his neck. He could afford to indulge his asshole mood for a few minutes; people expected doctors to be assholes. He used to, anyway.

The house was as beautiful inside as out. The wood floor had been polished deep and glimmering as lakewater where it wasn't covered with expensive rugs. The walls were dark, too, painted— and in a couple of rooms papered—in tasteful reds and deep golds. A fire burned in the living room fireplace between built-in floor-to-ceiling bookshelves, probably mahogany. Only the furniture was incongruous—too low and squared and modern for the house that contained it.

Lorraine was talking airily; Allison was exclaiming at the end of every one of her sentences.

The house actually had a built-in bar, in a corner of the living room. Lorraine had set a bottle of wine atop the counter, and several glasses, and offered them each a drink.

"Thank you," he said. "What a gorgeous house."

Lorraine smiled toothily, handed them glasses. "Oh my," Allison said, after a sip. Mark tasted his own; he could happily have sat at the bar, with that bottle, for the rest of the night.

Lorraine was fishing, now, trying to pull information out of

Allison. Mark kept half an ear on them and walked to the bookshelves, which had been filled with Reader's Digest Condensed Books.

"—And Mark's a surgeon," Allison was saying, walking to him and taking his elbow. "Up at Riverside." Mark turned and smiled in what he hoped was a distracted, doctorly kind of way.

"Oh my," Lorraine said. "Aren't you two something. What kind of surgery?"

"Hearts," Mark said.

Allison smirked and turned to examine the shelves.

Lorraine put a hand to her chest. "My father passed, last year. Four blockages—he never got tested."

Mark said, "Past forty, you get tested for everything. I tell everyone—see your family doc so you don't have to see me. I'm the bogeyman."

Lorraine did her best to smile, then led them upstairs, where she began her spiel anew, walking backward down the hallway. They glanced in and out of the rooms, each more ridiculously appointed than the last. The master bedroom opened up on a bathroom containing a whirlpool bath the size of an outdoor hot tub; Mark heard Allie's breath catch.

"Four bedrooms," Mark said, back in the living room, when the tour was over. "Too much space for us, I think."

"Not necessarily," Lorraine said, her voice curling. "You're both professionals; one or two of the bedrooms could be offices. Or guest rooms." She smiled slyly. "I know quite a few young couples who were glad to have a house they could grow into."

Allison's hand slid warmly against Mark's. "That's a ways off."

Lorraine pressed her lips together. She paused that way, Mark thought, maybe a second too long. He got it. Lorraine was telling Allison, *The clock's ticking, honey.* Allie squeezed his hand, too hard, so he was pretty sure the message had been received.

"Well," Lorraine said, "either way, it's nice to have space. Our kids are grown, but my husband? He's decided he's a book collector now!" Her laugh had a theatrical trill. "He's taken over two whole rooms."

"Mark builds ships in bottles," Allison said.

"Really?" Lorraine leaned closer to Mark. "What an unusual hobby."

"Keeps my hands steady." He held out his hands in front of him. "See?"

Allison pinched his lower back.

Lorraine cocked her head. "I've always been curious. How do you get all those little parts in there?"

"That's a good question," Mark said, bouncing on his heels. "I use my surgical tools."

"Lorraine!" Allie said, pinching him hard enough to bruise. "Thanks so much for your time."

⌣

When they were safely in the car, driving away, they both laughed for a long while. Allie's laughter grew louder and louder, and finally she pulled to the side of the road. When the car was in park she leaned across the seat and kissed him, hard, her hands pressed against his cheeks. He held her tightly—and when her arms were around him he breathed deep, suddenly relieved. Because he'd laughed, because Allison had helped him laugh.

"That felt good," she said at last. "I've been worried about you."

"I know," he said. "I've—"

But he didn't know what to say. That his mind had been somewhere else, ever since Connie Pelham had appeared? Allison already knew that. Could he tell her that he didn't believe in ghosts, but that he couldn't stop thinking about them? Or about Chloe?

"I'll be okay," he said. "I'm not going to let her get to me."

"Connie? Or Chloe?"

He froze.

"Sorry," Allison said. "But...you said she was mad?"

He regretted telling Allie that; in fact, he'd hoped she wouldn't remember. "She was."

"So what did she say?"

"Not much. She told me to leave. I did."

And then she called, drunk. And Mark had called her honey.

"So I told Bill," she said. "Last night, after work."

Allison hadn't talked to Bill in almost a year, as far as he knew. He had remarried and now lived in Pittsburgh.

"What did he say?"

She shrugged. "Congratulations. And that his wife was pregnant." Allie took his hand. "Don't look like that. I saw you about to tear that woman's face off in there. That's not why I brought it up."

"Sorry. I just—"

"I know. It's okay."

He shifted in the seat.

"He was unhappy," Allie said. "Of course he was. I've been..." She leaned her forehead against the window. "This is weird, right? Doing this again—getting *married* again?"

He couldn't lie. "Yeah."

"I miss...not Bill, not like that. But I guess I miss, you know, the *romance* of it. The first time."

He could understand that. Yes he could.

"How'd you propose to Chloe?"

"In bed," he said, reluctantly. "I was going to ask more officially, but I was twenty years old and getting laid and just...blurted it out." He rubbed Allison's fingers, trying not to remember how Chloe had clutched at him, crying, saying, I'm so happy. "What about you?"

"I asked Bill. We got in a fight, actually—he was mad that I'd asked him. Said it was the man's job." She lifted Mark's hand and kissed his knuckles. "I guess what I miss is the big deal. I mean, everyone's happy for us, sure. Everyone I know thinks you're better for me than Bill was. But the first time, I spent three weeks jumping up and down and squealing, and now, this time, I'm at a bar with all my girlfriends, and two of them have to go home and pay the babysitter, and Lana's getting divorced..."

"I know," he said. "Lewis and Dad were both pretty subdued. All told."

Steam bloomed up along the window glass when she sighed. "I wish I'd met you first," she said. "Instead of Bill. I wish the big whirlwind thing had been about *you*, and that you were the guy I brought home to Mom and Dad, and said *This is the one*. And I can't even say that to you. Because—"

She stopped, maybe because of the look that must have crossed his face. He knew what she had almost said: Because of Brendan. Because he couldn't—wouldn't—unwish his son.

"I know," he said.

She nodded and rubbed at her eyes.

"I can't imagine Connie Pelham's helping any," he said.

"Oh, fuck her." Allison shuddered. "No, she's not helping."

"Allie."

"Yeah?"

She wanted him to tell her it was the same, this time. That it could be the same. That they could be as happy as they'd been, during their first engagements. And if he didn't mean it, the least he could do was lie to her. When he'd said her name, he had planned to.

But he didn't.

"Thank you," he said. His voice sandpapery.

Allie stared at him a long time before nodding, then released his hand and put the car into gear.

Nine

Two days later, after an exhausting day's work, Mark sat in a stuffed chair at the Cup O'Joe, reading the arts listings in *The Other Paper*: all the gallery shows he promised himself he'd visit, but never would; reviews of artsy movies he knew he'd never rouse himself to see. He was bone-tired. He'd barely slept, even though his work schedule, so close to Christmas, had stretched out to twelve hours a day. And even when he did manage sleep, he was beset by dreams—his old nightmares, given fresh energy and vigor. Brendan, lost. Chloe screaming—in loss, and at him.

He would have no real rest until after the holiday. In three days, on Christmas Eve, his father and Helen would be coming to stay with them. Allison had been nervous, subdued, ever since their talk after the open house; the thought of Sam and Helen coming to stay in the townhouse had stretched her patience even thinner. Tonight she would expect the two of them to clean and decorate until bedtime.

Mark stood up to leave; it was nearly five. Allison was due home from work soon; if he didn't have the kitchen cleaned already, he'd catch needless hell. They were on the verge of a fight—he could sense it—and he wasn't sure he could handle their first big fight, not right now.

He turned for the door just in time to see Connie Pelham walking through it.

She made a beeline for him. Her face was drawn and some-how bloodless beneath its tan. She'd probably been staring at him through the window again, building up her courage. He felt a rush of pure, coppery hate.

"I'm not talking to you," he said.

"Mr. Fife." Her voice was hoarse. "Please. Just two minutes, that's all I ask."

This was a lie. Connie Pelham would always need more than two minutes, and then another two minutes more.

"Whatever you have to say, I don't want to hear it."

The barista, a shaggy-haired kid Mark joked with every morning—who only knew Mark as a friendly, happy guy who talked about basketball, who tipped well—was staring warily at them.

Connie followed his glance but didn't lower her voice. "I'll beg you if I have to. I'm desperate."

"Look—"

"I have new information," she said. "I think you need to hear it."

"Absolutely not," he said.

In response Connie sat heavily in the nearest chair and began to weep.

"Jesus Christ," he said. "Stop that."

She blinked over and over, before her voice started up again like a sputtering motor. "Do you know how hard it is to do this? Do you think I *want* to do this?"

"So don't. Move out of the fucking house."

Heads lifted across the shop. "Hey!" the barista said.

"I can't," Connie said. "I can't."

He said, slowly, "You can if you really have to."

She shook her head. "My ex—it's tied up in litigation—"

"Get an apartment."

"We're broke. And my son—"

"Stay with a fucking relative, then."

Was it a flicker of anger he saw in her eyes? "I'd really appreciate it if you wouldn't use that language with me."

He gave in. "You *appreciate*? You're in no position to appreciate anything. You—you're following me like some goddamned *stalker*."

She was shaking her head. "I'm telling you. Brendan's in the house. This is real."

Mark felt the barista's eyes burrowing into them both. A couple sitting by the door were staring with disgust.

"My son—" she began.

"*My* son used to see ghosts," Mark said. "You know why? Because he was a *little boy*."

"Don't you think I've thought of that? I've—"

"Your kid's what, six?"

"Nine—"

"Nine-year-olds lie. They don't even know they're doing it. It's up to you to see through it." He pushed a button he knew he shouldn't: "It's called being a parent."

"Don't tell me how to raise my son!" she cried. "Don't you dare!"

The barista emerged from behind the counter, his hands held out in front of him. "We got a problem here?"

"No," Mark said. "No we don't."

"I think you guys probably ought to go outside."

"She's just leaving," Mark said. "Aren't you, Connie."

Connie pressed her lips together. "Mr. Fife, please—"

"Out," Mark said.

"He's calling for his daddy," she said, in a rush. "That's what Jacob says."

Mark stared at her. "What did you say?"

Her voice was coming to him as if through a tin can and string. "Just—just come to the house. Please. Come over and see—"

The world blooming back up into full volume. He was shaking—he'd never in his life felt such rage. "Get the fuck out of my sight."

Connie lifted her eyes. "I've heard him, too."

"If you come near me again I'm calling the police."

"I'm desperate," she said. "Do it for my son, if not for yours."

"I think you're a very sick woman. I mean that." He turned for the door.

"Mr. Fife," Connie called. "Can I at least talk to Chloe?"

If the barista hadn't been present Mark might have hauled off and punched her in the face, over and over, and fuck the consequences. He stepped closer to her; she gasped.

"If you contact her," he said, "I'll have you arrested in front of your son. I'll have you taken away from him. Do you understand me?"

He didn't know where these words came from, or whether they carried any weight. But Connie flinched away, and he was sickly pleased.

"Leave me alone," he said. "Leave my wife alone. Or I'll make you suffer." Then he fled.

He was over a block away, shivering in his coat, before he realized he had just called Chloe his wife.

⌒

Inside the townhouse Mark locked the doors, shut all the blinds, then took a glass of Allie's wine up to his office. He sipped from the glass and tried to think of what to do. Go to the police? He still didn't know what he'd say. He texted Allie: come home soon? Even as he typed the letters he remembered that one of her college friends was a lawyer, here in the city. Maybe they could get some advice from him—someone who knew them, whom they could trust to be discreet.

He'd have to tell Chloe now. He realized this and sank back into his chair.

He opened an email, Chloe's address at the top. For half an hour he tried various inroads. I was contacted by a terrible woman. No. I have disturbing news. No. Chloe, be on the lookout—No and no. This woman says Brendan is a ghost, and that he wants his father—

He erased everything and closed the email.

Asking for his daddy. Fucking hell.

He opened his phone, highlighted Chloe's number. At this time of day, on her holiday break, she would probably be sitting on the couch, reading. Or making herself dinner. She might be brooding, still, about Steve, and maybe about Mark and Allie, too.

He'd dial her number, and she'd answer. *Chloe, a crazy woman believes Brendan's a ghost. Goodbye, and Merry Christmas.*

And that was why he didn't call her.

He had been imagining Chloe not in an apartment, but in the living room, back in the old house. Sitting on the couch, opposite their tall pine tree strung with pale yellow lights, the space under its lowest boughs packed tight with gifts.

It was Christmastime, and Chloe wouldn't be there. Mark wouldn't be there. Connie Pelham and her little boy would.

But what if Brendan was there, too? Watching them, somehow, from the shadows, as they laughed, as they handed each other gifts, one by one?

Mark drained the wineglass in a gulp.

Brendan wasn't there, couldn't be there. Because ghosts weren't *fucking real.*

⌢

When Allison came home and heard the news, she called her law-yer friend's office right away; he agreed to come by on his way home from work. Mark showered and shaved in preparation, mov-ing the razor with deliberate care. Downstairs Allie cooked them pasta, almost comically quiet. What must she be thinking? Mark had no idea.

Calling for his daddy.

Henry Aldridge, the lawyer, stopped by at seven, still dressed in his work suit. He was a square, good-looking man, his hair a rich, coppery brown, parted neatly as a politician's—he was a far cry from a scruffy graphic designer who spent most of his workdays in sweatpants and yesterday's socks. Mark had never wondered before, but he was now sure—watching Henry kiss Allison's cheek, watching the admiration in Allison's eyes as she withdrew—that, once upon a time, they had dated.

They sat at the kitchen table. Mark poured Henry wine, one of Allie's good reds. Henry pulled a notepad from his briefcase and smiled at Mark. "So what's the trouble, Mark?"

Allie had only told Henry they were having an emergency. Haltingly, Mark told him now what he could bear to say.

Henry jotted notes for a while; when Mark said the word "ghost" his eyes jerked up, then narrowed. He listened to the story of Mark's latest encounter with Connie with raised eyebrows.

When Mark had finished he said—after a long sigh, "I'm not sure there's much we can do. This woman didn't threaten you, correct?"

"No," Mark said.

"Well, you might be able to sue her," Henry said, "but that would require a lot of money and time. Also, I have to say it's a dicey case. Did she inflict pain and suffering? You could make that argument. But she found you in a public place—"

"She came here once," Allison said.

"Got any proof?" Henry asked, and gave them a sad smile when they didn't answer. "And if you're this upset, by the, the topic she raised—" Henry glanced toward Mark, without meeting his eyes. "—then I have to wonder whether you'd really want to be deposed about it."

"I just want her to stop," Mark said. "Whatever it takes."

Henry leaned forward. "Mark," he said, "do you believe in ghosts?"

Mark said, "Of course not."

"Let's say you sued her. And I'm not saying you should. But if you did, and I was on the other side, that's the question I'd ask. *If you don't believe in ghosts, why are you so upset?*"

Mark shook his head, too upset—*unfair! unfair!*—to answer.

"We could investigate a restraining order," Henry said, "but that's maybe not necessary. I know you're upset, but I don't think you're there yet." He put down his notepad. "Here's what I can do. I can write a very, very vague cease-and-desist. It'll be on my firm's letterhead, so I can't threaten her for real. But I can let her know you've contacted me, and that anything she does in the future might result in litigation. That's all technically true, since you called me and I'm a lawyer and we have, as of now, discussed it." Henry smiled again. "I'll send it certified mail tomorrow. That'll be a lot of scary stuff said to her. I bet she stops, after that."

Afterward they chatted and finished the wine in their glasses. Henry was surprised to hear that Mark and Allie were engaged; he smiled more and more broadly while they told him their plans.

At the door Henry shook Mark's hand, hard, and swore Mark owed him nothing for the letter. "Think of it as a wedding present if you have to." He looked Mark in the eye as he said it. "This'll blow over," he said. "Nobody wants a lawyer around. You watch."

⌒

After he left, they watched television. Before bedtime Allie got up to put away their dinner dishes. Mark lay down on his side and listened to her running water. On the television smoke was billowing out of a subway tunnel, somewhere in Europe. In Iraq the streets still ran with blood, and would tomorrow. Allie returned, slid into the small space behind him, and curled her arms around his chest.

The question he'd been avoiding all evening rushed out of

him. "Do I need to take this seriously? Do I need to go back to the house?"

Allison waited a long while before answering, "Would it make you feel better? To see for yourself?"

"I don't know."

"Do you believe there's anything to it? Really?"

"No," he said. Because he didn't.

"I can't tell you the right thing to do," she said. Which was true, but he was suddenly angry that she wouldn't. Couldn't. That no one could.

He could only tell her what he'd been repeating to himself all night: "It's not fair."

"No, it isn't." She squeezed him, pressed her cheek against his shoulder blade. "You've been through too much."

⌒

Later Allison tried to cajole him into bed. Mark told her he'd be up to the bedroom soon, but he knew sleep was an impossibility, tonight. He remained on the couch, watching television, the sound turned low.

You've been through too much. Allie meant well, saying so.

But Allie didn't know—couldn't *begin* to know—why Connie Pelham's words this afternoon had hurt him so deeply.

His sudden anger both shocked and pleased him: Allison had no fucking *idea* what he'd had to overcome.

Carefully he reminded himself that Allie didn't know because she hadn't suffered. Not like he had. And this was a good thing. Gayle, his therapist, used to ask him: Do you *really* want other people to understand your loss? No, he'd always said—no, of course not. He wouldn't wish a fraction of that pain on anyone.

Allison knew a great deal about him; no sane woman would have taken on a case as sad as his if he hadn't been prepared to bleed in front of her. He had told her about finding Brendan's body in the stairwell; he'd told her about Brendan's blank, staring eyes, about the impossible angle of his neck. He had told her how he'd hesitated, torn between the need to gather up Brendan in his arms and the knowledge that he shouldn't move him an inch. Mark had told her about getting angry at Brendan that Saturday morning, while Chloe was out having lunch with her friends. About how Mark had sent Brendan upstairs to his room, after Brendan had thrown a tantrum. About how he'd lost track of time in front of the television, watching a Buckeyes basketball game, alone. How Brendan was supposed to have been watching the game with him. How ordinarily—if Mark had been paying attention, if he hadn't already drunk a couple of whiskey-and-Cokes—he might have noticed the sounds of Brendan opening his door, of his sneakered feet creeping down the upstairs hallway. How—if he'd noticed—Mark might have stood and called upstairs: Brendan! Get back in your room!

How instead, he'd heard only the sudden, sickening thumps from the stairwell. One sharp cry, cut suddenly silent. How, afterward, Mark had—for a long time, too long—sat still on the couch, waiting for the ascending siren's wail of Brendan's crying. What it felt like to listen, instead, to silence.

He'd told Allison all of this.

And he'd told her about losing Chloe, too. How in the year before the accident they'd lost sight of their marriage, in ways that had left them confused and sullen with each other. How they'd fought in the weeks before Brendan's accident. How, the afternoon of the funeral, Chloe had jerked away from his touch. How they had spent months trying to live in the old house, and failing—even after Mark and Lewis had spent an afternoon moving Mark and Chloe's bedroom into the downstairs study, so they wouldn't have to climb the stairs anymore.

He'd told Allie about the months he and Chloe spent trying to mend themselves in a small apartment in the Short North. About how he'd drunk too much, spending his evenings as soused as he could make himself and still function. How he drank instead of talking to Chloe, instead of insisting that they talk. He told Allie about Chloe's sudden decision to ask for a divorce. About how he'd wept, begging her to change her mind, even as he knew the decision had been coming all along.

He had told Allie about the women he'd met, and failed to love, in Chloe's wake. How the first time he made love to Harriet he'd felt like an adulterer. How after dating her a year, he'd shamefully stopped answering her calls. He told Allie how he'd spent whole months rising and working and falling asleep without any hope of feeling, like some monster animated from the dead by borrowed lightning.

How he'd felt he was watching his life, and the world that enveloped it, from a low, quiet orbit, never touching ground. How, in the end, it was anger that finally woke him. He told Allie that, more than once—first on the morning of 9/11, then more and more as that event led the country into madness—he'd been astonished to realize the rest of the world could be as shocked and bruised as he was. That anyone else could be. That it felt as though everyone else had joined him, at last, in the world he'd been living in all along.

He'd even told Allie about an old, treasured paranoid fantasy: that Brendan's death had somehow prefaced the longer, slower death of the whole world. How, during the long years when Mark had lived alone, he used to stay awake late into the night, browsing the web, seeing more and more evidence of the End of It All: The evils of the Bush administration. Peak oil. Hurricanes, tsunamis. Preachers sounding more and more like politicians; politicians sounding more and more like preachers. No one, he saw, had a hand on the tiller. Brendan's loss had only been the first seal, broken; and now the world was set to burn and die.

He had told Allison, too, that she had helped awaken him. That through her love he had remembered what it meant to hope—for himself, for a future. That she had saved him from himself.

I was alive before I met you, he'd told her. Now I'm living.

⌒

He had told her all of this. But he had never told her about the week he'd spent alone in the old house. He didn't know how to explain that week to himself, let alone Allie.

Whatever had happened, happened six months after Brendan had died, only days after Chloe had told him she wanted a divorce.

When Chloe finally left him—when, one night, she called him from her parents' house and told him, I can't do this anymore—the thought of staying in their tiny Short North apartment without her, without any hope of her, was too much to bear. He spent a little less than a week trying, moving numbly through the motions of his day. But on a Friday night in late July, Mark lay down to sleep, listened through his open window to a group of women laughing drunkenly on the sidewalk below his window, and reached his limit. He hastily packed a small bag and drove the mile back to Victorian Village and the old house.

He didn't return there with any sort of plan. He was still technically on leave from the ad agency that had employed him for a decade, but he'd begun taking on the occasional project at home— easy jobs his bosses could use to justify a tiny paycheck. He was living off his savings—and why not? What was he saving for, now? He had thought this with a dreadful pain: He was no longer beholden to anyone. Maybe that was why, before reaching his old street, he stopped at a liquor store in the Village and bought a bottle of Maker's Mark—then his liquor of choice.

The old house's cable and phone lines were turned off, but not the heat and power; he and Chloe still held out vain hope of finding a buyer. Mark lay on the couch, holding a tumbler of whiskey. He took a burning sip and felt—for the first time in weeks—the sweet unknotting of relief. He had spent nine years in this house; he knew its drafts, its smells, its plaintive creaks. He could find his way around it in the dark. Even the shadowed mouth of the staircase didn't bother him, the way it had when he and Chloe had been trying to live here together.

Mark hadn't brought any of his work, and never once tried to go upstairs to his former office in the second-floor turret. He never opened any of the books that remained on the shelves in the upstairs bedroom and study. He ate bachelor food—chicken wings and cheese fries, delivered to the door at one in the morning by disinterested Ohio State students. He listened to jazz records on the old turntable he'd had since high school. He wrote letters to Chloe but threw them away before they were finished. He wanted her back—but to talk her into this required a vision: a future he could convince her was real. And what might that future be? Could they have another child? Could they move to a different state? Any suggestion seemed offensive. All Mark wanted was Chloe's belief in him, again; without it no vision would cohere.

Mostly he drank whiskey, in greater quantity than he'd ever drunk before.

During his second day in the house he was frightened, just for a moment, when he poured out the last of the Maker's into his glass. He'd never gone through a bottle so quickly before. He guiltily buried the empty at the bottom of the trash bag he'd been filling, before reminding himself no one was here with him to see it. He could do whatever he wanted.

He told himself that maybe what he needed, to get through Chloe's absence, was a few days of oblivion. He told himself he *deserved* this—he'd been through *so much*. So before darkness fell he walked three blocks to the liquor store on Michigan Avenue. He picked up two more bottles of Maker's, as well as some beer, expensive imports he'd always wanted to try. Before long he'd filled a shopping basket with bottles, liking the sound of them clinking together, the way the light from the front windows of the liquor store grew wet and glowing in their depths. He checked out and hurried home.

He hadn't used to drink very much. As an undergraduate he'd gone through his share of beer, but no more so than most of his friends, and a lot less than Lewis. Like any college student, he'd gone on a couple of bad benders, at parties where he was alone and trying not to be. He and Chloe had certainly drunk together while they dated—she beat him to twenty-one by two months, and with her new powers bought a bottle of cognac, because she liked the sound of the word. They sat cross-legged and naked on her bed, toasting each other with glass after glass.

When they were first married they drank when out to dinner, or when watching movies. After Brendan was born, they both scaled back—Mark had a few beers whenever he saw Lewis, and wine every now and then with dinner, and for a long time he didn't miss the rest.

But in the last two years of Brendan's life this had changed. Mark was promoted at work, began leading a design team of his own; he'd thought this would make him happy, but in the end the job cost him an extra ten hours per week. Because Chloe had to be at school at six every morning, she went to bed early; Mark returned home, often, just in time to kiss her goodnight—they made love less, then, than they had even during Brendan's infancy.

Many nights, by the time Mark came home Brendan was already in bed; Mark wouldn't see him awake until breakfast. Work was leaving him wired, tense, so—lonely, horny—he got in the habit of drinking a beer, or a shot, or both. Many nights after his work was done, he'd take a tumbler of whiskey upstairs with him to the turret office, where he'd drink it while surfing the net in the dark, or playing *Quake*. For a long time this ritual had sustained him. Relaxed him—at least until Chloe had begun to criticize him for it, those last months before Brendan died. To accuse him of hiding it.

But that week alone in the house, without Chloe or Brendan, the old comfort, the deep nothing of sleep, never arrived. The booze brought only numbness. Mark floated half an inch away from himself, and soon was glad to be there.

In this hazy nowhere-time, odd things began to happen. One night—his second? His third?—he walked carefully up the stairs and, after rummaging in a couple of boxes, found enough bedding to make up Brendan's old bed. He lay down on it, holding his half-full tumbler on his chest. He spoke into the air, talking to Chloe and Brendan both. Sometime later he woke in darkness, the whiskey soaked into the hollow of the mattress at his side, all the night in a whirl.

He remembered his cell phone ringing beside him on the bed, much later. He opened it, said hello, and heard Chloe's voice. Mark, she said, quick and clipped. Chloe, he said, his tongue heavy. She said, You called me six times.

Had he? When?

I wanted to hear you, he told her. She said, You're drunk, aren't you. This was Chloe as she had sounded these past months: emptied out, a doll's voice activated by a pull of string. I love you, he said. I've been thinking about you. Come back. No, she said. Please, he said. I can't do this alone. She said, I did it alone for months. Years.

A long silence. Both of them, he was sure, thinking of Mark in the house alone. Taking care of Brendan, alone. Drinking on the couch, alone.

Chloe hung up on him.

Mark remembered a little of what happened, after. He went downstairs to the kitchen and retrieved the last bottle of whiskey. He remembered guzzling long swallows right from the neck until he glowed from the inside, like a bottle held to the light.

He remembered coming to on the couch, his mouth as sticky as a strip of masking tape. Looking at the clock on the wall, and the angle of the sun outside, and realizing he'd slept almost a full twenty-four hours. He remembered, sometime later, sitting down in the bathroom to piss, and leaning sideways against the countertop, feeling the coolness of the porcelain against his cheek. Shitting out something that smelled like sour death, and probably was.

He remembered thinking: Keep this up and you're a dead man.

He remembered walking the length of the upstairs hallway, dragging his shoulder along the smooth plaster. He remembered not wanting to go back into Brendan's room, but not why.

He might have dreamed waking. He might never have woken. He saw Brendan facedown on the landing. He looked up once from the couch to see Brendan waving at him from the foot of the steps. He heard Brendan's small feet thumping up and down the upstairs hallway. In the bathroom mirror one of Mark's eyes had developed a small red flaw. Brendan was splashing in the tub. Brendan was in the hallway, at the top of the stairs. *Daddy*, he called, *Daddy come here!* And Mark tried to lift himself from the couch and see, but he couldn't, and he tried to open his mummy's mouth, and couldn't, he could only say Aaaahhh—and when he did, he heard the terrible crashing on the stairs, that awful, final concussion. He stood and walked to the bottom step and looked up into the darkness, but he could see nothing, nothing at all. Then Brendan's voice came from the shadows: *Daddy, I'm scared.*

But he'd dreamed that. He was sure.

And then, deep in nowhere-time, Mark found himself in the upstairs hallway, on his knees. His throat was still buzzing, his ears still pricked to the last echoes of speech. His cheeks were wet. He'd been talking, the words he'd spoken fading to ash on his tongue.

He wept, then, because he'd been dreaming—hadn't he?—of joy, of such great and beautiful joy. He *must* have been dreaming:

of finding Brendan in the hallway, of kneeling and embracing him. Saying his name.

He'd been looking for his boy, because his boy had been calling him.

And there, awake and on his knees, Mark was sure: He'd found him. *He'd found him.*

⌒

Drink, he told himself now. Drink and grief and loneliness. These had given him Brendan's voice in the dark.

Somehow, that night, he'd made it back down the stairs—the stairs he'd gone up and down a dozen times, blind drunk, safely, his neck intact—to the couch, to the half-full bottle on the end table.

You've been through too much.

He hadn't told Allie about any of this. About reaching, one last time, for the bottle.

He hadn't told her how surprised he'd been when, some unknown time later, he finally woke up, sunlight lancing his eyes, the inside of his head a battlefield, ripped and bloodied.

How he'd heard, from down the hallway, the sounds of the washer and dryer; how he'd smelled something savory and warm.

He'd opened his cottonmouth and said, Chloe, but not loudly enough for anyone but himself to hear. The running water in the kitchen stopped. Mark forced himself up. *Chloe had come back.* He forced his mutinous feet down the hallway. He could tell her—

What? The truth of it eluded him, then and now, but he remembered thinking he had found the answer, the secret that would make Chloe happy again. He would hold her, tell her, and she would love him for it.

But when he entered the kitchen, he saw—standing by the sink, drying a dish—his father.

Sam, it turned out, had been calling him, worried; when Mark hadn't answered he had driven out from Indiana to check on him, and had thought to visit the old house. His father had saved him.

Only Mark and his father knew that, when Mark had stumbled into the kitchen—when he'd seen the truth—he'd held up his hands over his face and cried out: No. No. No.

Only Mark knew that, in this moment, he had been wishing with all his heart never to have woken up at all.

Ten

The next day, a Saturday, Mark spent alone. Allison left him in the morning to go shopping, and then to meet a friend for coffee; she wouldn't be home, she told him, until dinnertime or after. He was at his computer, pretending to work, pretending he wasn't still lost in the old house, trying his damnedest to die.

Allison kissed his forehead, frowned down at him. "Do you want me to stay?"

"I'll be fine," he assured her—though when she was gone he felt a sudden, vertiginous loss.

But he had work to do. A life to lead. He didn't call her phone and beg her to come back. He settled in at the computer, opened up his files.

Calling for his daddy.

Don't do it, he told himself.

But he did: He poured himself more coffee—if he'd gotten more than an hour's sleep last night he wasn't aware of it—and returned to his office. After a glance out of the window—no sign of Connie Pelham—he closed down his work files and opened up his web browser. He typed the word *ghost* into the search field and hit return. Then he began to click some of the links that had popped up—over one hundred and sixty million of them.

There were a lot of people out there, he discovered, who believed fervently in ghosts.

Almost all the sites he visited were amateurish. Two separate addresses, each claiming to lead to galleries of "ghost photography," set off the virus protector on his browser. One page showed a "ghost investigation team" gathered around a table in a conference room, all of the members white and doughy and middle-aged, smiling with tremendous good cheer and innocence in identical blue polo shirts. Like some sort of outing from a group home.

Other sites—the people in them, behind them—tightened his heart.

People who'd posted pictures of themselves in graveyards at night, glowing lights hovering above them. Pictures of people standing next to mirrors that seemed to have extra figures reflected in them (NOT Tommy, who was taking the picture, he looks like THIS, so who is it in the MIRROR!??); shots of wedding ceremonies with an extra shadow floating in a line with the groomsmen (i believe that to be Will's grandpa Joe who was invited but had a heart attack and passed in May, look close the shadow has a hat on like Joes favorite—thanks for coming Grandpa Joe we miss you and pray for you); pictures of blurred faces reflected in television screens.

The desperation, the loneliness and need, leaked out of the screen like the smell of ozone. The modern photos all seemed to have been taken in trailers; on the steps of dilapidated houses in the country; in small, flat, treeless graveyards. The weddings were in VA halls and country churches. A few of the photographs were of famous or public places, but almost none were taken inside mansions, in homes supported by money.

Nearly all of these testimonials, these pictures and blurry YouTube videos, were obvious frauds. One old photo, in black and white, showed a woman sitting on a gravestone—a living woman, clearly, her head bowed in grief. And yet the website claimed that because her legs were faintly transparent, this was evidence the woman was a spirit. Historical records claim the photographer was sure he was alone in the graveyard. His chance composition produced one of the clearest shots of an apparition we have.

His father had a technical term for this: bullshit.

History, Sam had once told him, is ninety percent bullshit.

When had his father told him this? Maybe in his office at Butler—Mark had to have been young enough, still, to be shocked to hear that kind of language from him. Nine or ten. But he'd snapped to attention, as his father intended.

All I do, his father said—and that was it: Mark had asked what his father did all day, at his big wooden desk in his big building full of big-kid college students with frightening beards and breasts and bare legs—All I do is mine other people's bullshit, and try not to create any of my own.

By the time Mark's mother died, Sam probably would have phrased things a little differently. But he'd had a rough patch in his early years at the school, some trouble that Mark still understood only dimly. His father had been angry all the time, then. Some nights he had come home and poured himself a drink and put on his headphones and sat in the living room, his eyes closed, having never taken off his jacket and tie.

What would Sam think of him, now? Huddled frightened in front of his computer, chasing ghost stories? Again Mark was torn—he wanted to call his father, be comforted by him, but he could not imagine how to tell Sam any of this. He'd already made Allison promise not to say a word about it when Sam and Helen came to visit over Christmas.

Even so, Mark now clicked on another link: Real-Life Ghost Stories.

We were playing with a Ouija board our friend Will brought
back from his stepdad's house. We contacted a spirit who said
his name was Frank. I asked Frank to prove he was real, and the

light over the table flickered on and off and the planchette went crazy. It spelled out KILL YOU and KILL THEM, and then we put the board away and prayed. But I believe we opened a portal for Frank; my house has not been the same since. I later discovered that a previous occupant of the house, one Francis Hagen, had murdered his wife and son in it in 1946, and then hanged himself in the basement. My husband and I hear coughing in the night which I believe either to be due to Francis Hagen's emphyseema and or to the fact that he hanged himself.

...

In 1977 my wife Elizabeth and me bought a house in Hackensack, a little bungalow. Well we took a bunch of photos of it, of course, showing us moving in our things, the empty rooms filling up and such as that. We didn't develop the photos for two months, but when we did we had quite a start realizing that there was a third person in some of them, an old woman. Just visible through the curtains in one. Sitting in a chair, not ours(!), in another one. We believe after talking with neighbors that she is a woman named Jocelyn Krebs, who lived alone in the house for many years, and who died of lung cancer in 1974. Whoever our old ghost is, she sure does smoke, we can smell it all the time even though my wife and I do not ourselves smoke.

...

In 1985 my young daughter Leesie drowned in the above-ground pool in the back yard of our house in Mobile AL. She was four. Needless to say I was devastated, and my husband too. She was our only. Our little angel. But with strength from Jesus we persevered and had another angel, our baby girl Polly. I took this picture of Polly when she was four, playing in the back yard with her dolls, and if you look close you can see a shape over her that is another child playing with her. Its Leesie I know it is. I have often "felt" Leesie in the house. Like a breeze in my hair. Sometimes I

hear her laugh. Before Polly was born I was sometimes woken up
at night sure I heard her calling for me—

Mark clicked other links, as quickly as he could.

—Email me if you have had a similar experience, I know your
out there.
—Would you like to consult with a spectral investigator? Click
here for more information.
—What To Do If You Are HAUNTED—

He clicked on this one. A page full of text appeared, white letters on black, in a tiny, crowded italic font. His head immediately
began to throb.

I know you, read the first line.

I used to be you. I used to think it wasn't possible.
But it is possible. And if I can tell my story, as clearly as I can,
maybe I can save someone else all the heartache I suffered,
denying what in my heart I always knew to be true.
I grew up not believing in ghosts. My father and mother are
scientists who work at the University of Oregon. Once, a group of
my school friends set out on an expedition to find Bigfoot,
but I stopped them at the edge of the woods and explained to
them how Bigfoot was just a hoax. This was me. Up until I was
twenty-eight years old.
That was when a ghost changed my mind...

Mark leaned closer and closer to the screen, scrolling down.
The writer and his wife had purchased a house and began to
hear noises in the attic; simultaneously, they heard from neighbors

that a long-ago flood of the nearby river had trapped two young children in the attic, had drowned them even as rescuers tried to break open the roof with a pickax. The writer put off going upstairs as long as possible, but the noises persisted.

> …then, finally, I went into the attic and encountered something I can't explain.
>
> I had a camera with me, and a flashlight. When I entered the attic, the pounding had stopped, but I was filled, from deep inside me to the surface of my skin, with a feeling that I wasn't alone. I saw nothing, but began to aim my camera deep into the corners of the room, and took pictures at random.
>
> When I developed the pictures I was amazed to see what I'd captured.
>
> I don't want to prejudice your viewing of my photos. Click on the link below and judge for yourself what appears there.

Mark clicked the link. A black-and-white photo advanced slowly down the screen. It showed the inside of a small attic with a low, peaked roof, filled with a jumble of boxes and draped pieces of cloth, each splashed luridly by the flashbulb. In the center of the frame was a tiny circular window. Mark saw nothing out of the ordinary. He stared into the shadowed corners.

Then an earsplitting shriek filled the office, just as a horrible skull-face popped into the center of the screen. Mark only registered what had happened after he'd pushed his chair backward, slamming his shoulder into the corner of his file cabinet.

On his screen the skull-face was now spinning, above the blinking words: AND NOW I BELIEVE IN GHOSTS! The skull began to laugh, its lower jaw jouncing like a ventriloquist dummy's.

Mark didn't know whether to laugh or weep. He closed the

browser; the vibrating, crazy-eyed skull vanished, and was replaced by his desktop picture: the sun glistening, serene and warm, from the surface of Lake Tahoe.

⌒

When Mark's phone rang, three hours later, and he saw Lewis's name on the screen, he answered gratefully, guiltily. Lew told him he'd had dinner plans with his girlfriend, but she'd canceled—did Mark want to keep him company for a while? "I haven't talked to you in ages," Lew said, not bothering to hide the complaint in his voice.

Mark had in fact been avoiding Lew, in the same way he'd been avoiding his father. He'd been hiding from everyone in his life since Connie Pelham had found him. He thought of the grinning skull on his computer screen.

"I'm glad you called," he said. "Something—something's been going on."

Lew was immediately on point. He'd forgotten that, in Lew's eyes, he was still fragile, damaged, requiring constant care.

"What's wrong?"

"I'm fine," Mark said. "It's—not over the phone."

"I can take off now," Lew told him. "I'll come right over."

"No," Mark said. He looked from the computer screen to the drawn blinds behind him. "Let's get me the hell out of my house."

They agreed to meet at six, at a bar Lew had just discovered in the Short North, but Mark ended up leaving early; he truly couldn't sit in his office, stuck in his head, a second longer. With an hour to spare, he could sit at the bar, collect his thoughts, calm himself down. He could do what he used to, when he was grieving Brendan: walk among ordinary people, so he could be forced to act ordinary, too.

If he'd been thinking more clearly, he could have insisted Lew meet him closer to German Village. He avoided the Short

North—only half a mile or so from his old house, and the scene of much of his life with Chloe and Brendan, and of its dissolution—whenever he could. Coming here tonight, especially, was the wrong choice, and yet here he was, driving north on High Street, through downtown and out, across the 670 overpass, the shapes of the brick buildings on either side of him familiar and hurtful.

The neighborhood had been a slum when he was in college, but during the time he and Chloe lived nearby it had undergone a startling gentrification; now it was a mile-long stretch of trendy bars and galleries and bookstores, and the sorts of restaurants two well-off thirtysomethings like him and Allie got invited a lot to visit. When he and Allison came here he often—crazily, he knew—asked Allie to drive; he'd sit in the passenger seat with his eyes focused on safe places and sights. Otherwise he might be too tempted to see himself and Chloe and Brendan, as they used to be: walking the streets, ducking in and out of shops, eating ice cream on a wrought-iron bench.

Iron arches over the streets glimmered with braided Christmas lights, and the light poles were wreathed in plastic holly. Tonight the sidewalks were bustling with young hip people wearing expensive overcoats, packs of college students who had not gone home for the holidays. Two parents walked slowly down the sidewalk to his right, holding the hands of a young boy who swung between them like a monkey.

Did Connie Pelham and her son walk here, too? Mark's heart beat too fast as he nosed the car beside an empty meter—as though Connie's face would be waiting for him when he turned to his window.

The pub Lew had chosen was dim, narrow, with brick walls, polished wood, brass rails. Mark liked it immediately; the meat-market crowd seemed to have passed the place by, anyway, and the jukebox was playing Tim Easton. A row of booths with high-backed wooden seats ran parallel to the bar, and Mark slid into the last one, next to the swinging kitchen doors. After only a slight pause, he ordered a beer—a by-God Guinness, how long had it been? He pretended to watch the talking heads on ESPN, on the last of a row of televisions that hung behind the bar.

He told himself not to worry. He could tell Lewis his story, and Lew would take him seriously, no matter what he said. Even a few years ago, when Mark had been at his most desperate, Lew had never once wagged a finger, never told him how he ought to grieve. So tonight Mark would start where he ought to: by apologizing for being such a hermit. He would then lay out, simply, what had happened. And Lew would tell him—

He didn't know *what* Lew would tell him. What advice could Lew—anyone—give?

Lew would take Mark's side. He would be angry, too, at Connie Pelham. That was why Mark had come, wasn't it? To be reminded he was not alone? That Connie was the crazy one, and not him? Yes—but as he watched the game, finished his beer and ordered a second, a worry whose shape he could not quite perceive nagged at him.

Lew walked into the bar a few minutes before six, a hulk in his overcoat and black watch cap. Mark was still nursing his second beer; his face flushed when he saw Lew looking at it. How had his life gotten so suddenly compromised?

"That's a by-God Guinness," Lew said when he'd reached the table. "When did this start happening again?"

"It's nothing to worry about," Mark said. But his excuse sounded just like a drunk's—he felt caught, like he was taking a test he hadn't studied for.

Lew took off his coat and hat and slid into the booth. "You're going to drink again, you should let me come along, you know? Or else what's the fun in it?"

Mark let out his breath, smiled sheepishly. He'd been right—Lew couldn't judge him; he didn't have judgment in his genes. The waitress came by and Lew said, "Another one of those."

Lew was growing out his hair again; the stubble on his head was as gray as it was blond. The detail made him seem, suddenly, old. He dug into his pocket and removed a flash drive, which he pushed across the table to Mark. "Merry Christmas," he said. "It's music. Almost all pirated, but I didn't say that."

Mark hadn't even thought to buy Lew a present. "I'm an asshole," he said.

Lew shrugged, let his eyes flicker to Mark's. "I asked Santa for beer."

Mark smiled. "I owe you more than that. How've you been?"

Lew waved him off. "None of that. I'm worried about you." He glanced at Mark's glass. "Tell me you're not single."

"No," Mark said. "It's not that."

The waitress brought Lew's drink and set it in front of him. "Tell me," he said.

"I don't—I don't know how."

Lew's face bunched with worry. Again Mark felt a rush of odd misgiving, but he told himself this was what he'd come to do. He remembered what his therapist had once asked him: How long has it been since you've told *anyone* a secret?

So Mark took a breath and did just that. Instead of Lew's face, he stared at his clasped fingers on the tabletop. He started at the beginning, with Connie spying on him through the window. When Mark told him what she'd revealed in the bookstore, Lew erupted: "Fucking hell!" When Mark told him about what Connie had said to him yesterday at the coffee shop, Lew slumped back in shock. He told him everything he'd been thinking—almost everything. Lew knew he'd nearly drunk himself to death, once, but not what Mark had seen in the old house, along the way.

"Jesus," Lew said, when he'd finished. "Jesus fucking Christ, buddy."

"Yeah."

"You should have called me."

"I know. I'm sorry."

"What are you going to do?"

"Wait, I guess." Mark said. "Hope the letter does the trick. Threaten to sue her if she keeps it up."

Lew drained his glass, held two fingers up to the waitress. He thought for a moment, then said, "Shit, does Chloe know?"

Mark shook his head. "She didn't handle the news about the engagement all that well."

Lew let out a long breath.

"You know her," Mark said. "What should I say?"

"I don't know. But, man, you can't let this woman find her. The news has to come from you."

Mark nodded glumly.

Lew slowly shook his head. "Okay. The lawyer was a good call. But—what does this woman want you to do?"

"I don't know," Mark said. This question had been bothering him, too, since Allie had first asked it. "I think she wants me to come to the house, though to do what, I don't know. If there was such a thing as ghosts, I would. But—"

Lew was watching him intently. The waitress returned with their drinks. Lew took a gulp of beer, then said, "You're probably right. It's probably just her kid."

"But?"

The left side of Lew's mouth curled up, but not in a smile.

"Say it," Mark said.

"I don't know if I want to."

Mark's unease grew.

"I'm just going to say it. Since we're just sitting here talking." Lew stared at him. "Any chance there's something to this?"

Mark's mouth was dry. "No."

"Let's think about this. You're positive? There's a one hundred percent chance she's lying?"

Mark said, slowly, "There's a one hundred percent chance her kid is lying."

"Okay," Lew said. "I think you're right. I think her kid is lying. It's the most logical thing to think, here. But you know I don't—I don't know if I can just dismiss the whole idea out of hand."

"What?"

Lew gave him an odd, sidelong look. And then Mark remembered; the source of his unease came flooding back to him. *Lew believed in ghosts.* He thought he'd seen one, once.

How could Mark have forgotten?

He remembered Lew telling him the story for the first time in college—they'd been sharing an apartment, then. Chloe had been with them; they'd just watched a scary movie with Lew and whatever girl he was seeing. They'd passed around a joint, told scary stories. Then Lew had just announced: So yeah, I've seen a ghost. While Mark held Chloe beneath a blanket on the couch, feeling her body flex and squirm in response to the tale, Lew told them what had happened.

The story, as Mark remembered it, went like this: When he was sixteen, Lew had gone camping in Montana with a cousin. Deep in the mountain woods, they'd set up their tent inside the walls of an abandoned, roofless log cabin. In the middle of that night Lew had woken up—It was a feeling, Lew told them, a kind of command, I guess—and had seen, out the mouth of the tent, a figure on the far side of the cabin: an old, bearded man crouching, rubbing his hands, his face dully illuminated, as though lit from below by a campfire. The man glanced over at them, opened his mouth to speak, then vanished.

Lew's cousin, he claimed, had woken up, too, had seen the same thing. That's how we knew it was real, Lew told them. When he and the cousin compared notes they realized they had both noticed the same details: The man had been wearing a red flannel shirt. He had a gold tooth. He wore a feather in his hair, above his right ear. The firelight had gleamed in his eyes.

Lew's cousin later found out that a hundred years before, a fur trapper had gotten lost out in those same woods. The trapper had frozen to death, or been eaten by wolves—something horrible like that—but he had died alone, and Lew and his cousin weren't the first people who'd claimed to see him, still, crouched and rubbing his hands by his nonexistent fire.

Chloe, shivering beneath the blanket, had asked Lew, You're serious?

Mark had expected Lew to roar out a laugh, to give them, finally, a punch line. But Lew had answered with a soft seriousness: Chloe, I'd swear it in fucking court. This was real.

Mark hadn't thought of this story in what, fifteen years? If Lew had been a fucking Methodist, Mark would have remembered that. But not that Lew had seen a ghost.

Lew started to tell him the story again, now, but Mark stopped him. "I remember. So you still—"

"I still do," Lew said, quietly. "I know what I saw."

"Jesus, Lew, I don't—"

"You want me to shut up?" Lew asked. He meant it. "Tell me what you need here, and I'll do it."

But before Mark could tell him, *I need you to say it's all bullshit,* Lew kept talking: "Okay, forget I said it. But, man, I *know* you. You're not just worried about telling Chloe. This is eating at you."

Mark shook his head.

"Look," Lew said. "I'm going to ask a hard question. You can tell me to fuck off if you want. But—what if you're not a hundred percent? What if you're only ninety-nine percent sure?" He held up his hand. "Bear with me. I'm only asking because I loved Brendan. You know that, right?"

Mark's anger was sudden, sharp, overpowering. "So if I don't run right over there, I'm a bad father? Is that what you're saying?"

Lew's face darkened. "Do you think there's a chance in fucking hell I mean that?"

Mark couldn't answer.

"What I'm saying is, if there's any chance in your mind—any—like, even a one percent chance—that there's something to this, then do you have to go and see?"

Mark shook his head.

"Because I'm looking at you and I'm thinking it's ninety-nine."

"It's not," Mark said, hoarse.

Lew ran his hand across his head. His gray hairs glimmered like pelt. "Man—if it's ninety-nine, you can say it to me. You can always say it to me. You know that."

Mark was close to panic, now. This wasn't what he'd wanted, what he needed. Never mind his sleepless night, his searching on the net. Never mind the ache of Brendan's name in his throat.

"Look," Lew said, hunched forward. "I don't know what it's like. I can't imagine—"

"You can't."

"No. But I watched you go through—I watched you tear yourself up. About Brendan, about Chloe. I know what you can do to yourself. You should, too. I can see it on your face, Mark."

"It's not true. That's not what this is about."

"Just be sure," Lew said, very quietly. "We could go over there together, even."

Mark closed his eyes; almost imperceptibly, the room swayed. "I can't do that."

"You don't have to—"

He sounded so awful, so false. "You think I do."

"You asked me, I answered. Buddy, all I'm doing is asking *what if.*"

"And I haven't been?"

Lew's eyes were soft and wounded. "How could you not?"

And here Mark heard, truly heard, the judgment he'd been sure he never would—not from Lew. Not from a man who thought ghosts were real because he'd smoked a bunch of fucking pot when he was a teenager.

Not from a man who'd never had children, never had a son, never climbed up a flight of narrow stairs forever, toward that broken little boy.

"I have to go."

Lew's voice was thick. "Mark. Take it easy, I was just—come on. Sit."

Mark had stood, was reaching for his coat.

Lew stood, too. "Mark, man, I'm sorry. Just tell me what I can do."

"There's nothing to do." Mark pulled on his coat. If he wasn't outside in moments, he was sure, he was going to begin sobbing.

The weight of Lew's big hand fell on Mark's shoulder, as he squeezed between Lew and the bar, and he was tempted—more than tempted; he was *compelled*—to stop, to let Lew embrace him, to take care of him again, as Lew used to, when he'd show up at the door of Mark's apartment in the early-morning hours when Mark was pacing and frantic, his worst thoughts snapping and ravening at the door of their pen. Because he had called, and Lew had answered.

"I've got to go," Mark said. He buttoned his coat and hurried through the door, into the frigid evening.

⁓

Mark sat for a long time behind the wheel of his car. He wiped his eyes and watched through the fogged windshield as Lew appeared at the corner, his coat open, his head uncovered, looking quickly left, then right: searching for him. Lew pulled out his cell phone, and then walked south, holding his hand over his free ear. Mark's phone buzzed in his breast pocket, and he ignored it until it stilled.

He checked his watch. It was nearly eight; he should go home. He'd forgotten to leave Allison a note, though she was likely still shopping. She'd call him when she found him gone.

But the world was all wrong. He was all wrong. He'd just drunk three beers—more than he'd allowed himself in a long time. His movements were thick, his thoughts furred over. He might not even be legal to drive.

What he needed to do—had to do—was take a short walk. The night was cold, crisp. He could clear his head.

And not only that. This neighborhood had gotten to him—spooked him, and not just tonight. He'd been letting the place command him for years, now. If he walked for a while, he'd see there was nothing here—anywhere—for him to be afraid of. Maybe then, when he felt better, he could call Lew. Apologize for the way he'd just treated him. And tell him—firmly, absolutely—that he was one hundred percent sure.

Mark got out of the car and walked slowly back to the corner. Lew was nowhere in sight. He looked right and left. Every storefront, every bar and gallery, was new to him. All his old haunts were gone.

Haunts.

He couldn't go on like this. Jumping away from every dark corner, every diseased implication. He reminded himself: He was a successful man. He was engaged to Allison Daniel. Only two weeks ago he had been *happy*. Was it really Connie Pelham's fault that he wasn't anymore?

So what if the old house was less than a mile west of where he now stood? He was one hundred percent sure that it was, simply, a house he'd once lived in, but didn't any longer: Wood and stone and brick and the air they contained. And a man who was one hundred percent sure, who didn't lose himself playing silly *what-if* games, could walk anywhere he damned well pleased.

So he would.

He headed north on High Street, mingling with the crowds. So many people, happy; they smoked, drank, laughed; women pressed close to men. Mark passed the open door of an Italian restaurant, and the line of chattering people waiting for a seat; he smelled the rich garlic, the pillowy warm bread. He passed an art gallery; without thinking too much about it, he ducked inside, nodded to the cadaverous man in the bolo tie who sat at a desk beside the door, and looked at the terrible, terrible abstract art. He had half a degree in art; he liked art. So here he was: a man living his life. A member of this world. He had desires and opinions. His stomach growled.

He left the gallery, walked on down the sidewalk. What was there to fear? Every last shop and restaurant he remembered, from his old life, had changed. And he had changed with them.

Then he walked past the side street where his and Chloe's apartment had been. He glanced to his right, saw the building— now dingy, shabbier than he remembered. His old window dark, a cramped emptiness, a shadow above and behind High Street's bustle. It was the place a sad and lonely man would live, blocking his ears against the happiness outside.

That man was not him. Not anymore.

Mark walked on. And here was the old alley. The steps leading down from the sidewalk, beneath the brick arch. Beyond had been Dougie's Bar, where he and Chloe and Lew used to spend so much of their time. A student dive, favored by punk bands. Now it seemed to be an upscale jazz club. Mark leaned against the rail and listened to a rubbery, walking bass line rise up the stairs. He remembered his younger self—newlywed, safe and secure in his happiness—walking down these same steps. Chloe's hand in his hand. Lew on stage, face slicked with sweat, roaring, gripping his bass like an ogre's club.

Mark walked down the steps, into the bar. A combo was playing in a brick alcove cut into the east wall. The musicians were all men who looked like his father; his father would love them, their music. Of this Mark was one hundred percent sure—so sure he glanced suspiciously around, making sure Sam wasn't here, watching him.

Sam wasn't, so Mark went to the bartender and ordered another Guinness. The first sip slid easily down his throat. He followed it with another, and another, shutting his eyes, while his head filled with music.

An hour and two more beers later Mark climbed the steps back to the street. His feet seemed to float above the steps; he felt less like himself than he had before: a good thing, indeed. The night was much colder, but he did not walk toward his car—and why would he? Driving was out of the question now. Instead he kept strolling north. A crowd had assembled on a corner up ahead—some kind of formal event, everyone young and dressed up, maybe a fraternity party from OSU—and he turned down one side street, and then another, to avoid the mass. A heavyset woman, smoking in the doorway of a gift shop—a woman closer to his age than any of the women in the bar he'd just left—smiled and said, "Good evening."

"It is," he said, as Dr. Fife the heart surgeon.

And then—he couldn't believe it—he was at the corner of Buttles and Wall, at the exact dividing line between the shops of the Short North and the looming brick houses of Victorian Village.

At this corner, on this bench—the stone one, right here—Mark had once taught Brendan right and left, based on the way the cars turned onto High at the next intersection.

The blue Bug, he'd say. Which way's it going?

Left, Brendan would say. Then, with more certainty, his face tightening, as though being correct required courage: *Left.*

Good, Mark would say. Let's go for five out of six. He'd want to ruffle Brendan's hair, but that would mess up his concentration, annoy him.

If Brendan got it right often enough, the deal went, Mark would take him to his favorite place, across the street: Fitz's Old-Time Ice Cream and Soda Shoppe. Mark turned, lifted his eyes. Fitz's was still there, its windows brightly lit. Inside were adults, children. Fathers and sons.

Mark sat on the bench. He listened. Even though the Short North was to his right, dozens of people milling on the sidewalks, he heard only the cold wind moving across the roofs and treetops of the Village, the creak and sway of the trees. He was one hundred percent sure of this.

He stood and walked west, into the neighborhoods, mansions on his right and Goodale Park a black hole on his left.

Mark had only gone partway down the block when his shoulder bumped, painfully, the metal shaft of a stop sign. He counted, again, the beers he'd drunk. He'd have to call a cab soon. But he didn't want to spend the money, or explain to Chloe—Allison— what he'd been up to—

He'd just mixed up their names. He hated doing this. Allison was Allison and Chloe was Chloe. There was no mistaking one for the other.

A little while longer. To clear his head.

He walked on, past house after house, taking care with the cracked and upheaved sidewalk stones in the dark. Above him bedroom windows glowed orange and seemed to drip with heat.

When he'd walked four blocks, he was standing across Neil Avenue from Giant Eagle—which, when they'd lived here, used to be the Big Bear grocery. The Big Ol' Bear, they used to say. You had to say it in a certain voice—Baloo's. The big ol' redneck singing bear.

You went to the Big Bear for those bare necessities of life. Cheerios for Brendan and cases of Fresca for Chloe and Coca-Cola for himself. Countless boxes of diapers and rolls of toilet paper and the frozen pesto pizzas they all liked. Guinness, sometimes, and Merlot for Chloe. Once, humiliatingly, condoms, when Chloe'd had a reaction to her pills. Nothing like a box of rubbers to remind a man how much sex his wife wasn't having with him. He'd had to put a magazine in Brendan's hands to keep him from picking up the box and reading its contents aloud.

Brendan humming when he was allowed to push the cart.

Brendan singing tunelessly to himself on the living room rug, walking one of his action figures step by uncertain step.

Calling for his daddy.

No.

Mark turned north on Neil. Four blocks, then five. The appearance of each house as familiar as the ache of an old wound. The traffic murmuring by—Neil Avenue busy enough that, until he turned six, Brendan had always been required to hold Mark's hand alongside it.

His hand was empty, now. Fisted and cold in his coat pocket. And here was the old turn, onto Fourth. The way home.

A choice. Allie would be in the townhouse by now, and he hadn't called to tell her where he was. She'd be worried. He could call a cab and go home. Tell her he'd had too many with Lew. Apologize.

Or: He could turn left, and continue walking his familiar path home from the store. Within five minutes he'd be on Locust, and he'd see the house, his old house, *their* old house, which was not haunted, because there was no such thing as ghosts.

He was one hundred percent sure.

So left it was.

The streets here were darker, the sidewalks even more treacherous. He zigzagged across Harrison, then left again, into the stretch of streets named for the flyover states. The pavement soon gave way to cobblestones. He crossed Iowa. Pennsylvania. He was like a jet plane, speeding silently through the dark skies.

Then he was turning left onto Michigan. Another block and the big houses began—he was in the heart of Victorian Village, now, surrounded by the century-old homes, their small grassy front yards sloping past old oaks and maples to the sidewalk and the cobbled streets. Squared intersections gave way to manicured roundabouts. Here was quiet and stillness and old money.

One more right turn, onto Locust. And here was the little nameless park: exactly half a block in size, with seesaws and saddled ladybugs on big metal springs, and several lovely young birch trees and wooden benches. He took the diagonal path through it, past the rusted, quietly crying chains of the swings, past the sandbox, past the curving slide, and then: He was there.

Here. Standing on the sidewalk, looking across a roundabout at the house.

It had changed. Had become smaller in life than it remained in his head, less grand, less—less what? Welcoming? Maybe so. Sadly so.

Its shape had not changed. The house was still two stories high, still walled with dark brick. The wide turret still curved out from the corner of the house facing the roundabout and the park; the front porch was still made of concrete, on top of a stone foundation, its roof supported by square brick pillars. The front steps still descended from the porch to the sidewalk, between the two bare oaks that still rose from the narrow, banked yard. The two gable windows extending onto the porch roof still looked like eyes; the pillars of the porch still gave the whole the look of a gap-toothed, smiling mouth.

Happy house, Brendan used to say—though in the dark, like now, when he was afraid, he wouldn't have.

Several windows glowed. The tall chimney smoked. Connie Pelham was home.

Mark huddled close to the trunk of one of the birches. He couldn't tell, here in the dark, but he was fairly sure that Margie or Connie or both had repainted the shutters and trim. He and Chloe had painted all the wood dark green, with deep crimson accents. Christmas colors. Now the wood seemed lighter, the color probably garish—but that had always been the trend among the other owners in the neighborhood, painting Victorian houses in period colors, lavenders and pinks and lime greens.

The house's dimensions settled. His eyes adjusted. Yes. This was still his house. Theirs.

A car drove slowly past him and down the street; Mark turned his face from the headlights. He wondered if the driver had noticed him: a man in a dark overcoat standing next to a playground at night. What would he have thought, years ago, when he was a father in this house? If he'd looked out his study window and seen a man lurking in the trees?

He'd have called the police. He'd have kept his family safe.

He remembered any of a hundred nights: waking in the dark, beside Chloe in their bedroom, his breath and heartbeat suddenly quick, alert, even as his mind struggled to catch up. A vibration in the air, in the cells of his skin—had Brendan cried? And there, again—the barest tendril of sound, winding past the thick walls and the doors left ajar: *Daddy!*

Because in the night, in the dark—when he was afraid, when he'd been woken from a dream, when he feared the ghosts or worse—Brendan would only ever call for his father. He would not sleep until Mark tucked him back in, had told him a story.

When he glanced back at the house, a movement drew his eyes up, through the branches, to what had been Brendan's old window. A light had come on inside. The shade was up; the room's walls glowed whitely.

A silhouette appeared in the window. A boy's.

The hair rose on Mark's arms. The shadow of a boy, not very old—Brendan's age, maybe—standing in front of the window, looking out.

Mark knew he must be invisible, down in the park, but for the life of him it seemed as though the boy in the window was regarding him. Staring into him.

He turned and walked quickly away. His breath came very quickly, now; he could hear himself panting. He exited the park, onto Michigan Avenue. Don't run, he told himself. But he ran anyway. Up ahead the houses gave way to an intersection lined with businesses—a corner market, the liquor store, a yoga studio, all closed. The nasty all-night laundromat was still in business, too. Mark slipped inside. The air was slick, warm, smelling of detergent, wet mildewed cloth. One dryer tumbled forlornly in the back, but he was alone.

A pay phone hung on the wall just inside the door; a phone book in a plastic cover was attached to it with a braided cable. He flipped to the cab companies and called the first listing.

He'd have them take him to his car. He could drive home. He'd been very very stupid, but he wasn't drunk, not now.

He had not seen the ghost. He'd only seen Connie's son. Jacob—his name was Jacob. Jacob who slept in Brendan's old room. Jacob who had lied. Mark was sure of it.

⁓

He continued telling himself this. As the cab drove him through the darkened Village. As he carefully steered his car along the back streets toward home. As he unlocked the townhouse. As he told Allison—waiting for him, anxiously, in the living room—that he'd been out with Lew. As he apologized for not checking his messages. As he assured her that he'd been fine, driving like this. As she asked him, before climbing the stairs, if he was coming up to bed, and then again after he'd told her, Soon.

He had seen a living child, he told himself. Nothing more.

Eleven

All that week Allison had been preparing for Sam and Helen's arrival on Christmas Eve. She had decorated and redecorated the townhouse, stringing lights across the tops of the walls, had gone shopping—his father had insisted they not exchange gifts, but Allison wasn't about to accept these terms, and Mark figured Sam and Helen wouldn't, either.

Allie, in fact, had prepared for this Christmas in all the ways Mark had come to hate—ticking off a list of obligations, trying to hit the right aesthetic mark, as though German Village would run them out if they took a single wrong step, as though Helen and Sam would spit on the floor and return to Indiana in a huff.

So the morning after his walk to Victorian Village, Mark woke, his head thick and sore, and proceeded to spend a miserable Sunday out with Allie, hunting down the last of what she thought they needed, including—it was ridiculous to do so at the last minute, Mark thought, but her course was set—electric candles for the sills of their front windows.

He tried to maintain good cheer, patience. Tried to keep last night's adventure—his shameful fear—to himself. But in the parking lot of a Home Depot that had disappointed their quest, yet again, he snapped: "You know Dad doesn't care about this shit, right? We can give up."

Allison, behind the wheel, took a breath. She started the car, put it into gear, pulled onto the street.

"This time of year has to be rough on you," she said, almost to herself.

Mark bit down hard on everything he might have said in response. Allie was peering over the wheel, waiting for an answer, and because he had to say something—because Gayle would have urged him to answer, too; because it was fucking Christmas—he said, "It is."

He understood, then: Allie had held off decorating the townhouse for so long because she thought the holiday would upset him. All day she'd been patient with him for the same reason.

She wasn't wrong. Christmastime did upset him, and when he'd lived alone, these past years, he'd tried to ignore it. But now? He could not pass the piles of presents beneath their tree without remembering Brendan tearing into his own: A pouty toddler with Hitchcock cheeks, peeling away paper handful by solemn handful. A five-year-old waking him and Chloe at four in the morning, whispering, The presents came! A seven-year-old so excited by the bicycle Mark wheeled out from the dining room that he'd begun to jump up and down spastically, crying Dad! Dad! Dad!

Mark took Allie's hand, closed his eyes, let her drive.

So that evening, despite him, the townhouse was fully decorated. They had a tree and lights and tinsel hung from the boughs; under the tree were presents in silver wrapping paper and pale blue ribbon. Glimmering strings of lights hung in graceful waves along the walls of the living room. They had a frozen duck and a bag of yams and mulling spice. The air smelled of cinnamon. Electric candles shone in all the windows.

He deserved none of it, he thought, remembering the silhouette of the boy in the window, remembering how he'd abandoned Lew.

He took Allie into his arms beside the fireplace. "Thanks," he said, "for thinking I'm worth the trouble."

She softened against him. "You're not forgiven unless you take me upstairs," she said.

He nodded. Looked into her eyes. He was lucky. For a long time he hadn't been, but now he was. For the first time since Connie Pelham had found him in the bookstore, he felt a stirring of lust.

"Tell me what you want," he said to her. "Tell me everything."

Later, while they watched television together sleepily on the couch, the doorbell shrilled.

Mark glanced at Allie, who shrugged—and then her eyes narrowed.

"If it's her," Mark said, "call the police. Don't wait for me to get rid of her."

He handed Allie his phone, then walked to the window and pulled aside the curtain. A woman was on the stoop, and for a moment—steeling himself to see Connie Pelham—he didn't recognize Chloe, in her long black coat and woolen cap. But then he saw the blond hair spilling across her shoulders, the narrow pink blade of her nose. His first thought was that she had been caught up in a very Chloe-like spasm of holiday cheer; maybe she had come to make what peace she could, or to bring them cookies. That would be like her.

But then Chloe turned her head, saw him. Her eyes were red and wet and swollen, her mouth thin and grim. He knew this face. She was furious.

"Who is it?" Allison said, from the hallway behind him. Mark couldn't bring himself to answer. He unlatched and opened the door; frigid air rushed past him like floodwater.

"Mark," Chloe said, voice trembling.

Right away he knew what had happened.

"Come in," he said.

"No." She blinked rapidly. "I don't even know what to say to you."

He said nothing.

"I just talked to Connie Pelham. She came to my apartment a couple of hours ago." Chloe's eyes bore into him. "You weren't going to tell me?"

Mark felt Allison, a few feet behind him, registering who was at the door. Chloe's gaze slipped briefly over his shoulder and then back to him.

"Hi, Chloe," Allie said.

Chloe put a mittened hand over her eyes. "It's unbelievable. Except—no, I guess I do believe it. You'd do this. You would."

"Allie," Mark said, "I think Chloe and I better talk alone for a minute."

"We're not going to talk," Chloe said.

"You're sure," Allie said to him, a chill in her voice. He turned just long enough to nod, then stepped out onto the stoop and pulled the door shut behind him.

The cold was deep, cutting; he began right away to shiver. Chloe opened and shut her mouth. But her gears were jamming, and the frustration was making her even angrier.

"Listen," he said. "You were in bad shape when we talked, last. I didn't think it was the right time—"

"Oh, fuck you, Mark. You can tell me all about—about *her*?" Chloe pointed at the living room window behind them. "But this is too much for me? Our son might still be—might still be—"

He couldn't believe this. "Wait. You believe her?"

"I don't know!" Chloe cried. "They think Brendan's still there! And you think that's not—that's not important?"

"Jesus!" All the tension, all the sleeplessness, of the last weeks crumbled away the last of his restraint. "Connie Pelham's nuts.

That's why I didn't tell you. Think about it—her kid heard something about Brendan, and he got scared. He made something up. That's all this is."

Chloe was staring at him. "They've both seen him now."

He turned and looked down the street, toward the lights of downtown, the buildings lit up green and red. Victorian Village beyond.

"I don't believe anything that woman says," he said. "You shouldn't, either."

Chloe's eyes and nose were nearly the same shade of pink. "How can you say that? I told you this so many times—I keep *feeling* him, I keep thinking he's there—how can I not take this seriously? Why can't *you*?"

He kept his breathing deep, even. "That doesn't mean—"

Chloe was crying, now; he knew what was coming next. "You never took me seriously," she said. "You can't take Connie seriously, either. You think we're a bunch of silly women who—"

"Stop it," he said.

"I can't stop it!" Her fists balled up at her sides. "I was his mother!"

Here was their divorce, replaying itself again. Numbly, he said his line.

"And I wasn't his father?"

Chloe shivered, tense as wire.

"Yeah, Mark," she said. "You were. So why wouldn't you want to know? Why wouldn't you want to see? What's *wrong* with you?"

"There's nothing wrong with me."

A fractured, awful cry spilled from her. He'd heard this, too, as they'd cracked and split apart and sunk. Chloe would simmer and churn, and then finally he would goad her, to make her say her craziest thoughts aloud—*I just think, I just know, that if I'd been the one home*—and then she'd lose it, bend double; the cords would stand out on her neck as her moan grew and grew into a scream.

There was nothing he could do or say to her, now.

Chloe knew it, too—she turned abruptly and descended the steps, her hands over her mouth. She opened the door to her gray Civic and climbed behind the wheel. He watched her start the car; she convulsed, once, twice, over the wheel. She began to pull into the street, but then slowed at the curb in front of him. Her window rolled down.

"Everything is wrong with you!" she shouted. "Everything!"

Then she drove away.

Mark looked up and down the street. Chloe's outburst hadn't seemed to draw any neighbor's attention. He was tired. Not angry— not anymore—but sad, weary. He went back inside, into the cushiony heat. Allison stood in the hallway, arms across her chest, her mouth tightly set.

"You heard?" Mark asked.

"Most of it."

"I don't want to say anything I'll regret later. I don't want to bad-mouth her."

"You didn't tell her?" Allie said. "Is that what—"

He nodded.

Allison turned and walked into the kitchen. He heard the blowing heat of the gas jets, the ticking of the copper teapot. Only then did he follow her, rubbing feeling back into his hands.

"I should have told her," he said. "I'd been trying to think how."

Allison set a canister of tea on the counter with too much force. "I think she needs to talk to a psychiatrist. I mean that. But Mark—"

"It was the wrong time. It's Christmas."

Though that hadn't stopped Connie, had it?

"There wasn't going to be a right one," Allison said.

"Jesus!" he said. "I'm not the fucking problem here!"

Allie sucked in her breath. He held up his hands in apology.

She said, evenly, "I'm not trying to tell you what to do. I'm just really tired of crazy people coming to our house. That's all."

She held out her arm, but Mark didn't go to her. He didn't need to hear another goddamned word out of anyone, tonight, about what he did or didn't need to do.

"She's done this before," he said. "Made a scene like this. When she calms down, we'll talk again. And at some point she will—she *will*—apologize to you."

Allie dropped her arm. "I don't need that."

"I do."

"We don't have to humiliate her."

How had they reversed positions? "*She* humiliates *me*," he said. "She listens to Connie fucking Pelham for five minutes, and then she's on my steps telling me I don't love Brendan enough? That if I did—"

He'd what? Lose sleep? Have nightmares? Start drinking again?

Get drunk and visit the old house without telling anyone?

"I don't have to believe this," he said. "I don't have to believe *her.*" He wasn't going to say Connie's name, anymore. "Brendan's dead. It's not fair of them to ask."

Allie's face softened. "Honey," she said, and held open her arms again. This time he gave in to her embrace.

He knew what he had to say. What he had to do. He'd spent too much time in his head with Chloe: worrying about her, whispering to her, arguing with her. And now Allie, his fiancée, was upset in her own home, not an hour after hanging the last of their Christmas lights.

"It's time I cut ties with her," he said. "Overdue."

Allie shook her head. "I would never ask that."

He kissed her forehead. "You shouldn't have to."

This wasn't the romantic gesture Allison had been wanting from him. This wasn't when she'd most needed it. But he said, "Allie. You're my life, now. They can't do this to you."

Allie waited a long time before answering.

"Don't hurt her," she said. "Not because of me."

He told the truth: "She didn't give me a choice."

⌒

An hour later, just after Mark had switched off his bedside lamp, Allison said, "Poor Chloe."

When he'd come to bed, her eyes had been closed; her voice now took him by surprise. He rolled onto his elbow. "What do you mean?"

"This couldn't be easy news for her."

He had no idea what to make of this: Allie's pity.

She asked, "Is this why it's been hard for you to tell her?"

"Yes." He reached over and turned the light back on. "What, are you still mad at me?"

"No!" Allie said. "I never was. Just—"

"Just what?"

"You two. You're so different from me and Bill. That's all."

Mark heard no malice in her voice, but even so he couldn't imagine too many conversations he less wanted to have right now.

"Bill and I were only together four years," she said. "Start to finish. And I—I don't think I ever loved him."

He'd heard this speech before. The great shame of Allison's life: She hadn't understood love when she married.

"But even when he was cheating on me, I never—never screamed at him like that. I didn't love him enough to yell."

Mark grew frightened of what she'd say next.

Allie said, "I just get the feeling Chloe doesn't have anyone but you right now."

"She divorced me. She doesn't get a pass for tonight."

"No," Allie said. "But it's the holidays, and she's alone, and she's getting news that scares her. She was upset about us, when you told her. I just—" Allie sighed. "Do what you think is right. But try to go easy on her."

When he didn't answer, she asked, "Does that make you mad?"

"No," he said. In fact he thought what she'd said was pretty wise. He closed his eyes, considering. Caught a thread and followed it— because Allie was smart, very smart. She'd made—hadn't she?—a statement that he might hear two different ways. If Chloe's rage was due to the fact she still loved him, at least a little, then what was the source of *his*?

"I'll think it over," he said, his face burning. His thoughts spun, before finally settling in the darkest place. He'd asked her once already, but now he tried again: "Allie, tell me the truth. Do I need to go over there?"

"Where? To Chloe's?"

"To the old house." Allie's face tightened. "Is she right? Is something wrong with me if I don't want to go see?"

Allie sat up, the sheet pooling in her lap. "If you believed even a little bit, then you'd have to do something. But I think you're right. I really do. There's another explanation for what's going on."

He tried his best to smile at her, to remind her she was marrying someone sane and thoughtful. "When the sun's out, I can get there. But this late..."

"Just tell me what I can do."

"Be patient with me," he said. "It's not your fault. None of this is."

She pressed the tip of her thumb to his lips. Traced their outline with her nail, as though she were sealing them shut, the words into law.

～

At two in the morning, Mark slowly extricated himself from beneath Allison's arm and walked quietly to the living room. He sat down on the couch with his cell phone and dialed Chloe's number.

When he reached her voicemail he said, calmly, "Chloe. I should have told you about Connie, and I'm sorry I didn't. I really thought I was protecting you at a rough time. But I was wrong. This was your business, too."

He looked up at the light fixture above his head, glowing dim and yellow, its glass cover dotted by the shadows of dead insects.

"But you don't have the right to talk to me like that, not anymore. You don't have the right to come here and make a scene like that. So we're done. We're done for good. Don't contact me again. And you can tell Connie Pelham that if she tries, I will call the police on her." He closed his eyes to say the next part: "I loved our son, and I grieve him every day, and that's something *you've* never believed. So I guess we're even."

He'd had more to say, but now he'd lost the thread of his argument, shocked by the sound of his own voice.

"Goodbye."

He shut his phone quickly, looked at it in his hands. Despite his anger, he'd almost told her he loved her, one last time.

He sat still, waiting, expecting…what? For her to have been lying awake, waiting for his call? For her to hear his message and hurriedly call him back? For her to argue, to plead?

But his phone remained still and quiet. Mark waited an hour anyway before admitting to himself: Six long years after a judge had pronounced it so, he and Chloe were finally done.

He went to the kitchen. Allison had left a half-empty wineglass next to the sink. The wine was lukewarm, but he drank it in one swallow, then washed out the glass. He turned out the downstairs lights and carefully climbed the stairs.

His pulse fluttered against the satin edge of the blanket he'd pulled to his throat.

I'll never hurt you. He'd promised Chloe this.

You'll always have me, she'd once told him. I'm yours. Forever and always.

She'd said this at their wedding, in the summer sunshine at Whetstone Park, in the rose garden there. They'd written their own vows. My Mark, she'd said—her voice breaking, the paper upon which she'd written the words shaking. I wasn't a real person until I met you.

At the reception he'd been unable to move his eyes from her. He was no dancer, but he danced that afternoon, because Chloe loved to dance, and he wanted to be with her, to give her everything, his hand in hers as she swayed and shook her hair out of its pins and down her back.

Forever and always. Say it again, he'd told her, that night, in their hotel room.

I'm yours, she said, flinging her arms back across the sheets. Forever.

Mark's head had begun to throb. He imagined Chloe hearing his message, when she woke in the morning. He imagined her in her bed, weeping with anger or grief or both.

And he remembered, then—as punishment, maybe—the first night he and Chloe had brought Brendan home from the hospital. Mark hadn't been able to sleep then, either. He sat awake in the rocking chair that used to be his mother's, beside the bed where Chloe, just home from the hospital, slept; on the floor between them was Brendan in his bassinet, wrapped tight, not quite asleep and not quite awake. His breath came in squeaks.

Mark had been too amazed to sleep. By his son, swaddled. By Chloe, small again beneath the comforter, her face slack and, even in sleep, turned toward their child. Mark had leaned forward, his elbows on his knees, and he'd watched them both, in the glow of a night-light he'd hastily plugged into the wall beside the bed. His wife. His child.

Then Brendan had hiccupped, jerked. The sound sent contrails across Mark's vision. He reached down into the bassinet, but Brendan was merely squirming, working his lips. Mark touched his silken cheek with his index finger, withdrew it.

He looked up to see Chloe's open eyes.

She said, I heard—

He slid his hand across hers.

Go to sleep, he whispered. I'm watching.

She smiled, caressed his palm with her thumb.

I know, she said, and then slowly closed her eyes.

Twelve

Sam and Helen arrived late in the afternoon on Christmas Eve. Allison, in the kitchen stirring what seemed to be a dozen different pots, shouted upstairs to Mark when the doorbell rang. He trotted down the stairs—he'd been trying to work, to force himself alert with his third cup of coffee—wiped his suddenly damp palms on his jeans, and opened the door. His father was smiling on the stoop, holding two shopping bags full of gifts. Next to him was Helen: blond, tall—shockingly so. She was nearly the same height as Sam.

"Come in!" Mark said, his voice oddly booming.

"Mark," his father said, dropping his chin. "Helen Etley."

Mark wasn't sure what he'd expected in Helen—someone short and gray-haired, he supposed. Yet even though Sam had told him Helen was younger, he wasn't prepared for the woman in front of him now: thin, grinning, her eyes so green they seemed nearly feral. "Mark," she said—her voice booming a little, too—and took his hand in both of hers. "It's so good to meet you." She removed her long navy coat; beneath it she wore a long skirt and a blue sweater that—he couldn't help but notice—showed off a sizable bosom. And she was forty-eight? She could be forty. If he passed her on the street, he'd stare after her.

Helen greeted Allison, whose face lit up in happy amazement—she wasn't above staring after a statuesque babe, either. Then Allie was showing Helen around the townhouse, and Mark and his father were outside, carrying in suitcases and more bags of gifts from the back of the truck.

His father, Mark realized, was terrified: stiff-backed and grunting, refusing to meet Mark's eyes.

"Dad, she's amazing," Mark told him, shutting the truck's gate.

His father shook his head. "She's a pistol."

"A pistol? Dad, she's a goddamn shotgun."

"Don't embarrass me." The tips of his father's ears were red—and not, Mark thought, from the cold. "This is hard enough."

Mark made small talk with Sam and Helen in the living room until the food was ready, but it wasn't until all of them had sat down to dinner, and were listening to Helen tell a surprisingly funny story about a plagiarist student, that Mark finally understood why she had shocked him so much—why he'd spent the last half an hour forcing himself to smile: He had never considered that Sam might end up falling for someone so different from Mark's mother.

When he'd imagined Helen, he had pictured someone short, round, earthy. Someone who never raised her voice, who kept her counsel, always, until it was requested. And now here was Sam with a woman his own height, bold and aggressive, who—Mark heard it now—was speaking in a Voice much like his father's.

Helen finished her story, to much laughter, some of it her own.

"So how did you two meet?" Allison asked. She sat beside Mark, her knee pressed warmly against his, and was nearly vibrating with love for Helen Etley.

"You want this one, Sam?" Helen asked.

"She gives me the boring ones," his father said. "It was a committee meeting. A college bylaw-revision task force—"

"You're a liar. We met the night before."

Sam shook his head, slowly. "I *saw* you the night before—"

Helen touched Sam's hand. "I think Allison's asking for the romantic version."

His father was turning crimson again. "I saw her at a concert."

Allison had clasped her fingers in front of her, was sitting completely at attention.

Sam told them how he'd been at a little club in Broad Ripple, watching a jazz combo comprising some of Butler's music faculty. He'd noticed Helen in the audience. "Because one notices Helen," he said. "And I thought to myself, There's one woman I'll never speak to. She was surrounded by admirers—"

"Liar. I'd come with a date, but he wasn't a very good one."

"Did you notice Sam?" Allison asked.

Helen rubbed Sam's hand. "I saw him. He was sitting alone and looked completely at ease. He looked *cool.*"

This was news to Mark. His father: a man women noticed. Cool.

"At any rate," his father said, "the next day, as I sat down to this terrible committee meeting, I was, perhaps, thinking about the lovely Amazonian jazz aficionado I'd seen the night before. And then I looked up—and there the Amazon was, taking the very seat next to me."

"I couldn't help it," Helen said. "I got so bored I started writing him notes."

Helen was smiling at Sam, lifting her hair from her shoulder. His father, despite his embarrassment, smiled crookedly back. She said, "I asked him to dinner an hour later. And because Sam is Sam, I am forbidden from saying—"

"*The rest is history,*" Mark finished for her.

Helen beamed across the table at him. "So what about you two?"

Mark and Allie had rehearsed this. "We met at a conference," Allie said. "In Newark."

"Newark!" Helen said.

"Land of romance and intrigue," Mark said. Helen laughed, as she was supposed to.

He let Allie tell the story. The autumn before last, she and Mark had both been working for downtown design firms, and had both been sent to Newark for a professional conference. By chance they sat next to each other during a presentation. Mark had been wearing an Ohio State cap, and Allie, during a lull in the talk, had leaned closer to him and whispered, *O! H!*

"And I said what I was supposed to—" Mark began.

"You have to answer *I, O*," Allie told Helen, who looked lost. "It's kind of like a disease."

Helen nodded carefully.

Allie kept going: Neither of them knew anyone at the conference. When the presentation was over, they talked for a while at the bar. "We kept getting tangled up," Allie said. "We found out we were booked for the same flight home. We talked in the airport, and then Mark switched seats so we could talk on the flight. Then we shared a cab back from the airport, and by the end of the cab ride we decided we'd better have dinner. And we did." Allie was smiling her brightest smile. "And that was that."

They had already told this story to Sam, when he'd first met Allison. Like Helen, now, he'd smiled and accepted it. Of course Sam knew there must be more to tell; Sam, Helen—all the friends they'd told—knew that Allie was newly divorced, and that Mark used to have a family; no one who knew them could assume their courtship had been that easy. But putting a bow on the story—*And that was that!*—allowed everyone to smile and nod and never ask. It was a courtesy, and all their friends took it, but it bore little resemblance to the truth.

The truth was this: After leaving the presentation, Mark—lonely, possessed by courage that came from nowhere, and which he still could not explain—asked Allie, his fellow Buckeye, to dinner. She agreed, and after dinner the two of them went to his room to talk, and ended up having too-desperate, too-loud sex on the couch in his suite.

Allie, now, met Mark's eyes. The left corner of her mouth curled up.

He excused himself to the kitchen, where he divided a blueberry crumble into bowls and began to brew coffee. He listened to the voices in the dining room; in particular, Helen's carried, usually trailing Allison's laughter.

He reminded himself there was nothing shameful about Allison, about the way they'd met. They were adults; in certain company— well, around Lew—the story could even be a little funny. Even so, they'd developed the lie Allie was still spinning in the dining room.

The two of them hadn't, in fact, shared the same flight home, let alone a cab. When they woke the morning after, Allie had left his room in a state of obvious shame. Mark realized, as she gathered up her clothes, that he'd never learned her last name.

He might never have seen her again, if Allie hadn't hired on at his company that winter. Mark's boss called together the staff on Monday morning to introduce their new web-design specialist, and as he said, I want everyone to welcome Allison Daniel, Mark had lifted his face to find Allison already staring at him. She quickly directed her eyes to the floor, touches of crimson appearing in her cheeks, while Mark's boss discussed her qualifications, the energy she would bring to their team.

Allie came up to him in the break room at lunch. What were the odds? she asked.

It's a small town, he said.

She smiled, flushed. She'd grown her hair longer, was wearing granny glasses and a tailored gray suit and very high heels. He thought, I'm talking with a woman who couldn't run away from sex with me fast enough.

Allie Daniel, she said, and held out her hand. I don't—I don't think you know who I really am.

A weight had lifted from him.

Mark Fife, he said. I was just about to say the same thing.

A week after she'd hired on, Allie brought her lunch to Mark's cubicle. They ate companionably, and Mark was struck—as he had been in Newark—by Allie's wide, intense gaze, by the fullness of her lips and the hint of brown in her complexion, as though part of her genetic code had arrived via Bombay. The wicked force of her laughter.

Then her eyes passed over the pictures tacked beside his computer.

Is that—? she started to ask. His heart thumped as she bent closer to the picture. That kid's *got* to be related to you, she said.

She looked from Brendan's face to Mark's. And that moment, he knew now, was when they'd truly begun. He'd known he could love her when Allison saw the grief in his face, and understood, and did not recoil.

Tell me, she'd said.

Now, in the kitchen, Mark poured coffee into mugs on a tray. Laughter carried into the kitchen—Helen's, Allie's.

Was his father ever caught up in moments like this? Maybe it was different, for a man Sam's age. But when had Sam told Helen, *My wife died*? When had Helen realized that Sam had gone nearly two decades without remarrying? He wondered if their story was, in its way, as much of a sham as his and Allison's.

That didn't mean they were wrong for each other. Already he knew Helen was terrific—smart, funny, beautiful; the kind of woman he absolutely wished for his father to love. But he knew this, too: Apart from what was surely a basic goodness, Helen couldn't have been a more different woman than his mother. And that hurt him—so suddenly and deeply he could not bring himself to leave the kitchen and face the others.

He wondered, again, what his mother would think of Allison.

I can't imagine someone better for you than Chloe, she'd told him, only days before she died. *I can't tell you how happy I am that I had a chance to know her.*

Mark poured himself a glass of wine, gulped it down, then washed the glass and swallowed some coffee to mask the smell.

His father appeared in the kitchen doorway. "Need a hand?"

"You can watch me scoop ice cream," Mark said. Did Sam still have his old fatherly powers? Had he, from the other room, sensed his son's high-school-grade guilt? Mark's cheeks burned.

Sam was smiling. "Helen couldn't be having a better time. She adores you both."

"We adore her," Mark said. "Allie's about ready to follow you home."

Sam chuckled and leaned against the counter. "Tell me the truth, Mark. You really like her?"

"Yeah, Dad. I do."

"Good," Sam said. "Well. I need to tell you some news. Helen and I—we have decided to rent an apartment. Jointly."

Mark was suddenly stricken. He could have said any of a hundred things, but the one that popped inanely from his mouth was, "What about the house?"

Sam moved to the counter. He poured cream into one of the coffees and took a sip. "We'd live there in the summers and on weekends. But the drive's getting to be a lot for me. And . . . it's nice to be with someone, at the end of the day."

Mark could not falter. Sam hadn't, when Mark had told him about his engagement. "Dad," he said, smiling, "I'm happy for you."

He and his father embraced. "Plus someone can take care of you in your dotage," Mark said.

Sam faked outrage, but soon enough pulled Mark in for a sideways embrace—one he held for longer than Mark expected.

"Are you all right?" his father asked. "You look a little peaked."

A crazy woman thinks Brendan is a ghost. A ghost who calls for his daddy. And I told Chloe never to speak to me again. Also, I'm drinking.

"I've been working pretty hard," he said.

"That's all it is? You can tell me."

"I know. I'm fine."

His father looked into his mug and nodded. "Well, I wanted to tell you this, too. I called Chloe yesterday. To wish her a happy Christmas. She sounded...odd."

Mark stiffened. Nothing got past Sam Fife for long. "Odd how?"

"Hard to say. We didn't speak for long. She wished me a merry Christmas, more or less." Sam pursed his lips. "Do you...talk?"

"Not anymore." Mark weighed his words carefully. "We had— we had a little scene recently. I told her never to speak to me again."

The lines around his father's mouth deepened. "Can I ask?"

Mark could only lie. "I told her I was getting married."

Sam put his hand—heavy, more sandpapery than a scholar's ought to be—on Mark's neck. He seemed ready to say something else, but then Allison and Helen walked into the kitchen, laughing. His father gave Mark's neck one last squeeze; then he went to Helen and slipped an arm around her waist, but not before meeting Mark's eye. *I know*, the look seemed to say.

The four of them sat down again at the dining room table. Mark's father kept his arm around Helen's shoulders and gazed, smiling and fond, at Mark. Allie and Helen, new best friends, talked and talked across the table.

Mark wondered if his father, then, was thinking just what Mark did: that he sat opposite a wonderful woman, a beautiful, happy person—but that he couldn't help himself from missing, terribly, the one she had replaced.

Thirteen

The following week passed in a haze. The trip with Sam and Helen to see Allison's family went off without incident; in fact Mark found himself happy, during, caught up in the bustle and company.

But no sooner had Helen and his father left for Indiana than Mark came down with an awful flu. He spent three days moaning and sweating in bed. In the worst moments of the fever he dreamed scratchy endless dreams of the old house, of Brendan, of Brendan's body on the stairs. He dreamed of Chloe and Connie Pelham giving the infant Brendan a bath together. Sometimes Brendan called out for him—*Daddy!*—and each time Mark woke with a jerk, at once glad that he hadn't heard such a terrible sound, and—as he'd always been—grieving anew that he couldn't run down the hall and comfort Brendan, couldn't kiss him and say, *It's all right, I'm here.*

More than once, after he woke, he stared blearily into the dark and thought of Connie Pelham, and her son; he wondered whether they were asleep, or if, in their big, dark, creaking house, they had suddenly been wakened, too.

On New Year's Eve, Mark and Allie took Lew up on his invitation to meet him and his girlfriend, Heather, at a bar downtown. When they arrived Lew was, already, deep into his cups, and Mark was grateful; this was the first call of Lew's he'd answered since fleeing him in the Short North, and he'd hoped he wouldn't have to explain himself. Lew hugged Allie, and then Mark, and as they pulled apart he said, "You okay?"

"I'm fine," Mark told him. "Really." Lew looked askance at him, but said nothing.

He nursed a glass of wine while Allie allowed herself to get trashed. Mark was happy for her—he owed her a good time more than Lew—but even so he spent the evening standing still and quiet, watching Allie and Heather dance. At midnight Mark held Allie as the ball dropped on television, kissed her when it touched bottom—her breath was sharp with lime and tequila—and then they swayed together to "Auld Lang Syne." As always, he had to push down the song's creaking, maudlin sadness. Mark saw Lew watching him; he wondered if they were thinking of the same old acquaintance. Then the bar spilled into the street. Through gaps between the downtown buildings they watched fireworks arc lazily up, burst, and shed their cinders into the ink-black Scioto.

At one Allie tugged on Mark's hand, murmuring "Home, home," and they said their goodbyes. But Lew didn't let Mark leave without pulling him into an embrace. "Call me, okay?" he said. "No matter what." Mark assured him he would, his stomach tight.

Back at the townhouse, even though his fiancée was negotiating the front steps in a little black dress and heels, Mark was the one who slipped on the patch of ice; he fell on his side hard enough to knock the wind out of him. He managed to limp inside, to put the two of them to bed, but the following morning, the spectacular bruise on his hip was the least of his problems—when he tried to lift himself from the mattress, his lower back seized with wiry white pain.

Allison helped him downstairs to the couch, and he remained there, almost completely immobile, for two days, watching bowl games and reading. Allie tried to hide it, but he knew she was losing all patience with him.

"I'm sorry," he kept telling her.

"It's okay," Allie kept telling him.

But instead of talking to Allie, he brooded. One of the dreams he'd suffered during his flu took root in him, began to take on darker implications: the one where he'd watched, invisible, as Chloe and Connie Pelham gave Brendan a bath.

Chloe had believed Connie—or, at least, had not dismissed her. That meant that she would probably, by now, have gone to the old house, to see if Connie was right. And Mark had told her never to speak to him again. Chloe was in the place they had lived without him; whatever happened to her there, whatever she remembered, she was alone.

She did not need him. She did not want him there. He wouldn't have gone with her if she had asked. He told himself this.

For weeks he'd been avoiding the corner of the living room where a few pictures of Brendan still hung. But as he lay on the couch, his back pulsating, he felt those photos behind him; he would long to look at them, would sometimes twist himself painfully in order to make sure they were still there: Brendan on the front porch swing. Brendan dressed like a sailor and toddling toward an Easter egg. Brendan, five, pointing at the camera, his mouth open in a snaggle-toothed grin.

Calling for his daddy.

Everything's wrong with you, Chloe had said to him. Everything.

⌒

A few days after New Year's, on a Saturday, Allison's sister, Darlene, called. Mark heard Allie's cry of alarm through his office wall—he had been trying to work—and he hobbled to their bedroom, where Allie sat on the edge of the bed. Allie took his hand while she talked. "No!" she kept murmuring into the phone. "Oh, honey, no."

When she had hung up, Allie told him: Darlene's boyfriend,

Tim, had just moved out. They had been fighting for weeks, and on New Year's Day he finally told her he'd been seeing someone else.

Allison was in tears. "I really thought she'd marry him," she kept saying. Mark had, too. On Christmas Day, Tim—scruffy, dreadlocked, smelling of patchouli—had talked earnestly with Sam about his and Darlene's incipient business while wearing a present Darlene had made for him: a hand-knit sweater with a line of reindeer running across the chest.

Allison fretted for hours; Mark at last realized that the only reason she hadn't dashed to her sister's side was because of him and his injured back. "Go," he told her. He had finally agreed to see a doctor that morning; with his muscle relaxants he could feed himself, haul himself to the toilet, work. He could drive, if he had to.

"You're sure?" Allie asked.

"I'm sure. And Darly can come stay here, if she needs."

Allison pressed her forehead to his. "Thank you."

"No problem," he told her, and stroked her neck.

"Things need to be better soon," Allie said. "They will be, right?"

"They will be," he assured her.

Allison was in such a hurry to leave they neglected to check the weather. Almost the moment she reached her sister's house, a bitter snowstorm blew across the northern half of the state, burying everything, and closing most of the major roads, including I-75 between Toledo and Columbus. Allie called him early in the evening and told him Darlene's long driveway had drifted over, that she might or might not be able to drive back home in the morning. Mark sat in his office, the curtain pulled aside, watching the snow spiral wildly through the glow of the streetlight, and assured her over and over he would be all right.

After half an hour of listening to the wind howl, he called his father; Sam answered sleepily. "Oh, I'm fine," he said. "I'm at Helen's apartment. We went to the store and got all my staples."

Saltines. Coca-Cola. Gin and vermouth and olives.

"I was thinking of the first blizzard at the farmhouse, after we moved," Mark said, which was true; one of his earliest memories was his father holding him up to the windowsill, to see the drifts outside. "I keep thinking we should be there now, playing Monopoly." With Mom, he almost said. With Chloe and Brendan, too. All of them together, as they had never been, safe and sleepy and warm.

"I'd be very happy if we were," Sam said, after a pause, in such a way that Mark knew they'd both found their way to the very same thought.

The phone beeped, then, with an incoming message. Mark ignored it—probably Allison, calling him back.

Soon Mark bid his father goodnight. The streets outside were now blanketed; the snow was whipping past the streetlight in sheets, dense as rain. He turned on the news: twelve to sixteen inches by morning, and another eight before noon Sunday.

He thought to check who'd called him, then. The number was Chloe's.

Mark walked downstairs. Set his phone on the coffee table and lay back, away from it.

He had to admire her timing. She had picked exactly the moment he was lonely, nostalgic, Allison far away. Chloe, he thought, must be a fucking psychic—she had always known when he was weak. Whatever she had to say—whether it was about Connie Pelham, or an apology, or even more venom—it could wait for tomorrow.

Everything's wrong with you. Maybe he'd erase it.

He went downstairs to make himself dinner but found, to his dismay, that he was out of everything, especially his own staples: canned tuna and coffee beans and something salty he could eat by the fistful. The cold was getting inside of him; his back was stiffening. And he was stir-crazy. And Chloe had called him.

Just three blocks away was a little all-night convenience store. He could stock up there, before the worst of the overnight storm. A walk might be good for him—after days of immobility he could stand to stretch his muscles. He gingerly dug his backpack out of the depths of the coat closet and put on his boots.

The air outside was terrifyingly cold. It wasn't so bad as he tromped along the sidewalk along Erzelbach, his street—the rows of townhomes shut out the wind—but the moment he'd turned the corner he was leaning forward into a brutal, icy torrent. His cheeks, above his scarf, numbed and stiffened. His eyes leaked ice in horizontal streaks. He could have been the last man on earth; the other houses and apartments were all dark, seemingly vacant.

Like a ghost, he thought, a lonely ghost haunting a dead city.

The clerk in the convenience store, a college-aged guy with barbed wire tattooed around both his wrists, looked at him with outright anger when he lurched through the door. "Dude," he said, holding out his palms. "I'm closing down early."

Mark was panting. His back had not stretched at all; something in the angle of his walk, the resistance of the snow, had started a dull throb that traveled all the way to the backs of his knees. He was impossibly fucking stupid. "Please," he said. "Two minutes."

"If that," the guy said, narrowing his eyes.

Mark grabbed what he could: Coffee. A bag of frozen pizza rolls. Bread. A box of sugary cereal. A bag of Doritos and cheese dip in a can. And then—the shop had a little annex full of liquor—a bottle of whiskey. Maker's.

He shouldn't. He knew he shouldn't. But once he saw that bottle, he could have left everything else behind. A couple of shots, the warmth growing in his belly. His back loosening. The pain had been keeping him awake—this was what he needed, to knock him out until morning. He waited to hear his father's admonishing voice. The tickle of guilt. But he heard only the wind, shaking the front doors of the store.

"Goddamn," the clerk said, when Mark brought his haul to the counter. He picked up the bottle. "Now, this is a party."

"Got a glass?" Mark said. He couldn't believe himself. "I'm serious. I might need a shot to get me home. My back's killing me."

The clerk nodded several times, as though he was listening to thumping dance music, then reached over to a spinning rack by the counter and pulled down two shot glasses, each emblazoned with a scarlet Ohio State *O*.

They cracked the seal on the Maker's with the clerk's alarmingly large pocketknife, and Mark poured them each a shot. The clerk picked up his glass and stared at the liquor with something like love. They clinked glasses. "To Monopoly in a blizzard," Mark said.

The clerk shrugged and said, "To my girlfriend's big warm bed, in which I will shortly be."

The clerk's was better. "*Salud,*" Mark said, and they drank.

⌒

On the walk home Mark faced away from the wind; that fact, plus the embered warmth of the whiskey in his stomach, made the return more bearable. Alcohol, he remembered, thins the blood. Old Mr. Sorley, at Westover High, had taught him this. The warm feeling provided by alcohol in cold weather is a dangerous illusion. Saint Bernards with little oaken barrels on their collars? Lies, all lies. Alcohol gave you the illusion of safety, when your heart should be racing with panic.

He made himself stomp home faster. He thought of Chloe's message on his phone. His heart thumped in his chest.

When Mark reached the townhouse he discovered he'd locked himself out. He patted himself down, over and over, for his keys. For a moment he feared he'd forgotten them back at the store, on the counter. But he'd left the front hall light on, and through the long vertical window beside the front door, he could see his keys in a jumble on the hall table. He'd set them down to put on his gloves and hadn't picked them up again. His phone was beside them.

Good Christ, he was a fuckup. As if in response to the thought, his back flared dully.

He circled the ground floor, trying the windows. They were all locked. He walked to the back of the building and was just able to reach over the wooden fence that protected their small patio, to unlatch the gate. His fingers were as responsive as twigs. The snow on the patio was thick, protected from the wind; the kitchen door spilled out light. The stillness here felt colder, with that warmth so close.

But the kitchen door was shut fast, deadbolted.

He was shivering uncontrollably now. The phone and his keys were inside; there was nothing left to do. He dug through the snow until he found one of the decorative rocks Allison had put down to line her flower beds last summer, a hundred years ago. He considered the panes of glass on the back door. He threw the rock at the one nearest the deadbolt. The sound of the breaking glass was surprisingly loud, as though the air the stone passed through were breaking, too.

His aim was off. His throw took out not only the glass, but a part of the wooden frame. A spidery crack split the nearest pane to the right.

Fuckup.

He wrapped one of the straps of his backpack around his knuckles and cleared the shards of glass from the frame. He could almost see the warmth spilling out of the house and up the sleeve of his coat. He reached through—his back shrieked—and undid the bolt.

Mark spent the next half hour, once he could feel his hands, securing the house—sweeping up the glass from the kitchen floor, hanging a towel across the hole in the door, cutting a piece of cardboard to fit the hole, and duct-taping it in place.

When he was done he poured himself another shot. He took the shot glass and the bottle into the living room. He picked up his phone, saw Chloe's message again, and snapped it shut.

He watched the weather from the couch, wrapped in a blanket; the weatherman informed him the wind chill was twenty below. Whatever you do, the weatherman urged, stay inside! Mark switched channels until he found one playing *Dirty Harry*, which he'd never seen. Turned out it was pretty terrible, and he was sure he'd think so sober. But he sank back into the couch and watched anyway.

When it was over he poured another shot and lifted it into the air. It was midnight. He hoped the clerk was in his girlfriend's big warm bed. *Salud.*

He missed Allison. He missed Chloe. The townhouse was drafty at the best of times; now it was frigid. He shivered with the blanket pulled to his chin. Underneath the whiskey's fuzz and gloss, his throat was sore. That was all he needed, now—the return of his flu.

Mr. Sorley, from health class, told him: That's a myth. Cold weather doesn't correspond with susceptibility to illness. That's an old wives' tale.

There are no old wives here, Mr. Sorley. One wife in the past, another in the future, but presently? No wives in sight.

Mark sat up, opened the phone, and dialed his voicemail.

"Mark," Chloe's voice said. She was crying—he could hear it right away. And he heard something else, too, beneath her tears: something that alarmed him, that closed his eyes. She said his name again: "Mark, I—"

A sound, a smear of static that might have been her gasping.

"I'm at the house—"

He hit delete.

He forced himself to breathe in, to breathe back out. Chloe had gone to the old house.

She'd sat down with Connie Pelham. They'd talked about Brendan. Maybe Chloe had talked with Jacob, too. And then what had happened? She'd gone upstairs? She'd looked around? She'd visited Brendan's old room?

Whatever it was, she had then called Mark, crying.

He forced himself upright, poured another shot. How much had he drunk already? A good bit of the bottle was gone. But this was all right. He lifted the phone, turned it off, all the way off. There. Chloe couldn't call again. The roads were too dangerous for her to drive to him. No one could reach him tonight. He could do and think whatever he wanted.

Something had happened at the old house. Chloe had called him in tears.

He knew Chloe. Knew her inside and out. He had heard her cry dozens of times. He had heard her cry at weddings and he'd heard her grieve, from her bottomless depths, for her lost and broken child.

He'd also heard her cry when he proposed to her. As she spoke her vows. As she held their newborn son in her arms, while he sat at their bedside, watching her gaze down at Brendan, as she said *He's so beautiful, he's so perfect, Mark—*

She hadn't been crying, on the phone, out of sadness.

He'd heard it in her voice: A vibration, a richness. A wonder. Whatever had happened to her in the old house, Chloe had called him, crying—he knew it—out of joy.

III

The Mother of His Child

Fourteen

Mark woke to a different world.

The light around him was gray, painful. He was lying on the couch, and for a long while could not remember why. His stomach squeezed; the room began to turn sideways; he was just able to stumble—his legs rubbery, his back gnarled with woody knots— into the kitchen and vomit into the sink.

For a long time he sat at the kitchen table, shivering from the cold air leaking around the edges of the cardboard square that blocked the broken windowpane, and tried, as best he could, to piece together the previous night. He remembered the cold. The broken glass. Whiskey. Chloe's call.

Panicked, Mark patted down his pockets, then went to the living room and pulled aside the couch cushions until he found his cell phone. No new calls had come in.

He checked his call history—and, despite the sickness bubbling in him, was relieved beyond measure to find he hadn't called Chloe back.

⌒

Back in the kitchen he forced a palmful of Advil down his throat. Then, wincing, he ran water and bleach down the kitchen drain.

It was ten o'clock. Outside ropes of snow writhed snake-like across the street; drifts reached into the wheel wells of parked cars. Allison wouldn't try to drive home until the afternoon, at the earliest.

He picked up the half-empty bottle of Maker's from its spot beside the couch. He carried it upstairs, opened the toilet and—after only the slightest hesitation—upended the bottle over the bowl.

He ran a bath, then sat in the tub for a long time, the lights off, his face between his knees. He thought about Chloe's phone call. The joy in her voice.

The disappearing rabbit's tail of his own happiness, years before, when he'd woken in the hallway of the empty old house. What he'd always taken to be the cruelest moment of his grief: thinking—knowing—that he had found Brendan, at last, that his son wasn't really gone. And then opening his eyes, only to lose him all over again.

⌒

He dressed, went downstairs. Outside the snow still swirled and eddied. One new message had appeared on his phone, from Allison. The roads were still bad; she might or might not be home that night. "I miss you," she told him, abjectly enough that he guessed her visit with Darlene hadn't helped either one of them very much.

He'd call Allie back later. He still had a lot to do: Both the kitchen and the living room smelled like sickness and booze. He could tell her what he'd done—but he rejected the idea almost physically. He'd worried Allie enough already; she didn't need to figure out why he'd spent his time without her getting drunk. He scrubbed the floor and couch cushions, started a fire and lit candles, even though he wanted to lie down and close his eyes and sleep for a thousand years.

But he couldn't. So he sang to himself:

There's a job to do, and we're gonna do it; we're gonna do it because we're men.

A little shanty he'd made up, when Brendan had been—five? Six? On a fall weekend, the two of them had been raking up leaves from the tiny backyard, a chore they'd sworn to Chloe they would finish while she was out, before they could rent a movie that night. Brendan had concentrated, put in his share of work; Mark could still picture him, tugging bags of leaves across the backyard to the gate.

But first they'd raked the leaves into a big pile. This had been the way Mark enticed him to help. Brendan had never jumped into a pile of autumn leaves, and now, today, he would.

Brendan wasn't a very physical child—even at that age they knew he'd be bookish, like his parents—but that afternoon, over and over, he'd jumped, harder and higher and with more and more laughing abandon, into the piled leaves. Between jumps Mark wrestled with him, tickled him—he remembered Brendan's red-gummed grin, his face white with autumn cold; he remembered Brendan running in circles ahead of him, gasping, screaming: Daddy—don't—tickle! At the end of the game Mark had heave-ho'd Brendan by his wrists and ankles into the leaves—but when Brendan landed, his shoulder struck a hidden rock, and he rose up with his laughter breaking apart into a wail.

Daddy! he'd cried, drawing out the *aaa*, screeching it in accusation; there'd always been a fine line between Brendan shouting to him happily and naming him as the source of all his pain.

Mark carried Brendan inside, set him on the kitchen counter, fixed up his scrape—which was all it was, a sudden pain, three dots of blood. But Brendan had whimpered and gasped and carried on.

Even then—a year before the tantrum that had killed him—Brendan's whining had gotten to Mark. His little boy wasn't a baby anymore, and that afternoon—all the time, then—Mark had forced himself not to say so out loud. To be positive. A good father.

He straightened. Put on his jacket. Said, Okay, buddy. We've had a little break, now we have to get back to work.

Brendan's face blotched with tears, with cosmic unfairness. Daddy, no!

There's a job to do, and we're gonna do it. Just because it hurts doesn't mean we get to stop. We promised Mommy, didn't we? There's a job to do, and we're gonna do it.

Mark had started to sing it. Once, twice, again.

Then you sang it back. We sang it together. We swung our fists like pirates.

That's how I got you outside.

That's how I used to talk to you. When you were alive.

When you were real.

⌐

By two thirty the townhouse was more or less in order. Mark no longer wanted to throw up when he stood straight. He called Allie, both hopeful and reluctant.

She was on her way, she told him. The interstate was just barely passable. She was driving slowly, and might not be home until after dark.

Mark gave her an abbreviated version of last night's adventure: that he'd stupidly tried to run to the corner market, and had locked himself out, and had had to break a window to get in. Allie didn't scold him; instead, she laughed. He was lying on the couch, and the sound of her laughter brought all of his shame rushing up. He pinched his eyelids and said, "I wish you were here."

Right away Allie was on her guard. "Did something happen?"

Chloe's voice, rich and shaking with happiness.

"No," he said. "Nothing happened."

He hung up, returned to his cleaning. The light outside the window faded. He tried to focus on his work, on the television, on the thought of Allie driving carefully home to him. But he couldn't help himself.

Had Chloe seen him? Heard him? Had Brendan called her name? Mark's?

What if Brendan was in the house, had been in the house, all this time?

Jesus God, what if?

⌣

But Brendan wasn't. He couldn't be.

And that was because Brendan was dead. Dead and gone.

The facts were the facts. Brendan had fallen down the top flight of the steep, narrow stairs in their old house on Locust Avenue. Mark had been watching a basketball game in the family room downstairs. An hour before the accident, they'd argued; Brendan had refused to clean his toys off the living room floor, and then had thrown a tantrum when Mark insisted. Mark had sent him upstairs to his room. The last sight of his son, alive, had been this one: a red-faced, red-eyed Brendan, his breath hitching in his chest, glaring at Mark sideways before stomping angrily, recklessly up the steps.

While Mark watched the game downstairs and brooded, Brendan had busied himself. He filled a backpack with two changes of clothes, and with several of his favorite books and toys. He sneaked carefully down the hall to Mark's bedroom and used the phone; he called a friend down the street and told him he wanted to come over. Then he'd tried to sneak out of the house.

The heavy backpack might have unbalanced him; or, maybe, he had fallen because the laces of his right tennis shoe had been untied. Either way, Brendan tumbled down the upper flight of stairs. When he hit the landing his neck and skull had both been badly fractured. He had been unconscious when Mark found him, seconds after hearing the awful tumbling noise of the fall. His last, shrill cry. Brendan never woke; though paramedics arrived eight minutes after the fall—the house on Locust was only a mile from Ohio State Hospital—he stopped breathing almost the moment he was carried into the ER.

He had not suffered. The doctor who'd pronounced Brendan dead told Mark this—Brendan had almost certainly been brain-dead a fraction of a second after the shattering of his skull. The doctor (an older man, thin, kind-voiced, and matter-of-fact; he reminded Mark of Sam, and that helped, a little) had told him it didn't matter that Brendan had died in the hospital; the Brendan whom Mark had loved died even before Mark reached the landing.

He told Mark this some weeks after the funeral. Mark had gone back to the hospital and asked to see him, to ask guilty questions.

It was bad luck, Mr. Fife, the doctor had said. Every day children come into the ER with sprained wrists, with bruises, from falling down stairs. Then, just last night, a man died here of a fractured skull after he slipped on the sidewalk. We're fragile, that's all.

Maybe he knew this was not a comfort. He looked down for a moment at Brendan's file.

It would have been like a switch turning off, the doctor said. He leaned close to Mark, put a hand on his arm, made sure to look him in the eye. In this job, every day, I see children who suffer much, much more than your Brendan did.

He said this, too: There are fates worse than a quick death.

A switch, turned off. Apart from weak moments—moments he'd been on his knees, beside shards of broken glass—Mark had always believed this. Brendan Samuel Fife, his only son, had died of bad luck; now he was gone forever. Now he was nothing.

Nothing was left of him. Brendan's body had been buried, had by now decomposed in its small coffin. He was in the black, now, an absence that couldn't be described. Mark believed this utterly: His boy was not in a heaven; he was not sleeping a dreamless sleep. He was nothing, no more present in the world than the light of a switched-off bulb.

But *what if?*

The thought was a heartbeat, a malevolent, waking life.

What if Mark was only ninety-nine percent sure? What if—in

that one percent sliver, that terrible maybe—there was room for a little boy's ghost?

But *there wasn't*. Even if Mark had been wrong about everything—even if there were souls, and a God who made them, and a heaven where they were kept—then how could there be *ghosts*? If there was a heaven, then Brendan must be in it. He would be—as so many people had insisted, clutching Mark's hand in the hallway of the funeral home—in paradise, in the company of Mark's mother and a loving God.

But what if what Connie had said was true? What if Brendan really was still in the house?

Mark thought of the photographs he'd seen on the net. The testimonial of the young mother who was sure the spirit of her daughter remained, after her drowning.

If a child could become a ghost—if his child *was* a ghost—how could that story be a happy one?

What if Brendan had died, but he hadn't?

Maybe, not long after the fall, he'd awakened, confused. Maybe he thought he'd taken a nap, had slept too long.

Maybe his legs and arms had been numb, weightless. Maybe he'd tried to open his mouth and his voice came out wrong, like a whisper, or less. Maybe he had gotten up and walked through the house, room by room. Maybe he had seen what happened—maybe he saw Mark in the living room, being held back by a policeman, while paramedics rushed past him on the stairs, to kneel beside the odd little-boy doll that lay so still on the landing, wearing a backpack and his shoes just like Brendan's own—

When would he have known?

Maybe he had understood when he watched the paramedics carrying the little body out of the house on the stretcher, out to the ambulance, parked with its lights flashing at the curb. Maybe when he saw Mark leave with the policeman. Maybe Brendan had tried to run after them; maybe at the doorway he'd stopped, panicked. Trapped by doors he could not open. Maybe he'd cried out: *Here I am, Here I am, Wait*—

Daddy!

Or maybe it hadn't happened like that at all. Maybe when Brendan opened his eyes, he'd found himself in a different house: one filled with only cobwebs and fine gray dust. Maybe outside its windows he could see only fog. Maybe the handles of the house's doors refused to turn; maybe the windows refused to budge in their frames; maybe his own skin, like the walls, was the color of shadow and cold to the touch.

What would have happened to this Brendan, in this place, when at last he realized he was alone?

When he'd run from room to room, faster and faster, finding his parents nowhere, finding no exit?

Or, maybe—sometimes—this shadow-boy had heard his mother and father.

Maybe shadow-Brendan had pressed his ear to the dusty walls, straining to hear their muted whispers.

He'd have heard their tears first, their sadness. They had lost him; he would understand that. Then soon enough he would have heard their arguments—shouts and screams such as he'd never heard when he was alive. Then he'd have heard their silences, and then—horribly—the sounds of boxes closing, of furniture being moved. He must have cried for them, screamed for them. But they had not heard.

What would happen to a little boy who witnessed this? What would he become, during his long time alone?

If anything remained of his mind, the gray lonely thing, that little, boy-shaped tatter, would have begun to hear sounds again a few months later. He might scarcely have believed it; he'd surely been deceived before, over and over, chasing false creaks and moans around corners, jolted awake by dreams of the living.

But there! A sound, a real sound—footsteps, down below. *He was not alone.*

The shadow-boy must have crept from room to room, listening. And there: A man was in the house, muttering. The shadow-boy's heart might have begun to shiver, like being alive: His daddy was in the house again. Daddy was talking to himself downstairs—and the shadow-boy began to shout, to run from room to room, calling. But he could see no one—

Until, at last—there! *There* was Daddy: stomping slowly, heavily up the stairs, his outline wavering, shifting, like he was carrying his bottle across the bottom of a swimming pool. Daddy! he called, again and again, and then—*it was true, it was true*—his daddy saw him; his daddy knelt down, his daddy said Here I am, his voice blurry, too, yet full of joy, enough to light up the sun again. Oh God, Brendan, Daddy said, come here, and Daddy opened up his arms and Brendan went to them, and then Daddy—because Daddy was clumsy, sometimes, because maybe Daddy had been too surprised—dropped his bottle; it broke on the floor, and then the spell was broken; Daddy's shape flickered and went out, and then Brendan was alone again, screaming Daddy's name, but Daddy was gone—

—and even though Brendan kept calling and calling, Daddy never came back, even though Daddy had known Brendan was there, he'd left for good, and Brendan the shadow-boy remained, alone in his shadow-house for a million years—

~

It was dark. Mark felt, in his own panic, at the damp outlines of his face.

He rose from the couch, his heart still hammering. Shuffled to the kitchen, drank a glass of water, and then another. Cupped cold water in his hands and splashed it across his cheeks. The town-house was still empty. He picked up his phone and thought about calling Chloe, but did not.

A dream. All of this was a bad dream. He walked upstairs and lay down on the bed.

Later Mark was aware of light, of Allie, lifting the covers beside him.

"You're home," he said, his tongue thick.

"Finally," she said.

"I got sick again," he said. "I'm sorry."

"I thought I smelled it," she said. She put a cool hand on his forehead. "You feel hot."

He lifted his arm; she slid closer to him. He wondered if he still smelled like whiskey. If he did, Allie didn't say so. Instead she began to tell him about Darlene. Her visit had been awful, she said. Darlene had spent most of last night weeping. Tim, it turned out, had cheated on her with three different women. Darlene—never the world's most stable person—had mentioned to Allie that she'd thought about suicide.

"I drove her to Mom's before I came home." Allie let out a long, shaky breath. "I might go back up this weekend."

"Sure."

Allison said, "So what possessed you to go out in that storm?"

Maybe she had smelled the booze after all.

"You're marrying an idiot," he said. "That's the short version."

"Well, I'm glad I'm marrying him," she said, adjusting beneath the covers. "Whoever he is."

There's a job to do; we're gonna do it; we're gonna to do it till it's done.

"I'm happy to be home," she said.

"Me too," he said, though this made no sense.

Mark held her while her breathing deepened. His arm lost feeling beneath her.

He thought of Chloe's voice on the phone. The shiver in it.

That was happiness. He knew this. Remembered it.

Happiness was what you felt when you weren't lost anymore; when you'd spent a long time, crying out, in the loneliest and darkest of places—and then understood that the person you loved and longed for had, at long last, appeared.

Fifteen

Mark tried to be himself; he tried with all his might. But he wasn't. Not anymore.

⁓

During the day he worked. Business was starting to pick up again, now that the holidays were over, and they needed the money—he and Allison both had decent savings, but he figured the wedding would sooner or later cause them to hemorrhage cash, and afterward they wanted to buy a house. For the first time Mark began to hustle clients—he cold-called businesses throughout the city. How had their Christmas sales gone? How had their websites worked for them? Would they like to schedule a consultation?

All of this, however, felt like a show. He sat in his office and moved around his mouse and designed webpages that, in a few months' time, would be replaced by others; he spent his hours making pictures that could be erased with the swipe of a magnet, the flick of a switch. More and more he was aware that he made nothing: only pictures made of light, like dreams, like ghosts.

⁓

He spent every waking minute sure Chloe would try to reach him again. Two days after her message, he'd had his cell number changed, but still adrenaline flooded him whenever the phone rang; whenever his computer pinged, announcing a new email; whenever a car mumbled by on the cobbles outside.

He kept hearing two voices, speaking his two names:

Mark, said Chloe's—as full and whole and happy as it had ever been.

Daddy, said the other—terrified, needy, a clawing hand.

He did not sleep. He did not drink. He wanted to—God how he wanted to—but he didn't.

Every night he lay down on the bed and covered his eyes with a pillow. Please, he would think. Please let me sleep. Then his mind would turn to Allison's bottles of wine in the kitchen.

He'd think of the many nights he'd spent in the turret office in the old house, his family asleep. How in the springtime he'd open the windows on each side of him and sit in the flowing current of the breeze, the whiskey he'd drunk warming him, slowing him. And though he knew it was a lie—an old and valuable lie—during his long, sleepless nights he could only remember how relaxed that past version of himself used to be, how content, knowing that his work was done, that his family was asleep down the hall, before nodding off to the susurration of the trees.

Dismayingly, a wall had risen between him and Allison.

Every word Mark said to Allie these days came out wrong, false, as though another Mark, an impostor, had slipped unseen into the room and addressed Allie in his voice. When he meant to be kind, he sounded impatient; when he meant to be gentle, he sounded indifferent. Allie was frustrated with this Mark, sometimes hurt by him—but even his apologies to her came out halfhearted, undercut with complaint.

He knew he should tell her what was happening to him. A dozen times he was ready to go to her, to say: *Chloe went to the old house. She called me. I erased the message. But now—*

He could imagine no more. What had enveloped him, slipped

around his skin, into his lungs like fog, he could put no words to. Anything he imagined telling her sounded like a betrayal:

I'm dreaming about Brendan. I'm dreaming about Chloe, and how she said my name.

Chloe went to the old house and something happened to her there, and she called me crying and said my name.

She said my name. The way she used to.

⌣

Allie's response to this new, strange Mark was to throw herself full-bore at the wedding. She spent her evenings and weekends planning, talking about planning, calling her friends and Darlene to talk about their roles, about their travel arrangements, about which colors of bridesmaid dress might look best against the backdrop of a Tahoe autumn. One night Mark overheard her on the phone with a college friend; Allie kept saying how happy everyone would be, in September, at the lake; the wedding, she kept saying, would be perfect, perfect—and Mark, eavesdropping outside her door, understood she spoke so fervently about the future only because he was making her so unhappy, here and now.

⌣

One Saturday afternoon, a week after Chloe's call, Allie knocked on the door of his office. Mark was trying his best to get ahead of his work, to make up for the poor day he'd put in yesterday, and the day before that.

Allie stood frowning in the doorway. "I just got a message."

Chloe, he thought. She'd found Allie's number.

But she asked, "Did you send the check to the quartet?"

Allie had recently decided that for the ceremony she wanted real—and very expensive—musicians. She'd rhapsodized about how magical the music would sound in the open air, next to the water, and Mark had made himself care enough to agree, and she had asked him to reserve the quartet with a four-hundred-dollar deposit.

"I'm sure I did," he said. But now that he thought about it, he was sure he hadn't.

While she stood beside his desk, he made a show of checking his checkbook—and no, he truly hadn't. He'd written out the check, and for whatever reason had never torn it from the book and mailed it.

Allie turned on her heel and left the room.

Mark called the violist, right then, and promised he'd send the check priority mail, on Monday morning. He remained agreeable during a reasonable scolding. After he hung up he found Allie in front of the television downstairs, and told her he had fixed his mistake. He tried to apologize, wanted to—but the impostor-Mark appeared and said instead, "No harm done. So just relax, okay?"

Allie glared up at him. "I can't do this alone. I have to depend on you, if we're going to have a wedding at all."

He walked into the kitchen, poured a glass of water. Told himself that he couldn't be mad at her, that she was only angry because he was being a legitimate fuckup. That she'd been having a hard time of things, too—she'd been sick the last few days, having picked up his stomach flu; for days she'd barely been able to keep down her meals. That the hard time was his fault; that she was suffering for—because of—him.

But she was suffering nowhere near as much as him. He thought this, he did.

"Right?" she called, as he walked past her to the stairs. He didn't trust himself to answer.

Everything was wrong with him, everything.

～

A week and a half after her phone call Chloe's name appeared in Mark's email inbox. The subject line read: Please don't erase this.

It was evening. Allie was running water in the bathroom

through the wall of his office. A few minutes ago—after two days of chilliness that followed the forgotten check—she'd slipped her arms around his waist as he worked. Do you want to come up to bed? she'd murmured. Her tone had been almost formal, even as her warm hand slid beneath his shirt.

It's been awhile, she said. I miss you.

They hadn't made love since—when? Christmas? Since before he'd thrown out his back, on New Year's Eve, more than two weeks ago. And she'd made plans to spend the coming weekend at her sister's. If sex was going to happen, it had to happen now.

I miss you, too, he'd said. Let me just finish up here.

Again, he wondered if somehow Chloe knew—knew when best to undercut him, when to make him weak. Please don't erase this.

The water shut off in the bathroom.

Mark deleted the email, then emptied his trash file before he could second-guess himself. When the message was gone he felt a terrible, plunging guilt. He powered down the computer, stood, and walked to the bedroom. There he lay down beside Allison, curled on her side in a T-shirt and black panties. He tried to empty his mind.

Allie kissed him, stroked him, even took him in her mouth. Finally he rolled over on his side, exasperated.

"What's wrong?" Allie asked.

Everything. Everything.

"Nothing's wrong. Just give me a second."

Allie nestled close, but her eyes were pained, damp; she knew he was lying.

Hours later—the sex had never happened; Allie drifted off to sleep, or pretended to, before he could respond to her—Mark crept downstairs and stretched out on the couch. He was doing this almost every night, now. He'd programmed their TiVo to record old movies he'd always meant to watch, the ones that haunted the cable channels in the early-morning hours.

He shouldn't have erased Chloe's email. Now the what-ifs would come for him. Maybe Lewis had been right. Maybe he really *did* need to know.

No. Mark didn't believe in ghosts. Ghosts were not real—not a shred of evidence in the world said otherwise. It was late; he hadn't had a good night's sleep in weeks; he was sad about Allison, about whatever was happening to poor Chloe. That's all this was, foolish doubt. His own mind, playing games with him.

He turned on *The Maltese Falcon*. Watched Bogie stalk across the screen in his trench coat, fedora rakishly cocked. Bogie drank bourbon and smoked cigarettes beneath slowly turning ceiling fans. Bogie was made of cool, hard steel, and if his heart ever broke he had the words to dismiss the fracture.

Bogie lifting a glass to his lips. Mark could almost taste the sting of the whiskey.

He rose and walked to the kitchen. After the night of Chloe's phone call, he'd sworn he wouldn't drink anymore. But tonight, needing sleep as badly as he did, he'd have one glass of wine. Just one.

He was sure Allison would have a bottle open, but he didn't see one in the refrigerator. He looked in the pantry for others, but found nothing. He tried to remember if she'd had her usual glass with dinner, but couldn't.

She'd found out how much he'd drunk during the storm. She'd found out, had been alarmed, and had hidden the wine, or removed it from the house.

He remembered Chloe, her face still tracked with tears, holding up the half-full glass of whiskey-and-Coke he'd left beside the couch when he'd run to Brendan's side. Looking up from it to him.

Asking, Were you *drinking*?

Mark returned to the living room. Turned off the television. Walked slowly up the stairs. Slipped into bed beside Allison and lay staring at the ceiling.

Breathing deep. Relaxing his limbs, his fingers, the tiny muscles that kept tightening and tightening around the hinge of his jaw.

Sixteen

Three days later Mark was sorting the day's mail at the kitchen table when a small, pastel-green envelope fell from a stack of circulars into his lap. He knew what it was, who it was from, even before he picked it up and saw his name and address written on the front in Chloe's careful, looping script.

On the back, across the flap, Chloe had written a single word: *Please.*

He should, he knew, throw it out. Shred it and drop the pieces into the toilet and flush them away. But what would that solve? For two weeks he'd dreaded Chloe's next move, and now here it was. If anything he felt relief.

Relief—and something more complicated, too. He sat down at the table and squared the envelope between his thumbs. Chloe could have tried to reach him any number of ways, but that she had written a letter, he guessed—was supposed to guess—meant even more than whatever she'd written inside of it.

In their early days, before they were married, she had sent him dozens of letters. Wooing him, reassuring him. Playing with him. Chloe had been an English minor, an avid journal-keeper; the desk in her college apartment had been littered with stationery and notebooks and her grandmother's old fountain pens. Hardly a week went by, then, that he did not find an envelope like this one tucked between the pages of his textbooks, in the breast pocket of his coat, beneath his pillow.

Those letters had almost always been romantic, sentimental. The same small envelope he found in his boot might say *Meet me for dinner? XOXO.* The note tucked in his wallet might say *I spent an hour today imagining us married.* He might unzip his portfolio and find, clipped to a rolled-up sketch, a folded note that read *I wish you were inside of me.*

Chloe knew what he'd feel, seeing this. What he'd remember, feel.

Please come over. Come find me right now.

He slid his thumbnail under the envelope's flap.

Mark,

I know you told me not to contact you, but a lot has happened since you saw me last. Now I have to try to reach you, however I can. I'm guessing you never listened to my message to you, or read my email. I understand why, so I'm trying this. Please hear me out, Mark. Please read the whole thing.

There's a lot I have to tell you, but before I do, I have to apologize to you. I am really and truly sorry for that night when I came to your place. I'm ashamed of myself for that. I behaved like a child, and I deserved what you told me afterward. I probably deserve worse. I'm a hundred times sorry, a million.

I know this will be hard to believe, because of how I've acted, but I do care for you. It's so hard to write this. I can only imagine what this whole situation is doing to you. I feel all our history behind us, all that love and time and pain, and I have to invoke it even when I'm the one who broke us, I'm the one who told you not to care anymore. It's my fault, and I'm so so sorry.

I owe Allison an apology, too. I know she heard what I said to you, and no matter what happens between us, that was so wrong in so many ways. This isn't Allison's fault, none of it. I'll apologize to her myself if she wants. Please tell her.

This is already longer and crazier than I wanted it to be, but I've ripped up too many other versions. I'm just going to come out and say it. I've been to our old house. Connie Pelham asked me to, and I went, and I have to tell you about what happened.

I know you don't like Connie, and I know why. Under different circumstances I'm not sure I'd like her either. But in some ways that makes what I'm experiencing here, I don't know, a little more credible? If I liked Connie I'd worry I wasn't being critical enough. (And I _am_ trying to be critical, every step of the way.) For what it's worth, Connie's terribly sorry she made you angry, too, and you should believe her. This isn't her fault either.

But Mark—I believe her. I've had an experience in the house, too.

It's a weird word to use, <u>experience</u>, but how else can I say it? I don't know how to write about it. I want to talk to you about it.

Please don't think I'm nuts. This is Chloe writing this, the old Chloe, the one you used to like. I'm clearheaded and writing this in the teachers' lounge, in the light of day. I'm only doing it because I believe, deep in my heart, that you need to know what I know. I think that if our positions were reversed you would do what I'm doing, too.

I can feel you out there, doubting me. But Brendan is <u>here</u>. I've been with him, in his presence. I don't know how else to say it.

The first time it happened I was sitting in his old bedroom, late at night. I was talking to him, in my mind, like I always do. I was telling him about our lives, telling him that I love him, and that you love him, too.

I was telling him about you when I felt my heart—I felt my heart just <u>open up</u>. I started to shake. And then he was <u>everywhere</u>. I heard his voice, laughing. I smelled his hair. I smelled his skin, and it was like he was a baby again, and I was holding him.

Do you remember the time when Brendan was five, and he got away from us at Goodale Park? The time we took him to see Elmo? We both thought the other one was holding his hand, and suddenly neither of us had him, and we were surrounded by a hundred little kids and we couldn't see him. We both called and called, and both of us were so scared, we were both crying. And then finally we heard him calling us.

We both turned around and he was running to us. We hugged him and then all of us were crying. Do you remember that, how that felt?

What I felt in our house . . . Mark, it was like that. Only <u>better</u>, so much better. I don't know if I've ever been happier. It felt so good to be with him.

It's true, Mark. I promise you it's true.

Please call me. Please come to the house. I know you don't want to believe this. But this is <u>me</u>. This isn't the crazy Chloe who yelled at you. This is the person you were married to, telling you this is true. I want you to feel what I felt. You're going to be so happy when you do.

Our son is still here. Please believe me, Mark. <u>Please</u>.

Love, Chloe

Mark read the letter three more times. He looked at the clock. It was nearly six; Allison would be home soon. If she walked in the door right now he would crumble in front of her. He could not allow her to see this letter, or the man who had read it.

He stood, then gathered his keys and coat. He tucked the letter into his coat pocket, and—without any clear sense of his destination—he fled.

⌐

He drove for a long time. He circled 270 twice, three times, listening to music Lew had given him: loud, abrasive sounds that scoured away his thoughts. His cell phone buzzed—Allie calling, surely—but he sent it to voicemail, then turned the phone off. The city blurred by. A light rain began to fall.

He tried not to think about the letter, but what else could he do?

Chloe had apologized to him. If the letter contained nothing else but her request for forgiveness, he'd have called her right away. In their six years apart she'd never said a fraction of this, or hinted she ever might. He wanted to weep. *This is the person you were married to—*

But the letter contained more. Much more.

Our son is here.

Both his wife and son might be back from the dead.

On impulse he turned off the interstate, onto 670, cutting north of the glimmering downtown lights. He had pointed himself toward Victorian Village, even though he'd sworn a hundred times since entering the car that he would not.

Don't, he told himself. Don't. But a different Mark was driving the car, now.

He exited 670. To the right, on a dark hillock, was the same Goodale Park that Chloe had mentioned in the letter. Where they had, for a few grim moments—like a rehearsal—lost Brendan, the summer before he died. Chloe didn't have to urge him to remember that afternoon. Even now it recurred in his dreams: Brendan gone, suddenly, in a sea of two hundred children. The air a screamy mass of laughter and cries. Mark's own shouts lost in the din. Chloe's face gone the color of death. They had found him quickly; Brendan had been only feet from them the whole time, thinking another pair of legs had been his father's. But before he reappeared, Chloe's eyes had raked across Mark's face—and well before the accident that took the boy's life he understood: If they ever lost Brendan for good, the hole his passage rent in the universe would suck Chloe straight through. And so it had.

But what if Brendan had come back, and had brought Chloe with him?

Impossible.

The impostor-Mark turned north on Neil, the real Mark only a passenger.

Or was it the other way around?

Please believe me. Please come find me now.

Our son is still here.

Hiding was useless. Chloe had always commanded him, moved him from the soft core of himself into the world.

Mark turned the car down a side street, and then up another—and here was the crumbling brick duplex where, at a long-ago house party, he'd met Chloe in the front hallway, both of them shivering in their coats and waiting for their roommates—Lew and a girl named Carly—to emerge from an upstairs room. Mark was sober, sulking—he'd agreed to drive Lew home—and ordinarily, sobriety plus a pretty girl would have frozen him into silence. But Chloe's smile, the wry exasperation with which she'd said, You're looking for Lew? Big guy, kind of loud? was too much for him. She was smart, sly. Bored. Wanting something more from him than his nod, in order to pass the time. Mark couldn't have kept quiet then for all the world.

My name's Mark, he told her. Chloe never really knew how hard those words had been to say.

Chloe, she'd said. They shook hands, and smiled at having done so. So how do you know Lew? she asked.

I'm his handler, Mark said. He got off his leash. Sorry.

Chloe had laughed. In that laugh he thought he heard a bottomless kindness. What his mother would call *a good heart.* Chloe looked at her watch, then at the empty staircase. From deep within the house came thumping bass, laughter. Lew's happy holler.

I've got an exam tomorrow, she said. So how long...does he usually take?

They both laughed again. Her cheeks were flushed with beer. Her eyes blue and bright. Mark couldn't envision himself kissing her, holding her—and yet those eyes compelled him. He couldn't let her leave; Lew wouldn't even remember her roommate's name in the morning. Ohio State was too big; Mark had been to a dozen parties like this, full of pretty people who flashed before his eyes and vanished forever.

Tell you what, he said. Why don't *I* drive you home?

She'd smiled. Uncertainly, but not unkindly.

You shouldn't walk, I mean, he said. It's a bad neighborhood.

And you're not a bad person?

I really don't think I am.

Her eyes had searched him. Her smile had deepened.

I don't think so, either, she said.

The rest, as they said, was history.

Mark couldn't stop himself. He turned, aimed the car the direction he'd come, and then was headed south on Neil. He entered the Village; five blocks later he pulled to the curb beside the massive three-story house Chloe had shared with her roommates. Barely two weeks after he'd met her they made love for the first time, behind the third window from the left. The woman he couldn't have imagined touching, that night at the party, was then somehow naked beneath him, her breath quick on his cheek, her fingers light on his hips. They hadn't planned this—for two weeks, in fact, they'd planned nothing; their attraction seemed to pull them forward into each encounter, each conversation, each kiss. And now there they were on Chloe's bed, their books thrown aside, Mark's boxers still tangled on his ankle, the sole of her foot resting atop his calf. *I didn't bring anything*, he'd said.

We'll be careful.

Chloe—

She'd stopped him with a kiss.

It doesn't matter, she'd said, into his ear. *Tonight, tomorrow. It's going to happen. I've known since I saw you.*

He'd wanted to cry. He'd felt that, too. *Hoped* it.

But when he began to enter her she stiffened. There'd been other men, she'd told him, and they hadn't all been good ones. For the first time Chloe looked young, looked doubtful; a girl, one hand on his cheek, the other pressed palm-first against his chest. He knew—in the same weird, supernatural way he'd known how to do everything else, these last weeks—what she needed him to say:

I'll never hurt you, Chloe.

She nodded, unblinking. *I know*, she said. Then she smiled, pulled him close. Pulled him slowly, slowly in.

Mark was near tears, now. After Chloe left him he'd sometimes come here; he'd park in the same spot, remembering those old nights, his old promises. Losing himself.

But this was different, now. Now he had her letter.

Please come.

Our son is still here.

When he used to park here, before—his family lost into the sudden, ragged hole, his future a blank gray wall—he'd think maudlin thoughts. That this was a magic place. That the third window from the left was where his marriage had been born. Under Chloe's thick blankets they'd murmured to each other about the future Mark had just seen lost. They'd made themselves, here.

It was here, in her bed, that they had first imagined their son.

This is permanent, Chloe told him one night, after they'd been dating maybe three months. Don't you feel it? This is *special.*

Yes, he'd said.

I want kids, she told him. I want kids with you. Can I tell you that?

She'd begun to cry.

I want to make a baby with you, she said. I want to see you hold our little boy. I want him to call you Daddy.

He had balked. Maybe that was why Chloe's tears had come. He'd hesitated, and she'd clutched at him—had, while whispering, moved beside him, on top of him, her long body heavy and slick, nearly fevered.

Then she'd stopped talking, had moaned, had rocked, had woven her fingers into his hair.

Please believe me, she'd whispered.

Yes, he'd said.

What else could Mark say? He was a middling student. He'd already begun, shamefully, to plan an escape from fine art—he was ever more aware he didn't have the aptitude to pass his mid-program review—into graphic design. Chloe was prettier, smarter, kinder than him. Before he'd met her—he knew this now—he hadn't even really been alive. Chloe liked to talk wistfully about the life he'd lived without her, as though she'd missed out, having never seen him, never known him. But this was Mark's secret, his shame: Before he'd met her there had been no Mark to know. The man she had made of him was as new, as wide-eyed, as credulous as any infant.

He knew what she wanted, because he wanted it, too: *Life.* A house. A child: the two of them, joined inextricably in flesh and bone and mind.

He reached up to her. Took her hands. Said what he'd been practicing over and over: Marry me.

Mark put the car in gear again, pulled into the street. There was only one other destination, now. He turned, turned again. The Volvo shook across the cobbles; the houses rose up, bigger and bigger. *Please come. Please come.*

And here it was: the old house, again. Dark, cold. A single someone's-home light in the upstairs hallway leaked out the rounded turret windows, but the others were dark. Mark drove past, circled the roundabout, and stopped the car beside the park. He was breathing hard through his nose, as though he'd been running.

By the light of his cell phone he read, again, Chloe's letter. Then he stared up at the house. The dark window to Brendan's room.

Is it true? Are you there?

No one answered. But another voice he needed would.

He opened his phone and dialed Chloe's number.

While he listened to the ringing of her phone, he was startled to see, through one of the living room windows, a light come on in the house. Not a full light, but a tiny blue glow, just at the level of the sill, turning the white curtain on the other side of the glass pearlescent.

Chloe answered. Her "Hello" anxious, tense.

"Hello?" Chloe said again. Then: "Mark? Is it you?"

"It's me," he said.

A lamp was turned on behind the living room window. Beside it was a silhouette, withdrawing its hand. And Mark knew—was stunned to know—that Chloe was on the other side of the window. She'd been inside the old house, in the dark. She'd held up the blue screen of her cell phone. She'd turned on the light.

He wouldn't have been surprised, then, if Chloe pulled the curtain aside and stared out, right at him, sitting in the dark. If she could *feel* him.

But what was she doing here? Connie must be letting her sleep on the couch—but why?

"Mark," she said again. Her shadow-hand reached up and brushed at her shadow-hair, almost as though she knew he was looking at her.

"I got your letter," he said. "I read it all."

"Oh," she said. "God. You called. Thank you."

She stood; her shadow left the window frame. Chloe always paced while on the phone, one hand holding the phone, the other held at her hip, or molded to her lower back, fingers pointed down past the curve of her buttock.

Chloe didn't wait for him to talk. "So—do you believe me?" Her voice was as tender, as yearning, as the words in the letter.

"I believe you believe it," he said. "This isn't—"

"I know," she said, too quickly. "I know it's hard. Thank you so much for calling. It's felt so wrong to be doing this alone—"

"I—"

Her words rushed out: "I really want to meet with you. To talk about this in person."

He could get out of the car, walk up the sidewalk. Mount the steps of his old house. Knock, softly, so that only she would hear. She would open the door.

"I don't know," he said, resisting the urge to whisper.

I've missed you, she might say. *I've needed you.*

He said, "I don't know if that's a good idea."

"I at least owe you a conversation where I'm not screaming at you like a lunatic."

She was trying to sound nonchalant, but all the while—he could see this—she was stiff-backed, tense. She was terrified he'd say no.

"Let me ask you a question," he said. "If I did believe you, what would happen?"

"That's ... complicated." She turned a small circle. "Meet with me. Let's sit down and talk this out."

He said, "Do I have a choice?"

"What do you mean?"

"You're not going to stop trying, right?"

After a long while she said, "I don't think you'll *need* a choice. Mark, I'm sorry, I hate to cause you pain—"

"Well, I've been feeling plenty." The rest tumbled out of him: "I've been miserable ever since Connie found me. I want this to stop. I want things to go back the way they were."

With Allison, he could have said.

A long moment of staticky silence. Shadow-Chloe put a hand to her throat.

"I have nightmares." He couldn't stop his voice; it was as though they were first dating again, and they were afraid to hang up the phone, to stop spilling out their secrets late into the night. "I'm not sleeping. I'm drinking too much."

Was she crying? Was he?

"Can I tell you something?" Chloe asked. "What's happened to me—I won't say it isn't scary. It *was*, at first. But I see everything so much more clearly now."

He was shaking his head, as though she could see him.

"Mark. Just meet with me, and I promise—once this is over, I'll disappear. If that's what you want."

Chloe might not mean—could not mean—her words as a threat. But that's what they were, weren't they? If he didn't meet with her, she *wouldn't* disappear.

"Please give me a chance," she said.

Hadn't he said the same thing to her, when they were divorcing? He'd stood in front of the kitchen door in the old house, one night when Chloe was threatening to leave. Please, he'd said, and his voice was too loud, too full of panic. Please give me a chance to make this work. Chloe. Please don't leave me here alone.

All these years later, and now she was begging him.

"Mark," she said. "You'll be happy, when you know."

But there was a difference. Chloe's pleas, now, were working.

He closed his eyes. He gave in.

"Okay," he said.

⌐

When he arrived at the townhouse, an hour later—he'd been too restless to return home right away, so he'd driven aimlessly through the northern neighborhoods—Mark was relieved to find it dark: Allie was asleep. I'm sorry, he would say to her, when he slid into bed. A long story. I'll tell you about it in the morning.

He would certainly have to apologize. Allison's messages—he'd finally listened to them, while filling his car up with gas before finally driving home—had grown more and more worried. He had forgotten: She was leaving in the morning to visit Darlene in Toledo. They had agreed to have dinner out tonight—and he'd forgotten *that* even before receiving Chloe's letter.

But what would he tell Allie? The truth? He had agreed to meet Chloe the following day at Franklin Park Conservatory, a massive greenhouse just east of downtown, full of towering exotic plants, humid warmth, tropical fish, butterflies. It's so cold out, Chloe had said. And the conservatory's so nice in winter. We can talk some-place happy and warm and green.

He would go there, meet Chloe, while Allison would be away at her sister's. Could he tell Allie that?

Thank you, Chloe had said, her voice urgent and rich. Brendan will thank you, too.

She'd hung up first. He'd closed the phone, but kept watching shadow-Chloe.

She had left the living room, then turned on the kitchen light—her divided, stretched shadow appearing against the thick blinds over the sink. For a minute or so she stood still. Then she'd turned off the kitchen light and gone upstairs. He'd wondered again: Were Connie and Jacob in the house, too? Lights turned on in a progression: The stairwell, casting a faint glow out the upper-floor turret windows. Then the upstairs hall, just before the stairwell light winked off. And then the light went on in Brendan's old room.

Mark had imagined her, sitting on the edge of Brendan's bed—which of course could not be in the room, now, but this was what he saw—her hands holding one of Brendan's pillows to her chest. And, watching, he'd wished himself into the room. Into the space between her arms.

Could he tell Allison *that*?

He walked into his now-alien kitchen, his hand rustling across the wall for the light switch. His fingers had just touched the plastic of the switch plate when Allison called his name.

His body jerked, as though waking from a falling dream. A light clicked on in the living room behind him, and he turned and saw Allie wrapped in a blanket on the couch, her knees pulled to her chest.

"Where were you?" Her voice was raspy. She was blinking her eyes, too rapidly, but that might have been because of the sudden wash of light across the room. "God, I've been so worried."

He had to be calm. To seem reasonable.

"I'm sorry," he said. "I was just in a mood." But this sounded crazy, so he added, "I was with Lewis."

Her voice now stiff, alert. "Where?"

"We had dinner, then hung out for a while at the studio."

"It's almost *midnight*. We had plans."

He walked to the couch and sat down, beside Allie's feet. She was wearing the red silk pajamas he'd given her for Christmas. He touched her knee. "I'm sorry," he said again. "I just forgot."

Her eyes were wet, stormy. "Something's wrong. Something's been wrong. We've barely talked for weeks, and then you just—you just vanish on me?"

No use denying this. "I know," he said. "But it's not you."

"I left you three messages. I was sitting here wondering if I should call hospitals." She hugged her knees. "And by the way? I called Lewis, just an hour ago. He said he hadn't seen you."

He was so fucking stupid.

Allie stared into him. "You've never lied to me before."

Mark could do nothing but tell her the truth: "I was wrong to do that. I feel awful—"

She held up a hand. "Just tell me what's going on."

He said, "I was out—I was thinking about Brendan. About what Connie Pelham said. I can't seem to let it go."

Allison took in a long breath. "So why won't you talk to me about it?"

The excuses came too easily. "You've had Darly to worry about. And with the wedding, too—I haven't wanted to burden you. And...it sounds crazy. I don't know how to say this stuff. To anyone."

Her face crumpled. After a long time she said, "This—this felt like Bill, all over again. Wondering where he was. If he was even coming home."

"I'm not him," Mark said. "I have a problem I don't know how to fix, that's all."

This is Allie, he told himself; this is Allie and you love her. He made himself look at her: at the fine smooth curve of her jaw, her sweet dark eyes, her lovely Cupid's-bow lips.

He lifted his arm. "Come here?"

Allie shook her head—but she slid closer anyway, tears spilling down her cheeks. Ashamed—if he knew her, and he did—for needing him, for giving in.

She said, "I understand if you want to keep all—all of this—private. I get that. But why do you have to run away to do it?"

He didn't know how to answer.

She said, "Ever since this happened, you've only been partway here. I try to talk to you, and you look guilty, or you shut me out—"

"It's hard," he said. "I just try so hard not to let that life get out into this one."

"Is that even possible?"

He thought of Chloe pacing behind the curtain. How he'd promised to see her tomorrow.

"I don't know."

Allie's voice shook. "Do you feel better, being alone?"

He squeezed her, kissed her hair.

"I feel better coming home. I always do."

She buried her face in his shoulder. "I'm scared."

"About what? Us?"

She only shuddered. He held her tightly, sickened by himself.

"Hey. Come upstairs."

Allie's eyes dark and moist, distrusting, scared. But she nodded.

He reached across her and turned off the light. In the dark he took her hand and led her up the stairs. He quickly brushed his teeth, and was relieved to see the lines on his face in the mirror, the spots of gray in his hair and beard. All the years of his life. The man he was now.

"I don't know if I can," Allie said, after he'd climbed beneath the covers, reached out to stroke her hip.

But he slipped his hand around her side, to the spot where her waist sloped forward into her belly. Let his fingers follow her curve, her deepening heat, beneath the waistband of the pajamas. Her voice softened: "Mark."

Allison turned over, skimmed her underwear down her hips. Reached for the waistband of his boxers. Touched him. He kissed her, lifted himself above her. Allie pulled him down. Held her breath until he found her; then she moaned.

They caught a rhythm, followed it—and then Allie spoke, nearly panicked, in a way he hadn't heard in weeks. When he heard her he lost himself, too—because instead of Allie's voice, he heard Chloe's, saying the same words, that long-ago first time:

Mark I'm going to come I can't help it—

I can't help it either, he thought, holding her, his eyes shut tight. I can't.

Seventeen

Mark woke to Allie sitting beside him on the bed. The sun was up; Allie was already showered, dressed in a hoodie and jeans and sneakers, smelling clean and sweet. But her face was swollen, sickly with worry or pain.

"Can you wake up for a minute?" she asked. "I wanted to say goodbye."

For a long, terrible moment Mark was sure she meant she was leaving him for good. But then he remembered making love the night before. The way she'd gripped his shoulders, during, after. Allison was leaving for an overnight visit to Darlene's; that was all.

"Be careful," he said, sitting up. "Give Darly my love."

Allison looked down, for a long while, at her hand atop his.

"It was weird, last night."

Had Allie discovered what he'd really done before coming home? His cell phone—it was downstairs, on the table by the door. Had she checked his outgoing calls? She'd never been the sort of person who would. But then he had never before given her cause to suspect him.

"I'm sorry," he said. "I really am."

"I'm glad we—that we made love. That we could." That stung him. "But we didn't fix anything, did we?"

"I thought we did," he said, but the words sounded sulky, childish.

"I don't want to go to Darly's. I want to stay here and figure out where we are. We've got—there's a lot we have to think about." She lifted her eyes. "When I get back, can we talk? Seriously talk?"

"Of course we can."

Allie brought his hand to her lips. "I'll believe you, if you say so."

Which meant she still did not believe him.

"We'll get through this," he said. "I promise."

"You're just sitting there," Allie said, her voice shrunken and thin.

She was right: He was sitting still, watching the woman he loved as she began to cry. He pulled the blankets aside and sat up and held her. "I'm so sorry," he said.

He rose from bed and saw Allie to the door. The skies outside were surprisingly blue and clear. In the doorway he embraced her once more, kissed her chapped dry lips. Then he watched through the window as she loaded her duffel bag into the trunk of her little Honda, looking smaller than she ever had.

⌒

The parking lot at the conservatory was already crowded when Mark arrived, half an hour before noon—he had left the town-house early, to keep himself from checking and rechecking his clothing too often, from trying to talk himself out of going at all. He parked at the far edge of the lot, next to a wide swath of the art-fully kept Franklin Park grounds, its crisscrossed paths overlooked by leafless swaying trees, coated in yellow grass and sagging, dirty whitecaps of snow.

He was here; he'd done as Chloe wished. He sat in the car for a while, his hands still warming in front of the dashboard vents. Before he'd left the house he had re-read Chloe's letter. The urgency he'd felt the night before had dissipated; maybe this was because of how he'd treated Allie, but he didn't think so. He was nervous, now, and a little afraid. *Our son is still here.* Last night he'd lost himself in

Chloe's letter, her voice, her promises of happiness. This morning he could only think of the rest of the letter: about the shadow-boy who called for him in his dreams.

The one he might have spoken to, six years before. Who—if Chloe was right—might have been in the house ever since.

Please believe me.

Mark got out of the car, ducked into his collar, and walked toward the entrance.

This place always used to cheer him up. He loved the conservatory's sprawl, its elegance. The main building dated to 1895—only ten years older than the house on Locust—and had been modeled after the buildings at the Chicago World's Fair: It was a grand hall, a latticework of iron and glass with lofty curved ceilings, flanked by symmetrical rounded towers. A crystal castle, glowing now in the rare winter sun. Every artist and photographer and designer in the city came here—just as Mark used to—to take pictures, to take inspiration. Every parent brought his or her children.

They still did so. Children and parents were flowing in and out of the double main doors like the building's breath. Kids, especially little ones, loved the place—just as Brendan had, when Mark and Chloe used to bring him. Brendan had taken great pride in being able to read the names of each plant from its plaque. He loved the fish and the birds and the big flowers. One room even contained a long and intricate model train set; the engine chugged a complicated winding path among trunks and stalks, and Brendan had watched it, mesmerized.

Surely, Mark thought, this was part of his fear. He had completely avoided the conservatory since Brendan's death—and already, now, the old hurt was near to overwhelming him.

Still he kept going, through the doors, into the heat—into that old, familiar smell, of moisture and pollen, cut grass and sugar— and paid his admission.

He slipped by the attendants handing out brochures and up a flight of wide steps, then past the gift shop and through a room with a series of long tables set against its walls, where polo-shirted volunteers were teaching children how to plant their own seedlings. Mark closed his eyes, listened to the kids' high-pitched chatter, like the calls of gulls. Brendan had stood where those children stood, laughing, fascinated, his little white hands dirty with earth.

Coming here had been a mistake.

But what did that word even mean, anymore? Since last night, nothing that had happened to Mark felt accidental. The world, instead, seemed to be turning its gaze to him, its sequences forming a kind of pattern. *Letter. House. Call. Shadow. Yes.* These words seemed ready—as he entered a soaring humid vault, dense with flower and vine—to snap into a gridwork as precisely structured as the one now arching high above his head. But what did the pattern *mean*?

He walked down a long cylindrical hallway, a familiar one; he was surrounded on all sides by plant life indigenous to the Himalaya. Pine. Juniper. Tall rustling grasses. *Rhododendron*—a word Brendan had learned to say as Mark's finger paused beneath each syllable on the plaque. Rho. Do. Den. Dron.

He was starting to sweat beneath his coat. He passed through a room full of Japanese plants and arched wooden bridges and richly-stinking pools of koi as colorful as marbles. He took a seat on a bench in a two-story atrium full of palm trees, giant tiered trunks, exploding ferns. Two staircases curved down from the main floor to the tiled floor of the chamber; from this seat he'd likely be able to see Chloe at the top of them well before she saw him. It was eleven fifty. His brow and neck were damp.

Shadow. House. Letters. Mark. A meaning began to cohere; he could almost grasp it.

But before he did, Chloe appeared at the top of one of the

staircases, then walked slowly, dreamily down. Mark knew her shape, her gait, even before he recognized her features. She wore a blue sweater, a tan skirt, knee-high brown boots. Her hair was pulled back into a ponytail. A long cream-colored wool coat was slung over her forearm. She hadn't yet seen him; she stopped, her hand on the rail, and gazed out across the room.

He followed her eyes. Pieces of Chihuly glass were hung throughout the conservatory; directly across from Chloe, suspended from an alcove in the ceiling, was a twisted purple-and-blue piece. Its long, pointed tentacles swirled down nearly ten feet from a smooth jellyfish dome, like a flame burning upside-down.

All that had happened between them, to them—all that had happened in the last weeks, and what it must mean—and Chloe still could be stopped short by a pretty sculpture in her favorite colors. This meant something, too.

Mark waited for her eyes to leave the sculpture, to pass over the rest of the room. And so they did. She saw him, and her face softened.

How long had it been since she'd looked at him like this? Happily—with relief?

She'd told the truth in her letter. In front of him now was not the woman who had divorced him. Here, again, was the Chloe who had loved him so much, the woman with whom he had made a child.

Maybe Chloe wasn't part of the pattern. Maybe, instead, she was its answer.

Mark walked to meet her. At the base of the steps she threw her arms around his neck and pressed her cheek against his. Held it there. The muscles in her back flexed as she squeezed him. His mouth open and closed, millimeters from her ear.

"You came," she said. After all that had happened, she'd assumed he wouldn't.

Her body, against his. Her breath.

"I'm here," he said, and in that moment he would have agreed to anything.

⌒

They sat together on the bench in front of the giant palms. Unbelievably, Chloe began to make small talk. Did Mark want lunch at the café upstairs? She'd be happy to buy him a sandwich, if he wanted, or a coffee. How had he been?

How had he been? The question made him laugh; she laughed, too.

The past month had taken a toll on her. The lines at the sides of her mouth were more pronounced. Her skin was sallow; acne had broken out along one of the creases of her nose. Her hair, he was sure, was much more gray than it had ever been.

Chloe was probably thinking the same of him. He hadn't been to the gym for nearly a month, was eating poorly when he ate at all. His weeks of insomnia had put bags under his eyes, roughened his skin, loosened his jowls.

Chloe was saying something about the last time she'd been to the conservatory, about the board's purchase of a lot of the Chihuly glass—but then she must have seen the questions in his eyes. She exhaled, shook her head. "Listen to me. Mark, it's really good to see you."

He didn't say, You too. "It's strange, being back here."

She gave him a surprised, glancing look.

"I haven't been in years," he said.

"This used to be a happy place for us," Chloe said. "That's all I thought."

Her tone was just spiky enough to draw him back inside himself. Mark had loved this woman down to her molecules, and he had to remember how smart she was, far smarter than him; how she was—still—better than anyone at bending his will. Maybe all this was a ruse. Maybe she'd chosen the conservatory, really, because she wanted to talk to him while he was remembering. Grieving.

"I come here a lot," she said. "I mean, I remember him everywhere, but here..."

She didn't finish. Even that simple sentence was more personal than almost any other she'd spoken to him in the last five years. He pushed down his suspicion, but still he wondered: Which of them was crazier—the man who avoided the sites of his grief, or the woman who couldn't stay away from them?

"You're upset," Chloe said, watching him.

"This is hard," he said. "All of this. You, me. The reason we're here."

"I know. I do know that. I know I haven't made it easier. But when I tell you, it'll be better. Will you trust me that much?"

Trust her? When she spoke like this he wanted to hug her.

"Okay," he said.

Chloe dropped her eyes from his to her hands. Gathering herself.

"It's hard to say where to start," she said. "Maybe I should say that this—none of this was a surprise to me. Not really. I mean, not deep down." She still wasn't looking at him, but rather across the tiled floor to the next cluster of palms. "I've always had dreams about Brendan. I know, that's normal. Or whatever passes for normal, for people like us. My therapists all told me stuff like, 'Dreams of abandonment are common.'" Chloe shook her head. "I even had one tell me it wasn't unheard of—*her* words—for parents like, like us, to have hallucinations."

Gayle had never spoken to Mark about hallucinations. But then he'd never given her any reason to. He'd made sure of that.

"People kept saying it would get better," Chloe said. "They kept telling me I'd go on, that after a while I'd be able to get on with my life. But all along it's been as though I knew differently." She lifted her eyes. "And I've had such vivid dreams." The corners of her lips turned down. "That I'd left him someplace. Lost him in a crowd. And then after we moved out of the house...I had a lot of dreams about him being there. Calling for us."

Mark's heart pushed mercury through his veins instead of blood.

She said, "I—I've read about people who've lost limbs, who have phantom pain? I sometimes think, *I have a phantom son*. I feel his weight sometimes—like he's a little baby, and I'm holding him on my hip. I smell him." She nearly whispered: "Once or twice I could feel him nursing." She lifted a hand to her breast, then dropped it, quickly. "It was worst in the old house. Before—"

Before they moved out. Before she divorced him.

Chloe nodded sorrowfully, as though he had said the words aloud.

"That's what made me so crazy," she said. "It wasn't just that I was sad—it wasn't just that I missed him, or that I was grieving. It's that, down deep, I didn't ever feel like he was gone."

Mark could have told her what Gayle had told him, what any of Chloe's therapists had likely already said: That's what grieving *was*.

Chloe said, "Given what's happened since...I think, back then, I *did* feel Brendan there, at the house." She glanced up. "It makes sense. Now."

"Tell me," he said.

In front of them people were milling back and forth. A solitary ponytailed man with a camera, who knelt to take pictures of the sunlight through the palm fronds. Parents, alone and in pairs. Grandparents. Children. Bowlegged toddlers, babies in strollers, little boys.

Chloe said, "It's like I wrote in the letter. Connie had me over to the house. I talked to her and to her son—Jacob—about what had happened. And then they let me stay, there, alone. For an hour or two.

"I went and sat up in the room where they've been . . . encountering him. Brendan's old room." She gave him a significant sideways glance. "That first night I took along some of his things—pictures of him, some of his clothes. When I was alone I sat on the floor— they moved Jacob out of the room; it's empty, now—and I spread his pictures out. And then I—I talked to him. I told him that if he was really there, then he could come and see me. I told him we both missed him, and loved him.

"And then after a while . . . it happened."

She took a bottled water out of her purse and drank from it. When she was done she offered it to him. Mark took the bottle from her, drank a swallow, and handed it back.

Chloe said, "I've tried and tried to figure out how to say it, and I never can. It's not—there aren't words for it."

"Try."

She took a deep breath. "One second he wasn't there. I was just me, you know? The sad woman who'd lost her baby, looking at his pictures. And I was even sadder, because I was *there*. In our house." Her eyes lifted to his. "Alone. I—I started to get angry, at myself, at Connie. At you. I was feeling like this terrible fool who'd grasped at straws—I was crying and mad and wishing all kinds of things, and feeling sorry for myself, and I think—I think I remember saying, *Please come back to me.*

"And he *did.* He did, Mark. All of the sudden, I *felt* him. I *smelled* him. It was like he walked right through me. And then I heard him, too—a whole jumble of things he used to say: *Mommy. I'm thirsty, I'm hungry.* But not in—it wasn't scary, it wasn't sad. It was kind of like he'd hugged me, and we were remembering it all together." Her eyes were wide open, astonished. "Remember when we'd be doing something else, and he used to come in and hug us, out of the blue?"

The sudden grip on his pant leg. Brendan's toddler-face, round and gleeful, peering up at him. Surprise!

"It was like that," Chloe said. "I was sad, and I called for him, and he came. And when he was with me, I knew: He was happy to find me. He loved me."

Her eyes were closed; she was smiling.

"And then it was over. He was gone.

"It was like the wind was knocked out of me. I spent a little while, I don't know, *coming to*. Trying to get him to come back, but he didn't. Not that night.

"After a while I got up and I called you. It was all I could think to do."

Chloe's lashes were damp. She dug in her purse for a tissue and wiped at them.

She asked, "Do you believe me?"

Mark wanted to. So much of what she'd said reminded him of the feeling he'd woken from, those years before, in the upstairs hallway.

But he couldn't open his mouth, he couldn't say yes. Chloe had told him the same story she'd written him, and she'd made goosebumps rise on his arms. He wanted to put his arms around her, to rock her back and forth, to comfort her, to share in what she felt.

But that wasn't the same as belief, was it?

Chloe herself had given a possible explanation: She'd had a hallucination. She'd gone, for the first time in years, to a place guaranteed to tear her mind and heart to pieces. She'd concentrated on Brendan. She'd wanted to believe. She'd wanted it to happen. And then it had.

Mark had drunk himself nearly dead once, *wanting* that much.

He said, "I believe you believe it."

Chloe slumped forward, anguished. "Mark—you, you have to see for yourself. I know he'll come to you. He's—"

"Asking for me?"

She said, slowly, "Jacob heard him."

"But you haven't?"

She shook her head. "But I don't know if it means anything. When I'm with him, it's—it's intense, it's focused. On us."

"Do you trust Jacob?"

"I've had a long talk with him. He told me everything he could. He's—"

"Tell me exactly what he said."

She did. When this had all started—*the visitations* was Chloe's term—Jacob had been woken up in the middle of the night, over a period of a week or so. He'd told Chloe he heard quiet noises at first: footsteps in the hall, around the perimeter of his room.

Then one night he'd heard a voice—a little boy's, speaking just outside his door, though he couldn't make out what the boy was saying. Jacob thought he was dreaming, but night after night the voice kept waking him up. Coming closer and closer. Finally one night Jacob heard the voice in his room. He turned over in bed and saw someone standing next to his bed.

"In the dark?" Mark asked.

"He said it was like a shadow, between him and the window. But in the shape of a boy."

The shadow of a boy in the window. Chloe's silhouette on the living room drapes. The pattern, threatening again to cohere.

The rest of Chloe's story matched what Connie had told Mark about in the bookstore: Connie had accidentally frightened Jacob, and then had learned what he was seeing. Connie and Jacob moved his things out of his bedroom and into the spare room next door. But a few nights later Jacob heard the boy's voice again: through the walls, at first, speaking quietly, sometimes crying. And then Jacob had heard him call out *Daddy!*

Mark kept his gaze steady. "Does he still hear him? Since you've been coming?"

"Less and less. But I'm—" She paused, as though embarrassed.

"What?"

"I've been staying there, some nights," she said. "Connie's convinced a cousin of hers in Gahanna to take them in on weekends, and when they're gone, I watch the place."

"And it's happened again? What you—what you experienced?"

"Not every night," she said. "But a lot of them. And my dreams are different, too. Happier. Instead of looking for him, now...now sometimes I find him."

She shut her eyes languidly, as though she was being caressed.

He said, "Okay. Let's say it happens like you want. I go to the house. I have an experience, too. Then what happens?"

Chloe smiled, but thinly, nervously. "Then we'd try to help him."

"How?"

She took a breath, as though convincing herself she could say what she had to. "I've been doing some research. I think I found someone who can help us. Her name is Trudy Weill. She's—she calls herself a medium."

When he didn't respond, she said, "Don't think what you're thinking. Who else would I go to? The police? A priest?"

"I've looked up some of those people," he said. "They seem like con artists to me."

"I did my homework. I made calls everywhere. She's as legitimate as they come."

And how legitimate was that? he wanted to ask. Was she on file with the Better Business Bureau? Written up in *Consumer Reports*?

"I've met her," Chloe said. "I've talked with her. I've talked with people she's helped before. And I trust her. She's—she's not like those horrible people on TV. She's just a woman, up in Michigan."

A medium. Mark pictured candles and scarves and knocking on the walls. Holding Chloe's hand in the dark. Even as a boy

Jacob Pelham's age, Mark had read about how mediums faked their business.

"And the medium would do...what, exactly?"

"She would visit the house. And try to talk with him."

"So why doesn't she?"

"She said she needs to have both parents there, for this, this ritual, to work. She says, since you're—since you're being *called*, that you need to be present, too. With me."

Insane. Not a few minutes ago he'd been close to agreeing to everything Chloe wanted.

"Mark," she said. "One of the reasons I've been trying so hard to reach you—we're kind of on a deadline. With Trudy." Chloe was reddening. "She thinks she can do her job best on—on an important day. To us, to him. And the next big day..."

Chloe didn't have to finish. The anniversary of Brendan's death was January 23: only four days away. Christ almighty.

"So what happens? She comes to the house, we're there—"

"She talks to him. She tells him..."

The medium would tell Brendan to go away. To be at rest. Wherever that was, whatever that meant.

Chloe slipped her hand over his. "Mark."

His name, a piece of silk. He thought of Allison saying, We need to talk.

"I have to think this over."

"What is there to think about?"

"Chloe, I've never believed anything like this. Never. This is *hard*."

Her eyes narrowed—and here, at last, was a glimpse of the Chloe who had hurt him, the Chloe who might have picked the conservatory for a meeting because of its capacity to make him weak.

"I can't give you evidence," she said. "Not unless you come with me. Then either you'll see or you won't."

A tour group—a conservatory volunteer trailed by a pack of twenty or so elementary schoolchildren—walked into the room. The young woman began talking loudly, gesturing with her hands. The children laughed.

Chloe slumped, her face wan.

"Come on," she said.

She stood and led Mark up the nearest curving stairway. He watched the tender backs of her knees, just below the hem of her skirt, and the scuffing on the soles of her boots—boots he'd never seen before, yet old, worn.

Chloe turned down a narrow pathway, into a new chamber, smaller, lined by shoulder-high fragrant green shrubs and flowers in yellow and blue. Dozens of butterflies flitted among the blossoms, across the path. She sat down on a bench and patted the seat next to her. Mark sat. An elderly Japanese couple walked by, hand in hand. Water was trickling someplace he couldn't see.

Her eyes were huge, blue, direct; the cruel Chloe had vanished again. "I know why you won't come. It's because you don't trust me."

He was about to protest, but she kept talking. "You have every reason not to. I know that."

"Chloe—"

She touched his knee, as delicately as if one of the butterflies had landed there.

"It's wonderful to be with him," she said. "But it's also sad. And not just because he's there, and he shouldn't be. It's sad because I sit there with Brendan and I feel him, and—and I'm his *mother* again. I can almost convince myself that when I open my eyes, I'll have gone back in time, and everything will be like it was."

Mark began to realize, then, what Chloe was about to say.

"But it feels incomplete," she said. "I love to be with him, but sometimes I just can't stop crying. Do you know why?"

He shook his head.

"Because you're not there with us," Chloe said, her eyes wet. "Because I know—I can tell—he wants *both of us*."

He wanted so badly to take her hand.

"I did this to us," she said. "I understand that now."

"Chloe, no."

She said, very quietly, "It won't surprise you to know I blamed you."

She'd told him this, more than once, at her angriest. Maybe she'd forgotten. But even though he knew, hearing the words now was a blow.

"Everyone—my therapists—kept telling me not to. But I was sure. I convinced myself: If I'd been in the house with him, instead of you, it wouldn't have happened. If—"

He could recite the rest by heart: If she had been home. If they hadn't been fighting. If Mark had not been drinking while watching basketball. If he hadn't had so much to drink, the night before, and the night before that. If he'd been a good husband, a good father.

If he had loved them, Chloe and Brendan, the right way.

"But I always missed something important," Chloe said. "Something obvious. *I wasn't in the house because I chose not to be.* I was mad from the night before, and I went out to lunch with friends, and that wasn't any different from whatever I was mad at you about. Maybe it was worse. Maybe if I'd been there, the same thing would have happened. But I wasn't there." She swallowed. "If it was anybody's fault, it was mine. And I'm sorry it took this—Brendan coming back—to show me. To make me realize what I am, and all the things I've lost because of it."

His throat had closed. She took his hand between both of hers and squeezed. God, how he had longed to hear this.

"Even before, it was my fault," she said. "Ever since I left you I've been asking myself what happened. We were so happy, once. Weren't we?"

"Yes," he said.

"I don't know what it was," she told him, softly. "How we got to be so cold with each other. Maybe we were just too busy. Maybe if Brendan had lived we would have figured it out. But I want you to know. I want you—"

He waited, breathless.

"I want you to know I never stopped loving you," she said. "Even when things were so bad. Even after I left. I just couldn't hear you. I was too selfish, too mad. You kept telling me we could fix ourselves. You kept asking me to believe you, and I didn't, and I know what I'm asking you now is harder, but—"

He was crying now. They both were.

She said, "Please don't let what I did keep you from believing me now. I'm sorry I left. I'm sorrier than you could ever know. But please—"

He was sure she wanted to sob into his chest, in his arms, just as he was sure that he wanted her to, that he wanted—

To do what he had always done: to make it better.

She had forgiven him. All these years after the accident, and he had at last been absolved. All these years, and she at last wanted him to help her. She had never stopped loving him.

He could not help himself. No force on earth could stop him from encircling her with his arms. He held her and apologized to her, too. Told her again the story of his own blame, even as she shook her head.

When he'd finished she fell against him, pressed her wet cheek against his. "Please," she said again, but he shushed her, bent forward and kissed her hair and closed his eyes and smelled her and felt the pressure of her rail-thin arms, her ribs beneath the thin wool of her sweater—Chloe wasting away, like a cursed woman in an old story, Chloe, *his* Chloe, calling for him, needing him—and he nodded, his cheek pressed tight against her skull.

"Take me to the house," he said. "Show me."

Eighteen

They made plans as they walked out of the conservatory to the parking lot. Chloe told him that Connie and Jacob were leaving for her cousin's that very night. "We can go to the house tomorrow," she said. "If that's all right."

Mark was surprised by his disappointment; he was ready to go right now.

"What about later tonight?"

"I wish I could. I'm leaving here for Mom and Dad's. One of my uncles is in town. Plus Mom's worried—worried about me. I have to show my face." She smiled at him. "Tomorrow's okay. We can take our time, then."

"Your parents don't know?"

She shook her head. "They wouldn't understand." And it was true, they wouldn't. The Rosses were deeply devout; for their own reasons, they would find talk of a medium just as disturbing as Mark's father would.

As though reading his mind, Chloe asked, "Did you tell Sam?"

"No," he said. "Would *you*?"

She let out a tiny, frightened laugh.

There. They were alone in their knowledge, their plans. How else could it be?

"Tomorrow," he agreed, feeling dizzy. The same day Allison wanted to have a serious talk with him.

They were standing beside his car. A cold breeze blew Chloe's hair across his face. She squeezed his hands, then stood on tiptoe and hugged him, and before she let him go she kissed his cheek. "Thank you," she said.

She crossed the parking lot, got into her car, and drove away. The damp spot where she'd kissed him cooled until it stung.

⌒

He was in his warming car, just ready to leave the lot himself, when his phone buzzed: Lewis.

"Christ, finally," Lew said, when he answered. "Where are you?"

"Noplace," Mark said.

"So Allie called me last night—"

Mark winced; he'd forgotten that part already. Lew must have been worried sick about him. "Things are weird over here," he said, marveling at the inadequacy of the words. "What we talked about before, it's—"

"Come over," Lew said immediately. "Or I can meet you at your place. Doesn't matter."

Mark was nodding, even though Lew couldn't see him. He would rather do anything than return to the townhouse, to evidence of Allie and her sadness, past and future. "I'll be right there."

⌒

Lewis's apartment building, fifteen minutes away in Grandview, was a two-story U-shaped brick block he proclaimed to hate, but which he could never seem to bring himself to leave, as it was only a short walk both from the studio and from his favorite bar. Lew had lived here ten years, and Mark had always thought—unless Lew, somehow, got married—that he might happily stay another ten.

Lew opened the door even before Mark could knock. "Sit. You hungry? I'll order us sandwiches."

Lew kept the blinds shut in winter to trap heat; they let in only a dirty orange glow, and no air at all. Lew was a neat man, but not a clean one—his living room and his kitchen were free of clutter, but the air was thick with old smoke and beer and Lew's own animal-den funk. Even so, Mark was glad to be here. This place felt old, powerful. Safer in its familiarity than anyplace else he'd been of late.

"I owe you an apology," Mark said. "For running away, that night."

Lewis already had the phone in his hand; he waved Mark away, and then called a deli down the street. Mark sat in a chair at the kitchen table and closed his eyes. After the last twenty-four hours he was relieved to sit still, head empty, letting someone else make decisions.

Lewis's voice, ordering their food, was a little too insistent, a little too loud. Mark knew that tone as intimately as he knew the smell in the air: Lew had been putting back beer since the little hand hit twelve.

Lew hung up and sat down across the table. He gave Mark a long look. "You want to tell me what the fuck's been going on?"

Mark said, "You got a beer?"

Lew didn't answer.

Mark said, "Come on. This isn't easy."

Lew pushed himself up from the tabletop, rummaged in the refrigerator, and returned with two bottles of Amstel. He uncapped each of them against the edge of the tabletop, where the metal binding had gapped out from the Formica top. He slid a bottle across into Mark's hands.

Mark took a long, grateful pull. He'd begun imagining this as soon as he'd hung up the phone.

"Come on," Lew said. "Tell me."

Mark told him all he could bear to, from Chloe's last visit to the townhouse to her letter to the talk they'd just had. He left out only the most private details: How he'd imagined Chloe's voice instead of Allie's, last night. Chloe's cold, wet kiss on his cheek.

When he was done Lew said, sickly, "You don't need this. You of all people."

Here, again, was talk about what Mark deserved. After his meeting with Chloe the word seemed no longer to apply to any part of his life, past or present. He repeated a favorite phrase of Gayle's: "The world owes me nothing. It never did." He remembered the way Chloe had felt in his arms. "I'm no saint, Lew. You know that."

"Still—"

"Doesn't matter," Mark said, though Lew's sympathy—not to mention his beer—was warming him.

Lew stood and circled the kitchen and then sat back down again. "Okay. Let's think, here. It's still probably the kid, right? Making up a story. People have talked themselves into stranger shit than this, and Chloe's...Chloe's not exactly a stable person. Right?"

"I don't know. I really don't anymore. Lew, if you'd heard her—"

"You're really going to the house?"

"I have to," Mark said. "You were right. If I think there's a possibility, I need to go. I owe Chloe that much."

"*Maybe* there's a possibility. But you don't owe Chloe shit."

"She's—"

Lew's eyes narrowed. "Chloe can apologize all she wants. But she still divorced you, and she's been fucking you over ever since. I loved the girl, too, Mark, but *come on*. If you go, go because of Brendan. Not because Chloe finally had a moment of fucking clarity."

Mark felt himself flush. "You didn't hear her. This was the old Chloe."

"Think about it. Chloe's your weak point. She sends you a letter—to your house, where Allie might see it, we should discuss that—and then all of a sudden you're running to meet her? You're *engaged*."

"I didn't mean it like that," Mark said, his face burning. "I promise you, this is about Brendan."

Lew was silent for a long time, looking at his beer. He was agitated—this was a very different Lew than the one he'd run away from, weeks before.

"Can I ask you something?" Mark said.

Lew nodded, his eyes still agleam.

"When you saw your ghost—how did you know it was real?"

The question seemed to take Lew by surprise. As though he'd forgotten the story himself.

"It's hard to explain," he said at last. "You know, I tried to talk myself out of it at first. But I couldn't. For one thing, my cousin had seen our ghost, too. We compared stories; they matched up." He looked contemplatively down at his bottle. "I was a kid, too. And stoned. You know, I was the age where I *wanted* it to be real. There've been a lot of nights since where I tried to tell myself it wasn't." He shrugged. "But I can't talk myself out of it. It was real, and I knew."

"But how?"

"I didn't just see it," Lew said. "I *felt* it. I looked at it—at *him*—and I knew I was in the presence of something important." He took a drink. "I saw this guy, this figure, crouching by a fire, and—I didn't think, *A strange man is over there.* I thought—I felt—that *Over there is a soul without its body.*"

Mark had never heard him say any of this. Probably because he'd never taken Lew seriously enough to ask.

Lew said, "I've been thinking about this, for weeks. That last time we talked—I can't stop thinking about what it means. *If.* Everything I come up with terrifies me."

Mark didn't like the watery trouble in Lew's eyes.

"Whatever it is," Mark said, "tell me."

Lew stood and got two more bottles out of the refrigerator; he uncapped Mark's and set it in front of him. "You know I was raised

Baptist? I used to think that when you die, you go to heaven, you're at peace, you know?" He lifted his eyebrows. "I mean, I'm sure not a Jesus freak anymore, but you don't lose sight of heaven that easily. Even after I saw my ghost I didn't stop believing in it, not for a long time. But it just doesn't fit. That guy I saw—wasn't—*isn't*—in heaven. Or hell, or wherever it is we're supposed to go. And if I accept that, well—it opens up all kinds of nasty doors, right?"

Mark's neck prickled. "Like what?"

Lew's voice was very soft, and as sad as Mark had ever heard it:

"If Brendan's in the house," he said, "doesn't there have to be some kind of reason? And doesn't that reason have to be really bad?"

The doorbell startled them both. Lew got up and paid the deliveryman while Mark stared up at the yellowish ceiling, at a brown water stain that had spread slowly out from the corner above Lew's sink.

Lew handed a wrapped sandwich to Mark. "You should eat something."

Mark had never been less hungry in his life, but for Lew's sake he opened the sandwich and ate a few bites. The food was nearly tasteless in his mouth, but his stomach received it gratefully. Lew opened his sandwich, stared at it, and didn't eat. He got up and rummaged around on top of his desk in the next room.

He returned with a legal pad and sat down. He wrote down *Brendan* at the top. Lew circled the name, then wrote, *Ghost?*

"If he's in the house," he said, "there are a couple of ways to look at it, I think. One way is to say he's here because some accident happened."

"An accident did happen."

"I mean after death," Lew said. "Whatever was supposed to happen to him got disrupted. Brendan didn't go where he should have. Or he got lost, trying to find it."

Lew wrote *Accident* on the left side of the page. "Maybe that's all this is. A cosmic fuckup. He's lost and he needs someone to show him where to go. We leave aside the implications for now—which are pretty fucking plentiful. But if he's there for this reason then maybe—maybe—this medium Chloe found can help."

"But."

"But," Lew said, his voice dropping low, "we've only got a million stories floating around about ghosts that *aren't* accidental. Ghosts that have a purpose."

Why hadn't Mark thought to ask Chloe these most basic questions? *Why is Brendan still here? What does he want? Did he tell you?* He'd stumbled over each of them, these last weeks, staring into the dark. Surely Chloe had been mulling them over, too, in her own sleepless nights. She hadn't volunteered him any answers. Only that she was happy. That Brendan had seemed happy, too.

"So let's start with the most unlikely reasons," Lew said. "Nobody killed him, so we can cross *vengeance* off the list. But."

He wrote: *Bones/body not at rest.*

Mark and Lew had both been Brendan's pallbearers; Mark had watched, held at each elbow by Lew and his father, as Brendan's small coffin was lowered into the ground. And it had been Brendan's body in the coffin—Mark and Chloe had agreed on a closed-casket funeral, but between the service and the burial Chloe had asked to see him one last time, and Mark had gone, too, despite his misgivings, and they'd seen him, lying nestled against the velvet, so still and quiet in his navy-blue suit. Mark had had to wrap his arms around Chloe to pull her back from trying to pick up Brendan's body. He could still feel, if he closed his eyes, the way she had thrashed against him; the way she'd seemed full of lightning.

"No," he said to Lew.

Lewis nodded, then wrote: *Unfinished business.*

"An important task left undone," he said. "An important duty to fulfill. Anything like that."

Brendan had just turned seven. His concerns had been a child's. The last desire he'd expressed was not to clean up his toys. He'd wanted, instead, to play a fucking board game.

Brendan had badgered Mark all that morning: Can we play just one? Parcheesi? Just *that* one? Please? Dad, please?—his voice ratcheting up in pitch with each question, until finally he hit that whiny register that always made Mark squeeze shut his eyes.

Finally Brendan had kicked at the side of the couch, balled his hands into fists. I want to play a gaaame!

That's it, Mark had said. And then out came the last words he'd ever said to his son:

You get your ass upstairs and don't come down until your room is clean.

"He was seven," Mark said. "His whole life was unfinished fucking business."

"Sure." Lew's voice was as even, as reasonable, as a parent's. "But it might not have to seem important to *us*. Didn't you tell me something happened at school, around then? He was in a fight?"

Brendan had indeed been in some trouble the day before the accident. Brendan's second-grade teacher, Beth Reilly, had held Brendan off the bus, and called in Mark and Chloe to speak with her after school. Outside her classroom Beth told them: That afternoon, on the playground, she'd had to separate Brendan from a group of other boys.

He was fighting? Mark asked, stunned. Through the small square window inset high in the classroom door he peered at Brendan, tall and ungainly, making a Lego house beside a small blond girl at one of the play tables inside. His lips were pursed, his face composed, but—Mark could tell—his boy's shoulders were stiff with shame and misery.

No, Beth said, they weren't fighting.

She was a lovely, idealistic woman, fresh out of college, her glossy black hair pulled tightly back and tied with a ribbon at her nape. Her eyes were nearly spilling over with concern. She might have been Chloe, nearly a decade before.

She said, I'm sorry to tell you this, but Brendan was being bullied. The other boys were taunting him. He was very upset.

Chloe peppered her then with furious questions; Beth answered each carefully. No, she didn't know the cause, not yet; none of the boys was talking. Yes, she had reprimanded the other boys, and had asked to meet with their parents, too. And—she had to tell them this—she was concerned for Brendan. This sort of thing might not pass quickly. She knew Chloe, a teacher, would understand.

Chloe was livid, but she nodded.

Beth said: He's such a little gentleman, I don't know why the kids would do that.

Mark offered to drive Brendan home, while Chloe stayed behind to talk to Beth some more, teacher-to-teacher.

In the car Mark said, Rough day, huh, buddy? and Brendan sniffled, nodded.

Instead of going straight home, Mark detoured to Fitz's. They sat in the back corner and split a sundae, Brendan hunched forward over the table in his gray sweatshirt—his favorite, the one that showed Brutus Buckeye rearing back, ready to charge into action. Brendan, Mark saw, wasn't sad—he was furious. His mouth was pursed too tightly, and he held his spoon in a white-knuckle grip.

Mark tried to see an outcast in him. A boy who could be mocked. But Brendan, apart from his hectic color, seemed as normal as ever. He was tall, handsome. He didn't smell; he wore nice clothes, he had a cool haircut. A quiet boy, yes, a serious boy, but a loving boy. A boy who knew to hold the door open for the person behind him, to say please and thank you.

Gradually Mark got Brendan's side of the story. There'd been a contest out in the playground. A lengthy strip of ice had formed in the bottom of a ditch at the playground's edge, and, out of sight of the teachers, some of the boys had begun doing baseball slides along its length. One boy had even gone headfirst. Someone had asked Brendan to slide, but he didn't want to—he was afraid of hitting his head or scraping his hands, as others had done. And then—

And then David Helton called me a name, Brendan said.

Mark had been taunted, himself, on the playground, back when he was a serious, shy little boy, preferring to draw superheroes in a sketchbook instead of playing touch football. He'd been called a faggot and a gaylord and a pansy.

What name?

It's a bad word, Brendan told him.

You can say it.

They called me a *pussy*. Brendan quickly added, And I said not to say bad words, and then they *laughed* at me.

If Brendan had just brushed off the word, Mark was sure, nothing would have happened. But Brendan had reacted like a goody two-shoes—like his mother—and then someone had laughed at him, and Brendan had done the absolute wrong thing, which was to start crying. After that it would have been blood in the water.

Mark could imagine the ring forming. Several other kids taking up the shout. And Brendan—with his father's tendency to hide, to panic—would have covered his face, his tears. Mark ached for him, because he knew the truth: Brendan *was* a pussy. He was, after all, his father's son.

You know they're wrong, Mark said. Don't you, buddy?

No, Brendan said, and for a moment Mark had the eerie feeling Brendan was denying Mark's own thoughts: I *am* one. I *cried*.

All that night, and into the next morning, Brendan had been sullen, withdrawn. He wanted to stick close to Mark. And Mark—

Mark had wanted to be alone.

Unfinished business? A wrong left unrighted?

Mark had fought with Chloe the night before the accident, after Brendan was in bed. They'd argued about the taunting. Whether Beth Reilly had acted appropriately—whether she'd been fast enough to break things up, whether she'd been paying attention at all. What they should do next. Chloe—a fellow teacher, a mother—was a growling she-bear; she wanted to call the other children's parents herself. Mark tried to downplay things: A playground taunting, he told her, wasn't that big a deal; he'd been through plenty himself. He told her Brendan would have to learn from the pain, as he had. That he would grow up a lot, having to go back to class. But Chloe would have none of it.

Their fight wasn't unusual; they'd had plenty, that last year. But this one was especially hurtful. Chloe the popular girl, Chloe the fighter, would never understand. Mark couldn't make her. He couldn't tell her the damage was already done.

She went to bed angry, and Mark—as he had done so often, those last two years—stayed up late, drinking one whiskey-and-Coke, and then another. The next morning he woke late and hungover. When he joined Chloe and Brendan at the breakfast table, Chloe, still grim, said, You smell like a bar.

Pretty gross, Brendan agreed, pushing one of his cars along the edge of the tabletop, and it took all Mark's strength not to snap at them both.

When Chloe announced she was going to have lunch with her girlfriends—when, after her chilly goodbye, Mark wanted to sulk and watch basketball in silence—he instead found himself stuck with a clingy, traumatized Brendan. Brendan kept coloring at the kitchen table; Mark kept telling him to go clean up his room, reminding him of their standing Saturday deal: If Brendan cleaned his room first thing Saturday morning, then and only then could he watch sports with his father.

But Brendan couldn't be moved. Daddy, he kept asking, can we play a game? Please please please—

Brendan! Go clean your room. Otherwise we won't do *anything*.

Yesterday's problems still echoed in both their heads, and what had happened? Mark could only do a slow burn as Brendan lost himself to a tantrum. He followed Mark into the living room, first crying, then squalling; then he dropped face-first onto the couch, kicking his legs, and Mark, in his pain and frustration, could only stand and watch.

Thinking: This wasn't what he wanted.

Thinking: You little pussy.

He raised his voice—which he almost never did. He sent Brendan upstairs. Brendan had looked at him in utter betrayal before stomping away.

And then Brendan was upstairs, angry, slamming the door, throwing his toys, before finally—finally!—he fell silent. Mark could have gone to him, but he didn't. He poured himself a drink, finished it. Told himself, *Fuck it*, then poured another. He watched the game, his eyelids heavy. He thought about Beth Reilly, imagining her naked. He rehashed his argument with Chloe. He sulked, as silent as his boy.

He could have checked on Brendan. He could have called up the stairs: I don't hear you cleaning! Anything would have worked, except what he'd done, which was nothing.

And then those heavy, sodden thumps; that lone, sharp cry, suddenly cut off.

Unfinished business? A wrong left unpunished?

Mark had sent Brendan to his room before. They disciplined him this way a lot—if he couldn't act like a grown-up, he got a time-out. Mark hadn't beaten him, hadn't put him in harm's way. He'd yelled, yes, but that was no crime. Brendan had died only because he'd *disobeyed*. Because he tried to run away. Because he had an untied shoelace. Because he'd packed a backpack too full of toys and books.

All the while surely telling himself, I'm not a pussy. Throwing a stuffed animal across the room, thinking, I'm not I'm not I'm not.

Thinking: I'll show them.

I'll show *him*.

"Mark." Lewis was staring at him, his eyebrows knotted.

"No," Mark said. "Nothing."

Lewis wrote a question mark after *Unfinished business*. He said, "I don't guess you'd mind if I lit up a smoke?"

Mark shook his head. Lew reached into his breast pocket and pulled out a pack of cigarettes. He shook one out and lit it. He kept his eyes on Mark for a long second, then bent forward and wrote: *A warning? A message?*

"Ghosts sometimes carry messages," Lew said. "This is where it gets tricky, because there's so much we don't know. You know, about the rules. Has he been there all along? Or has he been, like, dormant? Or did he just now come back?" Lew exhaled through his nose. "Is there anything he'd want to tell you? To warn you about?"

"I don't know."

But then he remembered holding Allison to his chest. Telling her, It's not you.

"Because I can think of something," Lew said, watching Mark carefully.

And here, at last, was the pattern he had feared, revealing itself. He saw it clearly, horribly.

"I got engaged," Mark said.

The timing was almost perfect. Just as he'd begun planning to ask Allie to marry him, Jacob Pelham had woken up in the dark—

"It can't be that," he said. "Jesus Christ."

Lew tapped his pen against the pad. "I don't like to think about it, but it was all I could come up with."

Mark closed his eyes. Something Chloe had said, that afternoon—

He wants both of us.

Mark stood and circled the kitchen. If the story was true—if Brendan was a ghost—then Mark lived, now, in an entirely new world. One governed by its own meanings, its own logic. And that logic could lead down paths like this one.

His boy, come back to warn him.

About what? Marrying someone new?

Marrying someone he didn't love? Marrying someone he didn't love as much as *Chloe*?

Mark sat back down. "It can't be."

"It probably isn't," Lew said. "Which would be a problem, too, now. It's just that I wanted you to be prepared."

"It just can't be."

"Can you think of anything else?"

Mark, after a long while, shook his head no. Lew, his face soft and mottled with pain, looked away.

꙳

Lewis insisted that Mark stay with him, crash on his couch. He was right: What would Mark be going home to? So he went with Lew to the studio, sat silent beside him while the speakers, over and over, throbbed out a jingle for a furniture store's no-money-down Mondays.

In the studio he went over the same looping sentences. If-thens, what-ifs. He came to no answers. Either Brendan was in the house, or he wasn't. Either way, Mark himself was trapped. Either way, he would hurt Allison or Chloe.

If he was a good man—if the last seven years of pain had meant anything—he had to call Allison and confess everything: He'd been talking to Chloe. He'd agreed to go to the old house tomorrow.

But would that be enough? Allison didn't believe in ghosts any more than Mark did, and he'd been keeping the truth from her too long already. She might accept what he told her, or she might very well not.

This is crazy, she might say.

She might say, We're done.

He remembered Chloe in his arms, her lips on his cheek. The ways she had made him know she still loved him.

In the dark studio, Mark wasn't so sure Allison would be wrong.

⌒

When they walked back to Lew's apartment, the sun was setting; the sidewalks were glassy with the day's iced-over snowmelt. They didn't speak; Lew, for the last few hours, had been as quiet as Mark, his face almost as weary. Inside the apartment Lew preheated the oven for a pizza. Snow began to tick at the begrimed window above the sink. "This fucking winter," Lew said. He glanced at Mark. "Do you need to call Allison?"

When Mark didn't answer, Lew opened up a small cabinet above the refrigerator and produced a bottle of Maker's Mark, one shot glass. He glanced at Mark, then took down another.

"I shouldn't offer," Lew said. "Right?"

"Probably not."

"What would your dad say?"

"He'd tell you not to."

"Why'd you quit?" Lew asked. "Why, really?"

For the first time, Mark told him: "Right after Chloe left me, I got really drunk at the old house. In the middle of it I thought I heard Brendan. Maybe I saw him."

Lew looked at him pie-eyed.

"So," Mark said. "I guess I didn't trust my judgment. Do you?"

Lew looked at the bottle in his hand. "I trust you more than just about anybody," he said. "I wish you'd told me that."

"No, you don't."

Lew laughed at that. He poured the shots.

⌒

Two hours later—it was now past nine—Lewis went to the kitchen, poured himself one last drink, then capped the whiskey and put it away. They'd each had two shots, and several more cans of beer, and by now Mark's head was pleasantly insulated, his hands still and heavy on his thighs. He listened from the couch while Lew did the dishes. When Lew was done he stopped beside the kitchen table and looked at the legal pad upon which he'd written earlier, and shook his head.

They'd been quiet, watching television, for an hour. Watching Lew now, Mark wanted to keep it that way. "Maybe it's time we crashed," he said.

Lew nodded slowly—he'd drunk enough to be thick-lidded, too careful—then went to the hall closet and returned with sheets, a blanket, and a pillow, and dropped them on the couch beside Mark. He sat back down in his recliner and puffed out air. "I just don't know," he said.

"Don't know what?"

"I mean. I mean I can't stop thinking. I didn't tell you everything, before."

Mark spread the sheet out onto the couch cushions and lay back down. His own head was light, airy. He thought he just might be able to sleep, if Lew shut up.

"There was one idea I didn't write down," Lew said. "I figured it didn't count. But now I don't know. And—it's maybe the worst one."

Mark didn't answer him.

Lew said, "Ghosts *want* things."

"What—"

"Selfish things," Lew said, as though confessing to a sin of his own. "It's in so many of these stories. They want things they can't have anymore. What they had when they were *alive*."

The little shadow-Brendan, crouched in his empty room, listening for the voices of his parents through the walls.

"They get lonely," Lew said. "Desperate."

"Lew—"

"Listen. All these stories—so many of them end up with somebody dead."

"No one's going to die."

Lew was blinking furiously. "You're not listening. Ghosts want *company*. Except ghosts can't come back to life, right? But living people can always become ghosts."

Mark thought of Chloe, so thin she was nearly worn right through.

"This is Brendan we're talking about," he said.

"I don't know anything." Lew was slump-shouldered, his face slack, sad all the way down to his bones. "I mean, you're different, these days. Do you know that? This has changed you. You look sick."

Mark didn't answer.

"I was with you," Lew said, "all these years. I watched you live through it, and I didn't always know if you would. And now you're right back there again."

He knew Lew was right. Hadn't this been Mark's own fear, these past weeks? The one he'd been trying so hard not to admit to himself?

"You're my oldest friend," Lew said. "I just want you to be careful. That's all. That's all I'm trying to say."

"I'll be careful," he said. "I promise."

"You're still not getting it," Lew said. "It's dangerous for you. No matter what you do. No matter if it's true or not."

"What do you mean?"

"Allie's a good girl," Lew said. "She loves you. You love her. Don't fuck with that."

Mark said nothing.

Lew stood, then walked to him and hugged him. "So here's the deal. You have to check in with me tomorrow, or—"

"Or what?"

Lew drew himself up. "Or I'll call your father."

Mark was tempted to laugh, but Lew's face was grim.

"You think I'm kidding," he said, then lumbered down the hall-way to his bedroom and shut the door.

⌐

When he thought Lewis might be asleep, Mark put on his coat, went out to the walkway overlooking the courtyard, and called Allison while there was still some chance of catching her awake.

While Allie's phone rang he watched an old woman on the other side of the courtyard leaning against the iron railing and smoking a cigarette. She wore a housecoat and a white knit cap, and held a cell phone to her ear. She was smiling and shaking her head—as though listening to a long, elaborate joke.

Darlene answered: "Allie's phone."

"Darly," he said. "It's Mark."

Darlene said, not in a friendly way, "Allie's in the bathroom."

Mark tried not to think about what Allie had been saying to her sister, these last few hours. "Can she call me back? When she has a minute?"

The old woman in the courtyard suddenly cackled, then spoke in what sounded like Russian.

Darlene said, "Look. I know it's not my business. But Allie's not real happy, right now."

"I know," he said.

"I don't know you that well," Darly said. "I'm taking Allie at her word, you know, that you're different."

"I love your sister," Mark said. "Very much. That's what I called to tell her."

Darly's voice was now even colder. "Talk's cheap, Mark. My sister's been through a lot."

"This *is* different," Mark said, gritting his teeth. "Look, I'm not—I'm not cheating on her, okay? I'm not Bill. We just have to figure some things out."

Darly's volume increased: "Well, hurry it up. You don't even know how—"

Mark heard Allie's voice, then. Both sisters spoke, muffled; one voice rose, sharpened. Then Allie said to him, "Hey, sorry about that."

"Hi," he said. The cold had penetrated his jacket, and he was shivering.

"Where are you?" she asked.

"Lew's," he said. "I really am this time. I can put him on if you want."

"I—Okay. Thank you for calling."

"I'm sorry it wasn't earlier. Lew and I have been talking."

"Okay." Then she said, "About me?"

"Only good things," he said, and tried to smile when he said it.

"Well. Thanks."

A stone blocked his throat. He could tell her nothing, not yet. But her voice was so small, so hurt. So many people in this world gave him love he didn't deserve.

"I just wanted to say goodnight," he said.

He heard her breath, drawn quickly in, and felt shame. He'd shocked her with a kindness.

"I miss you," Allie said.

His eyes stung.

"I'm going to fix this," he told her. As always, the sound of his voice, spoken through tears, made him sound like a child, like a liar.

"Okay," Allie said—cautiously, as though she'd just heard a lie.

They told each other *I love you* before hanging up. When Mark looked again, the woman across the courtyard had vanished, as though she'd never been there at all.

⌒

Mark turned off the living room light and lay still in the darkness. His head swam. Right away he knew sleep would be impossible. He wanted Allison with him. When he remembered the conservatory, he wanted Chloe, too. He wanted not to think of the words Lewis had written on the legal pad. *Unfinished business. Warnings.*

Selfish things.

But if Chloe was right, what choice did he have?

I'll call your father.

Lew knew exactly how to make him feel guilty. Sam still had heard nothing of Mark's troubles. If Mark had his way, Sam never would. He'd gone, these last weeks, to a place where his father could not help him.

He was lying to himself. He *had* gone to a place like this before, and his father had not only helped him, he'd swooped in for a rescue.

In fact, the only other time Mark had ever come close to thinking what he now thought, he had asked his father's opinion.

After Sam had found Mark, alone and nearly dead, they had lived together for a while. Sam had taken a semester off from school, and had moved to the small apartment in Columbus. For weeks he stayed with Mark, caring for him, watching over him. Sam had only let Mark live alone after he made—and kept—an appointment with a therapist.

But just after Sam had rescued him, for almost a full month, Mark had gone to live with him in Indiana. Surrounded by his boyhood house, lying in his boyhood bed, the fact that for seven years Mark had been a father, and a husband for longer, seemed less definite, more a theory than a fact. Sometimes he could even allow himself to believe that he was, really, a teenager again, waking from nightmare visions of a terrible future. At other times, however, he was wholly, painfully himself—Sam's house, after all, was filled with pictures of their losses: Mark's mother, Brendan, even Chloe.

Mark and Sam spent every evening together. Some nights they talked on the stone porch; others, they watched baseball or football in the living room. But even when they were seemingly comfortable, Mark could feel that his father was alert, ready to agree to whatever Mark might say he needed.

But what did Mark need? He didn't know. He was sober, yet his dreams from the house were still close, still red and painful. They robbed him of his sleep; they followed him through his long and logy days. The world around him seemed inconsequential. Flimsy, not worth trusting.

One evening, he'd said, Dad, can I ask a question?

They were sitting on the porch steps, watching the woods and the newly harvested field across the road, rawly black, smelling sweetly of rot and chemicals. His father set down his book, turned to him, expectant.

Do you ever think about where Brendan is? Mark asked.

His father smiled tightly. If there's a heaven, he said, I'm sure it's populated by children.

But you don't believe in heaven.

Sam sat up straight. No, I really don't. Last I checked, you didn't, either.

No. But this—it's different.

Sam's voice was very soft, and surprised him: How could it not be?

So what do you think happened to him? Mark risked this, too: What do you think happened to Mom?

Mark, I don't know. Ask a priest. A philosopher. Ask a biologist.

He'd expected a more vehement denial. His father's voice: *Think about it, Mark.*

I know what they'd say, Mark said. I'm asking *you*.

Sam sighed.

Mark said, We have to think of them as *somewhere*, right?

His father thought for a moment, then said, Thinking doesn't make it so. Gone doesn't mean gone *someplace*. But I suppose I *do* imagine them in a place. A nowhere-place, where they can't think of us. Which is the same difference, maybe.

His father stared across the field. Mark was aware, as never before, of the deep lines in Sam's face, the jut of his knuckles. How his hair had almost entirely gone gray. He was fifty-three then, closer to his death than his birth. Soon he would be an old man.

I guess what I'm asking is whether you think—

But he couldn't finish. Sam did it for him:

You want to know whether I think I'll see Molly again. And Brendan.

Yes.

I don't think I will. But I wish I could.

Mark's disappointment tightened his throat.

Sam looked sideways at him. I really do imagine my death as an end. As a blackness. The deepest of sleeps. A sleep without dreaming.

But does that comfort you? Mark asked.

It does, now. Very much.

Why?

Sam spoke carefully, as though the words were spilled coins he was picking up, one by one:

I do not know what purpose there may be to my life, beyond what I see of it here in front of me. But it is very difficult for me to imagine that we die, only to go to a place that allows us to remember our lives. Even if there is a heaven. Even if death is a sleep filled with dreams—only happy dreams—I would dream of Molly, and of you, and of my brother. Of Brendan. My job. My house. What I'd left behind.

Mark could say nothing.

His father said, Even if I was to die tonight, and be reunited with your mother and Brendan in a heaven, I would miss *you*. I would miss sitting here on the porch, talking with my boy. So I ask myself, if this is true, would heaven *be* heaven?

Mark closed his eyes.

His father said, The only happy death I can imagine is one that severs me entirely from this life. Annihilates me. I think any other would be too cruel. For me and for the living.

His father took a sip of tea.

That's what comforts me.

Mark reached over and put his hand on his father's shoulder. Sam lifted his own hand, set it over Mark's. Maybe his father was right, but even so Mark, had he been offered it right then, might have chosen to live forever in that moment, to have it serve as heaven.

Me too, he said.

❧

The pattern had grown out; it was too big now, with too many variables. Either there was an afterlife, or there wasn't; either ghosts were real or they weren't. Either Mark would keep an appointment with Chloe tomorrow, or with Allison. Either his son was suffering, or he was not. Either Brendan was a ghost, or he was not. Either he wanted Mark to come, or he did not. His son was trapped on this earth, or had long ago traveled to another, or he had been erased.

So many visions in front of him. A different man seemed required to believe in each one.

So which man was he?

Please believe me, Chloe had said—her voice the possibility of something like heaven.

Mark opened his phone; a picture of Allison was his screensaver. In the picture she was dressed up for Halloween, like Dorothy from *The Wizard of Oz*, wearing a simple ponytail and a blue gingham dress and red slippers. She held a stuffed dog in a basket.

Mark had gone as the Cowardly Lion.

Words rose from a far corner of himself in a playground voice: taunting, cracked with contempt:

You'll never figure it out. You know why?

Because you're a *pussy*.

A solution came to him then. Sudden and whole and thrilling:

He didn't have to wait until tomorrow. He could find out tonight. *Right now.*

The old house on Locust was, at the moment, empty. Chloe had said so, hadn't she? The Pelhams were staying with relatives tonight, and Chloe was at her parents' house. Mark—if he could stop being a fucking pussy long enough—could go to Victorian Village, and he could see for himself what was inside the house. And he could do it without Chloe beside him. Touching him. Influencing him.

He could find out what he really wanted. Who—or what—really wanted him.

Mark sat up on the couch, his heart pounding. He reminded himself he'd been drinking. He reminded himself that people who'd been drinking often had very unwise ideas.

He told himself that in the kinds of ghost stories he'd liked as a child, a man in his position—drunk, too reckless—would be almost certain to end up dead on the landing of the old house, his neck broken and his skull caved in, just like his son's. He would be doomed, then, to live in the dead gray house, to roam its halls, the companion of his mad little child. The living would become the dead. He knew what Lew had meant, in his warning.

But Mark had come up with a *plan*. After all these weeks, he could *do* something. And how hard would breaking into the house be? At worst it meant a broken pane of glass, and at best—

At best he would *understand*. The pattern had been pointing here—he saw this now—for much longer than he'd supposed, maybe ever since he had last stayed in the house, that long week alone.

He had to go to the house, and he had to go alone.

At the kitchen table, by the light of his open cell phone, he wrote Lew a quick note on the legal pad: *Couldn't sleep. Talk to you tomorrow. Don't worry, and thanks for everything, M.* Then, quietly, he pulled on his shoes, his coat.

He should call a cab, he knew—but he couldn't very well ask a taxi to drop him off at the house he wanted to break into. He'd be all right, driving, if he went slowly, if he kept off the main roads. His plan had focused him, made him move with a purpose.

He was nearly out the door when one last idea came to him. He went to the kitchen and, by the light of his phone, found the bottle of Maker's just inside the cabinet on top of Lew's refrigerator. The big side pocket of his coat was just spacious enough to hold it. Mark dug in his wallet and left a twenty on the countertop, and then, before he could stop himself, he slipped out the door and away.

IV

Visitation

Nineteen

Mark crossed into Victorian Village a little before midnight, his breath fogging the inside of the Volvo's windshield, its heater struggling against the chill. A few stray flakes of snow curved from the darkness across the cobbles to his headlights. He'd driven here slowly, taking side streets. He'd seen almost no one else out, except a solitary salt truck rumbling north on Olentangy River Road.

When he reached the old house he drove past it—act casual, he thought, and nearly laughed aloud—and then circled the block, stopping finally alongside the curb at the far side of the park to the south. He turned off the headlights, but kept the heater running.

The old house was a hulk behind its protective trees; only the squat curve of the turret extended into the streetlights' glow. Two lights shone out of the house's mass: A lamp had been left on in the living room; another burned upstairs, in Brendan's old room.

Chloe must have been here. She had stopped by the house before she left; she must have turned on a light there and forgotten it.

That was an easier explanation to accept than this one: That Brendan, somehow, knew Mark was coming; that he had turned on a welcoming light.

Mark dug the bottle of whiskey out of his coat pocket. Without taking his eyes from the lit window upstairs, he tipped the bottle to his lips and swallowed once, twice.

Then, eyes tearing, he crammed the bottle back into his pocket and got out of the car. He jogged across the park, the sparse snow pricking his cheeks, the bottle bumping against his hip. He passed by the front door, walked to the east end of the block, turned left onto Pennsylvania, and half a block later turned left again, into the alley that cut the block in half, east to west. It was darker back here; only one solitary security light shone from a pole at the alley's midpoint; only two porch lights shone over the wooden fences of neighboring yards. The shadows at ground level were impenetrable, dizzying. Entering them was like wading into dark, cold water.

Mark walked forward. A dog, close but unseen, growled. A trash can not far away stank warmly, almost visibly, in the gloom. He tripped once, his foot coming down in a pothole, but he waved his invisible arms and did not fall.

He moved in slow motion, thinking: What had Chloe done, here? Had she talked to Brendan? Had she said, Daddy's coming?

In minutes Mark stood at the rear of the house, beside the six-foot-high plank fence and gate. He and Lew had built the fence themselves, the summer and fall Chloe spent pregnant; a child meant they needed a contained yard, a place safe from the occasional stray dog or college student staggering down the alley. Homeless drunks.

He pressed down the lever; it didn't budge. But he hadn't supposed this would be easy, had he? He had not.

Mark looked both ways, confirmed he was alone, then grabbed hold of the top of the fence and—his feet scrabbling too loudly on the boards—heaved himself up and over into the dark yard. Luck was with him; instead of landing on a pile of tools or a jagged rock, he struck only frozen earth, pitching off his heels onto his side.

A security light flashed on above the porch. Mark crouched close to the base of the fence, then glanced up and around. He was only visible to one of the upstairs windows of what used to be Kurt

Upchurch's place next door. But that window remained dark, its curtains still. He waited several long minutes, but no hue and cry went up. He was still alone, invisible.

He allowed himself to look over his old backyard. It was different, now. What had used to be mostly grass was now sectioned off; half the yard was tilled, bare earth: flower beds, bordered by chunks of quartz, lined the fences—he'd jumped at just the right spot to avoid breaking his ribs on one. In the center either Margie or Connie had planted a small tree—he didn't know what kind, but its bare branches were already twice as high as Mark's head. The half of the yard closer to the house had become a patio. The grass there had been replaced by concrete and pavers, and a white wrought-iron table and chairs were in its center, frosted by thick ice. Beyond this was the smaller, raised wooden porch that led to the kitchen door.

These changes *hurt*. Of course this would not be the same house, of course others had lived here, too, and still did. Mark had been preparing for this. He and Chloe had long ago relinquished any claim. And yet the old house—the yard he knew, the house he knew—seemed a prisoner here, trapped behind the new trees, behind the very years that had grown them. Behind the decisions Mark had made. His neglect.

No. He had no time for this. If he'd injured himself in the fall he felt no pain—so he gathered himself and scuttled low across the yard to the foot of the porch steps. He sat on the bottom one and caught his breath. While he did so he considered how he might get inside the house. Break out the window beside the kitchen door? Force the door with his shoulder?

But would getting inside really have to be that hard? Connie had a young son; she raised him by herself. She was a worrier, overprotective. What if she worked late? What if something happened to her? Jacob had to have a way into the house. She'd give him a key. But little boys lost keys. Little boys were unreliable.

Wouldn't she keep a key hidden? And if she did, wouldn't it be here in back, where no passerby would ever see its location revealed?

The back gate had been locked. Maybe she'd hide a gate key in the alley, and another one here, for entry to the house. He checked the top of the door frame. No. Too obvious—and nine-year-old Jacob wouldn't be able to reach that high.

But the flowerpots set in a line along the porch railing? The one with a molded Pooh Bear on its side, and raised letters spelling HUNNY?

Mark tipped the flowerpot toward him; inside was only a small semicircle of ice. But in the damp circle beneath it? A folded-over Baggie, containing a key.

Not bad. Not bad at all.

Mark's fingers, thick with cold, fumbled the key out of the bag. Quickly he opened the screen door—it shrieked—and slid the key into the lock of the kitchen door.

And, because he was not afraid, because he had nothing to fear—because he wasn't a pussy—he turned the key; the bolt shot back. Mark pushed open the door, and then, for the first time in years, stepped inside the only house he'd ever owned.

Twenty

The air inside the kitchen was sweetly, thickly warm. Mark listened carefully, trying to still his breath, but the house was quiet, hushed. No alarms sounded; no one cried out, *Who's there?*

Except for the light leaking down the hallway from the living room, the kitchen was dark. Mark's hand, by old habit, felt to the side of the door for the light switch there. But he stopped himself from lifting the switch.

The house felt *odd*. More different, even, than the yard. He was afraid to see its new strangeness revealed.

Still the differences assailed him. Mark smelled, still—in gratitude and in grief—the house's familiar odors of old varnish, paint, plaster. But it was missing *their* smells—his and Chloe's and Brendan's.

When Chloe had cooked here the kitchen had smelled of tomatoes, of garlic, of coffee; they grilled most of the meat they ate outside. Now the air smelled slightly of grease—of cheap hamburgers, of food gone bad in the refrigerator. Meat left in the garbage.

The house smelled of different people, different lives, different skin and sweat. Connie and her son, and Margie before them, had erased from the air a decade of Fifes.

Or had they?

Mark's fear rose up in him again: the reminder of what he had come to do. What he might find.

I promise you it's true.

Brendan?

The hum of the old refrigerator. The clicking of the furnace in the basement. If he cocked his head right—if he let himself—he could almost detect a sense of movement in the walls, the house gathering itself: a drawing in of breath, as if to answer.

The furnace clicked, rumbled, roared into life. Warm air from the hall vent rushed past his neck, his hands, caused his scratched and warming hands to sting.

Mark took the bottle from his pocket, drank a swallow.

Throat still burning, heart still thumping, he walked down the hallway, past the doorway to the half bath and into the living room. Here a tall lamp shone in the corner, casting long shadows up the white walls. Mark stood beside the base of the stairs. The stairwell was narrow, steep; the landing was inky with shadow. It seemed—he was sure of this—to pull at him.

Not yet.

The living room—like the yard—was too different for him to ignore. The furniture was wrong, arranged at different angles; their old sprung couch, buried in multicolored throws, had been replaced by a low, gray cubist sofa. The walls, formerly light blue, were now stark, eggshell white; they held no pictures or artwork, and so caught the shadows and stretched them longer, higher. The glass-topped coffee table was empty of toys, of coffee mugs and old rings where they'd been careless; on top was only a stack of magazines in a bamboo tray.

In this room, where the light was on, he could only see the Pelhams' house, not the Fifes'. Here, Mark Fife was himself: a man who lived somewhere, some*when*, else; a man who was no longer Brendan's father, or Chloe's husband. In this room he was the man who loved Allison Daniel—which made him a liar and maybe a fraud.

Or was he? Once—in this very room—he'd taught Brendan about how vision worked. They'd sat on the couch, blinking one eye and then the other; Brendan had been awed by the way the picture of his grandparents on the wall shifted back and forth.

Maybe it was the whiskey, but Mark thought the house might be shifting this way, too; his heart shifted with it. If he concentrated he could see the old couch, the old stuffed chair, the bookcases, the braided rug, made of concentric ovals, where Brendan spent so much of his short life: playing his games in the center of a bull's-eye.

Old house, new house; husband, fiancé. At any time Connie Pelham's house could blink away, leaving Mark and Chloe's exposed. If that happened, he could step out of this life and into the old one, where Chloe and Brendan were both asleep, upstairs; where he was only coming home late. He could wake them, hold them. Promise them, I am here for you both.

He could say to Brendan, I'll never take my eyes off you again.

He walked, unsteadily, to the fireplace mantel. Across its top stood candles, a whole line of them at different heights, and several photographs in metal frames. Hanging on the wall above the mantel was a painting, a hazy Parisian street scene, anonymous and horrible.

The first of the photographs was of Connie. She wore a swimsuit and a wrap skirt, standing on a dock in front of some mountain lake. Beside her, holding on to her thigh with both arms, was a boy in swim trunks. Jacob. In this picture he couldn't have been older than five or six, but he had Connie's round face, her curled dark hair, a natural pudginess. He was smiling with such force that his eyes were squinted shut.

The next photo showed Connie and a younger Jacob, sitting on a couch, reading together from a picture book.

A third photo showed Jacob, probably close to his present age, pudgier than before, sitting on the front steps of this very house beside a man who was surely his father. The father had dense black hair, both on his head and on his forearms, and big square glasses. One of his hands was draped across Jacob's shoulder.

This was the boy who had seen Brendan. An awkward little boy who missed his father.

Mark's throat was dry, constricted. He walked back to the kitchen; at the sink he ran cold water over his dirty hands, then cupped them and drank several swallows. When he straightened the darkness swayed.

He couldn't leave. Couldn't pussy out. The boy was one thing. Chloe was another.

Chloe. The woman he'd married. With whom he'd made a child.

Before Brendan was born they used to have quickies here in the kitchen, Chloe braced against the same counter Mark now gripped with his hands. The angle was good for both of them. Everything had been good for them, before he'd pissed it away. Before *they* had.

I never stopped loving you, she'd said, and kissed his cheek.

Allison hadn't stopped loving him, either. Not yet.

Mark took another swig of whiskey. He was already here, inside. He'd already broken laws. If he turned around now he'd have proven nothing except that he was a coward: That he didn't want to face what Chloe was asking him to. That he didn't owe Allison his courage. That he still, after all these years, wasn't prepared to do what a father must.

We have a job to do; we're gonna do it.

He listened again, stilling his breath, and heard nothing—the house was empty, he was sure, of anyone else living. It was time. He walked slowly to the stairs.

⌒

The stairwell seemed to darken unnaturally as Mark entered it. His own breath echoed wetly back from the close walls, like the panting of an eager, pursuing bully. The steps groaned beneath his feet.

He stopped at the landing, that dark knot of air where the stairs turned back on themselves. This place. He sat on the bottom step of the upper flight. The landing, four feet to a side, was at almost the exact center of the house. The house's gullet, he'd always thought, or its heart.

He tried not to see. But here was Brendan in a tangle, sprawled across the space where Mark's feet were invisible in the shadows. One arm trapped beneath him, the other splayed out beside his face. His neck kinked to the side. His chin pressed to the landing. One blue eye staring out from beneath a wild tangle of hair.

The house seemed to contract, to tighten its throat.

Was this it? Was this how it had happened to Chloe?

"Brendan," he whispered. "I'm here now."

Mark knelt, pressed his hand down against the empty floorboards. He looked up at the steps, the yellow square of light at the top. He was sure—so sure—that a silhouette of a boy would step into it. But he saw nothing.

"I'm alone," he said, so shockingly disappointed he nearly began to weep.

He stood. He tried to tell himself: It's a hoax. A story.

But the house did not feel empty to him. It felt *sly*. As though someone was hiding, watching, as Mark muttered in the dark.

He tightened his fist around the railing. The stairs above him seemed to steepen.

"Are you here?"

No answer.

You come to your mother. But you'll call for me and then hide?

Because your mother's not with me? Because I'm marrying someone else?

Because you want selfish things?

"Selfish," he whispered, and then waited, his ears straining. He heard nothing but the house's restless shifting, his own sandy breaths.

He climbed, his heart a stone.

The stairs opened just to the right of the crook in the L-shaped hallway that divided the second floor. Directly in front of him—he faced the house's prow—was the wide, dark archway to the circular turret room: his old office. Enough light spilled down the hallway from the open doorway to Brendan's room that Mark could see inside. Connie Pelham, like him, had made it a workroom, but instead of a desk and computer, it was now mostly filled by a heavy wooden table topped by a sewing machine and haphazard piles of fabric: swath after swath of patterned silks.

Did her son stand sometimes in the doorway, watching her while she worked—like Brendan had sometimes watched him—deciding whether or not she could be bothered?

Did Brendan still watch?

The shadow-boy might stand in the hallway, bewildered by the strange woman in his father's office. Or, maybe, he couldn't see her at all. Maybe he only knew someone was in the room where Mark had used to be. Maybe, then, he called out *Daddy*.

Mark turned. The doors to the other upstairs rooms were all firmly shut. For a long moment he thought about opening the door to the master bedroom. But he couldn't—he couldn't bear to see it missing its big bed, the rocking chair in the corner, the long scratched bureaus. Even when he and Chloe were trying to live here, after, they had not used that room.

He stared down the hall at Brendan's doorway, the warm light stretching out from it across the floorboards.

Ghosts only want things to be like they were before.

"But they're not," Mark said.

Even though he knew he wouldn't see Brendan's room as it had been—his unmade bed jutting out from the wall beneath the Ghost-Killer switch; the low shelves to either side of the window, stacked full with books; the *National Geographic* maps of the moon and earth tacked to the walls they'd painted a rich, flecked gold—Mark was still surprised by the room as it was: harshly lit, the floor bereft of furniture but full of clutter: Boxes. Draped clothes. A long chest flush against the right wall, stacked high with more clothing and pairs of women's shoes. Everything cast deep, broadening shadows toward him, because of the lamp, its shade yellowed by age, that glowed on a wooden crate just beneath the window.

But no sign of Brendan.

Mark crossed the dusty floor and stood next to the window, beside the lamp. Here the boxes had been pushed aside. Right below the windowsill was a large cushion. On the floor in front of it was a stack of folded clothing and a neat pile of photographs. He saw right away what they were: These were the things Chloe used to concentrate on Brendan, to make him appear.

The room was chilly. The window was barely cracked open below the pulled shade. An ashtray sat on the sill. Chloe's? She hadn't smoked, apart from the occasional joint, since before he'd met her.

Chloe had come here after leaving him at the conservatory, and had sat on the cushion and smoked, thinking of Brendan. Of him.

If Mark had come here tomorrow, he knew, these things would have been put away. He was looking now at something private. Intimate. Chloe's most secret self.

He sat down beside the cushion, leaning against the wall. Icy air dripped down from the windowsill. He pulled the whiskey bottle from his pocket and set it beside him on the floorboards. He was here. This was what he'd come for.

Brendan had appeared to Chloe when she turned off the lights and concentrated. When she talked to him. He would do that, too.

But not yet. First he wanted to see what Chloe had brought.

The stacked clothing was Brendan's. He'd known she saved some, though he had not seen it since they had divvied up

Brendan's things. On top of the pile was a pale blue T-shirt—the color Chloe had most liked to dress him in. Beneath it were a pair of jeans and what Mark guessed was probably Brendan's old gray Buckeyes sweatshirt, the one he'd died in. Beside the stack was a pair of Brendan's sneakers.

He stroked the fabric of the T-shirt. Smelled his fingertips. He could detect no trace of his boy. He picked up one of the shoes: a Nike trainer, white with red and black detailing, its seams and wrinkles still traced with grime. These had not been the shoes Brendan had been wearing—the ones that might have killed him. Those they'd thrown away.

Mark lifted the shoe to his face. Its smell had faded, too. But there—an old tang. A wisp of little-boy stink. The hair on his forearms lifted.

He closed his eyes, held his breath. But nothing else happened. Nothing entered him. *Visited* him. Mark set the shoe down. His hand was trembling. Carefully he opened the bottle and drank a long swallow.

He willed his hand to pick up the stack of pictures. There were maybe twenty of them. He was sure he'd know them—they'd had multiples printed of nearly every photo of Brendan they'd ever taken, to send them to his grandparents, and Sam had returned many of them, once Chloe left, without Mark having to ask.

He flipped through the stack:

Brendan, a toddler, submerged to his waist in the kiddie pool at the water park in Clintonville. Beside him a kneeling, bikini'd Chloe, her hair dampened to the color of honey.

Brendan grinning, showing his few teeth, in the hall outside his kindergarten classroom, his good citizenship certificate held just beneath his chin.

One of his school portraits, from that same year—the photographer had told him to fold his hands in his lap and smile, but

Brendan had pressed his lips together, and turned up the corners like the Mona Lisa's. Mark had loved this photo; in his tan but-tondown shirt, his neatly combed and parted hair, Brendan looked serene, older and wiser than his six years.

Brendan a toddler at the zoo, leaning forward in Mark's grasp, across a curving red rail, toward the extended trunk of an elephant.

The next photos surprised him.

Chloe had brought along photographs of *him*. Of him and Bren-dan, of him and Brendan and Chloe—their whole family, together.

He wants both of us.

On top of the stack was a picture Mark hadn't seen in seven years, one nearly too painful to consider: he and Brendan nap-ping on the couch, side by side. Mark, bearded, wearing a white T-shirt, one arm flung up to expose the pale underside. His other arm cradled the toddler Brendan, who pressed his cheek to Mark's ribs, smiling in his sleep.

He and Brendan, sitting on the porch swing, reading a book Mark held between them.

And then, at the bottom of the pile, another surprise: a single photo of Mark, alone.

In it he was a college boy again, shockingly young and skinny, wearing a jacket and a white shirt and a narrow punkish tie. His hair was longer, grown out nearly to his shoulders. His glasses were owlishly round. A dark goatee covered his chin.

This had been taken during his last year of college. Chloe had convinced him to emcee a bachelor auction to benefit the elemen-tary ed program. Just before he took the stage Chloe had said, Turn around, handsome! and then had snapped the picture.

He put this photo on his left knee, and the one of him and Bren-dan sleeping on his right.

He saw, then, crumpled up beside the pillow, a pile of pale blue denim: a jacket of Chloe's, dating to college, that was as comfortable to her as a baby blanket. She'd worn it on their first date. She'd worn it the first time they went out to dinner after the divorce; it had broken his heart—this jacket, he'd thought, had remained closer to her than he had.

He picked it up. Pressed it to his face. Smelled her detergent, her soap, her sweat, a hint of her occasional perfume. Cigarette smoke.

He took a long drink from the bottle. Looked again at Chloe in her bikini, the dark wet drips of her hair crossing her cheeks, her bare shoulders, the swell of a breast.

But he hadn't come here because of Chloe. Not *just* because of her.

And not just because of Brendan. He'd come because he was *engaged*.

He pulled his cell phone from his pocket and called up—after two or three fumbling tries—all the pictures he kept saved on it. Allie's face glowed up at him. Dark-eyed Allie, in her spaghetti-strapped black dress, kissing Lew's cheek on New Year's Eve. Reading a book at the coffee shop, one hand lifting her hair from her neck. At the airport just before their spring vacation to Seattle, wearing her travel outfit—sweats and tennies, a pink ball cap—and sweetly smiling.

He was marrying her in September, and she was only a picture on his phone. If he died right now, she would be appalled and hurt to know that he'd been here, pictures of Chloe at his feet.

As he thought this, the house seemed to clench, to hover over her image, like a giant with its brow furrowed, having finally discovered a tiny, hated intruder.

He picked up the stack of photos again. Brendan, two, tearing open a Christmas present beneath the tree; Mark and Chloe sitting cross-legged on either side of him, smiling; Mark holding a pre-made bow above Brendan's head.

A professional portrait, in black and white: Mark and Chloe

lying down with infant Brendan, chubby and close-fisted, his face agonized and squalling between their own.

Mark had shown Brendan this picture, once. Brendan had been what? Five? Six? Brendan had picked up the photograph carefully, by the edges, staring down with pursed lips and a kind of suspicion.

That's you, Mark had told him. That's you as a baby.

Brendan reached out a hand to touch his own face.

I look so mad, he said, and giggled.

All babies get mad, Mark had said. But see how happy Mommy and me are?

Mark closed his eyes, but still saw the photograph. Smiling Mommy and Daddy.

Little bitty baby boy.

The house, close. Attentive.

Yes, he thought. Yes. Lew had been right. Chloe had been right. Brendan wanted what he'd known when he was alive: Mommy and Daddy. Mommy and Daddy who were always there for him; Mommy and Daddy who slept together every night in their big bed; Mommy and Daddy, sun and moon.

Chloe came here, day after day, with these pictures. She sat here and cried and told Brendan exactly what he wanted to hear—which was *Yes*. Of course Mommy and Daddy would help him. Both of them would. She told him she wished she could go back in time.

Of course he could have both of them, as they were, as they had been. Perfect, whole.

But they hadn't been perfect, he and Chloe. They hadn't loved each other perfectly. They hadn't loved Brendan perfectly.

Or else he would be alive.

⌒

Don't you know that?

You've had enough time. You should have figured it out, by now.

259

Mommy and Daddy have argued about it for years, and both of us were right. It was our fault.

It seemed like an accident. Your big backpack. Your untied shoe. Your sneaking.

But it wasn't. Not really. You were trying to run away, but that was only because, that morning, Mommy and I were worth leaving.

Because we didn't love you the right way. Because I wanted to drink and watch the television more than I wanted to teach you. Because your mother wanted to punish me with you.

But we loved you, little man. Oh we loved you. When you were gone we knew how much.

It nearly killed us, finding out.

Mark was crying, now. He drank more of the whiskey and lay down, his head nestled into Chloe's jacket. The room rocking, rocking, rocking. He reached for the lamp and pulled its cord.

Like a light, turned out.

"I'm sorry," he said.

Do you know that? It's true. I'm sorry and Mommy's sorry. We're so sorry, little man. You have no idea how sorry we are.

And oh he wished for another chance, then. He wished it with all his might. He would give anything. Yes. *Anything.* The thought went from his brain into his tingling fingers: He would trade, if he could. He would walk away from Allie and his new life, if only he could return, if he could walk through the front door of this house and into his old life again. If he could replace the Mark who sat at his chair in front of the basketball game, his second drink in his hand, his head empty of anything except his disappointments. He wished with all his might that he could stand up and walk to the base of the stairs; he wished he could walk up them and into Brendan's room; he wished he could kneel in front of his surprised and guilty little boy, his cheeks streaked with dried tears, his hands shoved deep into his backpack; he wished he could say I'm sorry, I'm so sorry. Yeah, we were mad at each other, but it doesn't matter. We get tired of each other but it doesn't matter. Life's not like we want it to be sometimes but it doesn't matter. It's so much better than being dead. Than being without each other. He'd take Brendan's face in his hands and look into his son's deep blue eyes, his eyes like the sea, and he'd say, I know this. I know it in ways you never will. I love you, I love you more than life, and you can never leave my side, I hope you know that, because if you do, if you die, then I will die too.

I know this, little man: Without each other we'll *all* be gone.

And if Mark could have said those things—he knew it—then downstairs, right then, they would hear Mommy coming home: opening the door, setting down her keys. Calling out their names. Searching for them.

Mommy's home, he would say.

Let's go tell her, too, he would say, and then he and Brendan would stand, the two of them, and they'd descend the stairs to her, Mark walking in front of his son all the way down.

⌐

I'm sorry, he was saying, he was thinking, *I'm sorry*.

The room was close, spinning.

And then something touched his hand.

⌐

Mark sat up. His breath came in pants. His hand still tingled; he clutched it with his other. Something had reached out of the darkness and touched him, feather-light and fleeting.

The word was too big to say, but he gasped it out:

"Brendan!"

His smell. His laugh. His syrupy chirp: *Daddy!*

A hole in him, opening up, like a crack splitting quickly across a sheet of arctic ice. His skin crawling with light.

Oh God oh God Brendan it's you, it's you—

His stomach and his head whirled around each other. The smell was still in his nostrils: Boy-sweat. Dirt. But a sweetness, too, that last lingering baby-smell that Mark used to inhale when Brendan fell asleep against his chest.

He reached out his hand, expecting to touch the cotton of Brendan's pajama top, but instead knocked it against the lamp shade. The lamp creaked, then toppled; the lightbulb shattered.

Across the room he heard a sound.

He stared, straining, into the dark. He heard only the wind and the subtle creaks of the house and—

And there—

By the door, a delicate thump, like a pile of clothing falling to the floor.

"Brendan?"

And then, clearly: footsteps. Quick, pattering, leaving the room, fleeing down the hallway. Footsteps, heading for the stairs.

"Brendan!" he called, and then he was lurching forward. He plowed into a stack of boxes; they fell; the crash turned into fireworks exploding before his eyes. He stumbled, scraped his hand on something sharp, and then he was in the doorway. He ran by memory to the top of the stairs, turned the corner, grabbed for the smooth railing. His balance was still off; he swayed forward, fell, had to catch at the railing with the inside of his elbow.

With his other hand he clawed at the air in front of him; he was sure, as sure as he'd ever been, that his fingers would catch on Brendan's backpack, that he could reel his son back to him. But he toppled, and only his grip on the rail kept him from falling all the way down.

Mark pulled himself upright. He was trembling, crying. His side was sore where it had jounced against the step. He had never felt before what was in him, now—an excitement as bright and sharp as lightning. *It was all true.* Everything he'd hoped and feared was true.

Mark had told him the truth, and Brendan had come to him. He had apologized, and Brendan had touched his hand.

Brendan was *here.*

He could only do, then, what Chloe had done. He pulled his cell phone out of his pocket and dialed her number. It was now two thirty in the morning; she was at her parents' house in Marysville. She'd probably have the phone turned off. If she didn't answer, he'd leave her a message; then he'd go outside and down the street to the laundromat where, those weeks ago, he'd called himself a cab, and he'd do so again. But he wished for her to answer. He wished it with all his might.

Chloe picked up. Her voice pure, kind, good, said his name.

"Honey," he said, his own voice breaking. "It's me."

V

The Ghost-Killer

Twenty-one

When Mark first woke, he did not know where he was.

Sunlight pierced his eyelids; soft cotton pressed against his cheek. A net of smells hung in the air: Food, thick and sweet. Coffee. And a softer smell, too, familiar. Feminine.

He was still in the old house. Sleeping on Chloe's denim jacket.

No. No he wasn't. He remembered: He had called Chloe, last night. She had come for him; she had found him in Brendan's old room. He remembered that. Then she had brought him here with her. He was in her apartment.

Mark tried to open his eyes, but the light was too bright; he groaned. What he saw of the room was a painful brown blur. Then he heard footsteps. He was caught in a loop: Footsteps approaching, footsteps, leaving. Fuzz and echo.

Brendan had visited him last night. He hadn't dreamed this. *He was real.*

Chloe's voice—close, tender—said, "Are you awake?"

Mark risked cracking his eyes again, shading them against the sun. Chloe was sitting in an easy chair beside the couch, bent forward, smiling at him.

"Your glasses are on the coffee table," she said.

He fumbled for them, fit them to his face. The room came into focus, as did Chloe. She was wearing jeans, a sweatshirt, thick white socks on her feet. Her smile—happy, sly—suggested he was, at the moment, comically unkempt. He tried to smile back, but his stomach bore down on itself.

"How do you feel?" she asked.

"Sick."

"You were pretty drunk when I found you."

"I'm sorry." He drew the quilt under which he'd slept around his shoulders. "What did I tell you last night?"

Chloe sat with her back straight as a schoolgirl's. "You weren't making a whole lot of sense. But . . . you said Brendan visited you?"

"He did. Just like you said." Again, he was struck by the fact of it: *It was true.* "Chloe. I'm sorry—"

"Don't be. God." Chloe was grinning. She reached out and pried one of his hands from the quilt. Her fingers were cold, strong.

"I'm sorry I didn't wait for you," he said. "I needed to go by myself."

She shook her head. "You broke in."

"Connie keeps a key under Winnie-the-Pooh."

Chloe's smile, now, was glorious: conspiratorial, proud. She squeezed his hand, then released it. "I can't believe you."

"I had to know." Feeling surged in him, and he said again, "I'm sorry, I'm—"

"Hush," she said, and pressed his hand. "Do you think you can drink some coffee? I've got a new pot on."

He nodded.

"Water and aspirin first," she said, with such humor and care they might have been sitting again on the edge of the bed in her college apartment, bedraggled and cold, debating who was going to have to fetch breakfast.

Chloe stood and walked through an archway to his left: the kitchen. He swung his legs off the couch. They were bare. And so—he saw, as the quilt fell away—was the rest of him. He glanced around in a panic before spotting his clothes in a neatly folded pile on the coffee table. Chloe had stripped him and washed his clothes. And, since he wasn't covered in his own filth, she might have washed his body, too.

Chloe returned with a plastic cup of water. He pulled the quilt across his lap.

She ducked her eyes. "You threw up on yourself. Out on the sidewalk."

How much did he have to apologize for? *Everything.* "I'm so sorry."

She waved a hand toward his body. "Old news."

His face warmed, but he drank some of the water. Then Chloe handed him two aspirin, and he swallowed them, locking his jaws. His head pounded and he sank into the cushions.

Chloe went back to the kitchen, and Mark now allowed himself his first good look around the apartment. Her living room was tiny, lit only by a window just behind his shoulders. The easy chair where Chloe had sat was in the corner, under a reading lamp. The couch faced a small television. An archway to the left of the television opened into a hallway. The ceilings were high and the floors were dark, glossy hardwood; the walls were all painted a creamy white.

She lived in such a small place. The townhouse was much, much nicer.

The same townhouse to which Allison was returning today.

Chloe returned bearing a coffee mug. "Careful," she said, and closed his fingers around it with her own, as though he were blind.

She sat down on the easy chair, knees pressed together. She smiled, but he could see she was exhausted. She would be: She'd driven an hour in the middle of the night to rescue him.

"It's true," he said.

Chloe pressed her lips together and nodded.

"It was like you said," he told her. "I felt him. Heard him."

She touched his arm. He was remembering as he spoke. Mark had been crying—apologizing—and Brendan had come to him, had filled him up like a lungful of warm air, and then—

And then Mark had stood, and Brendan had run. His footsteps had pattered down the stairs.

"Chloe," he said, but the rest of it—the beautiful, gorgeous mystery of it—could not be put to words. The world had changed; he could not see a single part of it as it had been. Brendan was real; Chloe was here, with him; for the first time in years they knew each other's hearts. He didn't have to pretend. Brendan had come back.

Chloe gave him her hand. He took it and clutched it to his chest and cried like a child.

⌒

After a while Chloe stood and walked down the hall; he heard her washing her face. She returned with a wad of tissues and pressed them into his hand.

He blew his nose, then asked her: "So what now?"

"You really mean it?" she asked. "You really want to do this?"

"Yes," he said.

"Let me make some calls," she said. Her voice was gentle, thick with her own tears, as warm as his hollow of the couch. "I have some errands to run, too. You rest here, and I'll get us some dinner—you'll need food in you soon." She straightened. "I mean, if you stay. For dinner."

"Dinner?"

She said, "Yeah. You were out awhile. It's four."

He sat up. "Jesus Christ."

"What's wrong?"

"Allie," he said.

Chloe said, "But you told me—you said last night that Allison's in Toledo—?"

Mark had no memory of saying any of this. "Last night she was. She's home now."

Chloe watched him carefully.

"I'll call her. We...I've still got to tell her about what's been happening." His head squeezed down on itself like a damp fist. "I haven't been very honest with her about all this."

"Oh," Chloe said. "Well, if...if you have to go home, I can drive you back to your car. Whenever you need to."

"Where's my phone?"

"In your coat." Chloe walked down the hall and opened a closet door, then returned and handed it to him.

He opened it. Seven messages: Three from Lewis, and four from Allie.

Chloe was watching him, as though he were a machine that had suddenly begun to clank and emit smoke. "I'll be okay," he told her, though he was sure this was a lie. "If you need to go."

Chloe said, "You can call me if you need me back. Or, I can stay. I—"

"Chloe. What happened, happened. I'll still help. Whatever it takes."

She seemed about to say something else, but stopped herself. She reached out and touched his cheek, her eyes pained and guilty, before walking down the hallway and putting on her coat.

⌒

Even after Chloe was gone, Mark couldn't bring himself to call Allie, just yet. The damage was done; he might as well experience the blow when he was fully alert. He picked up his clean clothing and found Chloe's bathroom; he winced at the bright slap of the fluorescent light against the black-and-white checkerboard tile.

The bathroom was small. Half its space was given over to an enormous claw-foot tub; Chloe's soaps and lotions were arrayed on a little tile window ledge above it. Her sink and mirror were both sparkling clean, though the sink was stained with spots of rust. He lifted the toilet lid and pissed out burning orange poison. Then he washed his hands, ran hot water through his hair, pressed it down to his skull.

Only then did he look at himself in the mirror. His skin was sallow, his eyes sunken like a plague victim's. His cheeks were stubbled, grimy; his eyes were bloodshot. He thought about borrowing one of Chloe's razors. When they were married, he would have.

But they weren't marred. He was engaged to Allison Daniel.

Maybe she'd already given up on him; maybe, right now, she was crying onto the shoulder of one of her friends. Or maybe she was driving to Lew's, to grill him about Mark's whereabouts. Maybe she was trying to find Chloe's address—or driving by this apartment, craning her neck to spot his car.

Allie, he'd say, *you don't understand. Everything's different now.*

Mark took a quick shower, then dressed, grateful for the clean clothing, amazed that Chloe was still using the same detergents and dryer sheets she'd used when they were married, by their familiar enveloping smell. He looked in the mirror again. How strange, that when his eyes were open he was Allie's fiancé—but when they were closed, he could imagine himself, once again, as Chloe's husband.

⌒

Back in the living room he called Lewis.

"Jesus!" Lew said immediately. "I've been waiting all goddamned day. Are you all right?"

"Hung over. But I'm okay."

"Where are you?"

"I'll tell you," Mark said, "but first you have to tell me if you've talked to Allie."

"No. She's left me a bunch of messages, but I figured I'd better talk to you first."

Thank you, thank you.

"I was with you," Mark said. "On the couch, all night."

"Fuck," Lew said. "You're at Chloe's, aren't you?"

"It's not what you think," Mark told him. "I went to the old house last night. And—Lew, it's all true. Brendan's there."

The words sounded amazing—thrilling—even now.

Lew waited a long time before saying, "You're sure?"

"I'm sure."

"What *happened*?"

"I'll tell you soon. It's—it's not like you guessed. This was a happy thing. It's okay."

"Mark—"

"I'm fine, I promise."

After a long while Lew said, "Okay, sure. But what are you going to tell Allison?"

"I don't know. But she can't know I was here. Nothing happened, but—"

"Mark."

"Just back me up on this, Lew. Please."

"One condition."

"Name it."

"You get your ass over here. Stay here with me. For real this time."

This request made sense, of course. Chloe's apartment was no place for him to be for long. "Sure," he said.

"Give me the address. I'll pick you up."

"Not yet. Soon. Chloe and I have things to talk over first."

"You can do that over the phone."

"I can barely stand," Mark said. "I'll call you as soon as she gets back."

Lew's silence, then, made Mark wonder whether he'd believed anything he'd said, after all.

It wasn't until they'd hung up that he realized: Whatever else they'd discussed, both of them had assumed he wouldn't be going home to Allison tonight.

⌒

The sun had nearly set. Mark turned on a lamp in the living room, and then another in the kitchen. The kitchen was small, but neat, with yellow-painted walls and white enamel appliances that must have been fifty years old. A window over the stove looked out at a snarl of branches. A door, painted a glossy red, opened upon a small wooden balcony barely big enough for a squat gas grill and a chaise longue blanketed in iced-over snow. Over the balcony rail he could see only rooftops, trees, and beyond them a rising hillside: a wave of brown leafless branches whose crest was lost to the dusk.

He had just finished setting a new pot of coffee to brew when his phone rang. Allison's name appeared on the screen.

The sky outside was dark enough that he felt like an astronaut in a tiny tumbling capsule. He swallowed hard and answered.

"So you're alive," Allie said.

"Just barely."

He waited, imagining the dozens of replies Allison might be considering. None of them was friendly.

Her voice was a pinprick. "Tell me where you are."

"I stayed at Lew's last night."

"Where are you *now*?"

"Allie." He stood and walked into the living room. "Something's happened."

She was quiet.

"I haven't been totally honest with you," he said. "And I'm sorry. But I guess I just have to say it. I've been to the old house. Brendan..." He stopped in front of a photo hung on the wall: Brendan as a fat, happy baby, sitting in his zigzag Charlie Brown shirt, showing his toothless mouth. "Connie Pelham was right. He's there, in the house."

Allison waited so long to reply that he wondered whether their call had been dropped. "Oh, Mark."

"I know it's hard to believe. But it's me, saying this. Please bel—"

"Are you with Chloe?"

Just below the picture of Brendan as a baby was one of him as a toddler at Sam's house. Brendan sat beside Sam at the picnic table on the back patio; Sam's fingers were draped across the crown of Brendan's head like the arms of a starfish, and Brendan was sticking out his tongue at the camera. At Mark, who'd taken the picture.

"She convinced me to go see," he said. "I went last night."

Allie didn't say anything.

"I have to help him," he said. "He's—Allie, what this means—"

"Okay. *Okay.* But why aren't you *home*?"

"I'll come home soon," he said. "But Chloe and I have to talk some more. We have to come up with a plan." He could only hear himself now as Allie must: crazed, lost. "Honey, I know we were supposed to talk, but—"

She was silent.

"I don't want to hurt you," he said. "But I have to take care of this. Right now."

Allie said, "I need you here. I told you that. And you're not here."

"Allie, I *felt* him—"

She sobbed, then, into the phone.

He would never forgive himself for this. He would not deserve to be forgiven.

"I'll come back soon. But right now—"

"You can't. I get it. Jesus, Mark. You have no idea how much trouble—"

"What?"

"Nothing." He could hear it in her voice: She'd given up on

him; she was done. "You don't need me, that's great. I'll go back to Darly's tomorrow and be out of your hair." She was crying harder, now. "Just don't fucking come home tonight."

Then she hung up.

⁓

Chloe returned half an hour later. "Sorry I took so long," she said, bustling down the hallway, bearing paper sacks. He stood in the doorway to the kitchen and watched her set groceries on the counter: chicken breasts, pasta, olive oil.

"You look better," she said, when she finally turned to him.

"I'm all right."

"I'm going to make us some pasta. Can you handle that?"

He told her he could. While Chloe set out a skillet and cutting boards and knives, he poured them both some of the coffee he'd brewed.

Chloe was scrubbing her hands at the sink. "Did you make your calls?" Her tone chatty, offhanded.

"I just got off the phone with Allison."

Chloe didn't look up. "And?"

"It was bad."

She dried her hands. Her eyes were soft, sad.

"I did what I did," he told her. "I'll live with the consequences."

She leaned against the counter, her hands folded in front of her. "I don't get to tell you anything about Allison," she said. "I wouldn't dare. But I do want to say I'm—I'm grateful. That you went and saw. I know it wasn't easy." She looked right into him. "I couldn't do this alone anymore. I just couldn't."

He wanted badly to put his arms around her. For weeks Chloe had known what he now knew. Could he have held on as long as she did? Could he have written her a letter as kind? What he'd put her through—

He could only begin to understand what she must have suffered. Allison, as much as he loved her, as much as he deserved her anger—well, Allie could not.

"Can I help with dinner?" he asked.

"No, just sit. It feels good to make dinner for someone other than me."

So he sat with his coffee at the kitchen table and watched Chloe cook for him, take care of him. Thank him, with every movement of her hands.

Mark thought about calling Lew back, but didn't. Chloe hadn't yet asked him where he was staying, tonight.

The kitchen filled with good smells. While she cooked, Chloe hummed: a song he ought to have known, but couldn't place. A happy little tune.

⟳

They ate on the couch, side by side. The food was wonderful; smelling it cook, his appetite had returned, and now he wolfed it down. Chloe turned on the news—as fastidious as she was, she loved to eat while staring at the talking heads. A silver-haired newscaster talked ominously about the upcoming elections—Hillary Clinton had won Nevada, but, shockingly, Obama was probably going to toast her in South Carolina. Meanwhile the real estate market was more of a disaster than before.

When the news was over Chloe took the empty plates into the kitchen. Then she came and sat back down, her feet tucked beneath her—and she still did this, too: She picked up one of the throw pillows and hugged it between her knees and chest and looked at him over the top of it.

She said, "So I called Trudy Weill when I was out."

It took him a moment to remember the name: Trudy Weill, the medium.

"She wants to meet you," Chloe said. "We can drive up and see her tomorrow, if we want. So I guess I need to know if—"

"I can do that," he said. Made himself say.

"She's up in Michigan. It'll take a few hours, each way."

"I'm in. Whatever Brendan needs."

She let out a breath. "Okay. I don't know what happens after that—we'll have to see what Trudy says. But I think we should both go over to the house as soon as we can. The Pelhams are back in it for the week. I think maybe it would be a good idea if we all sat down—you and me and Connie and Jacob. Cleared the air."

Agreeing to see the medium had been easier, but Mark nodded—because Connie had been telling him the truth, hadn't she? And he'd been awful to her. "So what do we tell them? That I broke in?"

"No." Chloe squeezed the pillow. "I just went over there and cleaned up a little. There wasn't any sign of you. A little spilled booze." She shrugged. "I'll tell them we went over together." He heard no judgment, and was—again—deeply, shudderingly grateful. "Maybe we can go tomorrow? After we get back?"

"Sure." By tomorrow night he could make himself be ready. Then he had to say it. "Chloe, about the booze—"

She waved him away.

"I'm not like that," he said. "I mean, I still drink a little. But I thought—one time before, when I was drunk, I thought I heard him. I figured maybe—"

"Stop." She was still staring at him. "Jesus, I'm on enough anti-depressants to sedate a bull. I take pills to help me sleep. What can *I* say?"

He nodded, close to tears again.

"It doesn't matter," she said. "It really doesn't."

He said, "I felt last night like he forgave me. Like that was what he wanted to tell me."

Chloe's eyes welled up. "I'm so glad."

"I don't know if I deserve it—"

"Stop that." She wiped at her eyes with the heel of her hand. "We've been over that, Mark." She took his hand, squeezed it. Looked right at him.

Don't, he thought.

"Chloe, thanks for doing all this—"

She untucked a foot and kicked softly at his knee. "Of course."

"—But I should really go."

Chloe's throat worked. "You're going home?"

"I'm not sure I'm welcome at home. Lew offered to put me up."

"Does he...?"

"Most of it. He's been a good friend."

She said, "You know you're welcome to take the couch again."

"I don't know if that's a good idea." He added, "Given how much trouble I'm in."

Chloe kept watching him. "Mark, I trust you. Us. And Lew's all the way across town."

An odd thing to say, wasn't it? And anyway, it wouldn't be *Chloe's* trust he was endangering.

But she was right—Lew's apartment was half an hour away. Chloe would have to drop him off at his car, parked by the old house. It would need scraping, and maybe even a jump; the Volvo didn't much like the deep cold. And Mark was still tired to his bones.

And this, too: Chloe knew what he had seen, what he had felt. He didn't want to have to explain any of this to Lewis. He didn't want Lew's questions. What he was sure would be Lew's doubt.

"Allie can never know," he said.

Chloe nodded solemnly, like a child sworn to a secret.

⌒

He retreated to the bathroom while Chloe put new bedding on the couch. He'd meant to brush his teeth with his finger, but on the sink he found a toothbrush, still in its box. He opened the medicine cabinet and found toothpaste. While he brushed his teeth he read the labels on the pill bottles arrayed above the toothpaste and swabs. Nexium. Ambien. Xanax. Heartburn, insomnia, anxiety: Chloe, these days, was a woman after his own heart.

When he left the bathroom, Chloe's bedroom door, just down the hall from the bathroom, was cracked open. He saw a jumble of clothing on the same low dresser they had once shared. A stack of books on her bedside table. The barest glimpse of the wide, white bed where she slept alone.

In the living room Chloe sat in her easy chair, her eyes turned toward the news.

"World still there?" he asked.

"Such as it is." She stood up. "I'd better crash."

"Goodnight," he said. "And thanks. Thanks for everything."

Chloe reached out to him and opened her arms. He'd told himself not to hug her goodnight, but now he went to her anyway. Chloe rubbed his shoulders. He slid his hand down her bare upper arm, to her elbow—thrilled at the touch of her bare skin, frightened at how close her bones were, now, to the surface.

"I'll see you in the morning. If you need anything—"

And then she touched *his* arm, right at the elbow, and ran her fingers down to his wrist. He thought for a moment she might take his hand, lead him away; if she did, he was sure he would follow.

But she withdrew her hand. "Goodnight, Mark," she said, then went alone to her too-big bed.

⌒

He lay down on the couch, pulled the covers to his chin, and closed his eyes. In the place of his earlier headache was a gentle giddiness. The empty space, after a twisted ankle. The absence of a very particular pain. He hadn't felt like this in a long while.

He reminded himself: He didn't deserve to. He didn't deserve any good feeling. He was doing what was necessary, yes, but he wasn't doing it as he should. Allison, after all, certainly wasn't happy, wherever she was. And he'd forgotten to call Lewis back; Lew had to be worried about him, too.

He reached for his phone and sent Lew a quick text: Am fine, I promise. Don't worry. Then he turned off the phone before Lew could text him back.

He wished he could send Allie some kind of promise that mattered. But he couldn't. She hadn't believed him, on the phone—not a word of what he'd said had touched her. He had much to answer for, yes, but she hadn't even tried to listen to him. Allie knew how skeptical he had been. No matter how much reason he'd given her to distrust him, she could at least have listened to him explain.

They'd learned something about each other, hadn't they? For all the love they shared, they'd handled their first crisis—and it was a doozy—as poorly as any couple could. Mark was at fault, but when he'd finally told her what was going on—when he'd given her the truth—Allison had been furious, had told him not to come home, had hung up the phone.

They *did* need to talk. Maybe they would make it through that talk as a couple. But—and he thought this with deep sadness—they probably wouldn't. Too much had happened. Brendan had come back. No aspect of Mark's life would ever be the same again.

He turned now to the memory of Brendan's room. He had been saving it. So much of what had happened last night was patchy, eroded—but when he opened himself, as he did now, he could still feel the core of it: the surge of understanding, of love, that had overtaken him when his son had come.

Brendan still loved him. Brendan still *needed* him.

Mark had turned away from him for too long. Not just after Brendan's death, but before it, too. But now Mark could help him. Brendan had forgiven him, and Mark would repay him for that, a hundredfold.

Brendan's presence. His love. His laughter. His very scent.

Mark shuddered, remembering. Tears ran down his face into the cushions of the couch.

No matter how much it hurt them both, Allie would have to understand the same truth that Mark had just learned so painfully: No other love in his life, no matter how much he'd wanted it, sought it, tended it—no matter what promises he'd made—could ever be as strong as this one.

Twenty-two

He woke to the sound of Chloe talking on the phone. Mark lay still, calm from the gentle emptiness that had just held him; the peace and safety; the pleasant fullness of his penis, erect from some half-remembered dream. Chloe's voice lilted, and he was so taken with its sound that it took him many minutes to realize she must be speaking to the medium, Trudy Weill.

Yes, Chloe told her, they were still coming, but they were getting a later start than they'd hoped. Would Trudy mind? No? Great!

Mark smelled coffee. Pancakes. He sat up, then stood, his legs aching and wobbly, and visited the bathroom. When he returned to the kitchen Chloe was off the phone, spooning batter into a pan. "Good morning," she said, smiling, and he almost went to her, to nuzzle her neck beneath her hair, to smell her sleepy warmth.

"You let me sleep in."

"You needed it." She handed him a plate of already-done pancakes. "So did I."

"Was that Trudy Weill?"

Chloe nodded.

"She didn't already know we were late?"

Chloe looked at him strangely, then barked out a laugh. "Eat your damned pancakes."

He sat and did so, his heart full. It had been a lot longer since he and Chloe had shared a joke—especially a dark one—than since they'd last made love.

He ate, then showered and dressed. Afterward it was Chloe's turn. He sat on the couch and watched the news and tried not to listen as, down the hall, the water hissed over and around Chloe's naked body.

⌇

Half an hour later Mark followed Chloe out through the front door into a cutting, windy morning. The sky was sealed by dark clouds; even so, he'd been inside so long he had to shade his eyes at the sight of this new world.

Chloe drove them out of Columbus, onto the highway and north, as she'd always driven: with the posture of an old woman, hunched forward, hands at ten and two. When they were on the interstate she told Mark to pick a CD. The binder she handed him was, he discovered, full of the music she'd loved in high school and college; he couldn't find anything he and Chloe hadn't once made enthusiastic love to. Finally he picked Tears for Fears's *Songs from the Big Chair*, which he hoped would be mournful enough to keep his mind in the right place.

Two songs in, the highway flowing past, he asked, "So what's Trudy like?"

Chloe considered this, frowning. "She's . . . odd."

"You mean apart from being a medium?"

"She's fine. Likable. Kind of . . . intense."

"How so?"

"Well . . . she's sort of religious." Chloe eyed him; he kept his face neutral.

"She's going to mention Jesus to you," Chloe said. "But I told her you're a—a nonbeliever. She said—I quote—'That's not an obstacle.'"

"So what did she say about *you*? Are you an obstacle?"

Chloe sighed. "I don't know what I am, anymore."

This, from the woman who'd told him, firmly, on one of their first dates: I was born Methodist, but have since undergone a Christectomy.

"I mean," Chloe said, "this changes things, right? Knowing what we know."

He remembered, queasily, his long conversation with Lewis. "Brendan being in the house isn't proof of anything but ghosts."

Chloe said, "No, but . . . it makes me wonder, you know? About how much Brendan knows, and what he can do. What it all *means*."

"Yeah," Mark said. "You go into that maze, it's a long time before you come out."

Chloe nodded—eagerly, he thought. "Trudy wants to talk about all that. She says she can see a little bit of the big picture. But . . . to her this is all God's plan. You should prepare for that."

Chloe glanced at him and—as she always used to—jerked the car to the right along with the movement of her eyes.

He said, "I just don't know what to think about . . . about all this."

Chloe patted his knee. "You're not an obstacle. Just remember that."

He leaned back into the seat. The countryside opened up, growing flatter, the clumps of trees more sparse. The sky thickened and puffed, and occasional gusts buffeted the car. He thought about Trudy Weill. Other questions came to him, too, but he didn't want to ask them—not while he and Chloe were so strangely comfortable:

What *did* it all mean?

What if Trudy couldn't help them?

What if she could?

He glanced at Chloe, bent forward, peering at the road.

What would happen to the two of them, once Brendan was gone?

⌒

In Toledo they stopped for a bathroom break. The sky was darkening, and traffic was sparse; the Starbucks they chose was nearly abandoned. Mark took his phone with him to the bathroom, and sat on the toilet checking his work email. He'd been neglecting his job for days. He fought back the urge not to care—or, worse, to send the same answer to everyone: My son's ghost is real! Instead he chose more measured language: I'm sorry, I've been unexpectedly sick, and I should have been in touch with you earlier. I'd appreciate a little more time with your project, but I understand if you can't wait for me, and in that case will be happy to recommend another designer, and issue a refund. Thanks for your patience.

It occurred to him that Chloe's school must be back in session by now. This was a Monday. Had she called in sick? Was she even still employed? If he lost a client or two, he could replace them with a little hustle. Chloe might be risking a lot more.

But what else could she do? Brendan needed their help, and Trudy Weill thought he needed it now. Chloe would do whatever she had to. He could see it in her face.

Of course, he'd been promising the same.

He hesitated before returning to the car. His euphoria from yesterday had faded, just a little. He knew—knew in his bones—that something had happened to him in the old house. But the sensations that had burst through him, that had sent him plunging like a madman down the stairs—all he had of them were memories barely more real than a dream. *Brendan had come to him*—he knew this today, but he didn't feel the surge of wonder that yesterday had left him giddy.

But it had happened. It had.

Can you hear me, all the way from here?

I'm coming. Mommy and I are coming to help.

He whispered the next words out loud: "I promise."

An hour later they crossed the Michigan state line. Chloe handed Mark a folded piece of paper with directions to Trudy Weill's place from the interstate. She lived a good thirty miles west of the highway, past the small city of Adrian, in gently rolling farm country.

Chloe asked Mark to play the Cocteau Twins: *Heaven or Las Vegas.* She sang along in her airy high-school-choir voice. Mark closed his eyes and listened to her, not quite awake, not quite asleep. She used to sing this way to calm Brendan, when he'd fussed in the backseat. It had always calmed him, too.

They passed through Adrian; ten minutes later, they were crawling down the main street of an even smaller town: a strip of storefronts that, apart from the cars parked in front of them, probably looked the same as they had in the fifties.

Chloe turned off the main drag, then stopped the car in front of a small one-story ranch, one of a long line of them, all the same model. Across the street from the houses was a line of young elms, planted at equal intervals, one facing each house. Beyond the trees was a vast field, chocolaty brown, streaked with snow and broken, canted cornstalks. At its far end new snow was falling, smudging out the horizon.

The house's siding was painted white, its shutters blue; the roof was slate gray. A young tree stood in the sloping front yard, emerging from a dark circle of earth. One of those absurd stone geese certain Midwesterners loved so much squatted beside the front door, wearing a maize-and-blue vest.

Chloe turned off the car. "Ready?"

"I'm ready," he said, reminding himself that he really was.

Trudy Weill opened the door as they mounted the steps. "Hello!" she called.

Mark was taken aback by the woman's height; Trudy was tall,

almost eye-to-eye with Mark, and bone-skinny. She wore a brown jumper over a T-shirt and too-big, flapping blue jeans; her bare arms were stretched, knobby. Her dull red hair was pulled back into a bun, and she wore heavy, squared tortoiseshell glasses. Her skin was densely freckled, except for a whitish streak on the left side: a massive scar, Mark realized, curling from beneath her eye, along the jut of her cheekbone and then up into her hair, where it made an unnatural part in the shape of a knife blade.

"Mark," she said. "Chloe. Welcome to you both."

Her voice was ruddy, warm, disconcertingly like Helen Etley's. She held her hand to him, and he shook it. Her grip was strong, but her fingers were slim and light. Her eyes—magnified behind her glasses—had warm green irises, and though the scar tissue beside her left eye was smooth, her right eye was surrounded by tiny wrinkles, the kind that implied a lot of laughter.

"Come on in," she said. "I've got a fire going that needs souls beside it."

Mark followed Chloe into a small living room. The furniture was overstuffed and beige; the carpet was a dark brown. The air was warm, and sweetly scented—too sweet, almost as though, hidden somewhere in the house, was a baby.

A small oval picture of Jesus—the white, well-groomed Jesus, gazing up into a warm glow—hung beside the mantel, right where it had hung in all the houses of Mark's childhood friends.

"Sit anywhere you'd like," Trudy said. "Juice? Coffee? Soda? I've only got Diet Coke."

Chloe asked her for a water, and Mark asked for more coffee. When Trudy had left the room, he glanced at the top of the mantel and saw many pictures, but only of adults—Trudy herself, and many family members in bad suits. The coffee table in front of the couch was bare; on an end table was a basket of potpourri and a white leatherette Bible.

A man materialized then from a hallway leading away from the living room. Chloe took Mark's hand; Mark was startled, too.

The man wore a crew cut and a fringe beard that, if it were longer, could have marked him as Amish. His face was tanned and deeply lined; his eyes were squints. His dark blue polo shirt was pulled nearly skintight across considerable muscle in his arms and chest.

"Hello there," he said. His voice was reedy, mild. "I'm Trudy's husband. Warren."

They introduced themselves; Warren's handshake was surprisingly delicate, his palms smooth. "Trudy told me about you both," he said. "I am so very sorry for your loss."

He touched Chloe's shoulder on the way past her to the kitchen—almost a professional touch. A deacon's, or an undertaker's.

Moments later Trudy came back; she carried drinks on a tray, and Warren followed, carrying a cookie tin.

"Mr. Mark," Trudy said, "I know you're nervous, but if you don't sit down, you'll get me in a tizzy, too."

Mark began to sit beside Chloe on the couch, but Trudy said, "Next to me, please"—the space on Chloe's other side, in the corner. He did so. Trudy sat down in a high-backed wooden chair at right angles to the couch and crossed her long spindle legs. She was wearing gleaming white Nike sneakers—this, of all things, made him want to laugh giddily.

Warren leaned against the wall beside the front door, his chin lowered to his chest.

"Thank you so much," Trudy said, "for driving all this way. Warren's got a bad back, and it's nice to stay at home if we can."

Chloe said, "It was good of you to make time for us."

"Well, dear, this is what I do."

Trudy smiled broadly at her, then at Mark.

"Chloe, dear," she said, without looking away from him, "I wonder if I could speak to Mark alone?"

Warren lifted his chin. "Ms. Ross, why don't you come on with me into the kitchen? We'll have a chat."

Warren held out his hand, and Chloe stood—reluctantly, Mark thought—and walked ahead of him, into the kitchen. He fought down a sudden irrational panic—that Chloe was being led away from him to be killed.

Trudy said, "Please be at ease, Mark. We don't bite."

"I apologize. This is all...new to me."

"So I gather," Trudy said. "None of this could have been easy for you."

Mark was taken aback, again, by Trudy's gentle, lined face, by her easy tone. These people wanted to help them; Chloe trusted them. "Now that I've had...an experience, it's easier. But getting to this point—"

"I can only imagine." Trudy leaned forward and tapped his knee. "Chloe has told me a great deal about you, you know."

Mark was intensely curious as to what, exactly, Trudy had been told. She reached out and covered his hand with her weightless fingers. "Don't worry," she said. "Only good things."

The skin on his arms prickled. "I sincerely doubt that."

Trudy patted his hand. "Has Chloe been frustrated with you? Yes. But this way is not so easy for some of us. Our world is not receptive to the sort of news you and Chloe have received. Many of us—people like you—have never been prepared to hear it. That isn't your fault."

Only a month before, hearing something like this, he might have risen to his feet, left the house insulted and furious. But he found himself nodding.

He *trusted* her. He had been bracing himself for someone more obviously odd, or who presented as a con artist. Not whatever, who-ever, Trudy was.

"Now, don't think of me as a flirt, Mark, but I'd like to hold your hand for a moment. It won't take long."

He nodded, extended his hand. Trudy cupped his hand between her dry palms, and bent her head over it. The scar on her face shone in the firelight. She moved her lips, and then her face hung slack—just for a moment—before she straightened and released him.

"I can help you," she said. "You're ready to be helped."

Just like that? "Can I ask—what did you—?"

Trudy plucked a tissue from a square box on the end table between them and wiped at her eyes—she was crying.

"Your Brendan has asked for you," she said. "You are a neces-sary part of what must be done for him. But you are an unbeliever by nature. It might be possible for you to talk yourself into taking part even if you were not ready to. I had to look inside you and make sure."

Was this real? What could she have found in him that both reassured her, and had put tears in her eyes?

"You're thinking about your doubts," Trudy said, and sniffled. She smiled at his alarm. "No mystery, there—I saw it on your face. Faces are easy to read. Hearts are harder."

"You're crying," he said.

Trudy's smile vanished. When she did not smile her face was deeply, heartbreakingly plain, and ten years older. "Hearts are full of pain. Every one of them. But especially yours, Mark Fife."

To this he had no reply at all.

"You have questions, now," Trudy said. "I do wish you'd ask them. Be at ease. I assure you it's been a long time since a human being found a way to offend me."

"I don't know what to ask."

"Mr. Mark, don't lie to me."

She was right. He had a hundred questions. Five hundred. All right, then. "Why did you have Chloe go into the kitchen?"

Trudy gazed at him for a beat longer than he liked.

"I met with Chloe for over an hour last week," she said. "We spoke of Brendan, and we spoke of you. By the time we were done, I was a little bit in love. And why not? Chloe Ross is a remarkable and charismatic woman. I wish she and I could be friends. I wished—and still wish, with all my heart—that I could mend the hurt in hers." Trudy blinked; to Mark, caught by her gaze, this carried as much force as the touch of her fingers on his hand. "I can imagine how difficult it might be for you—who were married to her, who fathered a child with her—to say no to her.

"It doesn't matter that you're divorced. You two are *bound*."

She took his hand, kneaded it. His heart thumped guiltily.

"To know your true will, I had to see you alone."

He was alarmed by her frankness. "How do I know you're not conning us?"

She grinned, leaned forward. "You don't. I'm not able to"—she looped her hands in front of her face in a magician's flourish—"do any kind of hocus-pocus. I can put you in touch with people who will vouch for me. But the proof is going to be in the so-called pudding."

"How much do you charge?"

"Charge?" She lifted her eyebrows. "I ask that folks I assist make a donation to my church. I don't ask for a specific amount— whatever someone thinks my help is worth, it is worth. You can speak with Warren about that, if you'd like, or Chloe—she's already made a donation. May I ask you a question?" She smiled wider. "Make that *two* questions."

Chloe had already paid? "Yeah. Sure."

"One. If I were a con artist, don't you think I'd live in a nicer house?"

She'd begun to laugh even before she reached the end of her question. "You don't have to answer that. But do answer this one. Chloe said you're—an atheist?"

Mark straightened. "Yes. I always have been. Chloe—Chloe said that wouldn't be a problem for you."

"It won't affect what we do. You only need to be convinced of the truth of Brendan." She straightened, too. "But I *do* believe in God. I believe in the sacrifices of His Son, and that Son's teachings. I spend hours a day at my church. It is my entire life." Her smile turned wry. "I'll be honest with you, Mark. My church is not very big. Not many so-called Christians accept me, and what I do. So you might say I am a Christian who has had to learn the value of *adaptation*.

"I don't believe, for instance, that a man like you is bound for hell. I believe that anybody who lives a life of care and sacrifice is doing God's work. I do believe I am in possession of good news, for anybody—even a man like you—but in the end I am most concerned with good *acts*. Mine most of all.

"I believe I have a gift, Mark. I mean that word: *gift*. And I would be a terrible Christian if I auctioned off any gift of God's for profit."

She seemed to be waiting for him to ask her more questions. But a single word she'd said had caught at him. Thinking of Allison, he said, "But I haven't sacrificed. That's not how—"

"You *haven't*?"

He fell silent.

Trudy locked her fingers around his hand. "God took your *son* from you, Mark. He took that beautiful woman in the kitchen from you. I have looked into both your hearts—I assure you, the loss of your family, the love that created it, is a sacrifice beyond price."

She whispered this: "And you've given up far more than just your Chloe and your Brendan. To be here, with me? To have gone to the house, and opened yourself? You've sacrificed your *beliefs*, too. Your very way of life." She stared into his eyes. "And the woman Chloe told me about—"

He whispered: "Allison."

"Allison. Allison who is somewhere else, while you're here. Allison who is probably terrified that you are with Chloe today." Trudy did not blink. "Am I wrong?"

"No."

"You have sacrificed, Mark. So, so much. I am praying, and praying hard, that by the time we are done, God gives you a little peace. I have to allow God His mystery...but even I believe you have suffered more than you deserve. I believe—but I am not blind to it, Mark. The cruelty of my God in heaven."

She released his hands, and sat back. He was dizzy.

"How do you know?" he asked. "Any of this?"

Trudy wiped again at her eyes. Fixed her gaze upon him again. "You might have noticed my scar."

"I—"

"Shush. Of course you have. Everyone does. The scar is how I know.

"When I was a little girl my father repaired farm equipment, not ten miles from here," she said. "He worked out of a garage behind our house. The summer I was five, I sneaked in and watched my father and my older brothers at work. They were raising up a truck on a hydraulic lift, and the lift failed. The truck crashed down, right on top of my brother Jack, who was sixteen. And when it landed, one of the tires blew out, and a big piece of rubber flew across the room and struck me in the face—it knocked me back against the wall and fractured my skull. I was in a coma for three days."

"I'm sorry," he said.

Trudy was smiling. "Why would you be? God acted, not you. There's no fault." She said, "While I was in the coma, a strange thing happened to me. I traveled freely, back and forth between this world and the next. I spent most of my time playing with Jack, in a wide meadow under a clear blue sky. We were both very happy, and time...time rushed past, and yet did not move at all.

"But then, all of a sudden, my brother didn't want to play. He sat down and took my hands and told me—I remember this very clearly—that it was not my time. I was needed back in this world. And he told me I would return bearing a gift."

Trudy's voice, for the first time, began to shake. "He was my great big brother, and handsome, and I loved him. And I was afraid to leave that meadow. Desperately afraid. I begged Jack to let me stay. But he said, 'Trudy, you have to go back. You have a life to live, yet. You have to tell Dad not to feel bad. That I'm all right.' He told me, 'It won't be easy. You're being sent into a world of pain and trouble. Be strong.' Then he kissed me, right where my scar is, and waved goodbye."

"I woke up, right away, and the pain in my head made me scream. It was more than I could bear. For weeks all I could do was beg the doctors to let me go back to my brother. But of course they didn't understand. They didn't listen; they kept fixing me up. Even so, as soon as I could, I gave my father the message from Jack. And once I had delivered it, I felt a glorious peace."

She pulled the tissue from her pocket and dabbed at her eyes.

"After that I realized that, sometimes, I could hear voices. If I listened very carefully, I could make out their words. It was a long time before I could understand, but now I do. The voices I hear have always been messages. Sometimes they come from inside of living people. Sometimes they belong to those who have crossed over."

Trudy smiled; her eyes were red. Mark's own body seemed to have vanished.

"How is it possible?" he asked. Then: "Why does this happen? Why is Brendan *here*?"

"We keep the dead close," she said. "I've learned this all too well. The bonds between parents and children, especially, are strong, and sometimes death does not sever them.

"I've seen it happen, but I won't know the exact reason why until I try to reach him. Maybe Brendan's death came so quickly that he did not realize he was gone, and he came to look for you. Maybe he got halfway down the tunnel and then turned back. Now the two of you—calling to him from different places—confuse him. His home is no longer his home. The people who live in it are no longer his family."

Mark rasped, "Is he...afraid?"

Trudy squeezed his hands. "This is very, very important for you to understand, Mark. Brendan is not flesh anymore. He is not alive. He is spirit—and the rules we follow, stripped of the needs of our bodies, are different. Brendan is now memory, emotion and dream. He does not know cold or hot or pain. He does not know time, not like we know it.

"Think of it this way: He is asleep, most of the time. But he is a fitful sleeper, and sometimes he wakes, and then—then, yes, he is troubled. He is tempted by peace. By the great rest that awaits him. By voices like that of your mother's—familiar to him, yet unknown—that call to him from the next life."

Mark's eyes filled with tears.

"But Brendan is aware of you, too. You two, his parents, who created his spirit, call out to him, and so he calls to you, too." Trudy's hands seemed hotter. "This is the trouble. He is dreaming, missing you. You are alive, dreaming, missing him. Your dreams call to him, wake him, and then he is calling you in yours, waking you. Each of you picks up the phone the moment the other hangs up."

Only the dry palms of her hands, their warmth, convinced him she was, herself, flesh.

"Can you help him?" he asked. "What do we do?"

Her voice lower, calmer, she explained: Had he seen a séance on television, in the movies?

He had.

The ceremony she would perform would be similar. He and Chloe, as well as Connie and Jacob, would all join her and Warren at the house on Locust—

"Even the boy?" Mark asked, alarmed.

"Jacob Pelham is a focus of Brendan's attention. Brendan trusts him, comes to him. Jacob must help us. I've spoken to his mother—he will."

Then, Trudy told him, with the help of concentration and prayer, everyone gathered would try to summon Brendan from his hiding place. To awaken him. She told him that Brendan might speak, then. Or, more likely, he would speak *through* her, with her voice.

This, she said, was sometimes difficult for a parent to hear. "But it will be him," she said. "You can address me, and Brendan will hear your voice, even if he answers in mine."

"And then what?"

"Then we will tell him what he needs to hear. We will guide him to his rest."

She turned her head toward the hallway that led to the kitchen. Both of them, over the crackling of the fire, heard Chloe's voice.

Trudy whispered, "Mark. There is another reason I had to speak with you alone.

"Parents and children are tightly bound. But they are tied to their fathers and mothers with different cord. Mothers carry children, bear them into the world, know them from the inside out. This is why it is easier for Chloe to feel Brendan. Chloe has likely known the truth—known it in her belly—all along. She always will." She squeezed his forearm. "This means you and Chloe have very different tasks ahead of you.

"I can guess why Brendan has been calling for *you*. Chloe told me: You used to make things right—you put him to bed, you scared away the monsters. You were the one who punished him, and who forgave him."

Mark's vision closed to a pinhole.

"He can see the open doorway, Mark. He can hear the voices on the other side. But he is afraid of it.

"Deep inside, Brendan calls for you because he knows you will tell him what to do. Because the part of him—like the part in all of us—that is wise and ancient, that is full of the voice and the memory of God—knows *this is what fathers do*.

"Mothers tell a child how to be born, and to grow. But fathers are closer to death. Fathers show us how to fight. How to die.

"Mark," Trudy whispered, "Chloe has been very brave until now. But the ceremony will be awful for her. She only thinks of the good she will do—and why wouldn't she? She has held her baby again, loved him again. She is a mother again.

"She might forget that our ritual will send Brendan away from her, into the next world, for good. I have my doubts whether Chloe is strong enough to do this. So *you* must be."

He wanted to pull his hands free of Trudy's and run out the door. "I don't—"

Trudy was rocking back and forth, now, as though listening to slow, soft music: a lullaby. "You can. This is not a betrayal, Mark. It is the way of things, and that is all."

Her voice now dropped so low that he wondered whether her lips were really moving.

She said, This is what you'll do.

You'll tell Brendan nothing is wrong. You'll tell him not to be afraid. That you and Chloe are all right; that you love him and each other. That someday, before he knows it, you will be with him.

He will know, then, where to go. We all know the way on, deep down.

She said, And in the next life we are all reunited—not only with one another, but with God. With time. Past and present do not matter there. There we are all safe.

Trudy smiled, pressed his hands.

On and on, she said, Forever safe. Isn't that a comfort?

Twenty-three

Trudy stood, then, and went to the kitchen, leaving Mark shrunken into the corner of the couch. Chloe emerged from the kitchen only seconds later; she saw the look on his face and immediately sat close beside him. He lifted his arm, pulled her close without thinking; Chloe's cool fingers slid around his own.

Before he could tell her anything, Trudy and Warren returned; Trudy sat where she had, and Warren leaned beside the fireplace.

Trudy asked, "So I understand you're going to sit down with the Pelhams, Chloe?"

"Yes," Chloe said. "Tonight."

"Mr. Mark," Trudy said—she was now all stagy smiles again— "I also understand you've had some...difficulty...with Ms. Pelham?"

He nodded.

"Then I have an assignment for you, an important one. You're going to have to apologize to her."

"I—"

"You threatened to have her arrested, didn't you? In front of her child?"

He couldn't deny it.

Trudy told him, "The circle through which we contact Brendan must be one of positive energy. One utterly free of strife. I've talked to Connie; she is a good soul. So clear the air. *Capiche?*"

Capiche? "Sure."

To Chloe she said, "Don't take Mark to meet her at the house. We must make sure all is clean and pure when we enter Brendan's space again. We can't risk any discomfort, before."

"I—Okay," Chloe said, unable to keep the disappointment from her face. "We'll go get pizza or something."

Trudy smiled. "Jacob will like that." Then, to Mark, she said, "The boy will likely be terrified of you. Be his friend. We will ask much of him, these next few days."

He nodded.

"Trudy," Chloe began, her face troubled.

Trudy held up a hand, looking first Mark, and then especially Chloe, right in the eye. "Avoid the house until the ceremony. This is how it must be. Brendan may only reach us through a struggle. Withhold yourselves from him, just for a while, and he will come more readily when our circle is assembled." Trudy walked to Chloe and embraced her—more intimately than Mark would have guessed Chloe would tolerate from anyone but a lover—wrapping her long spindle-arms around Chloe's chest, pressing her palms against Chloe's head from behind, and squeezing their cheeks together. "Remember. He does not suffer as you think. I promise you, Chloe. I promise."

Chloe's eyes flickered, almost panicked, to Mark's. Then a sob convulsed her, and she went limp in Trudy's arms.

"It's all right," Trudy said. "All will be well. Your son is loved. *Your son is loved.*"

Mark wanted to pry Chloe from Trudy's arms. To hold her himself. To be held, to sob as she sobbed.

Warren cleared his throat. "The boy's death anniversary is on the twenty-third, yes?" That phrase, in Warren's mouth, seemed horrifyingly uncouth, but Mark nodded assent.

And that was that. On the twenty-third—two days from now—

the Weills would drive down to the Locust house for the ceremony. Trudy gave them instructions: Mark and Chloe were each to bring with them a memento of Brendan—something that brought him easily, powerfully to mind. Each of them was to think of a happy memory, one that moved them to feelings of great love, upon which they could meditate when the ritual was under way. Apart from making peace with the Pelhams, this was all that was required of them.

Then they were standing, and both Trudy and Warren embraced first Mark, then Chloe—but before she released him, Trudy whispered in his ear, "Remember, now," and when she embraced Chloe she whispered into Chloe's ear, too.

Whatever she'd said, Chloe seemed awed, at once happy and sad beyond words.

⁓

Ahead of them was a three-hour drive back home, but Mark and Chloe barely spoke until they were back on the two-lane state road, ten miles from Trudy's house. The snow was swirling all around them. Every few moments Chloe sniffled.

Finally she asked: "So what did Trudy say to you?"

He'd been wondering how to describe his experience. Haltingly, he gave Chloe as full an account as he could, leaving out only his own special instructions—Trudy's worries about Chloe, now his.

Chloe seemed satisfied by what he told her. Much of it, she said, was similar to what she and Trudy had talked about during her previous visit. Mark wondered whether Trudy had given Chloe special instructions about him, too.

Chloe was telling him how strange she'd found Warren. "He says he's actually the minister of their church. Which makes sense, I guess. He handles the preaching and Trudy handles the spirits themselves."

Something had been nagging at Mark since they'd left Trudy's house: a question he should have asked, but didn't. "What do we do if the ritual doesn't work? Did you ask her?"

Chloe gripped the wheel. "Trudy told me it might take one session, or it might take many. It depends."

"But if not on the anniversary—"

Chloe glanced quickly sideways; the car jerked. "She said we wait for another big day. His birthday, or—"

"That's almost a year from now."

"She said we just have to be careful. If we do everything the right way, we should be fine. But she said none of this is certain."

"God's will?"

"Mark . . . you *do* believe her?"

When Trudy had spoken to him, all he *could* do was believe her. But now that the visit was behind them, Trudy's words were clattering against the insides of his skull.

"She said you made—a donation? To her church?"

Chloe nodded—warily, he thought. "Yeah."

"How much?"

"It doesn't matter." She stopped at a light and flicked the wipers; they scratched across a sheening of ice. "I took care of it. And I'm taking care of the Weills' motel room, too."

Chloe had misunderstood his question, but now guilt flooded through him. "Let me pay half. It's the least I can do."

"This isn't a competition. I've got the money. And—"

"And what?"

Her voice was barely audible. "You're planning a wedding."

⌒

They stopped for a late lunch at a Wendy's near Toledo. Mark stood in the vestibule to check his messages while Chloe ordered. Lewis had tried to call him. Allison hadn't.

He called her before he could talk himself out of it; he was sent immediately to voicemail. Allie had said she was headed back to

Darlene's sometime today, not fifteen miles from where he stood; he wondered if one of the cars he could see crawling along the interstate was hers.

"Allie," he said, "I know you don't want to talk to me. But I just wanted to say I'm thinking of you. I don't even know if you care, but—" He was botching it. "Look. This isn't anything I ever wanted. I do love you. I do. I'm sorry I've been so terrible, but I couldn't know—"

His voice had flattened. He pulled the phone away from his ear and saw it had gone dead. He counted back; he hadn't charged it in three days—since before he'd gone to meet Chloe at the conservatory. The charger was still on his desk in the townhouse.

He was relieved. He hadn't known what to say to Allison, and now he couldn't say anything at all.

He joined Chloe at their table, let himself be lifted by her gentle smile. He remembered, when they'd first begun dating, how he'd been astonished, over and over, to find her smiling whenever she caught sight of him, even if all he'd done was go to the next aisle in the record store and return to her.

"I called Connie," she told him. "We're meeting her for dinner tonight. If that's all right."

It had to be, didn't it? Mark had his orders. He certainly owed Connie an apology, but that didn't mean he wanted to go to dinner with her. He wanted—

He wanted to go home with Chloe. To spend the evening in her apartment. His phone was dead; no one could reach him. He and Chloe could be truly alone.

"You okay?" Chloe asked.

She had a tiny shred of lettuce clinging to her lip. He reached over and plucked it away; she blushed.

"I'm fine," he said.

Because of the snow, they arrived at Chloe's apartment late. Right away she began to ready herself for dinner. Mark lay back on the couch, rubbery with exhaustion.

Both of them had retreated into their thoughts for the remainder of their drive home. Mark couldn't stop himself from returning to what Trudy had said—all of it so strange, so new. He found himself puzzling more and more over the reunion—with Brendan, with his mother—that Trudy had claimed awaited them. He thought of his father, and their long-ago talk on the front porch, and the vision of death Sam had described to him: a sleep without dreams. An annihilation.

Mark had shared this vision with his father for years. Trudy Weill had—smiling, teary-eyed—told him to abandon it.

If Trudy was right, his mother and Brendan could, finally, know each other; his mother could take care of Brendan, love him as Mark knew she would.

Let it be true. Please let it be true.

Because if it were true, then Mark would see them both, again. And his father. And Chloe, soon enough. They could all be reunited as something other than memories.

Trudy was right; this *was* a comfort—imagining it, now, he could barely stand the rest of his life, the heavy burden of his own body.

He lost himself in this vision for a while, until Chloe's phone buzzed forlornly on the kitchen table. He started guiltily, and that was when he realized he'd made no room, in his heaven, for Allison.

⌒

The pizza place Chloe and Connie had agreed upon, Pagliacci's, was across town in Clintonville, a low brown rectangle of a building with shuttered windows and a red neon clown grinning over the doorway. He had not objected when Chloe told him where they were going, even though he'd always disliked the place. Pagliacci's was aimed at children—Brendan had celebrated a couple of his birthdays there—and they were going to be talking about a séance with a little boy; they had damned well better entertain him beforehand.

The hostess led them past wide windows into a kitchen where chefs wearing suspenders and puffballed clown hats, dots of rouge on their cheeks, tossed and spun disks of dough high above their heads. Even on a Monday night in a snowstorm, the place was noisy with the shrills of children: a honed trebly blade.

Connie was sitting with Jacob at a corner booth. When she spotted them, Connie slid out from behind the table and stood. For one fearful moment her eyes found Mark's; then she met Chloe in a fierce embrace. Connie's hair had been straightened, was now molded into stiff feathers around her circular face. She wore a sensible black suit over a cream-colored blouse. When she released Chloe she looked back to Mark, her mouth tightening.

Jacob Pelham remained behind the table, a small, frowning, dark-haired shape, his glasses reflecting the dancing candlelight. Mark had a hard time matching him to the picture of the wet, happy little seal he'd seen in the pictures on the mantel.

"Connie." He held out his hand. "It's good to see you."

"Hi, Mark," she said. "I'm—I'm glad to see you, too."

He might as well get the worst over with. He lowered his voice, though he was sure Jacob wouldn't hear him over the din, and put his hand on her padded shoulder. "Listen—I feel really bad about how I've been with you. Obviously I didn't know better. I'm sorry—"

"No!" she said. "Oh, Mark, don't. I'd have been just as upset. I did it all wrong—"

Even this reaction made him a little angry: She *wouldn't* have been just as upset. But he pushed this down. "I'm sorry, regardless."

She put a hand to her chest, let out a fluttery laugh, then turned to the table. "Jakey! Stand up and say hello to Mr. Fife."

Jacob came to stand beside his mother, his shoulder against her hip. The candle-reflections in his lenses blinked and darted.

"Mark," Connie said, "this is my son, Jacob."

Jacob's face was round—naturally plump, like Connie's—and his skin had the same glossy, olive tone. Genetics hadn't done Jacob any favors. He had a weak chin; his eyes, behind his glasses, were close-set and a little squinty. His bowl-cut hair was lank with oil. He wore faded blue jeans and a brown sweater that clung to his thin upper arms and the small bulge of his stomach—he looked, Mark thought, like a half-inflated balloon.

He reminded himself that this boy had spent nearly a month of his life confronting a ghost in his bedroom, and made himself smile and hold out his hand. "Do you go by Jacob or Jake?"

"Jake," the boy said. His voice was high-pitched and a little raspy. His palm was hot and damp.

Connie said, in a chipper singsong: "Well! Let's all sit down and have some pizza!"

Mark slid into the booth beside Jacob. The boy would not meet Mark's eyes, and for a quick, uncharitable moment, Mark remembered the picture of him on the mantel with his absent father. He wondered if Trudy Weill had held Jacob Pelham's hands, too. What she had found deep in Jacob's heart.

The waitress came; Connie ended up ordering for all of them. When she had gone, Chloe began to describe their trip to see Trudy. Connie nodded and exclaimed and pressed her hands to her breastbone in a way that, Mark was sure, would never fail to annoy him.

Chloe and Connie, Mark came to realize, weren't simply speaking out of convenience. Chloe's voice had happily lifted in volume; Connie laughed with genuine delight. The two women had become friends.

Why was he surprised? Two nights ago, they'd been the only

people in the world who understood an inkling of each other's troubles.

Connie seemed to have been prepared for the date of the ceremony. But she asked, "Did Trudy say...what was involved?"

While Chloe explained what they knew of the ritual, Mark watched Jacob. The boy seemed uninterested, even though he was going to take part. Each table had been provided with a jelly jar full of crayons and placemats featuring an outline of Pagliacci the clown. Jacob reached for a brown crayon, then turned over his mat to the blank side and began to draw. He bent myopically close to the paper, his fingers pinching the crayon so hard his nails turned purple, and quickly sketched two stick figures, ovals for fists and heads, each in an action pose.

Mark smiled. Jacob was good. He was nine—unpracticed and clichéd—but he understood depth and movement and perspective.

"Ease up on your grip," Mark told him.

Jacob started: "What?"

Mark was aware of Chloe and Connie turning to watch them. "Don't press so hard. You're very good, but a light touch is always better."

Jacob blinked at him. "My art teacher told me that, too. I forget sometimes."

"You're going to Parkhurst?"

Jacob nodded.

"Is the art teacher still Ms. Kyle?"

"You *know* her?"

"Sure. She was my son's teacher, too."

"Oh," Jacob said.

Connie said, "Jake wants to be an artist. Isn't that what you do, Mark?"

"More or less." To Jacob, he said, "You want to draw comics?"

Jacob didn't redden so much as darken. "I want to work for DC

or Marvel. Dark Horse, even. But mostly DC. Like, my dream is
I want to pencil Batman someday."

"I was strictly a Marvel guy," Mark said. "I wanted to draw the
X-Men."

"Really?"

"Yep."

Jacob turned a crayon between his hands. "So why didn't you?"

Connie said, "Jakey."

Mark waved her off, but still he was surprised at his embarrassment.

"I wasn't as good as you are." Mark tilted the placemat toward
him. "I got into graphic design, then computers. I mostly make
websites now."

"Making websites takes art?" Jacob asked.

No, Mark almost said.

"Sure."

"Do you like doing it?"

"It's all right."

"My mom and dad are both bankers," Jacob said.

Connie put a hand on Jacob's shoulder. "Your dad's a banker.
I'm a teller." To Mark she said, "That's how his father and I met."

Jacob was drawing again, adding a cowl and cape to one of the
figures.

"Honey," Connie said, "did you hear what Ms. Ross and I were
just talking about?"

Jacob didn't look up. "Ms. Weill's coming to our house."

"Yes," Connie said. "Do you remember what we have to do?"

Jacob glanced at Mark. "We're going to make the ghost go
away."

Mark winced, to hear it said like this. Chloe's throat worked; she
picked up her soda. Connie said, "That's not what we say, Jacob.
We're going to *put him to rest*, remember?"

Jacob lifted his head from his drawing, but only for a second. "I'm sorry, Mr. Fife."

On the placemat Batman was punching out a man wearing a business suit and a bandit mask. The businessman's head was tilted back, motion lines indicating the force of Batman's punch. In one of his hands was a sack of money with a dollar sign on it.

"Don't you worry about it," Mark said.

Soon their pizza came. Jacob offered Mark the now-completed drawing of Batman; Mark took it solemnly, folded it in thirds—careful not to crease Batman's middle—and tucked it into the interior pocket of his coat.

Mark couldn't take his eyes off the boy. Jacob would have fascinated him even if he hadn't been Connie's son. The boy went after a supreme pizza with the gusto of a dog; twice Connie reached over to pull strings of cheese from his chin. Between bites he told Mark the storyline of a Batman comic he hoped to begin drawing soon.

Mark kept up his end of the conversation, but he couldn't get over how nonchalant Jacob had sounded: *We're going to make the ghost go away.* He might as well have said, *We're going to the grocery.*

Jacob had been frightened of Mark, but not of the word *ghost*.

The pizza was mostly gone when Jacob turned to Connie. His voice was suddenly imperious: "Mom, I've got to pee."

Connie looked at Mark, who slid obligingly from the booth. When Jacob had gotten out he looked at all three adults and bowed. "I take my leave."

Chloe smiled into her napkin, but Mark was pretty sure Jacob had seen it.

The kid was acting. Enjoying the hell out of all this attention. Mark's stomach boiled.

It couldn't be. Not after what he had felt, not after hearing those footsteps on the stairs.

Stay away from the house until the ceremony, Trudy had told them. Now, sickly, Mark wondered why.

He cleared his throat. "Connie, I have a request, and I hope it doesn't offend you."

Connie turned to him and took a deep breath. "Um. Okay?"

"I was wondering if I could maybe talk with Jake alone, a minute?"

Chloe shot him a look—almost identical to the one she'd given him when Trudy asked her to go to the kitchen with Warren.

"I believe him," Mark said. "It's not that. But I'd really like to hear him tell me about Brendan." He seized on an inspiration. "Just a man-to-man talk."

Connie laughed, too loud. Then a sly look crossed her face. "I *am* kind of dying for a smoke. Chloe, you want to come with me?"

Chloe hesitated.

"Just a few minutes," he said.

"Sure," she said, unblinking.

When Jake came back, and saw both Chloe and Connie headed away from the table, his bravado left him; he began to gulp like a fish on a line.

"They'll be right back," Mark said. "Have a seat, and let's polish this bad boy off."

Jacob sat. Mark put a slice on each of their plates. "I'm pretty full," Jacob said.

"Really?" Mark picked up his slice and took a bite. "If you're anything like I was at your age, you could literally eat a horse."

Jacob made a sound like a laugh and ducked his head. "I guess I could find some room."

They each ate a bite. Mark swallowed queasily, decided he'd steal a tactic from Trudy Weill. "I really just wanted to give you a chance to ask me some questions."

"Questions?" Jacob said, around a thick mouthful of cheese.

"Sure. If I was you, I'd be curious about all of this. It's got to be confusing."

Jacob nodded and rolled his eyes.

"Is there anything I can tell you?"

Jacob picked up his fork and set it on its end, tines up, and began to twirl it slowly back and forth. Then he asked, "Why did you guys ever move out of the house?"

The kid might as well have stabbed Mark's hand with the fork. "That's complicated."

"Yeah, I bet."

Was Jacob being sarcastic? The boy wasn't smiling.

"There were too many memories for us. After Brendan died, the house wasn't the happy place it was before. For us."

Jake said, "I think it was probably the same for my mom."

"How do you mean?"

"Once Dad left, the house got different."

"I bet it did," Mark said.

Jacob said, more quietly, "Mom said Brendan died by an accident?"

"Yeah," Mark said.

"What happened?"

Mark told him. Jacob listened without looking up, then asked, "Why did he have his backpack on?"

The kid was a lawyer. Or maybe he was repeating questions of his mother's.

"He was in trouble, and was supposed to be cleaning up his toys. But he sneaked out. I think he was trying to run away."

The fork in Jacob's hands stopped spinning. "So he was being bad."

"Yes," Mark said, carefully. "But he wasn't a bad kid. Not at all."

"Are you mad at him?"

The question had come out of his therapist's mouth often

enough. Out of Jacob's it sounded strange, cruel. But Jacob had asked softly, simply, with real curiosity.

"No," Mark told him. "But I have regrets. Brendan was sad about something, and didn't tell me. Maybe if he had, he wouldn't have tried to sneak away. But yeah…since he didn't tell me, it sometimes feels now like he lied to me. Sometimes that makes me mad, but mostly I'm sad he didn't think he could trust me."

Jacob was quiet for a long time. Then he took a sip of milk. When he set down his glass he had a small mustache. "Wipe up, buddy," Mark said, and was shocked by the tenderness in his voice.

Jacob reached for his napkin, obediently, and wiped his lip.

"Can you tell me what you see?" Mark asked. "When Brendan comes?"

Jacob looked at the table.

"I'd really like to know," Mark said.

Jacob nodded. "He's just this dark shape. He usually stands by my bed."

"You don't see his face?"

"No. It's too dark. But I can hear him, sometimes. He's mostly crying."

Mark kept his gaze steady. And there: There. Jacob's eyes darted to Mark's, and then back to the fork in his hands, like a mouse into a hole.

Mark's throat was as dry as his crumpled napkin. "But sometimes he—calls for me?"

"Yeah," Jacob said. "Sometimes."

Mark wished himself back in time, back to the floor of Brendan's room, to that last moment, to the jolt of truth that had coursed through him, searing his doubts to smoke. The patter of footsteps on the stairs—he wanted to be seized by that sound again. By the certainty in it.

But here, now, was a different truth: Mark was the father of a little boy, and his every instinct told him that Jacob Pelham was lying through his teeth.

Mark said, "Can I tell you something? A secret?"

This word *secret*—as it always had with Brendan—caught Jacob's interest, like a shiny coin in front of a crow.

Mark looked up, theatrically, to make sure Chloe and Connie were still gone. "Both Chloe and I have gone through a lot of trouble, because of—of Brendan coming back. We're both spending a lot of money. We might lose our jobs. The woman I'm about to marry is really mad at me. This is very, very serious, Jake. I need to make extra double-sure you're telling the truth."

Jacob drew back, offended. "Chloe and Mom have *both* seen him. *You*'ve seen him."

"I *heard* him," Mark said. "But—look. Brendan used to get woken up by sounds in the middle of the night. He'd hear a branch on the window, or he'd hear a board creak, and then he'd think it was a monster. It's harder for grown-ups, but we can make ourselves do that, too. Especially if we *want* something to be true."

He couldn't believe how easily this explanation had come out of him.

"It's *true*," Jacob said—louder, now. "I *saw* him."

Mark had one more card he could play. If Jacob was telling the truth, he had nothing to fear. But if he was a liar—if he'd made them all suffer for nothing—then he deserved what Mark was about to say.

He leaned forward. "Jacob. Trudy Weill told me today that I *needed* to make sure. Because if we try to do the ceremony, and there's really no ghost, something very bad could happen."

Jacob had been jabbing the fork at the tablecloth; now his hand stilled.

"She wouldn't tell me what. All she said was, we had to make sure. She made me promise. *For our safety*, she said."

"Mr. Fife. It's *true*."

Jacob's voice wobbled; his eyes, rising to Mark's, shone with hurt.

"It's okay," Mark said, too quickly. "I just had to make sure. Thank you for being honest."

Jacob folded his hands in his lap and sniffled. He said, with no small measure of affront, "Sure."

⌇

"Are you all right?" Chloe asked Mark in the car, moments after they'd bid farewell to the Pelhams in the parking lot. She had to be deeply curious about his talk with Jacob Pelham, but he couldn't begin to explain his new and unnerving doubt to her, and he wasn't about to try.

Chloe, at the wheel, was drawn—thin, tired, hollow-eyed. A woman held together with fragile loops of thread. Yet she was as lovely as he'd ever seen her, her eyes soft and gentle. Worried for them both.

"I'm okay," he said, trying not to think of Jacob's guilty face. He reached for her hand. She took it and squeezed.

They were stopped at a light; Chloe was signaling a right turn, onto the entrance ramp to 315. She was taking them, without discussion, back to her apartment in Dublin.

Mark could, if he wanted, ask her to turn south instead—to take him to his car, still parked near the Locust house. He could drive home to the townhouse, now empty. All he had to do was ask.

Chloe's thumb brushed his knuckles. "Do you mind if I turn on the radio?"

"No," he said, and she did: the Cocteau Twins again, ethereal and sexy.

The light changed, and Chloe pulled carefully through, up the ramp and onto the highway.

Mark leaned back into his seat, closed his eyes, and listened to her sing.

⌒

It was almost ten when they entered her apartment. Mark sat down on the couch. Chloe walked to the kitchen and poured herself a glass of water.

"We should have stopped at Target," she said. "We could have gotten you some other clothes."

So she had been thinking about his real home, too; he had clothes there, but she didn't want him to go get them.

"I'll be okay."

"I can wash those for you tonight," she said. She must have seen the alarm on his face; she laughed. "Don't worry. I've got a robe that I think will fit you."

Chloe went to her bedroom, then returned with a fluffy white bathrobe. He was relieved to see it was a woman's—he'd been worried she was going to hand him some leftover of Steve's.

He went to the bathroom to undress; it really was a relief to strip out of his two-day-old clothes. He hastily showered, then put on the robe. Chloe wasn't much shorter than him, but her bathrobe only covered half his thighs, and he could barely close it around his belly. When he returned to the living room she covered her mouth.

"Don't," he said.

She held up a laundry basket, smirking; he put his clothes into it. "I can't help it."

Chloe carried the laundry away to the building's basement. When she returned she told him she was going to take a shower, too—and Mark knew, then, what was going to happen; when they were married, the only time they both showered at night was when she wanted to make love.

Mark watched television, listening to the water run, smelling Chloe's soap. Two sportscasters barked at each other about the top-

316

ics of the day. He turned to the news, found it full of wailing and flame.

He couldn't do this. No matter how angry Allison was with him, no matter if they were no longer a couple, the circumstances in which Mark was caught were tenuous, wild—he couldn't make a decision of this magnitude, not now.

The water shut off in the bathroom.

But he had decided already, hadn't he? He'd decided the other night, at the old house. He had remembered there how much he'd loved his family. Brendan—he was sure of this—had *wanted* him to remember.

Did Mark love Allison? He did.

But not like he had loved Chloe. Not like he had loved Brendan. That was what he had been shown. That was the truth glowing in his heart.

Chloe emerged from the bathroom, wearing a T-shirt and shorts, a towel turbaned around her head. Her legs gleamed in the warm, close light. She glanced at him. "What's wrong?" she asked again.

"Nothing's wrong."

She walked to the couch and sat down at the far end of it, smelling of lavender, then pulled off the towel and began to dry her hair. "Are you sure?"

He wanted to bury his face into her neck, to hide, which meant the answer to her question was—had to be—no. But he made himself talk. All these years he'd missed her face, her sex—but he missed this too, maybe the most: Looking into her eyes, revealing his secrets. This kind of intimacy had been lost to them longer than any other.

"Something happened at dinner," he said.

The towel paused in its rubbing. "What do you mean?"

"For a while there I—I couldn't shake the feeling that Jacob was lying to me. When I talked to him about Brendan, he got pretty shifty."

"He doesn't know how to talk with people. Plus it's a tough situation for him. I mean, would *you* know how to act?"

"No. I just—I had an intuition."

"So what? We went and saw for ourselves, Mark."

"Yeah." She was right, but he forged ahead anyway: "Chloe, I'm forgetting it. What happened the other night. I remember that it was wonderful, but—"

"You told me all about it, when it happened," Chloe said, firmly. "And what happened to you was just like what happened to me."

"I was drunk," Mark said.

"You felt what I did. I could see it all over your face. And I *wasn't* drunk." Her eyes were clear and sweet, staring into him. "I went through this, too," she said. "I kept looking for reasons to deny it. But it *happened*. It's happened for me, over and over again. It will happen again to you."

Chloe moved closer, her knees tucked beneath her, her hair stringy and damp on her shoulders. "Hasn't it helped, to know it's true?"

"Yes." It had. His problems were greater, now, far greater than they'd been before—but he was working to fix them, instead of running away.

Chloe whispered, "I was *happy*, today. I know we haven't made anything better, yet. I know we haven't done what we need to do. But it feels so much better—to *know*—than it did before." She let out a long sigh. "God, Mark. Tell me feeling like this is—is a mistake."

She mistook his silence, and leaned back.

"I'm sorry. You and Allison—"

"It's all right."

"Have you talked with her today?"

"I don't want to talk about Allison."

Chloe's eyes darted across every part of his face. He held his breath. Then she did exactly what he'd wished and feared she would: She scooted close to him and put one arm around his shoulders, then pressed her other hand to his chest. She tilted forward, her forehead leaning on his shoulder, her cool wet hair stinging his ear, his cheek.

"Is this okay?" she asked.

He breathed in the scent of her hair. "It's okay."

"Does this make you happy?" she asked. "Even a little?"

Her mouth only inches from his. Her breath sweet and warm.

"More than a little."

"Are you happy with Allison?"

"She's a good person, Chloe."

He lifted a hand to her shoulder. Stroked her there with his thumb.

"Were you happy with me?" she asked.

"How could you think I wasn't?"

He knew exactly how she could think it. Because he'd spent the year before Brendan's death sullen and sulky as a little boy. Because he'd spent his nights drinking and staring at the Internet instead of trying to explain to Chloe how he felt. Because he'd been a pussy.

"I always wanted you to be," Chloe said.

"I was," he said. "Were you happy with me?"

"As happy as someone could possibly be." A corner of her mouth twitched. Maybe she was thinking of her own lost time, her own failures. How little, at the end of every day as Brendan's mother, she'd had left to give him. "I wish you knew that."

He pushed a strand of hair from her cheek. "I knew."

She said, "Please don't doubt I loved you."

But he had. He'd doubted happiness, he'd doubted fatherhood—all his loves. He knew, now—he knew painfully and completely—how much of all three he'd wasted. Maybe this was what Brendan had come back to tell him: *Don't waste it again.*

He opened his arms and turned sideways; Chloe did the same, and they held each other tightly.

She said, "Do you think we'll ever be happy again? As happy as we were?"

"I don't know. I hope so."

"I keep telling myself that if I can help him, I'll be able—finally—to open my eyes. To live like something other than a crazy woman. But do you think that's really true?"

"I want both of us to be happy," he said.

"Do we deserve it?"

The question stunned him—maybe because he'd spent so much of his time apart from Chloe asking it of himself, every damned day.

"You tell me."

Chloe cupped his cheek in her palm, stared directly into his eyes.

"If we help him. If we do that, we might."

He inhaled her scent. Put his hand over hers, on his chest. His skin tingled; his blood surged.

She lifted herself, blotted out the overhead light. Her mouth opened and moved forward and pressed against his.

He thought this: Maybe they wouldn't ever be happy, he and Chloe. But whatever they were, whoever they had been, in the end they deserved each other.

Twenty-four

She had come to him. He'd opened his arms.

I found you, he thought. I found you.

⌐

Mark told her, that night, the only truth left in his mind: I'm happy. Right now, I'm happy.

She laughed to hear it. She moved her hand. Her body. She took him in and laughed again at the sound he made, held by her. She rocked gently beneath him.

What about *now*? she said.

⌐

Later, while she slept, Mark lay awake, curved forward, his belly pressed to Chloe's back, his face pressed to her still-damp hair.

Is this what you wanted? When you called us?

He imagined Brendan running through the dark, empty halls of the house. Laughing.

Because I wanted it, too.

Chloe stirred, murmured, kissed his thumb. Arched herself into the curve of him.

Mark could not say it enough:

Thank you. Thank you for this. Thank you.

⌐

They showered together, close and quiet under the hot spray.

Mark worked shampoo into Chloe's hair and wondered if, when

Trudy Weill entered the old house, she wouldn't lift her face into the air, pause, and then say, This house is empty of spirits.

Brendan got what he wanted, she'd say. Now he's gone.

⌒

He and Chloe left the apartment only once that following day, to buy Mark some new clothes. Neither of them suggested a trip to the townhouse, and Mark spent the entire time at Kohl's nervous, jumpy, looking too hard at every stranger's approach—as though Allison might appear, or Lew, to point and shout at him. Chloe seemed to have no such fears; she seemed to enjoy dressing him, holding up shirt after shirt to his chest.

Smiling at him in the mirror, as though seeing him anew each time.

Tugging his hand. Leading him into the dressing rooms.

Quick, she said, inside a stall.

You're nuts.

Her eyes on his. Her mouth. Her fingers on the buckle of his belt.

So tell me to stop, she whispered.

Once, in college, she'd pulled him into a dark corner in the stairwell of the library. Now, she'd said. Right now. When they'd finished she'd folded her panties into a neat square and tucked them into the breast pocket of his shirt.

He didn't tell her to stop.

Later, on the way to the checkout counter, Mark's heart still heaving, they passed a display selling phone chargers. Chloe's fingers were laced loosely in his.

They kept walking.

⌒

Can I ask you something? Chloe said that night, as they lay beside each other in her bed.

Sure.

What happens now? With you and Allison?

He'd been waiting for the question, considering it in every quiet moment. I don't know, he said.

Once again he was trying to weasel out of his responsibilities. He said, I know what you're asking.

Do you?

He said, This isn't some fling, is it? You want to know if—if we're together again.

Her entire body softened. Yes, she said.

Mark kissed her forehead, her salty lips. Chloe rubbed her thumb across his stubbled cheeks. When we . . . when we help Brendan. What happens then? To us?

He wanted to say: *We'll run off to an island together. We'll live in a grass hut by the ocean. We'll make love in hammocks and wade in the surf until we're old and gray. I'll paint landscapes that tourists will buy, and you'll teach the local kids fractions with shells, and we'll read bad novels to each other and at night we'll go listen to calypso and the natives will laugh at the crazy old gringos who love each other so much.*

He said, I haven't let myself think about this in a long time.

Can we think about it now?

I have things to take care of first, he said. With Allie.

Chloe said, She's not here now. And look at us.

He knew what Chloe wanted: for him to offer her himself and the moon. He was only hesitating because he would have to hurt Allie to do it. But he'd already hurt her, hadn't he? Allison knew what he was up to, here. She'd known for longer than he had.

I want us to stay together, he said to her. Can we do that?

She pulled him close. Yes, she said. Oh, yes.

She said, Mark, I can't lose you again.

⟳

Late, late in the night, when Chloe slept, while a new storm—the third in as many days—blew snow against the bedroom window,

Mark at last worked on the homework Trudy had given them. She'd asked each of them to bring to the house an item—a talisman—that reminded them of Brendan. She wanted them to retrieve a memory.

The talisman was easy enough. When the sun was up, he would go to the townhouse. There he could retrieve the pictures he'd drawn of Brendan on his birthday. He felt a thrill: He could show them to Chloe. They would please her. For the first time since college, he would show her something he'd made, lines he'd drawn that *meant* something.

And this was only one of the hundred realizations he'd had, these past days: that, all along, he had been drawing those pictures for *her.*

The memory was harder. He had to pick only one? He lay boneless beneath Chloe's arm, sorting through them.

Brendan, playing chess. Brendan dog-paddling in the community pool, straining his neck to keep his chin out of the water. Brendan at three or four—when he'd started developing his sense of humor, and had begun laughing dementedly at anything Mark made to sound like a joke.

The first joke he'd told that had ever floored Mark: Knock-knock!

Who's there?

Interrupting cow.

Interrupt—

Moo!

And of course there were the early memories: The day of Brendan's birth. Brendan sleeping in his bassinet, or in Mark's or Chloe's arms. His first crooked infant smile. The nub of his first tooth. Rubbing his twisted ankle. Stomping up the stairs—

No. Something loving, safe.

Then he had it.

The summer before he died, Mark and Chloe had taken Brendan on a hike, an hour south of Columbus in Hocking Hills State Park. There they'd descended carefully into the cool limestone channels, the big overhanging caves like moist, toothless mouths. Mark had lifted Brendan again and again so he could read the informative plaques the park service posted in front of old landslides and swamps of orange mud. At one bend in the gully a thin rope of cold water fell from an overhang fifty feet above, splashing into a marsh just off the trail. Mark had held on to Brendan's belt and leaned him back—while Brendan winced and shrieked and laughed—until at last the water struck him in the forehead.

Later they walked part of a trail that followed the upper edge of a deep box canyon. The thick creepers, locust trees, and tall grass enclosing the trail gave way, now and again, to flat plates of gray rock jutting out over the canyon. There were no fences; a hiker could walk right up to the edge of a hundred-foot drop into the canopy below.

Of course Brendan wanted to see; of course Mark walked with him to the edge and put a hand on his shoulder. Mark felt Brendan tremble as he peered out into space.

This is scary, Brendan whispered.

Mark squeezed his shoulder. Yeah, he said. Come on, now.

As Brendan turned to go, he slipped on a handful of gravel; he lurched backward, pinwheeled his arms. The drop yawned behind them. Chloe, who had remained on the trail, cried Mark's name.

Mark's arm shot out; he caught a fistful of Brendan's shirt. Then he sat down, hard, and gathered Brendan to him. Brendan wept, and Mark wanted to—he'd jammed his tailbone badly—but instead he held Brendan close to him and whispered, I've got you.

They stopped at a Buffalo Wild Wings on the way home. Brendan had, by then, overcome his terror, had turned into a chatterbox. He explained to the teenage girl who took their order what had happened: My dad saved my life!

Even if it was true, Mark didn't want to dwell on it. Better to sit and eat a sandwich and watch his son, alive and well, plow chicken fingers into ketchup.

The shakes came over him that night, after Brendan was asleep. Mark had never had them before. He poured himself a whiskey and showed Chloe, who was reading on the other end of the couch, his trembling fingers.

Chloe smiled. Kissed them.

Later Mark crept into Brendan's room and gently lowered himself onto the bed, curling to fit Brendan and his pillow inside the shelter of his body. Brendan stirred. Shh, Mark said, and put his arm over his waist. It's just your dad.

He lay awake for a long time. He listened to Brendan's breathing, his sleeping gasps and whispers. He was dreaming. Mark imagined him—wanted to imagine him—unafraid. Ready for anything. Brave, even. Adventuring.

Safe, in the company of his father.

Twenty-five

They woke late in the morning to the ringing of Chloe's phone. Chloe cursed, untangled herself from the sheet and Mark's limbs, then thumped barefoot and naked to her purse on the bureau, all angles and jutting bones. When she bent over the phone, the knobs of her spine cast shadows. "It's probably school," she said to him. "They're disputing my leave. If they give me any shit today I swear I'm quitting."

She squinted quizzically at the number, then answered.

"Wow, hi," she said after a moment, standing straight. "Um. Yeah. Hang on." She turned to stare at Mark. "It's your dad."

Lewis had done this. Mark had ignored him, and—as Lewis had promised—he'd called Sam to sound the alarm. And just like that, Mark's and Chloe's cocoon had been torn open to the world. He could have punched the wall.

Chloe held the phone to her chest. "I'm sorry—I didn't recognize the number—"

"I'll take it," he said. He had to, now; he was caught. He sat at the edge of the bed, naked too, and took the phone. "Dad?"

"Marcus," his father said—calmly, but Mark only ever heard his full name when Sam was deeply upset. "Good to hear your voice."

"Did Lewis call you?"

"I've spoken to him. He's very concerned about you. Honestly,

327

so am I. I've been calling your phone for a day now." His father was using the Voice: He was too aggressive, too loud, biting down too hard at the end of every sentence.

Chloe sat beside Mark, gathered one of the pillows to her chest, and stared over the top.

Mark said, "I'm sorry, Dad. I've maybe been off the grid a little, but I'm just fine."

"Are you?"

"I am."

A long, long moment. Mark reached out and took Chloe's cold hand.

"Mark," his father said, "I'll be frank with you. I know a lot of—of what's been happening. And I'm having a difficult time believing that you're involved in . . . all this."

So Sam knew it all. "Things have been . . . too crazy. I haven't known what to tell you."

"Maybe so," his father said. "But I'm afraid I've reacted rashly."

"What do you mean?"

"I mean I'm at a gas station on I-70, in Springfield. I'll be at your place in an hour or so. I'd like you to meet me there."

Mark glanced at what must be six inches of new snow piled on the branches outside the kitchen window. "You *drove* in this?"

Chloe covered her mouth, then began to dress.

"As I said, I've been worried. Will you come meet me?"

"Dad. Today's a bad time—"

Sam said, "I'm happy to come by Chloe's, if you'd like. I have her address with me."

They had trumped him. Mark couldn't very well tell his father to turn around and drive home, could he?

"Okay," he said. "Okay, sure. Let's meet at my place. But it'll take me awhile to get down there."

"I'll let myself in," his father said. Which he could do; he had a key. He sounded calmer now, but—Mark was sure—saddened. His own worst suspicions confirmed.

When Mark had hung up and explained the call to Chloe, she was sanguine. "We'd have had to tell him sooner or later," she said. "It'll be okay. He's your dad, not the bogeyman."

"He's going to think all of this is nuts," Mark told her. "I didn't want to have to argue with him. Not today of all days."

Because today was the Bad Anniversary: seven years since Brendan's accident. The day they were meeting the Weills at the old house, their memories in tow. The day they were sending Brendan to his rest.

Chloe put her hands on his cheeks and kissed him firmly. "We've got the truth," she said. "It takes some time for people to believe." She kissed him again. "But they will."

⌁

They dressed quickly, then Chloe drove him to his car. Ice had fallen before the snow last night, and the roads were dangerously slick; they passed several police cars, keeping watch over vehicles nosed forward into ditches, taillights glaring. Tree branches and power lines drooped under sheaths of ice that in the dim light were as thick and gleaming as metal.

It was almost ten. Sam must have gotten on the road around five, just as the storm was tailing off. Lewis must have called him yesterday— Sam could well have been awake the entire night, calling Mark's phone, before finally lighting out for Ohio when the snow tailed off.

But wouldn't Sam have tried calling Allison first? He would have. That meant he and Allie had surely spoken.

And what would Allie have told him? Mark might, now, be facing a lot more than a stern lecture about the reality of ghosts.

He put his hand on Chloe's thigh. She hummed.

When they were at last parked beside Mark's buried Volvo, Chloe said, "I can come, too, if you want."

329

This seemed dangerous to him—Sam having to face Chloe's serene belief—but Mark didn't say so.

"I'll take care of it," he said. "Then I'll come right home."

Home, he'd said—even as they both scraped the Volvo's windshield, in sight of the old house, its chimney smoking happily. He'd meant Chloe's apartment. No. Chloe's arms.

⌒

The drive to German Village, normally a ten-minute jaunt, took Mark well over half an hour. He passed two more accidents, and—not far from the townhouse—slid sideways through a fortunately empty four-way stop before coming to a gentle rest against a curb. When he finally reached the townhouse, he was so shaken that, for a long minute, he couldn't quite piece together why Allison's Honda was parked in front of his father's truck.

But it was. Allison was *here*, with Sam. More than that—his father's truck was buried under the new snow.

Allison had called Sam, not Lew. His father hadn't driven through the night—he'd been here longer. He'd lied, in order to make Mark come here. Maybe that was why Chloe hadn't recognized his number—Sam could have called her from Allison's phone.

Mark sat for a long time in his parked car, the motor still running. He didn't want to go up to the door, but what else could he do? He'd made his choices, these last days; this confrontation would always have to be their outcome. A man who wasn't sure of his responsibilities, his new happiness, would run away from a fate such as this. Mark would not. Not anymore.

Even so, before walking up to the door that in a few minutes would no longer be his, he tried to convince himself—somehow, anyhow—that Allison might not know, yet, where he had spent the night.

⌒

The front door was unlocked. Mark, not knowing what else to do, knocked softly while opening it. The air inside smelled of coffee and eggs; of himself and of Allison—what only a few days before had been the smell of home. Mark heard the happy chatter of a morning television show. He took off his wet shoes beside his father's old duck boots. "Hello?" he called, just as the television clicked off.

His father appeared in jeans, a black sweater, and stockinged feet. His beard was longer, bushier, than it had been at Christmas; he looked something like a sea captain. "Mark," he said, smiling tightly.

"Dad."

"Allison's here," Sam said. "I know you didn't expect her."

"I sure didn't."

"Can your father give you a hug anyway?"

Mark nodded, and Sam embraced him, thumped his back. His grip was tight—so tight Mark wondered, nonsensically, if he was about to be wrestled to the ground. Sam said into Mark's ear, "Allie's in the kitchen. I'm going to go to your office, if that's all right, and call Helen. I'll be here when you need me."

Sam released him—Mark staggered backward—then smiled his sad smile, before turning and slowly climbing the stairs. Mark wanted to call after him, *Don't go*.

Instead he made himself walk through the living room, past the couch with the rumpled sheets on top of it (so his father *had* stayed the night); past the television; past the pictures on the mantel of Mark and Allie in Seattle, in her parents' living room, laughing together in the Florida surf.

These were another Mark Fife's pictures. That Mark might, in any number of ways, be better than the one who now stood in the kitchen doorway; who saw Allison Daniel sitting at the kitchen table, lifting her face—swollen, beautiful, hurt—to him; who drew back from her red, mourning eyes. Who had to tell her goodbye.

"Hi," she said.

She wasn't actively crying, but her voice was thick, clotted.

Before he could speak she added, "You turned off your phone—I didn't know what else to do. I called Sam, and he drove out last night."

He'd expected anger from her—something like the venom with which she'd always spoken of herself and Bill. But instead she seemed drained, her fingers curled limply around a tissue on the tabletop.

He sat opposite her. "I'm the one who owes apologies. My phone's been dead, or I would have called."

"I know Sam called you at Chloe's," Allie said. "He didn't want to tell me, but I got that out of him."

With surprising calm, he said, "Yeah. I was there."

"You've been staying with her."

"Yes," Mark said.

Allison bowed her head, closed her eyes. She waited a long time before speaking, as though sorting through possibilities. Or maybe he'd been lying to her long enough that she hadn't expected a simple truthful answer.

"I want you to come back. Maybe I shouldn't, but I do." She lifted her eyes. "Is there any way that can happen? Is there anything I can do?"

Her red eyes searched his face, depthless.

"We've been happy," she said. "Haven't we? We've been good together."

"We have been," he said, and wished his voice didn't sound so flat, so final.

"Are we done?" Her voice shook. "Is that what this is?"

He made himself say the words.

"Allie, I didn't expect this. I really didn't. But things have—have happened. Chloe still loves me, and I still love her. What's happened with Brendan has made us realize—"

Before he'd finished this last sentence Allie had turned her face away from him, hands covering her mouth.

He couldn't dare tell her that he loved her, still. But he could have; watching her sob, he knew he did. Maybe it was a different kind of love than what he felt for Chloe—a calmer love, a more considered love—but still he hurt for Allison, *with* her. Nothing that had happened was her fault. He wanted to reach for her, to hold her to him, to reassure her of this if he could.

But he had given up that right. He'd chosen his happiness at the cost of Allie's pain.

He'd chosen this because he had to. Because a miracle, or something like it, had brought his lost family back to him. In a million years, how could either of them have predicted such a thing? This was new territory, to which very few people alive possessed a map.

If he had any courage left, he could tell her: I had no choice. I never did.

But then Allison's cries, physical things, ripped apart the air, and he knew that if he said so he'd be lying.

"I'll go," he said, standing.

"No!" Allie shook her head, clenched her fists on her knees, took in deep drafts of air. "Sit down, Mark. We're not done."

But we are, he almost said.

Her eyes were sparkling with anger. He sat down. If she needed to be upset, he would take it. Taking it was the very least he could do.

Allie wiped her eyes and nose with a wad of tissue. "I wish I could just tell you to fuck off. You deserve it and I deserve to say it. But that would be too easy."

"I do—"

"Quiet. I have to talk now. I have to tell you something."

"Allie, I—"

"I'm pregnant," she said. "What do you think of that?"

All his thoughts snapped apart. He stared at her lovely face, her blinking eyes.

"How?" he asked, and immediately regretted the question.

"Christ, I don't know," she said. "I took all my pills. To quote my doctor, 'This sort of thing happens sometimes.'" Her voice shook. "I'm at five weeks. So I guess the real answer is, five weeks ago you were telling me you loved me, and I believed you."

He remembered rubbing her back while she threw up into the sink. The strange way her sister had spoken to him when he'd called from Lewis's. The desperation in Allison's eyes and voice, the night he'd stayed away without calling.

His head throbbed. "How long have you known?"

"Awhile," Allie said. "The doctor called with definite results Friday. She said, 'Congratulations.'"

"But you knew the night—"

Allie's face darkened. "You'd just lied to my face! You acted like you were leaving me, and I chickened out! I went to Darly's for some moral support, and then—"

Allie didn't finish. She didn't have to.

"I'm going back to Darlene's now," she said. "I guess I knew what you'd say about Chloe. I've known it for a while. But now I need an answer from you about something else."

She didn't wait for him to ask what it was. "I'm not getting any younger. And I'm not convinced there's a sane man out there I might want to plan a baby with—you know, when it's fucking *convenient*." She shook her head and wiped at each eye. "I'm saying I might want to keep it."

He tried to make himself speak, but couldn't.

She was crying again. "I feel like some silly little teenager. *If I have a baby, at least I'll have someone who'll love me no matter what.*" She held up her hands, grimaced. "How'd you like that one?"

"I don't," he said. "I don't want you to think like that."

"I don't want to ask this," she said. "Right now I really don't want to give a shit what you think. But I have to. That's the cruelest part of this, you know? I have to. So here goes: Are you going to be a dad to this kid, if I have it?"

He stared at her for too long.

"So you can run away from me to hang out with—with a god-damned *ghost*, but—"

"Allie!"

"Does this make you mad?" she asked, leaning forward. Her fists were clenched. "Tell me it makes you mad."

He clamped his mouth shut.

"You want to know the irony?" she asked. "I'm only talking to you because of *Sam*. I figured I'd just call you, tell you to go fuck yourself. But Sam talked me into this. Whatever I think of you, I'm glad your father's in my life." She wiped the corners of her burning eyes. "So I get it, now. I do. I know what it means to make a *commitment*. I'll deal with looking at your face every week for the rest of our lives, if you tell me this kid's going to have a father."

He was crying, then. He couldn't stop himself.

"*It*," she said, her voice sinking. "Him or her." She pressed at her flat stomach. "So tell me the truth. I mean it. The honest truth. Will you help me raise *him or her*?"

"I will," he said. "Of course I will."

The answer seemed to displease her, even though it had to have been the one she wanted.

"At least let me say I'm sorry," Mark began to say—but Allie stood and stalked out of the kitchen before he could go on.

For a long few minutes he listened to Allie leaving: to the gathering of her bags, the jingle of her keys, the thump and squeak of her boots on the tile. Footsteps then sounded on the stairs, and he heard his father's low, sonorant voice, speaking gently. Then the front door opened and shut. A car started on the street.

His father appeared in the kitchen doorway. "She's gone," he said.

Mark didn't answer. Sam set a mug of coffee down on the table next to Mark's elbow. He scooted Allie's box of tissues closer. Mark took one and wiped his eyes. Sam sat where Allie had, holding his own mug next to his chest.

"You must be angry with me," Sam said.

Mark shook his head.

"Allie called me yesterday morning," Sam said. "She was… distraught. She said she couldn't find you, that you wouldn't answer your phone. She told me about—something about—what's been going on here." He pressed his lips tight. "She didn't think you'd come if she asked you. And she wanted to tell you her news face-to-face."

"I'm not angry. Not with anyone."

Sam leaned over his hands. "Is she pregnant?"

"You didn't know?"

Sam shook his head. "She kept saying she had news, that it couldn't wait. I frankly didn't know what else it could be, but I didn't ask."

"She's been trying to tell me for a while. I haven't been listening."

Sam took a long sip of his coffee, watching Mark as though he held a gun in his hands. "What are you going to do?"

"I don't know. This is all new to me, Dad. Things—I was telling her I was leaving her."

His father let out a long, measured breath, as though Mark had just spoken an obscenity. "So you and Chloe—"

"Yes."

Sam rubbed his chin and looked at the ceiling.

"I wish you'd go ahead and say it," Mark told him.

"Say what?"

"We haven't talked about 'what's been going on here.' About Brendan."

"No, we haven't. We're talking about you and Allison. You and Chloe."

"It's all the same thing. I need to tell you about it, if this is going to make any sense at all."

Sam said, "All right. I'll listen."

"Will you?"

"Do you think I wouldn't? Why did I drive out here, do you suppose?"

"Because you think it's ridiculous."

"I don't believe in—in *ghosts*, no. But I've failed as a parent if you can sit there thinking I wouldn't give you a chance to explain yourself."

"I would have told you." Mark felt himself reddening. "Do I look like a guy who's operating with some kind of *plan*?"

His father said, "To be honest, you look like you're in quite a bit of pain."

"All of a sudden Brendan and Chloe are in my life again. Brendan needs me, and Chloe—it turns out—never stopped loving me. What the fuck was I supposed to do?"

Sam reached a hand across the tabletop, almost to Mark's forearm. "I don't know. I don't presume to know."

"I knew this would hurt Allie," Mark said. "I was prepared for that. But I didn't know about *this*."

"Would things be different if you had?"

No, Mark wanted to say. But if he'd known about Allie's pregnancy a week ago the news might have frozen him. If he'd known, he might never have gone to the house, alone or with Chloe.

"Say something," he said to his father. "Come on, yell at me. Now's the time."

Sam said, wearily: "Yell at you? Why?"

"For keeping this a secret. Being an asshole."

Sam sighed. "All my life—from the moment you were born—I told myself to be ready for anything. If you came to me and said you'd tried heroin, I'd be ready. If you told me you were gay, I'd be ready. If you said you wanted to be a Catholic priest, or join the army, I'd be ready.

"But I wasn't prepared for death. Or for ghosts." Sam smiled, the tiniest bit. "I don't know what advice I can give. And anyway, I haven't heard the story from you. Only from Allison and Lewis."

Mark glanced up. "Lew too?"

"I called him last night, and he told me a few things. Among them that he's very worried about you, like the rest of us."

Mark shook his head. "I doubt Allie's worried."

"Mark," Sam said—with exasperation, as though Mark were ten again—"Allie is only angry because she *loves* you. Whatever else is happening, don't deny the woman her feelings."

Mark said, "It was because of her that I tried every way I could not to believe—in all of this."

"But you do."

"Not at first. But I went and—and saw for myself."

Sam's voice was soft, his eyes unblinking. "You've seen him?"

"*Heard* him. Felt him. Things have happened to me. Supernatural things."

Sam leaned forward. "I have to ask you a difficult question. I only ask it because you are my son, and I love you."

"Okay," Mark said. "Okay, sure."

"Are you drinking again?"

Mark thought of the flicker of Jacob Pelham's eyes. Mark's sudden certainty—a father's certainty—that the boy was lying.

He said, "I can't sleep. You don't know how bad it's been, thinking about him, in the house alone—"

"For how long?"

"A month. Maybe more."

Sam, agitated now, said, "The last time you drank—"

"I shouldn't be drinking. I know that." Mark made himself look his father in the eyes. "But it doesn't matter, now. Everything's different. Tonight Chloe and I are going to help Brendan, if we can. That's got to be the most important thing."

His father rubbed his temples, thinking, thinking.

"If this is what you believe, it's what you believe," he said at last. "I can't tell you what to do. But I'm disappointed in you, Mark. I still have the right to say that. Maybe even about this business with Brendan, even though I should leave it alone."

Mark was about to argue, but Sam held up a hand.

"You're a grown man. But I am here because your fiancée called me crying yesterday and told me she didn't know where you were. I'm not here because of Brendan. I'm here because you *vanished*. You abandoned people who trust you. And the last time you pulled that stunt you nearly died."

Mark couldn't answer him. This was all too, too much.

"Mark," Sam said. "I love Chloe like a daughter. There is a part of me that misses her in your life, and misses her in mine.

"But Allison's pregnant with my grandchild. And I'll tell you—I'm worried about that child's life. I'm worried about its family."

Mark said, as calmly as he could, "I'll be there for the baby. I gave Allie my word."

Sam pinned him with a long, watery gaze. "You're sure?"

"Dad! Jesus!"

"*Will* you?"

"I can make this work," Mark said. "I can do this."

"Maybe so," his father said. "Maybe so."

"It's true. You don't—you just don't get what I've been dealing with. What this is all like."

Sam took a deep breath and pushed aside his pain. Mark watched him do it.

"All right. Tell me what's happened," he said. "Make me believe."

⌒

Haltingly, Mark told him everything, from start to finish. And, compared with the last time he'd told the story—to Lewis—his omissions were different. This time he left out his talk with Jacob Pelham. His sudden doubt. The lie he'd left with Jacob to simmer.

The story took him nearly forty minutes. His father asked questions only for clarification; mostly he sat with his hand on his beard, gazing down into his coffee.

When he was finished Mark asked him exactly what Chloe had, and with the same querulous hope: "Do you believe me?"

His father gave the same answer Mark had:

"I believe *you* believe it," he said. "But I don't buy a word of it."

He held up his hand against Mark's objections. "And that is exactly why I should come with you, tonight."

Twenty-six

Before Mark could answer, Sam said, "I understand. I think I can. If I was in your shoes—if you had died, and I heard you were back—I'd go and see for myself. I'd want to know. I'd want that story to be true, no matter how much I doubted it beforehand—"

"My mind is made up," Mark said again.

"That is exactly why someone whose mind *isn't* should be with you."

"Dad—"

Sam leaned forward. "This wouldn't be the first time in history that a group of otherwise rational people decided, en masse, to believe in a falsehood," he said, before beginning to count them off on his fingers. "There's gold in them thar hills. A prehistoric monster lives in the lake. My neighbor is a witch. The Jews are vermin."

"Christ, Dad. I'm not about to—to commit genocide."

"No," Sam said. "But consider the larger point. What concerns me most is this, this psychic. She's a fraud—I'd stake a lot of money on that. And if Chloe's paying money to her church, then I am *very* concerned. Do you know how much she's handed over?"

Mark could only shake his head.

His father said, "There has been no more reliable source of fraud and confidence scams throughout history than those people who claim to speak to the dead. And do you know why? Because no one is more gullible than a person in grief."

Mark rubbed at his eyes. "I got it, Dad. Thank you. But I have to do this. I've come too far, and I've given up too much—"

"There." His father jabbed a finger at the air. "We agree. You *have*. That means they have you right where they want you. You ask this *psychic* what happens if her ritual doesn't work. You've got the ideal night, all the arrows lined up. But if it doesn't work? What's next?"

Mark didn't want to say that he'd already asked that question. That he'd already heard it might take more than one session.

"Would you have to keep, what, making donations?"

"I don't know," Mark said.

"You would," Sam told him. "I'm sure of it. Once you're on the string, they'll keep getting their money."

"Dad—"

"Let me come along," Sam said. "Let me observe."

Mark could tell Trudy: This is Brendan's grandfather. He's the memento I brought.

But what would Chloe say, if Sam came along? And if he brought a stranger—someone who might be an *obstacle*—Mark could imagine the way Trudy's objections might run.

"No," Mark said. "I can't let you."

His father, just as Mark did, worked his jaw when he was upset; his muscles pulsed below his cheekbones.

Mark said, "I'm on top of things. You didn't raise an idiot."

Sam's eyes were hard now. "I know I didn't. All right, let me ask you this. You're in love again, fine. But what happens to you two, you and Chloe, if this turns out to be a scam?"

Mark had no answer, and Sam could see it.

"Chloe loves you. But she loved you before—and she abandoned you. She needs you to help Brendan. So you meet with her, full of doubt—and just three days later you're both desperately in love, and you've left your fiancée, and you're meeting with a psychic." His father swallowed. "I could interpret that story a couple of different ways."

Mark stood up. "I can't even begin to tell you how wrong you are."

His father said, "So what's Chloe going to say when she hears about Allison? The baby?"

Mark had no answer for this, either. "I need to help Brendan," he said. "Everything else is secondary."

His father pinched the bridge of his nose. He bent forward. When he lifted his head again, Mark saw that his thin lashes were damp. Mark was stunned; he had only ever seen Sam cry twice: at his wife's funeral, and at Brendan's.

Sam stood, poured himself more coffee, and sat down. He wiped again at his eyes. "May I tell you a story? It has relevance, today, that I hoped it might never have."

Mark's anger dissipated into a sour vapor. No, he thought. Whatever it is.

Sam said, "I once tried to leave your mother. And you."

For a moment the words didn't register.

"I promised your mother I'd never tell you," Sam said. "But now I think I have to."

"Dad—"

"Shush." His eyes slitted, and Mark saw that his father's tears had risen from anger, not sadness. "I promised her when she was dying. But now might be a good time to say I don't believe the dead give a ripe shit about our promises."

Mark could only stare. His father stared back—maybe defiant, maybe frightened, maybe both—then began to speak.

⌇

His mistress's name, Sam would not reveal.

He first met her in 1980, when Sam was thirty—married, a

father—Mark was ten—and a junior professor at the university, his first book in the process of being written. The woman was twenty-five, a PhD candidate in history at Indiana University. They first spoke over the phone—she was a friend's student; she had called him about a research question—and thereafter they began corresponding about nineteenth-century American politics. Sam sent her books and articles. He invited her to submit a paper for a panel he was chairing at a conference; the paper turned out to be exceptional. Sam thought its author was probably a genius.

When he met her in person, at the conference—when she was no longer a student but a kind of colleague—he was smitten. She was a tall redhead, very much unlike his wife, and though she wasn't classically beautiful, she was pretty in a way that seemed to speak intensely, privately, to him. She was interested wholly in the very same tiny niche of human knowledge that interested him; she admired the parts of his mind that his wife didn't pretend to understand. They each, he came to think, saw the best in the other, in ways others did not. The woman had just broken off an engagement. And Sam—

"There's no mystery to it," Sam said. "Your mother and I, we were—"

"Were what?" Mark asked, hoarse.

"In a rough patch. She was involved in the raising of you and I was away, a great deal. She wanted more children and I didn't."

Mark had never known this. He'd asked his mother a hundred times during his childhood why he'd never had a brother or a sister. *Oh honey,* she'd always told him, *you're more than enough for us.*

Sam kept talking. His work demanded all the time he could give it, and some he could not. He had just grown old enough to realize, for the first time, the full range of his promises. His marriage and his career: Till death would he part from each. And each, in turn, had become troubled, harder by far than he'd ever supposed.

Even through his shock, Mark couldn't believe how similar much of Sam's story was to his own—to the way he'd felt with Chloe when, before Brendan's death, they'd begun to grow apart. He'd barely seen his wife, then; when he did see her they spoke only of Brendan, of bills and deadlines and schedules. His professional ambitions had led him in a circle. He worked harder than he ever had, yet looked forward to nothing.

Sam told him he'd begun to correspond more and more with the woman. Their letters turned to phone calls. Then she began to appear at his office door—she had family in Indianapolis; she had every reason to make the drive from Bloomington, and then to stop in for friendly chats. They had long talks about her dissertation, his book. They traded each other's work and offered comment. Once Sam asked her if she'd like him to serve as an outside member of her dissertation committee, and she blushed.

I think we're too close for that, she told him. I don't want to be afraid of you.

Sam was surprised, but he did not contradict her.

"And then, one afternoon," Sam said, "she surprised me again. She appeared at my office door after my last class and, without much preamble, told me she loved me."

Sitting in the plush chair in front of Sam's desk, she told him she knew he was married, and assumed he was married happily. She told him she didn't expect the response she really wanted. But, she said, she couldn't keep silent about it, and she hoped he understood. She was prepared never to see him again.

"She risked everything to say this to me," Sam said. "I was in a position to make her career very difficult. I could have, and should

have, told her to stay away. But what she'd done, in telling me…"
He stared at the front of the refrigerator as though it were a television screen. "That morning, driving in to school, I would have said I was happily married. I wouldn't have admitted any boredom or trouble. But then she was in front of me, saying what she said, and I was helpless—" He stopped himself, lifting a hand. "I was *sure* I was helpless to stop myself."

Sam gave no details, but Mark could imagine well enough what had happened: Sam shutting the big wooden door of his office. Turning back to the redheaded young woman who was maybe, probably, crying in front of his desk.

What his father meant was this: They'd fucked right then and there. On the rug, on the desk, maybe in the big chair in the corner where Sam did his grading, in the soft yellow light cast by the Tiffany lamp.

The same chair where Mark had spent many an afternoon, at that age, reading his Hardy Boys mysteries, his Troll paperbacks—his ghost stories—while his father did paperwork at his desk. His father sometimes taught in summer; Mark often went with him and spent the day at Butler. He read there, drew pictures, or even napped, alone, while Sam taught a class or attended a meeting.

Sometimes people had knocked on the door while Mark was alone in the office: colleagues, students. Almost everyone in the building knew Mark, knew he liked to come to work with his father. The students were charmed by him. He remembered several women—tall and beautiful and threatening—who'd stood in the doorway, smiling down at him, asking for Professor Fife.

One woman, whose face Mark could not remember, had asked, You're Sam's son? I've heard a lot about you.

Had the woman's hair been red? Mark thought perhaps it had.

Tell him——stopped by.

I will, he'd have said, and then he'd have written down the woman's name on the yellow notepad on his father's desk.

His father kept talking:

He and the woman, he said, grew obsessed with each other. Sam began working late—he lied to Molly, told her he'd taken on a night class—in order to meet the woman for an hour or two in a motel, two nights a week.

His father told him: Each time he left the motel, and this woman's arms, and drove the long forty minutes into the country, to the house where his wife and son slept, he found time to despair.

"I wanted everything," his father said. "Her. And Molly, too. And my life before I was married and had a child, before everything I did took on life-and-death importance. I wanted impossibility." Sam smiled ruefully. "And, of course, I wanted you."

His father carried on his affair with the woman for well over a year. She was coming up on the end of her degree, and, because of her brilliance, she was guaranteed to find a university job, somewhere—but likely far away from Indianapolis. The closer her graduation and departure drew, the more Sam promised her things he shouldn't have promised: That he loved her too much to let her leave him. That he would leave his wife and his child. That he would marry her, that they would have children of their own. That they would be professors together, king and queen of some campus far away.

"All my life," his father said, "I thought I had integrity. I prided myself on my word meaning something. Having value. But suddenly I heard myself saying things I couldn't make true. That had no value at all."

He stopped. Considered his words. He hadn't yet looked Mark in the eye.

"Molly caught me," he said. "An old, banal story. The woman

had slipped a note into one of my pockets that I didn't find. Maybe she was trying to get me caught. Maybe she knew I had bullshit spilling out of my ears and needed to be put to the test. In the end it doesn't matter. Your mother found out and confronted me.

"I would like to say I gave in easily. That I dropped to my knees and swore love and devotion and apologies. That I cried in regret. But I didn't."

Mark remembered this time, now—the period during his childhood when his father had been unaccountably angry, distant; when he'd often as not grunted at Mark as answered his questions. Trouble at school, was the story his mother and father both told.

He wondered now if he'd gone to work with his father so often because his mother had been suspicious.

Tell your father I stopped by.

Mark remembered another night, from that time. One summer night his mother roused him from bed and asked him if he'd like to go for a late dessert at the Dairy Queen, fifteen minutes from their house, on the outskirts of Westover. Of course he'd said yes. They drove down the dark dirt roads in his mother's little brown Monza, the windows down, the air smelling of fertile earth and kicked-up dust. Before they'd left the house, he'd asked her, Is Dad home? And she'd said, No. He's staying at his office tonight. Her voice mild—she was always mild—but her lips tight around a cigarette.

At the Dairy Queen they both drank milkshakes at a picnic table on the edge of the parking lot, the air still warm enough to make their plastic cups sweat. They didn't speak; instead his mother watched a group of teenagers—many of whom Mark knew from the school bus—laughing and punching one another's shoulders at another table.

When their shakes were done, his mother had asked, Do you mind if we keep sitting here? And he'd said, No. He was mystified by her behavior, by being allowed to be awake and out of the house, to be eating sweets at ten in the evening, but he didn't dare question it. The DQ closed even as his mother smoked and watched the cars rolling by. Finally she seemed to remember herself. Tell me about the book you're reading, she said.

His belly full, his veins surging with sugar, he happily recounted to her the story of Taran, an Assistant Pig-Keeper, and his slow rise to becoming the savior of Prydain. How Taran came, over the course of many adventures, to love Princess Eilonwy—a development that, at the time, had made him thrill in secret. He'd known of Taran's love even before Taran had.

When he'd finished, his mother said, Boys don't often get to have adventures like they do in books. You know that, right?

I know. That's why I like books.

She reached over and brushed his hair from his cheek. That's right, she said. Don't forget, okay?

Sam said, now, "I told her I wanted to leave her."

"Dad," Mark said.

"Here's your mother for you," Sam said. "She said I couldn't. Just like that. We had a terrible fight, but she stuck to her guns. She told me I was a fool. She told me—your tiny mother told me—that she'd rather kill me than have our son grow up with a father who'd left him. She said at least then you would know you were loved."

Mark covered his mouth.

"None of this meant I didn't love you," Sam said, watching him carefully. "None of it meant I didn't love Molly. But I fought anyway. I had a vision, and I fought for it.

"*Your son*, your mother kept saying. *Don't do this to your son.*

"And you know what? I never left. I gave your mother a list of grievances, and she pointed out that all of them were foolish. And I stayed to argue. The woman I'd been seeing called the house, and your mother told her not to call anymore. And I stayed.

349

"The woman I'd loved stopped calling. I stopped calling her. Your mother and I spent a summer frozen, each of us watching the other. And that was my time, Mark. I could have left, I could have asserted myself. But I didn't. One night I told your mother what she already knew. I announced I would stay, if she'd have me. And she said she would."

Sam's eyes were wet. "None of this meant I didn't love the other woman. I did. I loved her desperately. But I called her one last time and told her what she'd already figured out: that I could not leave my family."

"Dad," Mark said again. He could have kept saying it.

He saw his father in his mother's hospital room, bending over her wizened body—suddenly, unnaturally still—and pressing his lips against hers, and then Sam's living body shuddering and shuddering, his fists gripping the sheets of the hospital bed into bunches, before Mark at last went to him and put his arms around him and pulled him back.

His father, giving a kiss to his dead wife as though he expected her to wake to it.

"I stayed," Sam said. "And you never knew, did you? But even now, I regret the betrayal of you. The time I lost with you. The reasons I found to ignore you. I want you to know that. When I decided to stay, I told myself I was going to relearn you. To see you through to the man you would become. This was what I lived for. And watching that happen—watching you learn, and meet Chloe, and have a child of your own—"

Mark should be moved by this, he knew, but now he was angry; he felt a child's need to swipe away his father's outstretched hands.

Or maybe he was angry at Allison, for being pregnant, or at Chloe, for loving him again. Or at Brendan, for bringing these problems to him. For sneaking down the stairs; for forgetting to tie his shoe.

His father seemed to be waiting for Mark to say something. To judge him, maybe.

Mark asked, "What happened to the woman?"

Sam said, "She's married, now. She's a professor at a more prestigious university than mine, and she publishes more frequently than I do, and we see each other once a year or so, since we know all the same people and go to the same conferences. She never lets me forget that I'm a liar. She hates me, hates me utterly."

Sam regarded him. "But that's not what you want to know, is it? I still love her. I do. What I promised her was a lie, but what I felt was real." He shrugged. "The worst part is that she knows. She thinks of me not only as a man who broke her heart, but as a coward."

With this, Sam let out some final reserve of air he'd been holding in. "Well. Those are my sins."

He held out his hand on top of the table. Mark didn't swipe it away. He reached out, almost against his will, and held it. Sam returned his grip tightly.

"Last night, and on the drive out here, I fought with myself. Do I tell you? Do I not? Do I give you advice? Do I not? I had no answer, and I still don't. I don't know what to tell you about Brendan. You're right—I don't think I can make myself believe in a ghost. But I know that if Allison is pregnant, and has a baby, I will have a grandchild again. You will be a father again.

"It's a long and strange life," Sam said. "I have regrets. I miss two women now. But in the end I know this." He looked Mark right in the eye. "I didn't leave my son for a fantasy."

"A fantasy?"

His father did not drop his gaze.

"I'm not leaving my son, either," Mark told him. "You have to understand that."

⌒

After that there wasn't much more to say. Sam stood—older, now; deflated—and told Mark he'd stay in a hotel. Mark offered him the townhouse, but Sam refused. Still, he said, he wanted news. He wanted Mark to call him. He wanted Mark to promise him, and finally Mark did.

Then his father was standing, was pulling on his coat, disappointed and slow.

At the front door he told Mark to take care. He held out his hand, and Mark shook it—then pulled him into an embrace. "I hope someday I can make you understand," he said.

Sam didn't answer. But at the bottom of the snowy steps he turned and said, "Give my love to Chloe."

⌒

When he was gone, Mark walked upstairs, to gather as quickly as he could what he needed for the evening. He pulled a zippered portfolio bag out of his office closet, then retrieved his sketches of Brendan and slid them inside. After a moment's thought, he returned to the closet and, from a box far in the back, removed a few pieces of Brendan's own artwork: a Christmas card that opened onto a crayoned, bulbous Santa; a creased piece of construction paper upon which Brendan had, for the first time, scrawled his own name.

Mark held this piece of paper in his hand for a long time. Now he was overcome by the idea of himself with another child—a daughter. He saw her clearly: brown-haired, brown-eyed, pudgy-faced. A real child, a living child.

Mark tucked the zippered case beneath his arm, then walked down the hall to the bedroom, to pack his clothes.

The bedroom was a mess. Allie had packed her own bags,

today, and had left what she didn't need strewn across the floor and bed.

Mark tried not to think about Allie's curses, his father's arguments, but both reverberated. Mark was a bad lover, a bad son. Without ever quite meaning to, he had become the worst of liars.

He remembered Jacob Pelham's sly, guilty face.

Mark sat down on the edge of the bed and closed his eyes and cast his mind back to Brendan's old room, to the faint, flickering touch that had roused him, to the footsteps running from him, away and down the stairs.

Brendan.

I felt you, didn't I? You called for me and I came to find you. You came to me, and you ran through me, and I heard you and felt you and then your footsteps were on the stairs. You were real.

You have to be real. You have to be.

Mark could see Allie's last minutes in the room; he watched her throwing clothes into her suitcase; sitting, maybe, where he now sat; crying and crying.

You have to be real, little man.

Because if you aren't, neither am I.

⌇

Mark was almost to the stairs, carrying his suitcase, when he remembered his phone charger. He dropped the bag and returned to his office. The charger was plugged into the same power strip as the computer; he freed it, then tucked it into the inside pocket of his coat. Then he stared at his desk. He might not be back here for several days—as much as he didn't want to think about work right now, he should take his laptop with him, at least, to be safe. He turned on the desktop computer and began to sync his calendar, to transfer some of his smaller project files to a portable drive. He still had bills, deadlines—though they had come to seem more surreal to him than the memory of Brendan's bedroom had been.

Especially if he and Allie weren't going to be splitting the rent anymore. Especially if he was going to be the father of a child again.

A father, a father—Christ, Brendan, did you know? *If you know so much, how come you couldn't know* this?

Maybe Brendan didn't. Maybe he couldn't. And maybe that was because Jacob had lied, and Brendan wasn't real at all.

Witches in Salem. The Jews at Birkenau. The dead at Jonestown. The men and women and children who walked into crowded squares in Israel and Syria and Iraq, strapped to nail bombs. The men who'd carried box cutters onto those airplanes, certain of an eternity populated with virgins.

But those were the extremes. What about the more mundane people Mark had always pitied, mocked: the audiences at televised sermons? Every time he flipped through the backwater channels of the television he saw vast seas of them in their megachurches, their arms outstretched, their eyes closed, speaking to the unseen while their pastors exhorted them to give, *give.* Were he and Chloe any different from *them*?

He remembered Trudy Weill, his hands in hers. *Isn't that a comfort?*

The computer was running, now. For the first time since meeting Trudy, Mark was alone with an open Internet connection. Given what he'd done, what he still planned to do, he could afford to spend a few minutes checking up on her. Couldn't he?

He decided he could. He owed his old life that much.

His first search, for "Gertrude Weill," turned up only one credible hit: a crude website for a Church of the White Light, in Kent, Michigan. The site's main graphic was a photograph of the church itself: a single-story stone house, sandwiched between a bean field in sprout and a gravel parking lot.

Below this was a mission statement: The Church of the White Light is a spiritualist haven, open to all seekers who would find peace in true knowledge of Heaven and Christ. The CWL does not discriminate against any color or creed. Our only interest is in seeing the acts of Jesus Christ inspire as many of our brethren as possible. The CWL is founded on a positive principle: that the spirits of those who have passed, and whom He holds close, may offer our flock guidance in His will.

Farther down the page was a picture of Trudy and Warren, maybe taken at a Sears portrait studio—the background was mottled brown-and-white drapery. Trudy's scar had been turned away from the camera—the picture showed only two plain, pious, white Midwesterners, each attempting a beatific smile. The caption beneath it read:

> Pastor, Warren Weill; Medium, Gertrude Weill. "Love does no wrong to a neighbor; therefore love is the fulfillment of the law." Rom 13:10.

Other than a listing of service times—Sunday morning and Wednesday night—and directions to the church, the site contained little information, and certainly nothing about Trudy's private work.

He searched again, for "Trudy Weill medium." This time over a hundred hits came back, almost all of them linked to posts on message boards. By far the board with the largest number of links was one titled SpiritualistNet.

Trudy Weill's name first appeared, here, in a post titled: HELP Looking for reputable mediums? The poster believed his mother's ghost was still present in her apartment. How do I find someone worth my time + who wont take my money??

Someone from Waukegan, Illinois, had replied: Trudy Weill works through a spiritualist church in Kent, MI, and can be reached through the website for the Church of the White Light. She also works in private consultation, either to reach lost spirits or to cleanse homes with resident spirits.

My sister and I contacted her in 1997 to help us reach the spirit of our father, who remained in residence in our home after his untimely death in 1985. We went to a number of so-called mediums before Trudy was recommended to us. She is very kind and good, and traveled a long distance to our home and helped lead Dad to rest. You're right to be wary of frauds, but believe me, Trudy is the Real Deal.

Someone in Las Vegas answered immediately:

—What does she charge?

The original poster:

—A donation to the CWL (her church). But you might be too far away for her.
—How much did you donate?
—That is between me and the church. I donated what I felt was right. I was told what past clients had donated and did not feel pressured to match that. The amount was four figures I can say that but I was happy to pay it.

Another poster, from Indiana:

—Sounds like a lot.
—Not for what she did for us.

More testimonials piled up, almost all of them from people in Michigan or Indiana or Ohio.

A poster from Flint:

—Trudy Weill was a godsend to us. After three sessions we were able to communicate with Harold. We told him, through

her, to go forward into the tunnel (what she says They see), and
he finally did so. This was traumatic for us and for Trudy too but
in every case she was professional and kind and counseled
us before and after our sessions. Our house has been at rest
since, just as Harold has. I did indeed make a donation to the
CWL. I want to support the Weills in all they do. And if you live
in MI go to the CWL and attend a service. Trudy will ask the
spirits about Jesus and His Will and they answer. I wish her
church was in my town; It is the only one I've been to that makes
sense.

    —My child Marcy passed from encephalitis in 2003. Since she
has gone I have been sure I felt her in the house. We contacted
Trudy, and she was great. We are very poor and we didn't donate
much but I felt I should thank her and would give her more if I
could.

Finally, near the bottom of the thread, Mark saw that someone named KLovell, from South Bend, had posted under the title
BEWARE THE WEILLS!

    —I know this comment will be flagged or even deleted as it
has been before. I just want everyone here to hear our story. My
husband and I paid over 10,000 dollars to the Weills via the CWL
and had agreed to pay another 5000 for a new session before
we realized we were being scammed. After two sessions without
results I saw that what Ms. Weill does is clearly an act. Basically
these people tell you everything you want to hear. We fired them
in effect. Ms. Weill's husband contacted us and put the hard sell
on us for that extra five K and he was unpleasant to say the least.
I am sorry to have been talked into this and feel very stupid and
would urge anyone who is thinking of letting the Weills into their

home to contact me at the following address: klovell365@gmail
.com. I am thinking of filing suit to reclaim my money.

A response, from someone named pray2king, had been posted
right away:

—So why isn't your husband on here with his side of things? I
find that suspicious. Did you both agree or did you decide for him?
The Weills helped me and my wife! You have given up too soon on
giving your loved one her peace.

KLovell had replied:

—I will not comment except to note this type of statement is
typical of my phone conversations with Warren Weill.

A slew of postings had followed, almost all of them pro–Trudy
and Warren.

Someone from St. Ignace, Michigan, replied:

—I donated something similar. Warren asked that I donate
according to my means. I do not miss the money and feel at
peace with what has happened. Klovell, I'm sorry you had a
bad experience but as Trudy says you can't have a successful
session with so much negative energy in your heart. I would
suggest you try again only with a more open mind. Love knows
no walls.

Fifty happy people. One doubter, shouted away.

Mark remembered something he'd once read in a book of true
crime: The best con artists never leave anyone feeling taken. None
of their victims ever knows there's been a crime.

He powered down the computer and left the townhouse for good.

⌒

The roads had improved, but even so it was nearly two o'clock when Mark parked in front of Chloe's apartment building. The apartment, when she opened the door, smelled oddly of Christmas, of mulling spice. Chloe wore faded jeans and a red T-shirt; she was barefoot, and her hair was pulled sloppily back. She smiled, her eyes sad and sweet, and kissed him in the doorway.

Only his repeating thoughts—Allie's pregnant, Allie's pregnant—kept him from pulling her down to the floor right there.

She said, "I was starting to get worried."

He dropped his suitcase. "Allison was there."

Chloe was instantly wary.

"I told her," he said.

On the way over he'd decided—in the interest of confining any negative energy to himself—to say nothing yet about the baby.

"It was bad," he said. "I'm not a good person, Chloe."

She took his hand and led him inside, to the couch. "You're not going to convince me of that." She kissed him again. Her breath tasted of cinnamon gum, and behind it, maybe, a cigarette. "You did what you had to. Allison will survive this."

For the first time since he'd come back to her, Mark heard a coldness in Chloe's voice: *She'll get over it.*

He said, again, "She doesn't deserve this."

Chloe said, "Neither did we, honey. But here we are."

Honey. Would Chloe call him this when he told her that, in eight months, he'd be spending half his time with a child who looked like Allie? That this child would play on their rug, would sleep in a bed down the hall?

"Do you want to talk about it?"

"Tomorrow, maybe," he said. "Let's get through tonight first."

"You're worried."

"It's okay. Really."

Her shoulders fell. "They tried to talk you out of it, didn't they? Sam tried."

"Yeah."

"God*damn* it—"

"Don't be angry. What else would you expect?"

Chloe was shaking her head. "They don't know. They just don't."

"No."

"You really told her?" Chloe asked.

"I did."

Chloe kissed him again. Hard. She dropped her hand to the front of his jeans. He'd wondered, on the drive back, whether he'd be able to hide his news, let alone feel desire—but those thoughts were destroyed, now, as he pulled at Chloe's shirt, at her belt. Today he had earned a good woman's hatred, and yet here was Chloe, her body, her mouth, her wide cornflower eyes, blinking and soft, only inches from his own. Urging him on. Thanking him.

Rewarding him for his trust, his faith.

⌒

In the bedroom, once they'd finished, Mark couldn't stop himself: "Chloe? Can I ask you something?"

Chloe lifted her head from the hollow of his shoulder and nodded.

"What happens when he's gone? When he's there, and we're here?"

Chloe rolled up onto an elbow. "We go on. You and me."

"You're sure?"

She held his gaze. "I told you. I can't do without you. Not again."

He wanted to ask her more: Will you still love me if it turns out we're wrong? Will you still love me when I'm a father to Allie's child? Yet despite all that had happened between them, he was afraid.

Chloe said, "Can I ask *you* something?"

"Yeah."

"It's just an idea," she said.

"Say it."

She sat up and pulled the comforter around her shoulders. Then she told him, hesitantly, her plan. She had a lot of money in the bank. She'd always been good about saving money—in the seven years since Brendan's death she'd bought almost nothing beyond necessities, had taken no vacations, and she still had half her share of the money from the sale of the old house. All told, she said, she had a little over a hundred thousand dollars in the bank.

"That's a little less than half of what the house is worth now," she said. "Connie and her ex are desperate to sell the place. And he's a bank executive."

Mark began to understand.

Even without Mark's money, Chloe told him, she thought she might be able to get financing; Connie's ex would help the loan along. But—if Mark wanted to—the two of them together would be a snap to get approval for a new mortgage.

She stroked his hand. "What I'm saying is, we could start over. You and me, again. In our house."

He breathed in and out.

"It's *ours*," Chloe said. "I've never stopped thinking that."

"But," he said, finally, "wouldn't it be too strange? Being there when he's gone?"

"I don't know," she said. "But it was happy for us once. It could be happy again. That's up to us, isn't it?"

Mark saw Allison standing in the front doorway of the Locust house, bouncing a dark-eyed toddler on her hip. Saying, Hi, Chloe, like poison.

"It's ours," Chloe said, and rested her cheek against his chest. "It feels wrong without us there. That's all I was thinking."

⌒

Chloe slept. Mark wasn't tired at all. The day's events, the unguessable future, began to sway and loom. He got up and walked naked down the hall to the bathroom, then went to the kitchen, where he leaned against the sink and downed a glass of water.

The old house, theirs again: A future as inconceivable to him, right now, as a heaven. As being a father once more.

He had just put his glass in the dishwasher when he saw that Chloe's purse was open on the counter, not far from the cooling spice cake she had whipped up to take with them to the Pelham's. Just visible inside was a leather checkbook.

As far as he could tell, Chloe still slept soundly. Carefully, he lifted out the checkbook and flipped quickly through the last carbons.

He didn't have to look far to spot the check she'd written to the Church of the White Light. Chloe had filled it out yesterday—she must have given it to Warren in the kitchen. It was for five thousand dollars.

He flipped back farther—rent, Verizon, Kroger—but saw nothing else made out to the Weills. Chloe had made only one payment—one donation, rendered in advance of tonight's session. Five grand, just like that.

When he opened her purse again, to drop the checkbook back into place, he saw a small brown pill bottle with no label. He lifted it. The pills inside were oddly shaped, odd-sounding. He uncapped the vial and tipped the contents out into his palm.

Teeth, clicking together like yellowed pearls. Brendan's baby teeth. Five of them, tiny and impossibly smooth and cold. Chloe's talismans, for the ritual to come—he was sure of it.

He dropped them carefully back into the vial, capped it, and dropped it back into her purse. Then he crept down the hallway to her bed and held her tightly while she slept, and he did not.

Twenty-seven

At four thirty he roused Chloe. They prepared for their evening in silence.

Mark sorted through the jumble of clothing in his suitcase, trying to decide: How might one dress, in order to attend a séance for one's son? He ended up choosing black slacks and a buttondown shirt. He put on a dark sport coat, too, and wondered idly whether Brendan would recognize him.

Chloe dressed in a long black skirt and a white blouse, a dress jacket too, and black boots. "Ready?" she asked him, when she'd done her hair and her makeup. She was lovely, he thought, achingly so.

A piercing premonition racked him. Their time together, he was sure—despite their promises—was coming to its end.

"We can do this," she said, smiling, after a glance at his face. "Mark—It's going to be all right."

⁓

Mark drove them to the old house in the Volvo. The night sky spit handfuls of sleet at the windshield, and with each explosive patter, Chloe—who had never been a relaxed passenger—let out a gasp. They held hands but did not speak.

Halfway to Victorian Village, Warren Weill called Chloe's phone. She answered and relayed the message to Mark: Warren and Trudy were having trouble on the roads, and would be late. He'd suggested everyone have a glass of wine, to ease themselves.

Mark thought of Sam, frowning, insisting he should come along. Chloe slipped her hand over his knee. "You okay?"

"I'm fine," he told her.

⁓

When they parked in front of the old house, almost every light in the place was blazing, including the one in Brendan's old room. Mark saw a shadow moving there, behind the drawn shade, and tightened his hands on the wheel.

He opened Chloe's door for her; without saying anything more they mounted the slippery porch steps, leaning against each other.

Connie opened the door before they knocked. She had dressed up, too; she wore black slacks and heels, and a tight gray sweater. Large silver hoops dangled from her ears. "Chloe, Mark! Welcome. Or maybe I should say, welcome back."

Her line fell flat. "Thank you," Chloe said, smiling anyway. They walked past Connie into the house.

Mark followed Chloe into the family room, and glanced around him; he hadn't visited it, the other night. Connie had decorated it as a library; several tall, dark-stained bookshelves hugged the walls, which had been repainted a dark, coppery brown. A love seat and two deep chairs were arranged on a rug in the room's center. Behind him Connie was accepting the spice cake from Chloe. Mark glanced at one of the shelves nearest to him, saw Dickens, Austen, and even Wilkie Collins.

He had been misjudging Connie. She wasn't stupid. The more likely story—one he hadn't allowed himself to see—was that she was just like Jacob: bookish and shy, blinkered by the world as it was.

Connie appeared beside him. "I love this room," she said. Her voice was still nervous, tentative, as though she was afraid he might snap at her. "I can open the windows to the porch in spring. And we wanted—I wanted—someplace with no television, you know?"

They'd had the television in this room when they lived here; this was where Mark had been sitting, seven years ago today, when Brendan fell.

"I like what you've done with it," he told her.

Chloe filled Connie in on the Weills' progress as they walked through the living room—lit with scented candles, as well as the floor lamps—past the stairwell and to the kitchen. In the full light, the house seemed to have expanded out and up. As he'd been the other night, Mark was struck by the lack of artwork, the unfinishedness of the house; lit and inhabited, it seemed even emptier than it had in the dark.

In the kitchen Connie said, "Well, we should do what Mr. Weill asked, right?" and produced a bottle of wine from the pantry. She held it out for Mark to examine: an expensive-looking Pinot, filmed with dust.

"I'll be fine with water," he said.

"Oh," she said, taken aback. "Well, I have club soda?"

He thanked her. Connie poured his drink first, and was nice enough to slice a lime for him, too. Then she and Chloe wrestled the wine cork.

"Where's Jacob?" Mark asked.

Connie adopted a clownish, sour frown and said, *"But Mom, I just got my new comics."* She shook her head, walked to the stairwell, and called: "Jacob! Come down!" Then she sighed to Mark and Chloe. "I don't get him. Yesterday he was excited, asking me all these questions: *Mom, are there going to be candles? Mom, are we going to sing?* But he's been moping today."

Mark's stomach shrank on itself. "It's got to be a scary thing for a kid to think about."

"Well, sure." Connie lowered her voice. "I think meeting you was part of it, Mark. He's so weird about male figures, you know.

His dad and all." Then she smiled. "He asked me a bunch of questions about you."

"Like what?" he asked, as Chloe slipped her hand into his.

"Do you think Mr. Fife is nice? Do you think he really liked my picture? That sort of thing." She shouted again: "Jacob Pelham!"

His entire day bore down upon him: Allison's pregnancy. His father's talk of con artists. And now Jacob Pelham, in hiding.

Mark put on what he hoped was a warm smile. "Tell you what, Connie. Do you think it would be okay if I went upstairs and got him?"

Chloe squeezed his hand; he squeezed back.

"Oh!" Connie said. "Would you? He's got all his drawings up there—he'd be thrilled to show them to you." She sighed again. "He's such a complicated little guy."

"He reminds me a lot of myself," Mark said.

⌒

He walked slowly up the stairs, trailing his hands across the old, textured wallpaper. He'd been here only a few nights ago, but the steps seemed strange again, the weird echoey meld of Chloe's and Connie's voices fading behind him. He stopped on the landing; now, in the brighter light, the spot of Brendan's death seemed much smaller, much more innocuous than it had been the other night in the dark. Stepping through it, however, still left him light-headed, his palms damp.

Give me a sign. Brendan, anything. Don't make me do this.

Mark closed his eyes; his fingertips touched the walls. But Brendan did not come to him. The house—which just a few nights ago had felt like a pulsing, breathing, secretive beast—remained straight and warm and silent.

In the upstairs hallway the overhead light was blazing. The door to Brendan's old bedroom was shut. This time the only open doorway led to what had once been the guest room, but which now had to be Jacob Pelham's bedroom.

Jacob appeared then in the doorway, in jeans and a too-tight T-shirt and stocking feet. When he saw Mark standing in the hallway he drew back in fright.

Mark said, "Hi, Jacob."

"Oh!" Jacob said. "I didn't see you there."

Mark said, "I'm sorry. I didn't mean to scare you."

Jacob nodded, still blinking.

"Can I come see your room? Your mom says you've got a lot of artwork up."

"Um," Jacob said, "Sure." He pointed behind him. "It's—it's this one."

The room was a cramped mess: a riot of color and books and heaps of clothes. A pile of comic books were fanned out beneath a desk lamp, clipped to the top of a small drawing table abutting the foot of the bed. Along the other wall were a child-size bureau and several deep shelves that held long boxes full of comics. Jacob had papered the high walls with posters and drawings of superheroes— including, above his bed, a horizontal poster of Batman, crouched on the edge of a rooftop, his cape billowing out behind him like a storm cloud.

The air smelled, unpleasantly, of little boy—of unwashed clothing and grime and old, congealed soda pop.

Jacob said, "You can sit in the desk chair." He flopped on his bed; his jeans rode down on his hip, exposing a strip of elastic torn away from the rest of his underwear.

When he dropped down, what Mark had thought to be a small pillow on Jacob's bed turned into an enormous orange-and-white piebald cat, skittering sideways in alarm. It crouched in the corner, beside Jacob's jumbled pillows. The cat's eyes glowed like Batman's.

"That's one gigantic cat," Mark said, sitting.

"Oh. That's Bigwig. Here, kitty-kit." Jacob held out his fingers and made a *took-took-took* sound with his tongue. The cat rose right away and crept to Jacob, trilling. "I've had him since he was a kitten."

"*Watership Down*?" Mark asked. "That Bigwig?"

Jacob smiled, but only with one corner of his mouth, and rubbed the cat's buzzing throat. "Yeah," he said. "It's basically my favorite book of all time."

"One of mine, too," Mark said. "I even read it aloud to Brendan one summer."

"Really?" Jacob thought about this, and then asked, "Did he like it?"

Brendan had loved it. In fact, Mark doubted Brendan had loved anything in the real world as much as Hazel and Fiver and Bigwig. In that way he was a lot like his father.

Mark had forgotten that the book ended with the appearance of God. He'd had to explain that to Brendan, hadn't he? What had happened to Hazel, and the identity of the strange rabbit that had come for him in his last moments.

He'd said, Look at the rabbits Hazel left behind, all safe and happy. That comforts him. In the end Hazel's happy, even if *we're* sad.

"He liked it very much," Mark said.

They fell quiet. Jacob began to poke at a scab on his wrist. He was nervous. No—he was *scared*.

"Jacob," Mark said, "the Weills will be here in a few minutes."

"I know," Jacob said.

"Your mother says you've been a little nervous today."

Jacob shrugged. "I don't know."

"Have you—have you been thinking about what I asked you the other day?"

Jacob nodded, so slightly Mark could barely see it.

"Do you have anything you need to say?"

Jacob dropped his chin to his chest, then shook his head.

Oh Brendan, he's lying, he's lying. Look at him.

Jacob said, "It's like I told you."

"You mean that? Even though we're about to start the ceremony?"

Again the tiny nod.

Mark scooted his chair closer. "Jacob. Can I tell you something?"

"Sure."

"Do you know that I'm a liar?"

Jacob blinked, with a look of stubborn incomprehension Mark hadn't seen in a long time: Adults couldn't have *flaws*. It didn't compute.

"It's true," Mark said. "I didn't used to be, but since Brendan died, I've lied all the time."

How simple it sounded, when he told it like this. How awful.

"About what?" Jacob asked.

"Lots of things," Mark said. "But mostly I lie to make people like me. If I say something they like, I keep saying it. Mostly because I'm afraid that if they don't like me, I'll be alone."

"Oh," Jacob said. Air escaping a punctured tire.

"The hardest part," Mark told him, "the worst part, is when a lie keeps building on itself. I tell one, and then I have to tell another one to cover up the first one, and then another one, and another one. That's taken me a long time to learn—lies seem like they solve problems, but they don't. They never do."

Jacob stared at his fidgeting hands.

"I lied to Chloe, when she was my wife, and just this week I lied to a woman named Allison, who I was going to marry. And neither one of them liked it very much at all. And so I had to apologize."

Jacob said, without lifting his head, "Chloe must have forgave you."

"She did," Mark said, carefully. The boy was smart, so smart. "But not until I told her I'd lied. And even then it took a long time for us to trust each other again. Years and years."

Jacob furrowed his fingers through the cat's pelt.

"I want to let you know that if—if you're not sure about what happened, you can say so. I'll forgive you. I'm pretty good at it. Of all people, I *have* to be."

"I told the truth," Jacob insisted.

"Jacob. Look at me."

Jacob did so, but only for a moment, before his eyes jerked back to his cat.

"If you're not telling the truth, a lot of people will be hurt. Hurt in ways you don't understand, yet. But very seriously hurt."

"Mr. Fife," he said, "I *know*. I swear I'm telling the truth."

He stared at Jacob stroking the cat, avoiding his eyes. Mark hadn't raised a son for seven years not to recognize how scared Jacob was. But maybe he wasn't scared *enough*.

Mark said, "I talked to Trudy Weill again today. I asked her again what would happen, if there wasn't really a ghost. And she told me something that really worries me."

Jacob swallowed, but didn't answer.

"She has to open a doorway," Mark said. "And if Brendan's on the other side, he'll come through and talk to us. But if there's no Brendan there, Trudy says something *else* might."

This was language right out of some tattered comic book that— for all Mark knew—was sealed in a plastic bag in Jacob's collection.

Mark said, "The thing that comes through will be stuck here, then. We could end up haunting this place with something a lot meaner than a little boy. And it'll be you and your mom who have to live with it."

Jacob bent close to Bigwig, whose tail switched back and forth. "Oh," he said.

"So be sure," Mark said. *"Are* you?"

Jacob's voice was a salted whisper: "Yeah."

"If you change your mind, you have to tell me before we get started. That's very important."

"Okay."

"You'll tell me? If you change your mind?"

Jacob nodded. "Sure."

The boy seemed right on the verge of opening up—of collapsing, spilling out every one of his secrets. Mark waited, waited—but Jacob said nothing.

Finally Mark had to admit he'd lost. "Okay," he said, heavily. "Go downstairs and see your mother. And tell her I'll be down in a minute, okay?"

Jacob nodded and stood. Carrying his cat, he walked out of the room, past Mark, down the hallway to the stairs.

⌒

Mark walked down the hall, to the doorway of Brendan's old room. Halfway there he paused and listened carefully to Jacob's thumping descent of the steps. It sounded—he had to admit it—nothing at all like the sounds he remembered the other night. Nothing like Brendan running.

Please. *Please.*

Brendan's old room was different than when Mark had last been inside: Chloe's cushion and lamp were still arranged beside the window, but now a card table had been set up in the cleared-out center of the room, ringed by six folding chairs. In the middle of the tabletop stood two tall, unlit taper candles. Beside the candles was a book, and Mark didn't have to approach closer to know it was a Bible.

Of course they'd do the ceremony here, where the visitations had occurred. But these things, here—they felt like a violation. Unreal and untrue.

Mark crossed the room and pulled one of the folding chairs beside the window. He sat, pushed aside the blind, and looked down onto the street. The cobbles under the streetlight were silvery, brushed over with new snow; they looked like the scales of an enormous snake.

Jacob was lying. Mark's every instinct told him so. In the space of a day Mark had become suspicious of everything they were to do, everything that he'd cast aside his life to accomplish. Chloe was right: His father *had* gotten to him. Allie had gotten to him. His old self, too.

But he was suspicious, even, of this suspicion. How quickly, how easily, it had come. Here in this room, and in Chloe's apartment, he'd been suffused with belief, with a happiness and purpose he hadn't felt since—

Since Chloe had first loved him.

Chloe wasn't conning him, using him. His father was wrong about that; she couldn't be. Chloe had believed, heart and soul, in Brendan, in what they were about to do tonight. She had given herself to Mark. She'd offered him her future.

This had all happened because she thought Brendan was here. Because, for two days, Mark had told her he thought so, too.

So what did it matter, whether Brendan was here, now, or not? If both of them, in their way, had talked themselves into him? If Mark said nothing—if he let the ceremony go on, if he acted his part—what was the harm? Wasn't it worth five grand—more—to let the Weills give Chloe her peace?

To allow Chloe to stay with him? To give them both, at last, another chance?

Outside he heard a sound: an engine winding down, the whine of brakes taking hold. He peered out and saw a black SUV parking just in front of his Volvo. The driver's-side door opened, and Warren Weill emerged, wearing a black overcoat. He stepped stiffly across the ice in order to open the passenger door and offer his hand to Trudy. She wore a black coat, too, and a long black skirt.

Mark saw it, now: All of them had dressed as though they were attending a funeral.

He released the shade. He should go downstairs, present himself. Act his part. Down below he heard the muffled exclamations of Connie greeting the Weills. He closed his eyes.

Brendan.

We don't have much time. I need a sign. I need you.

Mark remembered how happy he'd been, the other night. How he'd suddenly filled, nearly to bursting; how he'd heard laughter; how he'd flung himself heedless down the hallway and the stairs, chasing after Brendan and his pattering footsteps. He'd been so happy. He'd felt such love.

He'd been so sure, so goddamned sure as he ran, that when he reached out his arms he would grasp the skinny wriggling body of his boy.

Now he could only think: Just before hearing Brendan laugh, just before hearing his footsteps, he *had* reached out his arms, and closed them on empty air.

Brendan. Please.

Chloe's voice, calling up the stairwell: "Mark! The Weills are here!"

Mark stood, near tears, and shifted the chair back to the table. Its rubber-tipped legs skidded harshly across the polished wood of the floor.

And then he heard it. The hair on his arms rose.

The patter of footsteps, in the hall.

"Brendan?"

He walked around the table and to the doorway.

Oh, Brendan. Please.

He peered out the doorway, toward the corner and the stairwell. A moan left him—because even though he'd prepared himself for the sight of an empty hallway, or even for the figure of his son, he saw, instead, two green-gold gleams: two lambent eyes, staring up at him.

Jacob's giant cat was crouched in the center of the hallway, its tail puffed straight out.

He took a step into the hall. The cat immediately turned and ran from him, around the corner, then into the stairwell and down.

Mark heard every step of its quick, bumping descent.

Twenty-eight

His hand over his mouth, holding back giddy laughter or tears or both, Mark descended the stairs, too. A woman's voice—Trudy Weill's—grew in volume, and when he emerged into the living room he found all the others—Chloe and Warren and Connie and even Jacob—sitting silently, heads bowed.

All of them lifted their heads at Mark's arrival; all of them except Jacob smiled.

Trudy immediately walked to him and took his hand. "Mark! Join us!" Her palm was dry, warm. He wondered if she could know his heart right now, the horror trying to claw that heart to flinders.

"I hope, Mr. Mark, that you'll bear with me while we pray."

Trudy pulled him along beside her. Chloe read his face and began to rise from her seat; he shook his head. Instead he turned to Jacob—who sat beside his mother on the couch, staring intently at his shoes.

"O Lord!" Trudy cried out, with a shocking lift in volume. Connie and Chloe both dropped their heads; Jacob started, then stared gape-mouthed, first at Trudy, then at Mark. Warren dropped stiffly onto one knee, his hands clasped before him.

"At last," Trudy cried—and here she squeezed Mark's hand—"we are all assembled, to do Your work. To return a wayward sheep to Your flock, as You have called. O Lord, we ask of

You only Your patience and guidance—and Your forgiveness, as we knock upon the gates of Your kingdom. O Lord, please guide us as we reach out our hand to little Brendan. Please let us send him home to You. In Your name we ask this. Amen."

Connie's fervent squeak. Warren's louder baritone: "Ahh-men." Jacob's lips moving soundlessly. And amid the other voices Mark even heard Chloe's: "Amen," whispered, like the name of a lover.

Bigwig the cat emerged from under an end table. He hopped from the floor onto an ottoman in front of a low reading chair, standing as close to Jacob as he could. He glared first at Mark, and then at everyone else in the room.

"Well," Trudy said, beaming. "Shall we begin?"

Mark couldn't hold it in any longer. He took a deep breath. The five faces in the living room turned and regarded him. He opened his mouth.

Jacob spoke first: "Wait!"

The boy was bent forward, his fingers laced tightly together. He turned his wet eyes to his mother. "We can't."

Trudy released Mark's hand.

"None of it's true," Jacob said.

The excitement drained from Chloe's face, was replaced by something more uncertain—then pain. Hurt. She took a step toward Jacob—who launched himself from the couch, then ran past Mark and up the stairs. As he turned the landing a sob escaped him.

His cat gave the room one last, hateful stare, and followed.

"Well," Trudy said, "that was unexpected."

"No, it wasn't," Mark said.

Warren came to stand beside his wife, one fist pressed to the small of her back, his face stony.

"What's happened, Mark?" Trudy asked; her voice was like a suspicious high school teacher's, just beginning to harden around the edges. She reached for his hand, but he pulled it back. He had to applaud her acting—she seemed as upset, as shocked, as Chloe, who was staring at him motionless.

Connie stood, obviously torn between following her child and listening to what Mark had to say.

"He lied to us," Mark said. "He never saw any ghost."

"Mark," Chloe said.

"We just had a talk upstairs," he said. "That's what happened."

Chloe said, "Mark, we've—we've all—"

Mark could hardly bear to look at her. She leaned forward, one arm crossing her stomach, as though he'd punched her. In one day's time he had told the only two women who had ever loved him the words they could bear the least.

"Chloe," he said softly, "why don't we go talk to Jacob? He'll explain."

"Mark," she said again, but did not move.

Warren cleared his throat. "I think you misunderstand, Mr. Fife. This situation—"

Trudy cut him off. "Mark. I feel your son in this house. He is *here*, I assure you." Her scar stood out from her forehead like a smear of chalk. "I knew the moment I walked in. The energies here are considerable—"

Mark ignored her. He went to Chloe and took her hand, tugging her upright. She rose weightless as a balloon, but did not look at him. Connie, her shock finally broken, ran up the stairs.

"Connie felt him, too," Chloe said.

"I think we've all been fooling ourselves," Mark told her. "That's what's been happening here."

"Mark," Trudy said. "Please, let me—"

"We're going to go talk to the boy," Mark said, firmly. "Just the two of us." Trudy seemed to have no answer for this.

He walked toward the stairs, Chloe's hand gripped in his. She followed—but when they'd begun to climb the steps, when they were deep into the shadows, her fingers pulled suddenly back from his, as though they'd been bitten.

⌒

They found Jacob sprawled across his bed, crying. He'd taken off his glasses and was wiping at his face with the corner of his sheet. Connie sat beside him, rubbing his shoulder. His cat was curled between his feet.

Chloe walked past Mark into the room, and knelt in front of Jacob. She said his name.

Mark had forgotten how tender she could sound; how kind she was to the children she taught. He used to marvel at this reserve of kindness—how she could mother her own son so beautifully and still have love left over for the children of strangers. He wanted to reach out and hold her as she spoke. He wanted to apologize.

"I'm sorry, Chloe," Jacob cried. "I'm so sorry!"

Chloe's shoulders jerked. Connie covered her eyes with her hand.

"Jacob," Mark said. "Tell us what's wrong."

Jacob could barely force out the words, but he needed no more prompting. He was confessing now, and Chloe, her eyes tightly shut, took his hands and listened.

⌒

The boy's story did not take long, and it played out as Mark had suspected: Kids at the elementary school had told Jacob about Brendan, and he had done the rest. He hadn't meant to—he insisted this, over and over. He had told his mother about a bad dream that had woken him up: a dream about the ghost of a boy who'd died in the house. But his mother, he thought, had misheard him—had thought he actually *saw* a ghost—and was so upset over his story, so sad and frightened for him, that he didn't correct her right away.

Connie drew back. "But—"

379

"Mom," he said. "That's what happened."

He told them all he kept meaning to correct his mother, but he didn't. He just couldn't make himself, and after a few days of this, he knew she'd be angry at him for lying, for playing along. And anyway, what was the harm? It was a fun story he and his mother shared, exciting and scary. He didn't know that his mother was seeking out Mark and Chloe—he pleaded with Chloe to believe him about this.

And then one day his mother told him *she'd* heard the ghost, too. She told him, too, that she'd talked to the little dead boy's parents, and then one day Chloe came to visit—

"And then you *saw* him!" he said to Chloe. "And then it was too late!"

"Jacob," Mark asked. "Did you *ever* hear the ghost? Even after Chloe did?"

Jacob couldn't say the word. He looked at Chloe, then buried his face in the sheet and shook his head. Connie held her hands to her mouth, then slumped over him.

Mark reached to Chloe and lifted her up again—she was even more pliable than she'd been downstairs. He led her out of the room, into the hall in front of the turret office. As gently as he could, he said, "I think we should go home now, okay?"

She shook her head; her cheeks were wet.

"We can't do anything more here," he said.

"I want to talk to Trudy," Chloe told him. She was looking everywhere but at Mark's face.

"I don't think that's a good idea, honey. I don't think Trudy and Warren are who they say they are."

Chloe leaned against the wall. Some of her hair had come loose from its clip and hung in damp strands against her cheeks.

"What's done is done," he said. "Let's go home."

When she met his eyes, he drew back. He saw that what had

happened when Brendan died was beginning again. Her grief was turning to anger. Chloe's fondest hopes had vanished—and she was starting to suspect it was his fault.

"We *both* felt him," she said. "*I* felt him. You can't tell me that's a lie."

She turned abruptly, and, before he could reach for her, she'd run down the hall, into Brendan's old room, and shut the door.

At the same time, Connie closed Jacob's door; behind it he could hear both of them sobbing. Then all these sounds were drowned out by heavy footsteps on the stairs—Warren Weill's.

Mark met him at the landing. "Let's talk downstairs."

Warren's mouth was an angry cartoon frown, almost the exact shape of a staple.

In the living room Trudy sat on the couch, reading from a Bible perched on her knees. When Mark entered she closed the book and stood; Warren took his usual place beside her. His back was straight, his hands curled into fists; if Mark saw a man this tense in a bar, he would assume he was about to be punched.

"Mark," Trudy said, "we think you're making a grave mistake—"

He didn't want to give them a syllable more than was required. "I thank you for coming down here. If you haven't been paid for your room and your gas, I will do that now. But I'm going to ask you now to leave."

"Mark," Trudy said, "please. Your son—"

"Thank you, Trudy, but that's enough."

"Mr. Fife," Warren said carefully, "we've seen this sort of thing before. These are just jitters. In every case the family reconsiders, given time. I have to remind you that if we don't perform the ceremony tonight, we won't have another chance for a long while. If you love your son—"

Mark walked to the rack beside the front door and lifted their coats. He brought them back and extended them to Warren.

"Let's try real hard to keep things civil," Mark said.

Warren stared at his coat as though he were being offered a dead animal. "I would imagine Chloe doesn't feel as you do."

"Warren, how about you don't imagine my wife ever again."

Warren tried to stare him down, but Mark had bigger contests ahead of him; he wasn't about to back away from this charlatan now. Trudy's hand tapped against Warren's forearm. Her face remained so sorrowful—so full of genuine fear—that for a quick, panicky moment Mark wanted to fall on his knees and beg her to stay. But he did not.

"Warren," she said at last. "Let's keep the energies here pure."

Mark walked them to the door, and through it. When they were on the porch he turned the deadbolt behind them. He watched them walk all the way to their car, their breaths puffing out in vehement bursts. He didn't turn his back on them until they'd gotten into their SUV and driven away. Then he gathered his and Chloe's coats, and her purse, and returned upstairs.

⌒

Jacob's door was still shut. Mark walked past it to Brendan's old room. He knocked, softly; Chloe didn't answer, but when he turned the knob, the door opened easily.

Chloe had pulled one of the folding chairs beside the window; she had lifted the blind and was looking out at the street. Her thumbnail was pressed against her lower lip.

He crossed the room, then knelt and set her coat and purse beside her. "Chloe. We should go home, now."

"I don't want to." Her voice a wisp.

"We really should leave."

"I've been asking for Brendan to come, and he won't."

Mark's chest tightened. "Honey, Jacob made everything up. You heard him."

"I heard him," Chloe said, but she wasn't repeating Mark's words. She didn't mean Jacob.

He put his hand on top of hers. She drew her fingers away, but not before he was shocked by the iciness of her hand, cold all the way to the bone, as though her body had been abandoned by its heart.

"I heard him," she said, "and I felt him."

"Me too," he said. "But honey"—this time she flinched at the word—"I wanted to feel what everybody else did, and I found a way to do it. I got really drunk—"

"*I* wasn't drunk."

She said this without any anger at all. She was acting as she had right after Brendan had died, as if all the important parts of her were curled up in a tiny cave. Outside she was cold stone.

Then the Chloe he loved looked out of her eyes. "These last few weeks have been more real than anything else in my life. The last two days, we've been *happy*. Do you want to tell me that was a lie, too?"

"Of course not," he told her. "But if he was real, and we'd sent him away tonight, would that be any different? Either way we still have to spend the rest of our lives without him."

Her eyes kept boring into his. "Our son is here. I still feel that. I'll call Trudy and Warren back; they'll listen. Just do the ceremony, Mark. Do it for me."

Mark wondered if he would ever be able to explain to her why he couldn't. The harm it would do them, in keeping the Weills near, in pretending. His firm belief that sooner or later, in order to love him, Chloe would have to pretend, as well.

But they had loved each other without Brendan, these past days; they could do it again. He believed that, too.

He slid his hand up Chloe's calf, to her knees, to the hands that were linked in front of them. He grasped her fingers. She was stiff, her eyes now shut tight.

"I want you to listen to me for a minute," he said.

⌒

He told her, then, what he knew to be true:

He told her he loved her. He said this with words, and with his arms, his hands. He embraced her, rocked her. And while he spoke, she softened, she did; she slid off the chair, down and into his arms, and, made hopeful, he shut his eyes and pressed his face against her hair and murmured to her:

I love you, he said. I need you. You're real to me. You always will be.

After a while he stopped talking. He held her head to his chest. What he hoped she could hear now was not made up of words or sentences but, rather, his own heartbeat—rabbity and terrified, pattering like code.

⌒

Finally she spoke.

"I just—I just need to think." She put a hand to his cheek. "I can't just give it up."

He shook his head.

She said, "Let me try, one more time, to reach him."

"Chloe—"

"Go downstairs," she said. "Okay? Let me try."

"Tell me you love me first," he said, panicking now.

She lifted her fingers to his cheek. Looked into him, long and deep.

"With all my heart," she said. "Please believe me."

⌒

Downstairs, in the living room, Mark found Connie and Jacob sitting side by side on the couch. Jacob held his cat, and turned his blotchy face into the cushion, but otherwise seemed to have survived his unburdening. When Connie saw Mark she stood and said, "I need to speak to you in the kitchen."

The moment they were there, she turned to him, her finger jabbing painfully into his breastbone.

"That was some story you told him. If he doesn't tell the truth, some—some *demon's* going to come and *eat* us?"

"I regret that," Mark said. "But he wouldn't have told me, otherwise."

"That's—that's coercion. It doesn't mean anything."

Mark rubbed the back of his neck.

"You'll give him nightmares," she said.

"Connie," he said, "you and your son have just about ruined my fucking life. Maybe he *should* have some bad dreams."

Connie crossed her arms in front of her chest. She tried to look angry, but he'd gotten to her, he could tell. Her eyes kept skipping past his.

"I'm sure of what I heard," she said. "And the Weills—"

"The Weills are con artists," he told her. "If you call them back, they'll want a lot of money. But you won't have to call them. There'll be no more ghost after tonight. You watch."

"I know what I heard," she insisted.

"Voices?" he asked. "Bumps in the night? I heard those, too. It was the goddamned cat, Connie."

"You don't live here anymore. I'm the one stuck here with your son."

Maybe he was still being too kind to her. He seized on the worst idea he could: "Connie, none of this had anything to do with you wanting to get out of your mortgage, did it?"

Connie drew a sharp breath; she flinched back from him, blinking. But he saw no guilt in her face—only new anger.

She shouldered past him. "I want to talk with Chloe."

"She wanted some time alone," Mark said, softly. His anger

was gone; now he was only sorry—for himself, for Chloe, for Jacob, even for poor, deluded Connie. "Then we'll leave."

"Chloe can stay." Connie's voice shook, now. "But you have to go."

"I need to talk with her, Connie."

Instead of answering, Connie fled the kitchen, but didn't go upstairs after all. She collapsed onto the couch, next to Jacob, and wrapped her arms around him, her living boy.

⌒

Mark climbed back up the stairs. Brendan's bedroom door was still tightly shut. He didn't know how much time to give Chloe, so he sat in the chair inside the turret office and waited. He stared out the windows, down at the roundabout; at the streets under their patina of snow and ice; the occasional falling snowflakes, like warping stars, that bent through the cones of light dropping from the streetlamps. Superimposed over the window was the reflection of the lit hallway behind him. If Chloe walked out to greet him, he'd see her right away.

If he saw a little boy, approaching him in the hall, he supposed he'd see that, too.

He closed his eyes.

Here I am. Your mother's here, too. And this is it. If you don't come now—

He loosened his mind. He thought good thoughts. He opened the portfolio at his feet and pulled out the drawings of Brendan's face and held them in his lap. He thought of reaching out and catching a fistful of Brendan's shirt, both of them swaying at the edge of the cliff in the hot summer wind above the deep green abyss.

Come on, little man. Here I am. Prove me wrong.

Going once. Going twice—

Mark opened his eyes. The hallway behind him was empty of little boys.

Gone.

He waited a long time, maybe half an hour, maybe more.

Finally he stood, walked down the hallway, and opened Brendan's bedroom door. Chloe was sitting on her cushion beside the window, her back against the wall, her head tipped back; she'd turned off all the lights except the single lamp on the crate, which had painted her long throat a tawny gold.

She turned her head, slowly, and blinked at him. Her face was puffy. He knelt beside her; she slumped against his shoulder. She reeked of alcohol—and Mark saw, then, the bottle of Maker's he'd brought to the house the other night, empty beside her foot. She must have secreted it up here, the night she'd come by and cleaned up after him.

"He won't come see me now," she said. "He's mad at us."

"No, he isn't," Mark said. "We need to leave now, honey."

"No."

"It's for the best."

"I can't leave him," Chloe said.

"There's no one to leave."

She lifted her mouth to his ear.

"Stay with me. Please."

Chloe put her hands on the sides of his face, and tilted her head back to smile at him in the eye. Her skin had gone a deep, buttery white. One of her slick palms was pressing something hard and smooth against his cheek.

She dropped her hand, pressed it against his; the hard object was inside it. He closed his fingers around it and knew what it was: the vial of Brendan's teeth, from her purse.

No. It wasn't.

She slumped; he caught her around the waist, eased her back against the wall. Her head lolled. Her eyes were opening and closing. He looked down at the bottle of pills in his hand: Valium, two-milligram tablets. Quantity fifty. He opened it. Only a handful of the pills were left.

She'd taken the rest of them with the whiskey.

He pulled his phone from his coat pocket, his fingers already starting to shake. Chloe's hand fluttered between them, swatting at it. "Wait," she murmured. Her hand settled damply onto his forearm. She spoke again, with all the love he'd ever wished: "Mark." With her other hand she closed his fingers around the bottle.

"Come with me," she whispered. "Let's go find him."

Twenty-nine

When Mark had, at last, made his decision, when he knew what he had to do, he scooped Chloe up from the chair by the window and carried her down the stairs. She weighed nothing, it seemed, and he was worried that this was because whatever animated her, whatever gave her breath, had already left her. That he was, in the end, too late.

He carried her past Connie and Jacob, sitting together on the couch. Shouted to Connie to call the ER at Ohio State and tell them he was coming. What happened? Connie cried, and Mark said, Overdose, his voice ringing out. He kicked at the front door, forgetting he'd shut the deadbolt behind the Weills, but Connie's hand scrabbled at the lock, and Mark pressed Chloe close—her cheek lolled damply against his throat, where his shirt button was open—and moved sideways through the doorway so she wouldn't hit her head on the frame. He had not carried Brendan like this; he had not been allowed to touch him, not until his boy, Chloe's boy, their boy, was in the emergency room, not until after the doctor came into the hall and put a hand on Mark's shoulder and a hand on Chloe's shoulder, his face deeply lined, and Chloe had begun to pant, to say already No, No, to strike out, first at the doctor and then at Mark, and Mark had grabbed her, he'd held her to him, and she fought him, she began to scream, and the doctor shook his head and said, He's gone—

But here, now, he carried Chloe down the steps and the icy walk to the Volvo, and then Connie was in front of him, pulling open the door, and Mark slid Chloe into the passenger seat; he scrambled around the hood for his own door, dug with spasming hands for the keys in the pockets of his jeans, started the car and pulled squealing out into the road.

The hospital was close, only a mile or so up Neil Avenue, at the south end of campus. Mark kept his hand pressed to Chloe's breast-bone; she was shaking, either because of their speed, or because she was convulsing. Mark gave the car gas, felt it shudder like Chloe had, only the opposite—fighting against gravity, the pull of nothing.

⌒

But he couldn't go fast enough, he was sure he couldn't—

—because he'd already spent too long kneeling in front of Chloe in Brendan's old room, the bottle of pills in his hand, stunned by what she'd offered him.

Too long saying Chloe! Chloe! Listen to me!

Too long, thinking about how he could do what she'd asked. How he could close the door of the bedroom and jam it shut with a folding chair; how he could lower Chloe to the floor and take the rest of the pills, and then lie down, too, holding her; how this would be so easy—easier by far than deciding what to do with the next minute, the next hour, the next week, the rest of his life without her.

Easier than having to survive again.

What if, he thought, he'd been wrong?

Come with me, she'd said. Let's find him.

Maybe after he took the pills and closed his eyes, he would open them and Brendan would be standing before them, at the end of the long tunnel, holding the hand of Mark's mother.

Maybe *this* was what Brendan had wanted, all along: For them to come to *him*. In the tunnel their shadow-boy would at last run to them and hug them and take their hands.

He would smile, their Brendan, he would laugh; he would say, as though he had expected it all along, You came back.

How long had Mark imagined all of this? Seconds? Minutes? How many?

Too long, too long.

Now he drove through stop signs. Now he took a hard left onto Neil, laying on the horn, bracing Chloe hard against the seat with his forearm. His front right wheel clipped the curb. The rear end caught a patch of ice and fishtailed, too wide. Another horn sounded behind him, and lights loomed up, but they were not struck; the car scraped through a slow revolution and then he was pointed forward, punching the gas, and they were speeding up—

—No more than a minute or two, deciding. It couldn't have been more, before he knelt in front of Chloe and said, No—

And now: Lights flashing behind him; a police car drawing even beside him; Mark rolling down his window, yelling Hospital! as loud as he could; the cop nodding hard, then pulling ahead of him, siren wailing; traffic clearing from the streets.

The Volvo speeding, the streets clear, everything in the city in a matter of seconds pointing the way toward the emergency room like a tunnel lined with lights—

—and then there were nurses and a doctor running out of the ER's sliding doors, opening the passenger door, listening to Mark say Overdose, taking the bottle of pills from his shaking hand, and they were taking Chloe away from him, lifting her onto the gurney, putting oxygen to her lips, the cop who'd escorted him suddenly gripping his shoulder saying, Okay, buddy, you got her here, you did good—

Mark, his chest heaving, agreed. It did feel good. It did.

This was what it was like when you paid attention.

This was what it was like when you had time.

What it was like when you believed.

Thirty

For a while Mark had to wait alone in the lobby. He spent that weightless time planning.

When Chloe was awake again, he would tell her: I couldn't let you go.

He would say: Because you're stronger than you think. Because you loved me. Because your heart is too rare. Because you're you.

He saw himself beside her, stroking her hand; he saw her eyelids fluttering.

Please believe me, he would say. Please come find me now.

⁓

From the bank of pay phones he called his father, and Lewis; both of them arrived within minutes.

Before long his father had put his arms around Mark's shoulders, and he could feel Sam's grief in the shaking of his arms and chest.

Connie Pelham arrived, soon after, bearing Chloe's coat and purse and cell phone. Jacob was not with her. Lewis took Chloe's things from her; Sam wrote down Connie's number, saying very little. Connie seemed to understand she should not stay.

When she'd gone Sam opened Chloe's phone and found a number for her parents, and made the call to them. Lewis dug in Chloe's purse and gave her insurance card to the nurses, and spoke with them for a while, then sat beside Mark.

Before Chloe's parents arrived, a doctor—a young woman, dirty-blond and chubby-cheeked—at last called Mark's name.

Even before he could brace himself, the doctor told Mark that Chloe was awake, that she would live ("It's actually pretty hard to overdose on Valium," was what the doctor said, frowning); she said the hospital would need to keep her overnight for observation, and that—if Mark wasn't actually her husband—she was afraid they couldn't release Chloe to his care.

"Her parents are coming soon," his father said, beside him.

"I need to talk to her," Mark said.

The doctor's eyes moved away from his, to Sam's, and then back. Mark listened to her speak; then she turned and retreated to the innards of the hospital. He wanted to follow her, but his father and Lewis were already guiding him away, and Mark would have let them carry him, would have gone anywhere in time, would have vanished entirely in order not to have heard the doctor's words:

I'm sorry, Mr. Fife. Chloe doesn't want to see you.

VI

---- ❧ ----

His New Life

One

At the end of that August, Allison was vast, unhappy. Her pregnancy had continually been difficult—as though her and Mark's troubles had infiltrated the very blood of their baby girl. So when Allie phoned him one afternoon and told Mark he needed to buy a crib—right now, it couldn't wait—he quickly agreed, eager to give her whatever contentment he could.

"Do you need me to bring you a treat?" he asked her. "Ice cream? Anything?"

Allie said, "What I need is to have this goddamned baby."

He waited.

"Maybe a Reuben," she said. "A good one, from Katzinger's."

Her call cheered him; she'd asked him for a sandwich. These little moments of trust were like candies, treasures he could swirl around in his mouth and savor, before they dissolved.

‿

Mark had been on a campaign, in the months since Chloe's overdose. He had rebuilt himself. Since the night he had broken into the old house, he'd drunk not a single drop of alcohol. He had redoubled his efforts in the gym, had sheared ten pounds from his gut and jowls. He'd been working sixty-hour weeks, stabilizing his business, and banking a tidy reservoir of cash for the coming of his daughter-to-be.

He had also been spending time—as much as she would

allow—with Allison. Helping her, running errands for her. And, as of last month, making arrangements for the two of them to move to Denver, not long after their daughter would be born.

I need to get out of this town, Allie had told him one night in July, after a long rant about the humidity. I can't stand it here anymore.

What about Denver? he'd asked her.

They were sitting in the townhouse, on opposite ends of the couch, enjoying the AC and watching a bad comedy on the big television—just like they used to, except that now Allie wasn't nestled beside him. She paused the movie and stared.

You're serious, she said.

I'll go wherever you and the baby are. I told you that, and I mean it.

She didn't answer him that night, but a few days later she surprised him, knocking on the townhouse door just as he was sitting down to dinner.

If you're serious, she said, I think it's a good idea. Denver, I mean.

I am serious, he told her.

As far as they'd come, these last months, Allie still rolled her eyes.

He had not expected this future, this life. When Lew and his father had driven him away from the hospital, back at the end of January, he could never have imagined wanting it.

That night, his father and Lew had taken him back to the townhouse. One of them had cleaned Allison's clothing off the bed, and told Mark to sleep in it. He lay down beneath the rumpled covers, but never closed his eyes. He could only stare into the dark and think of Chloe, across town, drowsing and pained in her cold hospital bed.

In the morning, over breakfast, his father proposed a plan: Mark could come and live with him for a while at the farmhouse. Like he had, before. Just until things got themselves sorted out.

What about Helen? Mark asked, numb.

She'll understand, Sam said. She wants you to be better, Mark.

After breakfast Mark tried to call the hospital. Chloe's mother answered, and told him the same thing the doctor had: She was sorry, but Chloe didn't want to talk to him.

His father and Lew drove Mark to Indiana that afternoon.

The following morning, after another sleepless night, Mark called Allison.

He told her what had happened. He left out Chloe's overdose; he couldn't bring himself to say those words aloud. But he did try to give Allison the truth: that he had been played for a fool, not least of all by himself. That he would not be going to the old house anymore. That Chloe was angry at him, and that he loved her, but that he didn't know what to expect from her.

He told Allie, I'm not asking to come back. I don't expect us to be friends. But I meant what I said: I'm going to help you and the baby in whatever way you need. I promise you that.

Allison said, Your promises are worth jack shit to me.

I know, he said. But I'm at my father's, if you need me.

She had hung up on him before he finished the sentence.

Lew and Mark worked out a plan: Lew would move into the townhouse for the remaining six months of the lease, taking over Allison's half of the rent. Whenever Mark returned from his father's house, they could be roommates again. Lew seemed genuinely happy at the thought.

Mark holed up in the farmhouse for several weeks. During the day, when his father was at school, he worked. Sometimes in the evenings he had dinner with Sam and Helen, though Mark didn't care for this—Helen was nice enough to him, but he could tell she was suspicious of him, too. He was her boyfriend's weird fuckup son, a man who'd delayed her happiness, a man so inconsiderate he'd dumped his pregnant fiancée to chase a ghost.

He couldn't blame her. He wouldn't know what to say to a man like him, either.

⌒

During those weeks he thought constantly of Chloe. Missing her, worrying for her.

Sam called Chloe's parents every few days, gathering what news he could. Through him, Mark learned that Chloe had spent two days in a psychiatric care ward—but then, like Mark, had returned home to her parents' house, where she was still staying. Her mother wasn't particularly eager to give Sam details, but he pressed her: And so Mark learned that they considered Chloe out of danger, but that she remained almost catatonically sad.

One evening three weeks after her overdose, Sam returned home from school and said, So I talked with Chloe today.

Mark had been making them soup for dinner. He turned off the heat on the stove.

What did she say?

Sam sat down at the table. She's not well, Mark.

What do you mean?

I mean she's—she's not where you are. She's very sad and confused. She thinks that you—

What?

She thinks you abandoned her, Sam said, quietly. And Brendan.

A hole opened inside of Mark. I have to call her, he said. I have to talk with her, Dad.

I wouldn't.

Before Mark could finish objecting, Sam said, Mark, forgive me—I told her about Allie and the baby.

Mark sat down at the table, too. His heart pounded, slow and hurt.

What did she say?

His father put his hand on Mark's.

She said goodbye.

⌒

A week later Mark moved back to Columbus. In seven months he'd be a father; he had promised Allison he would help parent their child; this was not the purpose he'd sought, but it had to be purpose enough.

When he announced to his father that he was returning home, he could see that Sam, no matter how hard he tried to hide it, was relieved.

⌒

Some weeks later, he began calling Allison again.

I'd like to take you to dinner, he said the first time, when she picked up.

Her voice was cold. I don't think that's a good idea.

I don't mean *that*, he said. We should learn to get along. For the baby's sake.

She didn't answer.

How can I be this kid's father, he asked, if I can't even speak to you?

Allie agreed to meet him at a restaurant in Grandview. She was barely two months along; her belly had only just begun to bulge. He would have hesitated to call her radiant—she was too nervous with him, too angry—but the growing baby *had* made her more beautiful, her skin and hair more lustrous, her eyes deeper, darker.

He said, Can I tell you you look good?

She shook her head. Only if I get to say you look like shit.

They began to have dinner every other week. Allison spent the first three dinners tearing into him, then the next making sarcastic remarks in response to everything he said. He kept smiling at her—accepting, as he'd told himself he must, all he had earned.

During the fifth dinner she finally began to relax. He told her truthful things: that he was working, and hard. That he'd been going back to the gym. He told her, I want to get myself back.

That won't change my mind about us, she said at last. You know that, right?

I don't expect it to, he told her.

Allie stared at him over her water glass. Finally she said, Well—do you want to know she's a she?

A she?

We're having a daughter. She laughed—the first time he'd heard Allie laugh, since—and said, God, the poor chick.

A daughter, he thought, over and over.

Tell me what happened, Allie said then. Tell me *really*.

He'd been practicing this. Chloe wanted me back, he said. I went along. I was afraid of the future, so I picked the past. I always loved her, Allie. I know you don't like to hear it, but I can't say anything else. And all of a sudden she loved me too.

Allie looked into her glass, probably wishing it held wine.

Do you still talk to her?

No. Not since she tried to kill herself.

He'd been practicing to tell this story, too. It was a test, and he intended to pass it. So he told Allison everything. She sat stunned, her hands flat on the tabletop, eyes wide.

You're not the only one I hurt, he told her at the end. Do you know that?

Whatever was in her eyes, it wasn't anger. Not entirely.

I do now, she said.

⤳

In March, Sam and Helen came to Columbus for a visit, and Mark—at Helen's request—invited Allison to dinner with them. And why not? They would, after all, be the baby's grandparents.

Along with Lewis, they gathered at the townhouse, and when Mark had poured the wine (excepting himself and Allie), Sam cleared his throat.

I don't want to make too big a fuss about this, he said, but Helen and I married three days ago.

Good, Mark said, as they toasted. When he set down his glass he caught Allie and Helen sharing a sad smile across the table.

That night, after Sam and Helen had left, and Lewis had retreated to his room upstairs, Allison broke down on the couch in the living room.

It wasn't supposed to be like this, she said. Goddamn it, Mark.

I'm sorry, Mark said.

Over and over he said them, but not once did he see the words make a difference.

⤳

For the next month Mark called Allie twice a week, checking on her health, asking her if there was anything she needed.

Her anger at him had grown again.

I trusted you, she said, over and over. I fucking *trusted* you.

Mark didn't call Chloe, no matter how much he wanted to. He often fought the urge to go drive past her apartment, her school, to see if she had finally returned from her parents'.

He missed her; he worried about her. She had tried to end her life, thinking she could find Brendan. He kept asking himself a question he could not answer: What would stop her from doing it again?

It ate at him, kept him awake: What did Chloe believe?

⤳

One Friday night, at the end of April, Allison surprised him with an afternoon call: Can you come over, for a second?

He drove immediately into Grandview—Allie had been living with a friend there, in a duplex only a few blocks from Lew's old apartment. He braced himself for her venom, but the Allie who opened the door to him was cheerful, if wary.

She poured him a Coke and said, So she's kicking.

Really?

Allison took his hand and pressed it to her swollen stomach. See if she does it. Probably won't, now that I want her to.

Her hand was on his. His hand was pressed to the warm, taut curve of her stomach.

Come on, Allie said.

And then he felt what he'd learned to recognize, all those years ago, through Chloe's swollen belly: that peculiar flutter and pulse, that lightning on the horizon.

She's alive! Allie cried, in a horror-movie voice. Then she said, That's it.

She was looking down at Mark's hand, still pressed to her stomach. He dropped it back against his side.

⁓

Spring swelled into summer. The baby grew. Chloe did not call.

Mark imagined her laughing with her friends. Shopping for fabric with her mother. Opening her windows to the springtime air.

Shaking pills out into her palm. Swallowing them, one by one.

Pulling up in front of Trudy Weill's house. Knocking on the door.

Looking at the photos of him and Brendan. Thinking of his new child. Thinking, I am alone.

The weather warmed, dampened, clung. His daughter grew and grew. He imagined Chloe looking at his number on her phone.

If you don't call, he thought, lying awake, there's nothing I can do.

⌐

Mark and Allie had dinner, now, once a week. Mark asked for, and paid, some of her medical bills. Once the summer heat arrived in full, he began offering the townhouse—which had a much more vigorous air conditioner than her duplex—for her use. She and her roommate, Bella, often came over in the evenings and watched movies with Mark and Lewis. Mark didn't like Bella, and she didn't like him; he knew she was along only to chaperone. But he liked showing Allie that he could accommodate any demand. He was like a monk, he thought, taking pride, pleasure, in deprivation.

One night in June, Allie came by without Bella in tow. They watched *The Incredibles*, which Lew had been evangelizing about, and when the little animated baby was being threatened at the end, Mark felt Allie tense beside him on the couch, and he touched her hand, and she took it.

After the movie was over Lew bid them goodnight and retreated to his room. Mark and Allie ate ice cream he'd fetched for her at the kitchen table.

So, she said. Do you want to talk names?

Do I get to?

Her eyes narrowed. I just said so, didn't I?

They discussed several. Allie was partial to Melissa—the name of her aunt, who'd died when she was a girl—or Katherine. Mark proposed names he'd always liked: Rachel, Sarah, Elizabeth. Charlotte—which, he remembered, was the name of one of Allison's grandmothers.

I don't mind Molly, she said. I mean, it can be in the mix.

Mark? she asked.

He cried in front of her. I'm sorry, he kept saying. I'm so sorry.

Jesus, I get it, she said, and patted his hand. You're the sorriest man I ever met.

When she bid him goodnight he walked her to her car. Beside it she surprised him: She stood awkwardly on tiptoe and hugged his neck. Mark, before he could stop himself, turned his head, tried to brush her lips with his own.

Right away she said, No. You don't get to do that.

Okay, he said, already ashamed.

If I let you, she said, I'd hate myself.

I know, he told her.

She stared at him for a long time.

I'm not your fucking backup plan, she said, and got in her car and left.

One afternoon in July, not long after suggesting to Allison that they leave Ohio for Colorado, Mark did something he'd been neglecting: He drove with Lewis to Marysville, to visit Brendan's grave.

He did this because, all along, these past months, he had been grieving Brendan, too. For a long time he'd been trying not to—there'd been no new Brendan to grieve, after all—but Mark was human, and he was lonely, and whenever Allison remembered she hated him, whenever she turned him aside, he couldn't help but remember the happiness he'd felt back in January. It was easy to forget, now, that not all of it had been because of Chloe.

He had this to feel guilty about, too: He owed his son one last goodbye.

When they reached the cemetery, Lew accompanied Mark up a small grassy hill to the Ross family plot. They stood silently beside the low square stone, and after a while Lew shifted on his feet and said, You know what, I'm going to leave you to it. Then he walked downhill and lit a cigarette.

For the first time in nearly two years Mark sat beside Brendan's grave, ran his hand across the chiseled stone. BRENDAN SAMUEL FIFE. 1993–2001. BELOVED SON AND GRANDSON. A bouquet of flowers had been propped in the sconce: white lilies.

Chloe's favorite flower, so fresh that she might very well have placed them here this morning. Fresh enough that Mark looked quickly up, right and then left, to make sure he hadn't frightened Chloe away, that she wasn't observing him from behind a nearby tree.

He saw nothing. And this nothing pressed him flat against the stone. He would have given anything, then—anything—to see Chloe walking to him, happy.

This wasn't going to happen. It would never happen.

But Mark could walk away.

He touched the stone one last time, then went to find Lewis.

As Mark walked down the gravel path, and then again as they drove back to Columbus, he felt a strange and unruly lightness in his belly. And for the first time since January, he understood what he had really discovered, there in the old house: Brendan was *not* suffering. *Not* lost. *Not* in need of help.

His son was really and truly dead.

⌇

Mark invited Allison over for dinner that night. He told her jokes, tried his best to make her feel happy and loved. She still viewed him with suspicion, but their upcoming move had—he could tell— removed a weight from her. She liked to talk about Denver, about the life that awaited their child in Colorado. For her, he understood, these coming months were the beginning, at long last, of the life she really wanted.

Finally Mark smiled at her and said, I'm not trying anything, but—can I listen to her?

Allison regarded him for a long time before finally nodding. She stood and moved closer to him, then lifted up her thin cot-

ton T-shirt. Mark—carefully, as though nearing an antique vase—
tilted his head until his ear was pressed to her distended stomach.
He closed his eyes. Heard the odd, distant slurs and whooshes, like
a whale, swimming.

Do you know what I've done for you? he wanted to ask. What
I've given to be here with you?

He listened to his dark-eyed girl, shifting, stirring.

You won't, he told her. And you never will.

Two

He could not say where the idea came from, but, after looking at cribs that afternoon in August, Mark drove, easily and without very much fear, toward Victorian Village and the house on Locust Avenue.

Before he and Allison left for Denver, he thought, he owed one more goodbye. Mark had not come anywhere near the Village since that night in late January. Now, as he drove slowly along the cobbles, it occurred to him that he hadn't seen the neighborhood like this—in daylight, under a blue summer sky—since Chloe had left him, all those years before.

The old streets, beautiful as always, seemed as alive as Mark felt. So few days in a Columbus year were blue and crisp like this. People were out on their porches, sitting in swings, kneeling in flower beds. Two women sunned themselves on a blanket in front of their house. Yesterday the Buckeyes had won their first game of the season. Everyone he saw seemed happy, expectant.

He'd meant only to swing past the house—but the beautiful day and the cool air sweeping through his open windows caught him up, and he parked the car where he'd used to, back in the winter: on the far side of the park, now full of children. Several were spinning on the merry-go-round, and others rocked back and forth on the squealing metal horses. A young couple sat watching on a nearby bench.

Mark looked up at his old house through the passenger window. Someone was home: The living room windows were open; the curtains on the other side billowed in the breeze. The windows upstairs were closed, their shades pulled.

Was Connie still living here? He'd seen no FOR SALE sign in the yard.

It seemed like such a happy house, now, such a safe house. He wished this to be true, for whoever lived inside it.

He was ready to pull away when he realized one of the children had stopped playing and was looking right at him: A gangly boy with a round stomach, astride a bicycle, a yellow plastic helmet perched mushroom-like on his head. Before Mark could roll up his window, Jacob Pelham had walked the bicycle down the sidewalk to the side of the car.

"Mr. Fife?"

Mark made himself smile. Jacob's face was sweaty, wary, but he smiled back.

"Hi, Jacob," Mark said. "How are you?"

"I'm good. Riding my bike."

What on earth was he supposed to say to this boy? "I—I'm surprised to see you. I thought maybe you and your mom would have moved by now."

"We are, in a couple of weeks." He frowned. "I thought you knew."

"I haven't talked to your mother since—since this winter." Mark glanced again at the park. "Is she here?"

"She's inside." Jacob wiped his lip, thickly beaded with sweat. "She's packing."

The young man and woman on the bench were watching them.

"Mr. Fife," Jacob said, "I'm really, really sorry for what happened."

"Please, Jacob—there's nothing to be sorry about."

"But I *am*," Jacob said. "I really wish I could take it all back. I've been hoping you'd come by sometime. Mom took me"—he lowered his voice, walking the bike even closer to the car—"to confession, and Father McCormack told me I should apologize to you in a letter, but when I told Mom, she said not to. But I would have."

Mark leaned toward the window. "Jacob. I forgive you. I'm not mad, and I never was. I promise. We got it figured out in time."

Jacob glanced at the house again. Then back at Mark.

"But what about Miss Ross?"

Mark hadn't wanted to hear her name. "I'm sure she forgives you, too."

"No," Jacob said. "It's—I keep telling her I made it up, but she won't believe me."

Mark's stomach clenched. "You still talk to her?"

"Don't you know?"

"Chloe—Chloe and I don't talk anymore."

Jacob twisted his hand around the grip of his bicycle.

"Jacob, does she still come to your house?"

"Yeah." Jacob turned again and looked at the front door. "She's in there with Mom right now."

Mark tried to keep his face neutral. He had to leave, put the car in gear and drive. But he heard himself ask: "What does she do? When she comes by?"

"She talks to Mom. And…she goes upstairs sometimes, by herself."

Mark swallowed sickly.

Jacob said, "Maybe you could tell her again that I lied? She keeps saying I didn't."

Mark glanced at the house. "Jacob, I really have to go now."

Jacob's face fell. "Please? I could go get her."

"I'm leaving, right now." Mark added quickly: "I'm moving, too."

"But…moving where?"

Jacob was still a little boy. He'd tell Chloe everything Mark said, no matter what promises he gave.

"Florida," Mark said. "Tampa. With my wife."

"Now you're married again? To who?"

"Jacob. Just—please don't tell Chloe I was here. Will you do that for me? Promise?"

Jacob's face was pinched, sad. "I promise."

Mark looked at the house. How easy it would be for someone to notice him here. He had to go. He had to go right now.

But he asked Jacob: "Is she—does she look happy?"

"I guess so," Jacob said. "She's buying the house from us. She seems really happy, when she talks about it."

Mark said nothing.

"Do you think she's doing it because of what I did?" Jacob asked.

The young woman on the bench stood up, and, after one backward glance at Mark, began walking toward the house.

"It's not your fault," Mark said to Jacob. "Nothing's ever been your fault. Okay?"

"But—"

Mark glanced up at the house again. What he saw, this time, set his heart racing. Without saying goodbye to Jacob, Mark put the Volvo into gear, then guided it away from the curb, his eyes watering, his heart pulsing and pulsing, urging him on, like footsteps, like running.

⌒

He drove for a long time, in circles. He kept his hands firm and steady on the wheel.

As he drove, he made himself think, not of the old house, but of Molly: his little girl who would soon be born. In the rare moments of panic that still overtook him sometimes, he used her as a reminder of the life he had yet to live.

He could picture her, clearly—but not the infant she would be, in mere weeks; not that tiny, squalling bean. More and more, these days, it pleased him to see Molly as a young girl. Six, seven. Brendan's age. A little older.

He liked to imagine her, strapped into her car seat behind him, just visible in the rearview mirror. Her thick black hair, her dark eyes, like Allie's. Her chubby, heart-shaped face. Sometimes, like now, he'd imagine her expression as stormy as her mother's: her mouth pulled into a tight distrustful bow. She would do this whenever he displeased her.

Daddy, she'd ask, if she were here, now. Who was that little boy?

And what would he tell her?

Well, he'd say, That's a story, little bean.

⁓

Once upon a time, he might say, Daddy had another family.

Once, he might say, Daddy was married to a woman named Chloe. Together they had a little boy, named Brendan. He was your brother. They're gone now.

He pictured telling Molly this as she sat up in bed, too agitated by his story to lay her head down and sleep.

Chloe, his girl would say, rolling the strange name around on her tongue. Brendan.

I don't want you to worry, he could say—because wouldn't his daughter be tempted to worry, hearing this story? Learning that her daddy was not always the man she knew? That he had once belonged, heart and soul, to someone else?

He'd stroke her hair; he could say, Daddy's here with *you* now.

No.

I don't want you to worry, he could say. Daddy's learned a lot. He'll be a better Daddy this time around.

No.

Daddy loves you and Brendan the same, he would say. He

misses Brendan and Brendan's mommy, but he loves you, now. He loves you so very much.

But no matter what he said, his daughter would be insatiably curious, about this other family. She would ask if Mark had pictures of Brendan, and Brendan's mommy. He couldn't possibly lie and tell her he didn't.

I want to see them, she'd say.

He imagined them at home—some new home, like the townhouse and the Locust house combined, a place where Mark lived with both his daughter and her mother. In this place Mark would leave Molly—I'll be right back, he'd say—and walk upstairs to his office closet. He would retrieve his photographs, and then he would return and hand them to her, one by one.

His daughter would lay them flat on the covers, amazed by these strangers, and by him, too—her younger daddy, happy and smiling, proud.

What happened to them? she would ask.

He would explain that his first family had been a wonderful family, but that a terrible thing had happened. He would tell her, carefully, that her brother Brendan had had an accident, and had died. He would tell her that after the accident, her daddy and Chloe just couldn't stay together, no matter how hard they tried.

This would be a terrible thing to explain. For a child to hear.

It was very bad luck, he would tell her. It was an accident. It just happened. Then he would hug her and whisper, But it won't happen to us, I promise.

Daddy? she'd ask. Would I have liked them? Would they have liked me?

Yes, he'd say. Brendan was a wonderful little boy, and he would have been a great brother. He was smart and kind and curious, and he would have loved you and looked out for you.

And Chloe? his daughter would say. What was she like?

Is, Mark would say. She's still alive.

⌣

But would this be true?

Mark drove under the highway, entering German Village, and no matter how hard he tried not to, he saw what had sent him fleeing the old house:

The window of Brendan's old room. A flicker of movement there: the curtains being pulled aside. A shape, indistinct, behind the glass.

Someone looking out.

⌣

Maybe she was saying, Daddy left us.

Maybe she was opening herself to a world she could not see with her eyes.

Or maybe she was imagining herself at one end of a long tunnel. At its far end was a glowing light. A little boy crouched somewhere in between. A shadow: wary, afraid.

Maybe right now she was closing her eyes and breathing deep; maybe she was saying, Tell me how to find you—

⌣

No.

Mark imagined, instead, his daughter's room. It would be in Colorado; the mountains outside the window would glow, pink and orange, in the summer sunset. The wind would be clean and sharp with the smell of pine.

What's Chloe like? his daughter would ask.

He would bend close enough that Allie, downstairs, could not hear, and he would tell her:

Chloe is a wonderful woman, and she was a great mommy. She's tall and blond and pretty, and if she met you, she'd play games with you, and tickle you, and make you feel special.

His daughter's eyes—Allison's, big and dark—staring at the photos in her hands.

Brendan at his birthday party. Brendan with Grandpa's hand making a starfish on his head. Mark and Chloe, in their wedding clothes. Mark and Chloe and Brendan in his bassinet, sitting on the porch of the house on Locust in the green, dappled summer light.

Molly's finger, reaching out to trace Chloe's hair, so unlike her mother's and her own.

She sounds nice, she might say.

Mark, then, might smile and touch his daughter's nose. He might lean close and whisper to her his last, most precious lie:

Well. Maybe someday you'll meet her.